BOOK ONE

THE TWELVE RINGS

A CHANCE FOR HEROES

CHRISTOPHER W. PELL

Printed in the United States of America
First Printing, 2022

Pantheon Expects
www.the12rings.net

Publisher's Cataloging-in-Publication data
Names: Pell, Christopher W., author.
Title: A chance for heroes / Christopher W. Pell.
Series: The Twelve Rings
Description: San Diego, CA: Pantheon Expects, 2022.
Identifiers: LCCN: 2022913739 | ISBN: 979-8-9865541-0-5 (paperback) | 979-8-9865541-1-2 (ebook)
Subjects: LCSH Time Travel--Fiction. | Nashville (Tenn.)--Fiction. | Dystopias--Fiction. | Science fiction. | Bildungsroman. | BISAC FICTION / Science Fiction / Action & Adventure | FICTION / Science Fiction / Time Travel | FICTION / Visionary & Metaphysical | FICTION / Dystopian | FICTION / Coming of Age
Classification: LCC PS3616 .E368 C43 2022 | DDC 813.6--dc23

For Sidney

CONTENTS

PROLOGUE:
THE PANTHEON'S DELIGHT

Ours is an era of identity loss amidst infinite possibility. We are a generation cast directionless in space, yet to find ballast, teetering between isolationism and cynicism on one hand and indulgent groupthink paralysis on the other. We are desperate for the catalyst but wary of augury. We are skeptic beggars gone starving at the feast because we have been so warned: where history has known such periods of grace, weightless ascension ushers forward the exploitation of seekers.

But I say, rejoice my brothers and sisters; rejoice, for out there amidst battle lines and borders, where powerful agenda and multifaceted propaganda spangle dangerous and languid upon our social landscape, out there exists a chance for heroes to emerge, the shining beacons to guide the open way once we have outpaced the speed of light. Should only gods or nature dare to tip the scales, the pantheon's delight shall Myth rebirth, and we, its fingertips, shall unveil the heavens as we race toward our dreams in practiced strides.

Undelivered valedictorian speech MK Gandhi Magnet
High School, Graduating Class of 2003

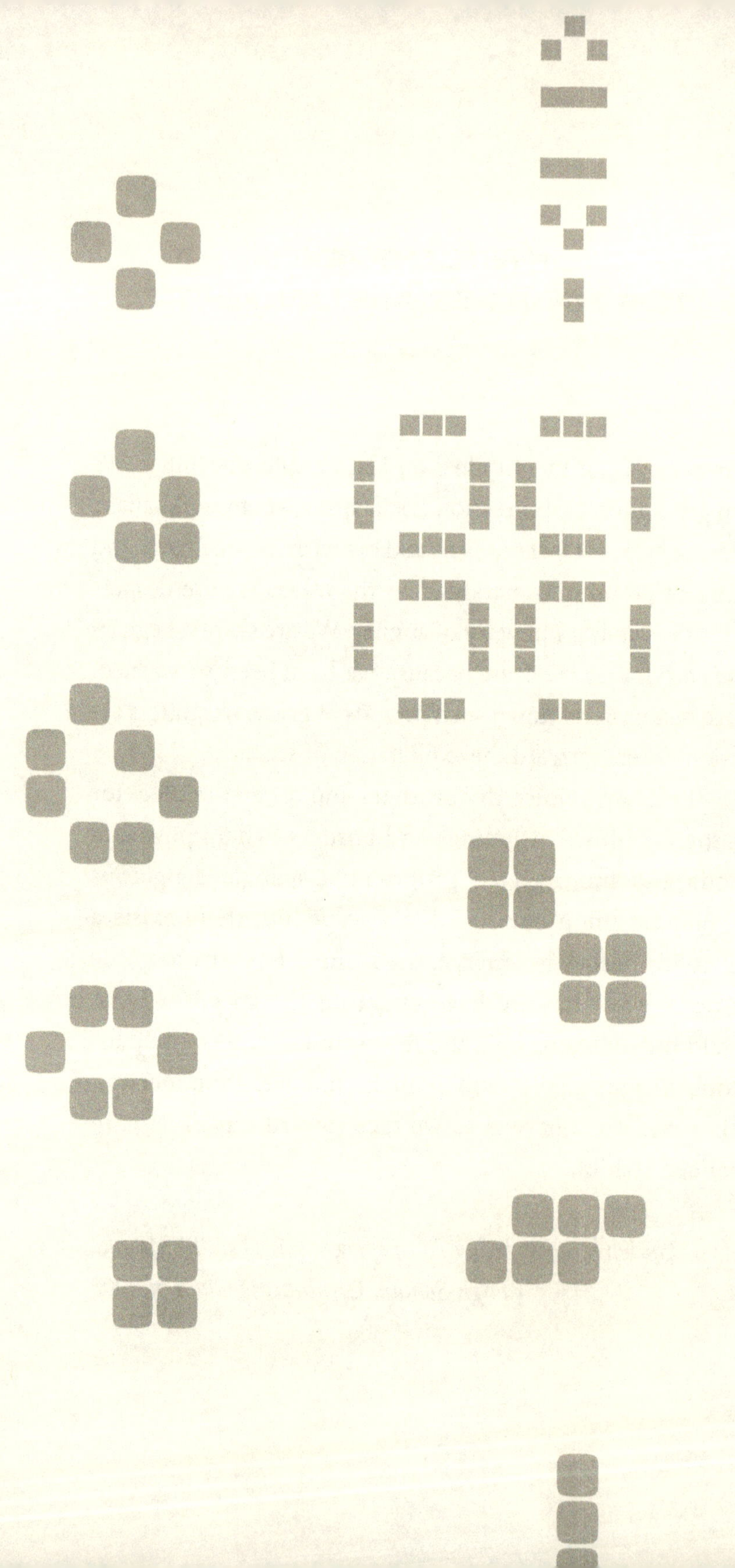

IF THE POLICE COME FOR YOU AT SCHOOL

Summer 1990–Fall 1995

The summer of his eleventh birthday, Roman Smith receives an invitation to attend a special school where he will obtain "the most up-to-date training possible in the fields of science, engineering, and computers." Unaware that every child in the city of Nashville with a decent fifth-grade GPA received the same invitation, Roman spends an isolated summer eclipsed in fanciful dreams of how amazing it is going to be when he is finally surrounded by other people that are as freakishly smart as he is. In his best imaginations, the school will be a think tank full of no-nonsense CIA and MI6 spy-wannabe types. Dotted throughout will of course be a handful of tech-savvy misfits, led by a slightly jaded upperclassman with plans to graduate early to tutor professors working at MIT. In time, Roman imagines, they will come to see him as one of their own ilk and provide him with the technological mentorship he so desperately desires. It is the best summer of his life.

When fall arrives at long last, Roman is completely disappointed in the school. MK Gandhi Magnet is neither a *Real Genius*–inspired hacker fantasyland, nor a hotbed of spies and covert operatives working on wall monitors. Located in an abandoned building on one of the worst drug-dealing and prostitution streets in the city, the magnet school is a social experiment at best. The student body is the direct result of cherry-picking the top standardized test scores from all over the surrounding county. While Roman had been hoping for an army of outlandishly smart peers, he finds a microcosm of a normal combined junior high and high school.

Or rather, it is a normal school except for it is missing the lowest common denominator of students. In theory, everyone at the school is in the top twenty-five percent of their feeder school, which means no one is technically "below average" in grades. While Roman does not experience any overt hostility for liking computers, and thank the Lord there is not anything like overt racism from teachers or classmates over his light-tan complexion and glossy black hair, he quickly finds there are still plenty of mouth-breathers and suck-asses to avoid in the form of the normal athlete-cheerleader-class-president types and a handful of punk-rock upperclassmen that look like they huff glue. In his entire seventh-grade cohort of two hundred students, only two people have any real interest in computers whatsoever: Sadakant Kassam and Seth Perez. As far as Roman is concerned, the selection criteria for his classmates are a joke.

And the school DOES NOT provide "the most up-to-date training possible" in the field of computers. Not by a long shot. The "computer lab" at the school is a six-by-six matrix of Apple Macintosh green-screen monitors and one orange-screen IBM propped up on the teacher's desk behind the lectern. And the languages? MS DOS. BASIC. PASCAL!!!

He had mastered those languages by the age of ten! The curriculum is a joke and not at all what he had been promised.

Roman delivers this exact tirade to his parents once they are home from work long enough to hear. Given that his parents are Vanderbilt researchers, Roman truly expects them to have his back when he informs them that he knows more computer languages than the teachers at the school do, but in a total surprise move, his parents take the prototypical parent stance of "you asked to sign up for it, now you have to see it through." Roman argues that this is his education, not a soccer league, but his dad just smiles his goofy professor smile and runs his large hands through Roman's bowl-cut black hair, and his mom gives him a squeeze around the shoulders and chimes in her sweetest voice, "suck it up, buttercup."

But over the next few years, school and life and mediocrity just seem to suck him up instead. By the time Roman is thirteen years old, he has grown his hair to the start of a decent ponytail, and his only comforts are found in his handful of friends and in computers. School itself is beneath him, and he refuses to think about it beyond it being a mechanical exercise; he does his work in short, neat script as quickly as possible, turns it in, and forgets about it immediately. While he would never cut off his nose to spite his face and toss a chance to at least get into a decent college, he most certainly is not going to fake interest.

For the entire school year, Roman ignores everyone, including his parents, and exclusively hangs out with Sadakant and Seth. Sadakant has a kind smile, but his mind is a dangerous laser sword. Behind Sadakant's moon-lidded, onyx eyes, which are set in his golden-orange complexion and offset by thick raven hair and eyebrows, silent judgement waits. Anything that does not meet his muster is deemed *bullshit* and is automatically cast aside. Apart from computers, Sadakant is into *Star Wars* and playing frisbee and *anything* not related to going to temple with his family, but most else is bullshit. Seth is the "pasty" variety of white boy that Roman suspects has only barely avoided getting beaten up his whole life because he's athletic. Slightly taller than most boys in class with dishwater blonde hair and green eyes, Seth is religiously into running track and competing against himself athletically. He does not run for the school team, however; he runs specifically because he can train without having to talk to other people. Before school, during breaks, and after school dismisses, Seth can be found running the steps in the gym and adding the day's information to the filing system in his brain. As far as Roman can tell, Seth's interest in computers does not seem much different. Roman can tell that Seth just wants to be good at himself, and Roman understands his friend, as self-centered as he is.

Within a few short months, the trio exhausts their collective knowledge about the computer world. Wanting more knowledge, the boys set out to adventure in the darkness of the World Wide Web. For a year they push each other to go further and further into unknown territory. They have only one code among them: anything one person learns they pass along to the others. One day in conversation, Seth makes the offhand comment that information should flow like the milk from mother to child, and from that conversation their moniker, The Mothers, is formed.

The following year, Cosette Rho and Katie Ward arrive to MK Gandhi with the new seventh-grade class, and the three Mothers become five. Cosette adds an artistic quality to the group that has been lacking prior, a quality she attributes to her rare upbringing. Cosette's mother was born and raised in France, but she moved to America twenty years ago with Cosette's late father, a Korean American journalist. Cosette is a prolific writer in all areas: stories and poetry, cookbook recipes, magazine articles, book reviews in the local newspapers, and computer code. At first glance, she looks like an average white girl with auburn hair hanging near her ears, choppy self-cut bangs hanging over her blue eyes, but closer observation of the angles of her face might cause a stranger to question her heritage.

When it comes to Katie Ward, however, no stranger in their right mind would question her about anything they did not absolutely have to, and no one would dare accuse her of being an average white anything, even though her skin is so pale white she rivals notebook paper. Katie Ward, with her ruler-straight long black hair and piercing black eyes, is the daughter of a certain breed of wealthy parents who believe in giving their children whatever they desire, without asking too many questions. As it happens, all Katie desires is a tech-based education designed to enhance her Machiavellian survival skills. Though Roman thinks of Katie as very pretty, elegant even, he cannot say he is attracted to her. Roman is certain she is okay with that; nobody exudes that "fuck off" vibe quite like Katie does. In short order, Katie's haughtiness and overt fondness for outgroup-focused cruelty make her the natural sword of the group; anyone hypothesizing they might want to approach the Mothers as friends begins to recheck their data. All three boys agree that the introduction of Cosette and Katie brings real balance to the force of the Mothers.

With minimum outside interference from school or meddling parents, the group begins to focus on growing their computer skills, and for a short time Roman is happy. Together they start diving deeper and deeper into the webs of connected information that exist inside of computers. The Mothers eventually take on screen aliases, and as a team, they learn to protect themselves better online. Together they learn how to take a good long look into computer systems. They never touch anything or do anything illegal. They know enough to know they do not want jail time for something as stupid as accidentally looking in a bank file.

As their screen names become more accomplished, Roman suggests that they take on better aliases and go deeper underground. One evening, Cosette takes the Mothers to an untended graveyard near her neighborhood. There they sit in the approaching twilight and smoke cigarettes in secret and debate names. Sadakant quickly renames himself Senator, and as he is wont to do, he decrees himself the judge on everybody else's name choice: they will either pass muster or be decried as *bullshit*. In the rising darkness of evening, the deep shadows around the eyes and cheekbones of the newly dubbed Senator lend him a slightly skeletal visage. Roman agrees Senator makes a striking arbiter.

Sitting cross-legged on the cool grass between two fading headstones both marked with the name McConnell, Cosette grins at Senator and intones, "I am Blue."

"The color or the mood?" Senator drags on his cigarette causing the orange firefly glow of the ember to expose his face momentarily.

"The color," she responds with a hungry smile in her voice.

"You sure about that?" Senator fixes her with a baleful look and blows smoke in her face; she does not flinch. "What color blue exactly?"

"I am all shades of Blue, from cobalt to aquamarine."

Senator looks deep into Blue's eyes, and after a long moment, he nods slowly and decrees resolutely,

"I judge this name worthy." Somewhere in the darkness, a cricket chirps once in agreement. Senator sets a smile back upon his face and turns his attention upon the remaining Mothers; no one else fares so well.

Senator rules *bullshit* three times upon Seth before he comes to reveal his name. Seth gets super-pissed, but he works through the anger, like he is running hard in his mind, using the adrenaline to his advantage, and with a clenched fist, he finally growls out, "I am Vercingetorix!" Senator gives Vercingetorix an approving nod, and Vercingetorix releases his fist and flexes his fingers, trying on the name like a glove, and finding he loves the fit. Roman thinks Vercingetorix could run a mile cold just trying on his new name.

Senator shifts to face Katie who is framed by a statue of a woman pouring out an urn. Katie's typical icy glare cannot shake Senator's stance tonight. She likewise suffers Senator's verdict of *bullshit* three times before she is rechristened, all claws out, hissing mad, HexxCat.

The night holds no moon, and it is the true dark of evening by the time Roman Smith is dubbed Kaldari. He feels the ground is a damp cool beneath his seat but not yet wet under his jeans. There is a sharp cleansing smell in the air mingling with the distinct smell of chimney smoke wafting in over the shadowy canopy of trees from the next street over. Kaldari leans in close to his comrades, and not knowing what else to do, puts his hand in the center like he used to do in little league baseball games. The others silently follow suit, each stacking a hand in the pile atop Kaldari's own: Vercingetorix, HexxCat, Senator, and Blue. The Mothers reborn. They hold for a meaningful moment, then break with all the sincerity of a team prepared to win.

In the company of tombstones, the five changelings slide on their new selves with canny ease. The only light now comes from the glow of their cigarettes and a were-light of streetlamp halos promising illumination from other neighborhoods rising beyond the trees. This nameless night, hidden from all eyes and the moon, the Mothers leave all old selves and early aliases behind in the graveyard, and they never go back to retrieve them.

The transition into their new lives is seamless and natural, like metamorphosis. With their new protective shells, the Mothers' power and reach increases throughout the school without a whisper. One Monday afternoon, while the computer teacher, Mrs. Brownie, is on her lunch break, the Mothers use her networked IBM to gain access to the front office's computer, and through it, the Mothers gain access into Davidson County's computer system. First, the Mothers change their class schedules in the school's computers so all five are always together, even though the girls are a full year younger. Then, they write a script to adjust their grades automatically in the county's system at the end of the year to reflect randomly near-perfect scores. They show up when they want to, study only what they want to know, and leave well before everyone else, all according to their official schedule, which nobody bothers to check.

Once they have school settled, they start learning how to build their own computers from scratch. The night Kaldari finishes his first hard drive, the Mothers celebrate by hacking into a nearby Domino's computer system and adding a few pizzas and a two liter of Mountain Dew to the call-in delivery order. They tip the driver well and stay up the entire night eating pizza and smoking cigarettes, laughing, and dreaming up new schemes for global domination. The next morning, they watch the sunrise together, and in that golden moment, it begins to look as if the world is finally ready to open and let the Mothers have their day.

But within the next year, the Mothers hit a wall. While the school's computer systems are a joke, and various low-level businesses are totally unprotected, any networked systems of value begin to show signs of sophistication, both in terms of protection and traceability. The more the Mothers search the perimeter lines looking for back doors, the more they find trip wires. The more the Mothers go searching for information in the dark of the web, the more they come back empty-handed. No one ever verbally expresses as much, but Kaldari knows the Mothers are growing bored.

To shake things up a bit, they branch out into school activities with moderate success. Vercingetorix and Senator enter the Mothers as a team in the school's Ultimate frisbee league competition, and to the surprise of all, the Mothers end up in a tie for first place. As a result of their prowess on the frisbee field however, people suddenly seem to know their names; random underclassmen stop to say hi to Kaldari in the hall, which he isn't certain he cares for. Blue and HexxCat also start to receive attention from other cliques and crews at school, most notably their new frisbee rivals, the Halflings. Secretly, Kaldari worries that the ladies like the stares and comments, but he always acts cool.

In winter of 1993, just before the blizzard shuts down the entire city of Nashville, Kaldari starts to develop feelings for Blue, but he does not tell her for fear of screwing up the team dynamic. He also is not sure if he is ready to face the rejection if she declines the offer, so he ignores his feelings and smiles and sticks to the script. He occupies his time instead looking out for something cool to challenge them. But nothing of interest ever comes along, and Kaldari and the Mothers start spending less time on the web.

Then, in spring of 1994, a few highly publicized arrests over hacking occur, and two moves by the school system bring the Mothers' progress to a grinding halt. First, the entire countywide school system decides to update their rinky-dink passwords and install some firewalls. Second, because MK Gandhi is a so-called "computer sciences school," they are specifically issued new rules for computer use, which require them to give all their account login and use history to the school board. While the password upgrade and firewalls do not directly impact the Mothers, the school-level sweep of computer history is an immediate threat requiring action.

Thankfully, the Mothers catch the news early by being hacked into the internal school reports, and they immediately erase what few visible footprints they have remaining in the system, but it is truly a lucky save. In an act of good will, Blue tips off Chance Black, a member of the Halflings that she knows dabbles in computers; he then informs a few other interested tribes throughout the school and on the web. By the time the school officials receive the student records, any signs pointing to internal mischief have been thoroughly scrubbed.

With the new internal monitoring of the school systems, all attempts at hacking the Mothers had been making during school hours come to a standstill. Until they write a script to mask their keystrokes and apply it to every machine in the computer lab, they cannot run any code through the school's system without setting off alarms. This restricts Kaldari to his home computer and means using his parents' server, which he deems is fine really, but muddies the waters as far as comfort level in web searching. By Kaldari's thinking, if the police come for you at school, you go out a legend; if they show up at your parents' house, you go out as that no-good punk kid.

Then in an even more inexplicable twist of fate, Kaldari's parents come home and restrict his dial-up access. They say that Vanderbilt is requiring all their work to be done on secure computers now. This means his parents will spend even more time away from home (which is awesome), but they are no longer allowed to give him access to the Vanderbilt servers (which totally fucking sucks). The Vanderbilt servers mask his location and allow him to work from home without giving away his true IP address. Now all exploring requires Kaldari to use an outside phone line, or else suffer the fate of leading the police to their front door. Kaldari has never felt so castrated. Tonight, as he cries for the first time in years, he finds his fixation with computers and science stupid. Tonight, his heart breaks a little as he is forced to grow up.

A BOOTY CALL
IN HER FILTH PALACE

August 1996

This story is a mystifying tale surrounding the life of a true hero. Now, heroes, by their very nature, are forever tied up in other people's affairs, for good or for ill, and as such, their stories are often convoluted, which is a fancy way of saying they are complicated. And this story is no different; it is complicated, through and through. In fact, to even tell this story to you correctly, requires you knowing that if a hero could just resist their "heroic" impulses, if they could not *help* people in need, if they just stayed out of other people's affairs altogether, then there would not be a story worth telling. Telling this story correctly also requires you knowing that when it comes to doing the right thing, a hero rarely thinks about the story that will be told later. A hero just flies onto the scene and takes care of business, consequences be damned.

Knowing those two facts about heroes starts us out on the right foot, as we are soon to see our hero, who has recently flown into action, trying to do the right thing without thinking about the consequences. And now things have become convoluted for him.

Where our story begins, we see our hero, a middle-aged man nearly six foot tall with rich brown skin and a small tight

Afro, wearing gym clothes and carrying a gym bag across his chest. He is presently walking at a very steady pace away from a fire truck and an ambulance that are parked in front of a dilapidated house on Wedgewood Avenue, which is a forgotten district in the very heart of downtown Nashville, Tennessee. Our hero is heading southbound, down toward the Melrose Bowling Lanes with the Nashville skyline to his back. It is early in the evening, end of August. The bugs hum indiscriminately, and it is so humid outside that walking feels like taking a swim.

Our hero, Tyrone Walker—or Supraman, as everyone calls him—is not feeling at all heroic right now. He is feeling angry at himself, furious at Sylvia, and confused about the day's events, which is to say he is slightly freaked out by them. He is also upset about Loni being upset over nothing. All in all, Supraman is very much in need of a drink. And maybe something to punch. But most definitely a drink first.

Supraman pulls out his pager from the waistband of his shorts and looks at the message again: 4234. Code: what in the hell. He sighs and slides the pager back on the elastic band. He is fully aware that this is not the best area to be walking at night, having lived here in the not-so-distant past, and he would prefer to not be on this street at all whatsoever, if possible. And certainly not in gym clothes. But impossible events seem to be steering his course today, and here he is, leaving Sylvia Tate's house, walking to the Rose to get a beer, as if he had stepped back in time to 1980 on some weird astral reset. As he walks, his head swims, and he wonders how he has suddenly ended up in the middle of Sylvia's mess today. He looks back over his shoulder and can no longer see the paramedics or the fire truck. He keeps walking with purpose, but his mind is racing.

Images of the last two hours flash in his mind, and he bats them away. He still isn't sure what went down back there, he just knows that he wants to get a safe distance away and have a beer and ruminate for a while.

Supraman's brain circles back around to Loni. Sweet Jesus, how did Loni even get involved in this? He hasn't been home yet to tell her what happened. He and Loni haven't heard from Sylvia in a decade at least. *Which was as it should be*, he thinks to himself, exasperated. Supraman is so confused, but one thing he does know for certain is Loni does not need a reason to hate Sylvia Tate, and this whole mixed-up situation might even lead to a divorce if he isn't careful.

Supraman hears the sound of a Zippo lighter flicking open, and a flame ignites, revealing a shadow-dark face on porch steps off to his left. He keeps walking, but his hand grips on his gym bag, and he glances up cool and slow. A soft sigh and exhale of smoke watch Supraman go as he moves forward; Supraman immediately snaps out of his rampaging thoughts and focuses on his surroundings. He is determined to make his goal before any weirder shit goes down.

Cars filter by with the changing streetlights, and before too long, Supraman can see the neon sign of the bowling lanes down on the left. Five minutes later, he walks through the door of the Melrose Bowling Lanes and makes a beeline to the men's bathroom to change clothes. Another five minutes and Supraman is sitting at the bar in blue jeans and an orange polo shirt, drink in hand. A thick cloud of cigarette smoke paints the room, and the muffled sound of bowling pins being clobbered in the adjacent part of the building plays on repeat. Supraman pulls slowly on his beer, though the urge to slam it back is strong. He nurses the bottle instead, trying to get his thoughts together as they collide and crash through his head like those same bowling pins he can hear. How in the hell has he ended up here?

Supraman looks down at his bottle and realizes he has not actually nursed it. He raises his hand to get the bartender's attention. From behind, he hears the familiar intoning of "Suuu-praahh-maaay-yan" with three syllables stretching well beyond four. Supraman turns around to see Eddie Sharpton walking toward him. Eddie is tall and slender sporting tight blue jeans and a slim black-and-red league bowling shirt with *E-Sharp* stitched over the pocket in white-gold thread. Behind Eddie, a group of men, two black and one Latino, all wearing matching black-and-red shirts, break away and grab a booth. Supraman gives E-Sharp a complicated handshake.

"What's up, E?" Supraman looks E-Sharp over to make sure all is well.

"Nothing, Supe. What's up with you, baby?" E-Sharp pulls off his bowling glove with a quick tear of Velcro. "I thought you and Loni were over in East Nashville?"

"I had some business over here. Figured I would stop by the Rose and have a sniff." Supraman nods to his drink.

"A rose by any other name …" E-Sharp chimes in.

"Exactly."

"Well say, Supraman, we are about to grab a pitcher or two if you care to join us."

Supraman looks over at the booth and glances back at E-Sharp. He wonders if E-Sharp knows anything about Sylvia but suspects that he doesn't. Supraman nods and closes his tab at the bar before heading over. He mostly wants to drink until he can't think anymore, but he figures he may be able to catch a ride later if E-Sharp is feeling generous. It would beat riding the bus back to East Nashville.

Then, unbidden, Sylvia's face from tonight comes flashing into his mind. Her eyes, wild and hungry for him, like when they were still teenagers, like it was the very beginning again, and all she wanted to do was give him everything, anything, right then and there. And then that putrid smell. A gag starts to creep into his throat and frost crawls over his heart and chills his spine. He shakes it off and joins his friend at the booth.

E-Sharp makes introductions. "Clarence, Robert, Ramone. This is Supraman. Supraman these are the Sharpshooters." Supraman greets each in turn as the waitress sets the pitcher and glasses down and moves on to another table. Everyone but Supraman takes a moment to appreciate her walking away. Supraman pours beer for himself and the others. The glasses clink, and they drink. E-Sharp lights a cigarette and blows the smoke out into the lamp above the table.

"How is Miss Loni Lore?" E-Sharp probes by way of polite conversation.

"She's good," Supraman answers, waving off a proffered cigarette. "Probably going to make me sleep on the front porch tonight, but she's good."

"Your lady really named Loni Lore?" Ramone gapes openly. It was a question he got all the time. *Are you really Supraman and Loni Lore? Is that how you met? Did you rescue her? Is she a reporter?* To which all of the answers are "yes, really!"

"Yes, really," he reveals, being extra cool and polite since this is a friend of E-Sharp, and not some random white guy at the *Nashville Banner* where Loni works.

"She black too?"

"Ramone," E-Sharp warns over his beer.

"My bad, my bad. I didn't mean nothing by it. Just a black Supraman and Loni Lore, that's cool as shit."

"Ramone!" everybody but Supraman snaps, but Supraman just waves it off.

"It's cool. It's cool."

"No. It ain't," Clarence croaks out. Clarence is the quiet type, Supraman can tell, but his voice, a deep baritone, carries authority.

"Hey, Supraman," E-Sharp interjects, "what they call it now when kids can't shut the fuck up at school?"

"Loudmouth," Clarence offers, glaring at Ramone.

"No, the new name for hyperactive? Supraman teaches up at the school system. He knows what I mean."

"A-D-D," Supraman spells out. "Attention deficit disorder."

"That's the one. Ramone's got the ADD. Ha ha!" E-Sharp laughs, his voice as sharp and high as his name. "Can't keep his mouth shut for nothing."

"Loudmouth," Clarence croaks resolutely again.

"What do you teach?" Robert inquires after swallowing a sip of beer.

"PE coach. Substitute really, but it's a steady gig. I swap schools every few weeks as they need me."

"You sub around here any?"

"I used to teach up at Rose Park some, back when they still bused in the white kids."

Everyone nods in understanding. Robert adds, "I went to Rose Park, but it was still all black at the time. My nephew goes there now."

Supraman does the math and puts Robert at about forty-five years old, and possibly the oldest man at the table by five years. "What about you?" Supraman motions around the table. "Y'all work at the Purity with E-Sharp?"

Two *yeahs* from Robert and Ramone. A *no* from Clarence.

"I run a secondhand furniture shop. Sam's over on Nolensville Road?" Clarence manages in his slow froggy growl that sounds like he is working around a mouth full of gravel.

"I know the place. How did you get involved with E-Sharp?" Supraman's eyebrows arch up slightly as he strains to listen over the crowded room.

"Church," Clarence offers. "We're in the instrumental section of the choir. I play the bass." He holds up his hand so Supraman can see the callouses on his fingers. Supraman nods in understanding. Having grown up in the church, Supraman and E-Sharp had both been in band and choir from early childhood up through high school. Supraman could still visualize a young skinny-faced Eddie Sharpton in his Sunday robes.

"Well, no church next week," Ramone interjects excitedly drumming his fingers on the rim of his beer glass, "because we have three shows booked at Ole Miss! My cousin said the gig is solid next weekend. Make sure you have the time off from the shop. He got us rooms to stay in and our pay in hand up front, so no bullshit hassle when we get down there—$225 each per set."

"It better be legit. I'm not driving all the way down to Oxford, Mississippi, for no good reason," Clarence huffs over his beer. Robert nods sagely and looks at Ramone saying nothing.

"I'm telling you"—Ramone is visibly excited now—"the gig is gold. Friday and Saturday night and Sunday afternoon. That's $675 each total. Plus, this could really get us established on the college circuit. This fraternity said they will just contact their organization at different universities. We go blow down the doors in Mississippi, and we are set. Then we can set a schedule and just jump from town to town playing this fraternity until December. Get the car paid off, play locally until spring break, then start hitting college open houses all over the South through summer."

"Well, we shall see, huh?" E-Sharp steeples his fingers and tilts his brow in mock finality, tamping down Ramone's enthusiasm.

"What's your sound these days, E? You playing jazz?" Supraman finishes his beer and sits the glass on the table.

"Funk," E-Sharp announces, slapping his hand on the table. "Good old 1970s funk. P-Funk. WAR. Baby Huey. Just like we used to play back in our high school days. These white kids can't get enough of it." Supraman nods and smiles. He bets E-Sharp is right.

The waitress delivers another pitcher, and Supraman sits back and listens as the Sharpshooters plan their sets, lay down rehearsal dates, and speculate about the legitimacy of

Ramone's cousins, of which it turns out he has no less than thirty. Only once does Supraman let his mind slide to Sylvia and Loni, but he quickly takes a drink and pushes the thought far from his mind. *Now is not the time,* he tells himself. *Enjoy your drink while you can, Supraman.*

Eleven o'clock finds Supraman sitting shotgun in E-Sharp's Pontiac heading north on I-65. E-Sharp has the window down and is smoking a cigarette in silence. The wind whistles a warm breeze into the back seat, causing the sagging roof lining to flutter in the back windshield. E-Sharp glances sideways at Supraman.

"I know it's not really my business, but were you with your ex-lady tonight, Supraman? I mean, you'd let me know if Loni might blow my head off when I pull in the driveway, right?"

Supraman looks up from the taillights in front of them. He puts his hand to the bridge of his nose and has nothing to say except, "Yeah, man, but it ain't what you assume."

"Shiiiit. It's no sweat off my back, Supe. I just put two and two together that you ain't been to the Rose alone in a hot minute. I figured though if you and Loni were fine, you'd probably be closer to your own crib."

Supraman lets out a long sigh and wipes at his face. "Today has been so very fucked up, Eddie. I haven't even processed it yet. Not really. I was down to do some serious drinking when you arrived."

"Well, lay it on me, man. Ain't that what friends do?"

"I don't know …," Supraman starts, but then he blurts out, "it was just a normal morning, E. I was substituting over at McGavock, which is great because I didn't have to take the bus very far from the house, and it was just a normal morning. Most trouble I had was a kid fell and skinned his knee."

He closes his eyes, pinches the bridge of his nose again, and sighs deeply as he retells it all to E-Sharp in vivid detail—how just after lunch today, he had received a summons over the intercom that he had an emergency phone call in the office. Of course, thinking it was Loni his mind had started racing wondering if something had happened to her. When he got to the front office, the secretary said, "Your wife is on the phone, and she sounds very upset." He recalls the secretary giving him the stink eye like he was wasting precious resources by being on her phone. Supraman had answered the phone nervously and said, "Loni, this is Tyrone. You OK, dear?"

And very quickly he had realized it wasn't Loni on the phone. Someone was crying and sniffling, and he started thinking it was prank call or something until Sylvia started saying his name, and he realized with a shot who it was.

Supraman tells E-Sharp, "She started moaning, 'Tyrone, Tyrone. I'm so sorry. So sorry to bother you at work, baby, but I woke up in a panic, and I was confused and couldn't remember where you were teaching today, and I feel sick and woozy, and I panicked so I called the school board to find out where you were. I really need you to come home. I don't feel OK at all.'"

She had started moaning again loudly and carrying on, and Supraman had not known what to say to her except "just be cool" and "I'll be over as soon as I can," which he really didn't want to do but she sounded really messed up. After he'd hung up the phone he felt he had to tell the secretary something because she'd been eavesdropping on him the whole time, and she'd heard the panic on Sylvia's part. So, he'd told her, "I have an emergency I need to attend to," and he just left.

"You just walked out of work?" E-Sharp echoes incredulous.

"Yeah, I was so stunned I didn't know what else to do. And thankfully I have a good record with the city because this is going to be a strike on it."

E-Sharp watches the road but squints his eyes as he thinks. "How did you know she still lived over here?"

"I didn't really. My brain just assumed she was still in the same place. I caught a bus over to Wedgewood almost out of instinct or old habit."

But the moment he had arrived and walked up to Sylvia's place, he knew something was not right. The yard was a mess. Trash was strewn on the lawn, and chairs were knocked over. On the front porch, there was trash piled as high as a human. It was real dark inside, but the front door was open just a touch, so he had nudged it open a little farther and glanced inside.

"Oh yeah, and get this," Supraman explains, "the door had no door handle, just a flat, rectangular metal plate where the handle should be."

"What? That's too creepy, man. I don't know if I'd be down for those haunted house vibes personally, even in broad daylight."

"Trust me, I agree whole heart, but other than the door handle and all the trash on the porch, the house looks normal-ish. You know, no homeless people in the front room, or anything, but something ain't right."

"Yeah, no shit, something ain't right. Sylvia Tate leaving her house trashed? Oh, hell no."

Supraman slaps his thigh with a small sense of vindication. "My thoughts exactly, Eddie! Sylvia Tate's house is a pigsty out front, which is insane, but inside it just looked abandoned like somebody had recently come in and stole and all the furniture." Supraman remembers waiting for something or someone to jump out at any moment. "Well, before I know it, I'm at the foot of our old stairwell. Now, mind you, I haven't been to this place since we split up back in '84, so twelve years ago, and I'm telling you, it looks like I just stepped into a horror film."

"Nope." E-Sharp declares resolutely.

"And I wouldn't even be here right now," Supraman continues, "except Sylvia sounded really messed up on the phone. I mean, what was I supposed to do? I couldn't just call the cops to come check on her, given that I didn't know what was up."

"Well, right." E-Sharp shrugs, eyes on the road.

"So then, I hear a rustle upstairs, and I'm kind of freaking out because what if she's dead or worse because by the look of her place, God only knows. But then I hear her voice, and she calls out, 'Tyrone, baby? Is that you? Are you home? I'm upstairs in the bed.' Now all kinds of things are going through my head because the stench of garbage, and what I believe is piss *and* shit *and* vomit, is everywhere. Not the stuff itself, not inside, just the *smell* of it. I don't know if some of it was from stray dogs or what, but all of my alarm bells were going off telling me to just go; get the hell out. But by this point, I have to see for myself, you know. I've come this far." Supraman shakes his head in disbelief at the sound of his own words. "So, I go up the steps, a little slow in case something jumps out at me, and I'm all in karate mode. I get to the top of the landing, and it's all dark, but I can smell trash funk up here too. It's horrible. The only light is coming from our old bedroom.

"'Hey, Sylvia,' I say really slow as I make my way down the hall. I push the door open, and a couple of things stand out immediately. One, this is the only clean, lit, and furnished room in the house. I mean, like spring-fucking-clean. The kind of clean you expect Sylvia's house to be. Two, the bedroom furniture is her old college décor from her TSU days. All the same bedding, same comforters and quilts, same dresser and nightstand, which is weird because I know for a fact, we sold some of those objects." Supraman takes a deep breath and sighs out in resignation. "And three, Sylvia is buck-ass naked on the bed."

"Oh shit!" E-Sharp calls out like he's been burned by something. He casts a look over at Supraman. "You are a dead man."

"I know."

"A dead-ass motherfucker." E-Sharp continues to watch Supraman and not the road.

"I know." Supraman pronounces with more conviction.

"Loni know about any of this shit?" E-Sharp grills.

"Some. But wait. I haven't told you the part that got me the most freaked."

"You mean other than your ex-lady hitting you up at work for a booty call in her filth palace? What else is there? I mean, you didn't actually fuck her, did you?"

"No, man!"

"Well, what then?"

Supraman takes a deep breath, rubs his forehead with both palms. "OK, this is gonna sound ludicrous, Eddie, but shit if it ain't the truth. Here goes. You remember Sylvia's motorcycle wreck?"

"Well, yeah." E-Sharp nods and shrugs.

"I mean, we all used to hang around a lot then, so I know she showed you her titties from where she came over the handlebars, right?" Supraman looks over at E-Sharp for confirmation.

"Yeah, man." E-Sharp laughs a little. "Yeah, she showed me."

"I know. She showed everybody." Supraman stares intently at E-Sharp. "The scar was gone, E." Supraman lets that sink in for a moment.

"Like completely gone?" E-Sharp scrunches up his eyes trying to envision it. "Like real good plastic surgery or something?"

"I mean, I guess so, but how did she afford it?" Supraman shrugs. "And … this is gonna sound stupid, but seriously she looked way younger than the last time I saw her. Like in her twenties."

E-Sharp drives in silence as they coast down McGavock Pike. Supraman recounts how he left immediately, trying to abort mission, but Sylvia had followed him out of the house, all but naked. She had tied a red silk bathrobe around herself but just barely. Meanwhile Supraman had spent the rest of the afternoon trying to find a neighbor, or somebody, who could tell him how long she's been like that. All with a half-naked, twenty-something year-old-looking Sylvia hanging on his arm and saying things that would make a marine blush.

"Her whole neighborhood situation was wrecked," Supraman paints the picture but figures E-Sharp already knows living only a few blocks west of Wedgewood Avenue. "Nobody from the old days lives there anymore, so none of her neighbors knew her. I walked to the nearest gas station and tried to telephone Sylvia's mom's house, but the old number was different."

He'd also called his own house to try to talk to Loni, but no one picked up, so he just left Loni a message saying he was handling something messed up and would be late. Not knowing what else to do next, he'd called the paramedics.

"But when the paramedics arrived, they wouldn't take her because she wasn't hurt, and she wasn't in danger. Then she flipped out, kicked everyone off the lawn, and ran inside leaving everyone standing there in the dark. About that time, I got a page from Loni 4-3-4. 'What the hell.' I knew I was fucked already. She only sends that message when she is truly pissed off. That's when I left and walked to the Rose."

Supraman stares out the windows at the passing houses in the neighborhood. "So, here's my situation, and mind you, I'm just laying this on you because we happened to run into one another, and you actually know everyone involved, but here it is. This is some Twilight Zone shit." Supraman raises one finger. "Sylvia needs some for-real help." Supraman raises a second finger. "And Loni is going to mess me up, even though I had nothing to do with it." Supraman raises a third finger.

"I concur," E-Sharp states with finality as he turns off Cooper Lane and on to Bobby Avenue.

Supraman glances at the house as E-Sharp pulls in the driveway. It's a one-story Craftsman home painted white with black trim, black shutters and porch awning, and a black wrought iron security door protecting a red wooden door.

Loni's car is parked at the end of the twenty-foot driveway, and the porch light is on, which he thinks may be a good sign until he gets up to the porch to find a box on the steps and a note. It reads "She called my work. Then I called your work. I can't believe you." Supraman snatches up the box and knocks on the door. Hearing nothing inside, he pulls out a key, and just as he gets it to the lock, he hears Loni through the door.

"Go on now, Supraman," she growls, low and dangerous. "Don't open that door tonight unless you lookin' for a fight." She slurs her words slightly.

Supraman wants with all of his might to just tell her his side of the story and have her hear him and have her see that this what not what it seems. But he chooses to listen to Loni, because he knows Loni, and he knows that she is not kidding. She will not listen in the present moment, and she will put someone in the hospital if he opens that door. He turns with his box and walks back to E-Sharp's car. He gets in and closes the door.

E-Sharp pulls out of the driveway and makes his way back to McGavock Pike and then onto the interstate back over to Belmont and E-Sharp's apartment. When they get inside, E-Sharp offers Supraman a beer, a blanket, and a clap on the shoulder.

"The dairy calls early, my man."

"Hey, speaking of calls, I need the phone to see where I'm teaching in the morning."

"Sure thing. It's in the kitchen on the counter."

"Thanks, E."

E-Sharp turns and heads into his bedroom. Supraman picks up the cordless phone. He thinks really hard about calling Loni but decides to dial the school system instead. He enters his six-digit code and listens in mild disbelief as the recording tells him he will be substituting at Rose Park Middle School in the morning. Head spinning from the day's events, Supraman lays down on E-Sharp's couch. It's a nice couch, Supraman thinks, probably because E is a bachelor and spends his money on different things. Supraman thinks about how he's going to be a bachelor if the shit with Loni doesn't get resolved soon.

Then he thinks about Sylvia. And unbidden, the images flood over him. Sylvia. Naked. Young. Like someone lifted the needle and reset the record. Hungry. Savage. On that bed. That bed. But then the smell returns. He gags a little and opens his eyes, remembering.

He had backed out of the room instantly, telling her he was going to the bathroom, and then he had fled down the steps and out the door to find a neighbor. That putrid smell covering everything in the house. Supraman went outside and knocked on the doors of three houses, but all of the neighbors were new and none of them seemed to know Sylvia or show the slightest concern.

He closes his eyes again. Lips. Eyes. Breasts. No scar. The smell.

Supraman forces his eyes open. He tries to visualize something else, but each thought comes back to Sylvia. Sylvia said she had phoned the school board to find him. What had she told them? And Loni said Sylvia had called her at the *Nashville Banner*. Dear God in heaven, when exactly had she called Loni, and what had she said to her? And why? Why? Why was this happening now? Sylvia hadn't bothered them in over a decade. Why now? Supraman wonders for the two hundredth time. His mind races, but each time he closes his eyes to try to sleep, he sees Sylvia naked and poised on the bed and the lingering smell comes back.

He fights the images until he is too tired to resist, and his brain can take no more. Then, somewhere in a bedroom from twenty years ago, Supraman is with Sylvia, and she will have no more waiting. He is young, and they are still children, perhaps too young even for this scene, but their naked bodies do not care that the dream has got it wrong as they topple softly over each other, over and over in the cool remembrance of another's flesh. Sylvia laughs in his ear, and it echoes.

SHE STILL HAD HER WHITE GLOVES ON

Summer 1972–Fall 1972

When Loni Lore was sixteen years old, she and her best friend Sylvia Tate got summer jobs at the new theme park that had just opened near their house. It was a quick bus ride to work, and Opryland provided all of their work outfits on-site, so every day the girls rolled out of bed, walked to the bus stop in sweatpants, and did each other's makeup on the bus while sharing a bacon sandwich and a cup of coffee that was three-quarters sugar.

Once the girls were safely off the bus, they would sneak around the corner and smoke a cigarette where no one could see them from the street. Then they would head to the main building where all the employees got costumes. They worked at the same station, securing people into their seats on a water ride called the Flume Zoom. They spent most of the day looking for cute boys in line and chatting amiably between the log boat loadings.

On lunch breaks, they were not allowed to be on the rides in uniform, and it was too much hassle to cross the park to change clothes for a quick ride (even if you were allowed to skip the line). So, Loni and Sylvia would usually wind up sitting in the petting zoo with the baby fawns. Even though they were pretty sure the animals were drugged up to keep them docile enough for toddlers to pet, the girls found them irresistibly cute.

Perfect as the picture was, Loni had begun to worry that they were drifting apart. Loni worried that their distance was due to Sylvia developing a woman's body practically overnight while Loni remained the same. Sylvia started coming up with little games and challenges for herself. She would first try to get particular boys to look at her, then smile at her, then talk to her, and inevitability she would convince them to give her little things. Some days they would linger near the pretzel stand just to see if the vendor would talk to Sylvia and offer them some food to share on the way back to the Flume Zoom.

Loni never noticeably received the same attentions as her friend, which was OK, she guessed. At most, boys would comment on her name when Sylvia introduced her, some iteration of *"Loni Lore? Really? Just like in Bionic Comics?"*, and then they'd go back to flirting with Sylvia. Loni was a little envious of Sylvia sometimes but not all of the time. Loni was well aware that Sylvia's looks sometimes got her unwanted attention from older men, and once the scene had turned a little scary when a drunk man on the evening bus home from work persisted in harassing Sylvia until another man stepped in and intervened. Loni didn't want any such attentions like that, but she wouldn't mind a stuffed animal or a little attention from the pretzel guy without the obvious line about her name, she supposed.

If Loni ever complained about Sylvia to her parents her dad would only shrug and remark that Loni would be able to count her real friends on one hand, and he cautioned that family tend to take up most of the fingers on that hand, and not get too caught up in friends. Loni always suspected her father didn't care for Sylvia, but he was just too polite to say so. In the long run, Loni really didn't have any other close friends and certainly nobody who lived as close to her house as Sylvia. As far as Loni knew, Sylvia didn't have anyone who would be counted as a close friend either. Loni tried to talk to her mom about how she felt regarding her looks and her body and Sylvia, but her mom was too invested in wrangling her baby sister to say much beyond, "You're going to grow into your face and your body in time. And Miss Sylvia is going to get more than she bargained for if she doesn't watch herself."

Being best friends, of course, Loni talked to Sylvia about her looks and her body plenty, but those conversations always turned into talking about Sylvia's body, which did mildly fascinate Loni but was ultimately unhelpful. Trying to discuss or analyze their friendship or relationship together would also just become a discussion about Sylvia, so Loni had long ago just opted to talk about boys, movies, music, school, and boys. Loni just shrugged and chalked it up to different strokes for different folks, like her dad always said.

Loni decided to leave Sylvia be. If Sylvia wanted to be boy crazy and self-centered and flirt with every guy in East Nashville, well that was her prerogative. May she get all the pretzels and stuffed animals she desired. In the meantime, Loni just followed Sylvia's lead, only occasionally giving herself sidelong looks in the mirror, waiting for her face and her body to do something interesting.

Wednesday, July 26, 1972, had begun just like the Tuesday before with a bright sun in the east and large puffs of white clouds over the river to the west and the promise of humidity and sticky sweat by afternoon for everyone in the park. Sylvia had counted forty-six cute boys by 10:30, and two of them had come through the Flume Zoom line three times just to talk to her and exchange phone numbers.

Once the boys had embarked on their third log ride, Sylvia leaned over to Loni and said, "They want to meet us when we go on break." Loni's eyes grew wide at this news.

"Both of us?"

"Yeah. I told them we'd meet them by the giant swings. What do you say?"

"Oh. OK. Sure," Loni said, resolved to take a better look at the two boys when they came off the ride.

Before another minute passed, the boys were scooting toward her in their fiberglass and bumper log boat. They both were pretty cute actually, and one of them looked right at her and smiled. She managed to hide all her panic and shock and kept her regular kind smile on her face as she turned from him to her next guest in line on the platform, preparing to put them in a boat. She was eternally grateful that her job required her to look away from him without being rude so she could keep her composure in that moment. And by the time she had her people seated, the two boys were down the stairs of the ride exit and away.

When Loni next got the chance, she leaned over to Sylvia and asked, "What are their names?"

And in between putting guests in boats, Loni learned all that Sylvia had learned in their three turns through her line.

The boys were Michael and Tyrone, ages sixteen and fifteen respectively. They went to East High, rising juniors.

Mike plays football, and Tyrone is in the marching band. Trumpet and saxophone. Sylvia really was focused when she wanted something, and Loni realized that in a few minutes she would be talking to boys with Sylvia. What was she going to say? How was her hair? Was she showing how sweaty she felt? Oh my God, she was in her work outfit! American flag vest motif with hair in braids with red, white, and blue ribbons woven in the ends and slip-proof shoes that gave her an extra inch at least.

She hoped he wasn't too short.

They stepped off shift, and she'd never noticed the trellis path leading off the ride with such detail, but perhaps the adrenaline in her bloodstream was heightening her senses as they exited the ride and entered the park.

The giant swings were just across from the exit, and the boys were posted up nearby watching and saw them as soon as they emerged.

"You should've told them to wait for us by the bumper cars, so we would have a chance to stop at the bathrooms first."

"That's our escape plan if we don't like them."

"Oh, good thinking."

"I read it in a magazine."

"I didn't know you could read," Loni said dryly.

"Bitch," Sylvia said with a genuine heartfelt laugh.

The boys reached them just as they were cracking up laughing at Loni's joke. And like a chemical reaction destined to occur, summer's late blossoms opened, and the two boys and two girls spent an hour sitting on a bench in the shade of the concession stand. Loni spoke to Tyrone as if she spoke to boys every day. Boys with beautiful eyes and eyelashes and noses and lips and collarbones poking out of the edges of their maroon jersey with a large number five stickered on the front. Collarbones and necks adorned with the telltale chain of dog tags, which must be hanging somewhere close to their chest. She did this all the time, she thought, as she fell in love with Tyrone, his face framed by the list of ice cream flavors on the wall behind him and the line of families ready for lunch. She recorded every word he said, every syllable and pause, every laugh, each smile, each moment when he would look right into her eyes and turn her to liquid gold.

An hour's eternity passed, and Loni knew what heaven was, and then it was time to go. To go where? Back to work. *But I was in love*, she thought then and again so many times later. *But I was in love.* They should have sat right there for the rest of their lives and just talked, so she could watch the colors of the setting sun pass slowly across his eyelashes as he spoke. But then she was moving. Why was Sylvia dragging her by the arm? And they were laughing and talking and moving back toward the Flume Zoom, and the boys were going to run to the front of the line to ride and talk more, and Sylvia was pulling Loni up the steps.

"Hurry up, we're late already. God, I have to pee so bad," she said, but Loni was still sitting in concessions. This was the reason she was not responding to her shift manager's complaints of her tardiness. The reason that she had floated into position quietly, relieving her glowering coworker, and then escorting the next guest onto the ride. She saw Tyrone and Michael in the line below the platform that zigged then zagged up to the front of the turnstiles. Soon they were too close to the wall for her to see clearly from her vantage point.

Suddenly Loni realized that a guest needed help at the back of the line. A stroller wheel had become snagged on the railing somehow, and the mother couldn't pry it loose. Loni excused herself past the other waiting guests and moved to the mother's position, which chanced her to look down to see Michael and Tyrone beneath her. Loni saw that the stroller was snagged on a loose metal rod at the bottom of the pole and bent to unhook it, but just as she worked it loose and was in the motion of standing up, an impatient man reached past the mother and yanked up on the stroller, deciding that what the situation needed was a man's touch, and he accidentally smacked Loni clean in the face with the stroller, knocking her backward over the rail.

As chance would have it, a photographer from the *Nashville Banner* happened to be standing at the entrance of the Flume Zoom ride snapping pictures for the morning edition article on the prosperity of Opryland's opening summer, and he squarely framed three photos: one of Loni coming over the rail, one of Loni falling, and one of Loni landing in Tyrone's outstretched arms.

It all happened so fast, and then crowds were gathered around Loni and Tyrone. Loni was pulled by someone else out of his arms like some bizarre twist in a perfect dream, and she was whisked away to the back rooms at the Opryland complex where waiting medical staff probed her and flickered flashlights in her eyes while swabbing her forehead with alcohol and asking her if she knew her name. But she just wanted to go back to his face for a moment.

Then Sylvia was with her and helping her out of her work clothes, and she told Loni that Loni's dad was on his way and would be waiting out front. Sylvia winced when she looked at Loni's head.

"Dang, girl. That looks ghastly."

"Where is Tyrone?" Loni finally managed to say through the fog surrounding her.

"Who? Oh him. I think he got interviewed by the newspaper for saving you."

"Saving me?"

"Lolo, you almost died, girl. At the very least you would've been crippled. You fell ten feet headfirst. Tyrone scooped you right out of the air apparently. I couldn't see it. I just saw your feet as you went backward over the rail. I almost peed my pants."

She had almost died? And Tyrone had saved her?

Yes, he had, Loni thought dreamily.

Loni hadn't even realized what she'd been needing until she saw his eyes. But just seeing and knowing would have been enough to swim in content for years; that's how it felt that evening and for the next week as she recovered in the inpatient wing of Baptist Hospital. She was swimming in memory, looking out the window across some street into another set of reflective windows. Eating tiny cups of ice cream after each meal. And receiving so many guests and interviews. The room was covered in flowers from the Opryland staff. Somebody had brought her the copy of the newspaper with the photo of Tyrone catching Loni on the front. And underneath that a photo of Tyrone face front in his number five jersey with his perfect eyes and smile and short Afro and "Supraman Saves Loni Lore" in giant block letters.

Loni spent hours ignoring other people and just staring down at the photo in between catnaps brought on by her medications. Much to her alarm and resentment, she learned that Tyrone had visited her while she had been asleep, but no one had woken her, and she had missed him. She had missed her young Supraman.

As her hospital stay converted to bed rest at home, Loni was unable to return to work for the end of the season and resigned from Opryland. She spent the last two weeks of summer letting her sisters crawl all over her bedroom while she sketched pictures of Tyrone in her lock-and-key journal.

When school started back, Loni saw Sylvia for the first time in days, and Sylvia was acting strange. She wasn't chatty or excited about the first day of school or showing off her new clothes. She just stared down the street waiting for the bus. When Loni asked her if she was OK, Sylvia shrugged and said she just didn't feel like talking.

On the bus, she just stared out the window. But when they got to school, Sylvia made a beeline to the Jennys (Virginia and Jennifer), and the three were immediately engaged in an animated conversation. Loni went to her locker, confused, but almost immediately class was starting, and she was swept up in first-day inundations of homerooms, book assignments, assembly, and learning class rotations. By the time Loni was going to get back on the bus, she looked up for the first time and realized that Sylvia wasn't in line. She looked all around and couldn't find her, but the line trudged forward and up the steps, and then she was on the bus heading home with two unknown freshmen girls gabbing away excitedly in the seat next to her.

The next morning at the bus stop, Loni asked Sylvia where she'd been, and Sylvia told her that she joined the cheer squad and wouldn't be riding the bus home anymore and she thought she told Loni sorry. And again, Sylvia was distracted and aloof. When the bus came and they got on, Sylvia bypassed her normal seat with Loni and went to join Sissy Gifford in the back seat. Loni felt as if Sylvia had just punched her in the nose. She was so stunned she barely took her seat before the bus started to roll, and she almost fell. Sinking into her seat, she stared out the window to their houses below, and as the rooftops pulled away from view, Loni wondered what in the world had happened. Had she done something wrong somehow? Had she offended Sylvia somehow? Maybe by not calling or coming over. But that wasn't right because Sylvia had been at work most of the time, and Loni had received a head injury for Pete's sake. And then Loni started to get mad as she thought about how she'd been injured and now Sylvia was upset at her because of it. She just up and decided to join the cheer squad? Sylvia hated sports, didn't she?

But whatever, right? What does a lifetime of friendship mean after all? Loni thought as she stared out of the school bus window and blinked back hot tears. Flaring her nostrils one time, she saw her reflection in the window. Loni reached up and pinched each cheek to put sensation back in her face, and slowly she began to transform her righteous indignation into a low, low burn unlike anything she'd experienced prior. By the time the bus arrived at the corner of Trinity Lane, Loni was literally seeing red. She laughed and thought, *I used to think it was just a saying.* When the bus pulled into the school, Loni Lore stood up, grabbed her book bag, and resolutely did not look back at Sylvia Tate as she exited the bus and made her way into the building and the next phase of her life that did not include Sylvia Tate as one of the five fingers on her hand.

If Sylvia avoided Loni, Loni didn't know because she avoided Sylvia and the cheer squad completely at school. And because of cheering, Sylvia was never on the afternoon bus. In the mornings, Loni would take the newspaper after her father would finish it, and she would bury her nose in it until it was time for the bus to arrive. When the bus rounded the corner, she would fold it long enough to climb the steps and take her seat, then unfold it and continue reading.

This routine lasted about two weeks until one morning while Loni was eating a piece of toast and getting her bag ready, she heard a car honk outside and through the thin gauze of the window hangings, Loni saw Sylvia get into a black Chevrolet and leave. When Loni got on the bus, she noted that Sissy Gifford was conspicuously missing and assumed this meant her daily life was now 100 percent Sylvia free.

Junior year was more than enough to keep Loni's mind off of the fact that Sylvia had ditched her. Because of the combined forces of science, advanced math, and joining the school newspaper (which was the result of her carrying a newspaper around every day), Loni was always reading something or writing something or running between locations to interview someone.

Loni quickly learned how much she never knew about her school, its history, her fellow students, the teachers, or the different activities that existed until she was assigned to write about them. For example, Loni had known about an auto shop existing in their school, but she had never had a reason to approach that end of the school building in the two prior years she'd been a student. Loni had marveled to learn that two entire garage bays opened up to hold cars in a classroom setting. She wondered why it was kept a secret. It had to be more exciting than learning geometrical proofs. She interviewed class president nominees, asking hard-line questions about their campaign promises. She wrote advertisements for the blood drives on behalf of the candy stripers, and she posted classified ads for the theater department. Loni, however, was not allowed to write about sports events. She was told by an editor that she lacked a basic understanding of the game objectives, and that her adjectives were entirely inappropriate. This suited her though, as she would never have to interview the cheer team.

In late September, the newspaper began lead-up stories to homecoming, which meant Desmond and Derek were interviewing football players and coaches and Loni was interviewing the homecoming court. Loni agreed to attend, but only so she could write about it for the following week, even though she had no clue what to wear. The blue sequin dress her cousin loaned her was a bit uncomfortable and scratchy. And she had a fit trying to get her hair to cooperate. And she wasn't sure if wearing the long white gloves actually complemented the outfit or if it was over the top. When her father inquired about the young man accompanying her, she squirmed as she explained that she didn't have a date as such but was attending with a few others from the newspaper, at which point Loni realized that dances were some bizarre form of torture.

Loni had only recently gotten used to seeing the school after hours for different events, but her eyes popped in amazement observing how the homecoming committee had decorated the halls and the gymnasium with white streamers and garlands and little strands of white lights dripping from the ceiling like jellyfish tentacles. It was breathtaking. Loni was overwhelmed with the simple joy of seeing her class-mates dressed up in suits and gowns, transformed for the evening into the kings and queens of the court with all the pageantry properly devoted. She was suddenly ashamed of herself for having never wanted to take part in it before, but she resolved to make up for lost time by taking photos and interviewing as many people as she could. She waited by the bleachers for people to naturally filter over, and she would ask if they were enjoying themselves and if they wanted to do a quick interview for the school newspaper. She was always pleasantly surprised when someone said yes.

By 8:30, Loni felt like she'd had her fill of note gathering, and she settled in to watching the crowd. She was observing the slow-dancing couples all around her when a figure approached. He stepped into the circle of light, and she realized with a jolt that it was Tyrone. It was her Supraman! But before she could consider what to say, he was already to her.

"Loni Lore! It's good to see you."

"Hi, Tyrone," she said, shaking her head, dazed. "Fancy seeing you here."

She winced inwardly. What was she supposed to say? *How have you been? Oh good. I love you by the way. Yeah.* But he was talking to her again.

"Yeah, I hoped that I would get to see you tonight. I never got a chance to properly check up on you, though I did come by the hospital."

"Yeah. I heard. Thank you." Loni smiled.

"No worries. But I didn't think they were going to let us in at first. I expect you must've been the first black woman ever to lay in Baptist Hospital's bed. Probably thought you were staging a sit-in. Lucky they didn't send in the dogs, which they normally would, but it might disturb the other white people."

Loni liked the way Tyrone just kept talking, not like he was nervous but instead like he just couldn't stop himself. She looked up and said, "Tyrone, ask me to dance."

And he said, "Yeah, do you want to dance?"

"I thought you'd never ask," she said dryly, and he extended his arm and led her to the floor. Loni never once looked away, and she let him guide her in easy circles with his hands on her waist and her long white gloves extending behind his neck. Her shoes once again gave her an extra two inches, allowing her to gaze easily into his eyes. And once more, in an instant and without warning, Loni's mind was dragged beneath the undertow of stars that pulled her down and down, further down, until she and Tyrone were left isolated for a slow, beautiful eternity around a blue pulsing light, his hands pressed against her sequin waist and the pleasure of how the dress scratched against her skin, reminding her to breathe. And when she stared into his eyes, she was complete again where she had forgotten something was missing. And then the song was over, and Tyrone and Loni found themselves standing beside the white glow of the hallway leading out of the gymnasium. Tyrone was looking around, unsure.

"Loni?" he asked.

"Yes, Tyrone?"

"Where are the bathrooms in this place?"

Loni laughed. "Come on, I'll show you."

Loni took Tyrone by the hand, negotiating the languid crowd of smiling faces and moved toward the front of the school. She had just rounded the corner into the Language Arts hall when she heard off to the left, "Hey, I wondered where you'd run off to."

And turning naturally to look, Loni saw Sylvia in a black-and-gold dress walking toward her. No, walking toward Tyrone! Tyrone let go of Loni's hand as he turned, and Loni was drawn up short of breath. She never asked why he was here. She hadn't cared. It was enough that he was here. But he was here with Sylvia! Loni gawked, stunned as the sum total understanding landed upon her heart.

Sylvia was dating Tyrone.

If she stood there or if she ran or if she screamed, she did not recall. All Loni knew were the vivid colors that assaulted her visual field and the noises like a Ham radio searching for signal in the quiet space. When Loni came to her senses, she was in the bathroom gently cupping handfuls of water over her mouth, eyes, and nose. She still had her white gloves on, but she didn't care.

Her oldest and dearest friend had stabbed her in her heart no sooner than she had discovered it. How, she wondered in that moment, would she ever feel again.

***

DELIGHTED TO BE FRIENDS WITH YOU

October 1995

As Kaldari sits in his bedroom and toils over his keyboard, plugging away at a stupid piece of script, he thinks about how high school has amounted to so very little. He continues to plunk away at a series of code segments, rearranging ones and zeros late into the night, and as he does, he sighs deeply at his monitor. He now doubts college will be any better.

He is at home alone on a cold Friday night in October, chatting on the net with Senator, struggling to create a script that, when completed, will show a running display of the game Minesweeper being beaten indefinitely. *Yay.*

Why is Kaldari scripting the unending domination of Minesweeper? Because Kaldari thinks Minesweeper is a dumb game—a game so dumb that it deserves to be beaten on repeat. And because Kaldari is limited to hosting private chatrooms and writing video game code, so what else is he going to do? But mostly because he ran his mouth to Senator, and Senator called *bullshit*.

One evening, after drinking a few beers lifted from Senator's dad, Kaldari shares his opinion of Minesweeper with Senator, arguing 1) that the winning script should be created as a matter of principle and 2) that anyone with a modicum of talent could write it. And Senator being equally bored claims Kaldari is bullshit. This leads to a drunken argument, and eventually an all-out contest to prove whether it can be done. And so Kaldari, finding himself obliged to put his money where his mouth is, sits at home writing the code.

It's been more time consuming than anything, but it really can be done, just like Kaldari bets it can, because it's a logic puzzle (damn it), and therefore runs off an algorithm. And so Kaldari turns it on again, and the script works again.

Until it doesn't. *Dammit.*

The first time Kaldari finds that the program has stopped running, it is early Friday afternoon when he gets home from school, and he assumes someone has interrupted his computer while he was away. But then it happens again later that evening when nobody else is around. He sets down his ramen cup on the edge of his desk and contemplates answers. When he looks at the screen, two mines are still covered with a pattern of blocks arrayed around them. The algorithm should have easily solved them. But why isn't it solving them?

He clears the screen with a few clicks, and the algorithm starts up again. It runs for a few hours, then stops again. Kaldari looks up from his calculus homework and glowers in frustration. He is just going to have to recode. Damn it. What time is it even? 11:30 PM. *Ugh.*

But then, just as he leans in to restart his computer, the shape of the remaining mines catches his eye. He leans back in his chair and examines the screen again. It is silly really, but Kaldari tries to remember if the configuration of bricks has been the same every time the algorithm stopped.

Because when he looks at it now, the arrangement of the five remaining blocks covering the mines resembles what is called a "glider" in the old computer game *Game of Life*. Which is nothing special at all because that pattern exists everywhere. He can go to IHOP right now and find the same pattern in the ceiling tiles if he looks hard enough … but for some reason it nags at him. Kaldari restarts the algorithm again.

Almost an hour later, the program stops in the glider formation again. But the pattern is not the same as before. The glider has "walked forward" a single step on the screen. Kaldari starts to get an uneasy feeling.

He hard restarts his computer, and then runs the program again. It runs again for almost two hours, presenting new screen after new screen of a gray minefield, a yellow happy face, and a red mine count that decreases in quick succession as the invisible cursor uncovers the pattern of numbers and flags. Kaldari just ignores the fact that he is suddenly anxious for the program to stop, when up until now all he'd been wanting to do was make it keep running. It is completely ridiculous, and he knows it.

But the program stops again. The blocks covering the remaining two mines are in a glider shape again, and the glider has walked forward another step from where it was when he turned the computer off. Kaldari gets up and examines his screen closely. He looks at his dial-up which is connected to the Mothers' private chatroom. He sees Senator online. He chats with Senator to see if he is working in real time. All systems seem normal.

Kaldari imagines if the glider were to walk one more step forward. He flips his homework over, and on the back, he calculates what the next configuration points would have to be. On a guess, rather than solving the mines to restart the algorithm, Kaldari clicks the mouse five times into the boxes where he calculates the glider should appear next. Kaldari gasps as he watches the little glider form begin to tumble end over end down the Minesweeper screen. It begins to change into vibrant colors as it repeats a path down screen again and again.

Another hacker.

Holy shit! Another hacker! Inside his machine!

Kaldari is still chatting with Senator online, so he immediately sends the High Alert message to get the Mothers and come over to his house ASAP. Kaldari doesn't even know what time it is. When he checks, it's 5:30 AM. Jesus, neither of them had slept. Kaldari walks into the hallway, tempted to grab a quick shower before the Mothers arrive, but instead returns to his bedroom; he doesn't dare look away from the monitor in case the glider disappears.

Senator arrives within the hour, a very sleepy trio of Blue, Vercingetorix, and HexxCat in tow. They are all five up very early for a Saturday morning, and in short order, they are all squinting at the Minesweeper pixels over cups of coffee. The Mothers watch the animation repeat down the screen for a few minutes at a time, then retreat outside in groups of three or four where they can smoke cigarettes openly on the back porch and pace and deliberate and discuss while always leaving someone inside to watch the monitor.

Kaldari's parents are away at a conference in Banff and won't be back for a few days, so they decide to just make a day of smoking and thinking and coming up with a plan.

Car doors slam around the corner to signal the neighbors are leaving. The two elderly families on either side of his parents' house, Mr. and Mrs. Nasim on the left and Mrs. Cole-Jean on the right, have openly remarked that they consider he and the rest of the Mothers to be "no-good punks." Kaldari believes that is only because they have never seen real punks.

Leaves drift down from the giant red-orange maple tree in Kaldari's backyard. Vercingetorix and HexxCat are bundled in matching tan trench coats and black toboggins; Kaldari notes that they have a thing for matching lately. They dart playfully around one another and make patterns with the leaves on the porch railing. Meanwhile, Senator sits in a lawn chair and stares quietly from behind his wraparound Ray-Ban sunglasses. The lenses fall just below his prominent eyebrows and hide his thoughts. Blue steps out for her turn to smoke and runs her fingers through her wavy auburn hair; she keeps talking about shaving it off, but it's down to her shoulders now. She lights a cigarette and suggests they all go back inside and give it a try. Kaldari supposes that she is right; he cannot drag the suspense out any longer.

The Mothers finish smoking and file in the back door. Kaldari enters his bedroom last and joins Verse and Cat on the neatly made bed where they perch like little birds. Blue sits in a folding chair that is pressed up against the bedside nightstand, causing the lamplight to glow out from behind her in a halo. Kaldari gives Senator the seat at his desk as he types the fastest, but he keeps a stack of floppy disks near to hand in case Senator needs code quickly.

Senator clears the desk of paper scraps, ramen noodle cups, and any technical debris that belies actual human occupancy. Without fanfare, Senator clicks onto the glider. Nothing happens. He clicks on the remaining mines in succession. Nothing happens.

"Try the smiley face," HexxCat suggests, and when Senator does, the whole screen dissolves. The black of the monitor hums and the C: prompt appears. They all groan, and HexxCat moans "Noooooooooo!" and buries her face in Vercingetorix's collar. He cradles her head in sympathy.

Suddenly text appears under the C: prompt one letter at a time. It reads "Complex conjugate?"

They all come to attention in a chorus of "Oh shit!"

Beneath the first line of text, another line of text appears all at once. It reads "Tick-tock." A digital clock readout of 2:00:00 appears and starts to count down. They all start jabbering at once, spitballing ideas.

Kaldari thinks over his recent homework. "They want the inverse of the denominator … but for what? Of what?"

Senator states the obvious: "They want us to make the inverse of their glider function. Make it run backward."

Vercingetorix barks out a laugh. "That's not possible in two hours. We don't even have their code anymore or a picture of it. They wiped the Minesweeper screen."

Blue smiles. "Of course, we do," she says, and she pushes Senator over from the keyboard. She pulls up the history from Kaldari's computer and reveals the script for the hacker's glider. "Right here." And with the push of a button Blue revives everyone from the doldrums of the last six months, and the scent of the challenge is in the air. 1:57:31.

Senator scowls at the screen. "They asked for the reciprocal function. So, let's make the pattern go in reverse."

While the others loudly debate the formula for reversing the glider, Kaldari sits next to Blue and thinks to himself quietly about how some samurai has hacked his personal rig with impunity. Whoever it is obviously has the class advantage. He wonders for the first time what might be waiting for them at the end of this challenge; he hopes they are up for it, but he articulates nothing about his reservations. Soon, the Mothers have a plan. They handwrite the basics, then Senator begins to copy the code into a text box arranged under the timer. 1:22:50.

Senator finishes typing and launches a test of the reverse glider program. It crashes. 1:03:22.

They scan the script and catch a simple mistake. 0:59:26.

They run the script again. It runs, but the output is not reversed; it is translated. They know what to fix now. 0:47:13.

All loops look correct. They go back and check all the script again for any glaring clues or codes or Easter eggs. Nothing stands out. 0:29:12.

Senator copies the reverse code into the C: prompt and hits enter. 0:28:57.

On the screen, their reverse glider appears and begins walking back up the screen. It repeats this loop twice before a series of glider patterns and shapes from Conway's *Game of Life* emerge from the sides of the screen, including blocks, beehives, traffic lights, and eaters. The stand-alone shapes begin to dance around the screen slowly at first, then quicker and quicker, before finally colliding into one another and forming into more complex shapes.

Before the entire screen goes diehard, the monitor dissolves again and returns to the black screen, and the C:

prompt reappears. The word "STARDATE?" types itself into the C: prompt just as the counter of 0:28:57 reappears and instantly drops to 0:28:56.

They try to keep cool as they hurriedly cast about for anyone they can contact who knows anything about *Star Trek*. They are on the verge of trying Chance Black of the Halflings when Senator slaps the desk and shouts, "Bill Jenkins! I heard him in a debate with Steven Carol about Picard and Riker! His number is in the directory." 0:19:45.

Senator calls Bill's house, and Bill's mom answers the phone.

"Hi, Mrs. Jenkins. This is Sadakant Kassam. I go to school with Bill. I need to ask him a quick question if he's around. Please, ma'am."

They all hold their breath and stare at the popcorn ceiling. The Mothers exhale a collective sigh when she replies Bill is home and awake and able to come to the phone. 0:17:21.

Bill Jones is amused that they are eager to learn about *Star Trek* this early on a Saturday morning, but sensing the urgency in Senator's tone, he quickly explains how to calculate a stardate. As Senator hangs up, they all yell to Bill that they will see him on Monday, and Kaldari can see Bill's kind smile radiate through the receiver.

Glancing over to Vercingetorix, HexxCat, and Blue with sincerity, Kaldari states, "Please remind me to buy Bill a doughnut on Monday from the snack table. You know, Chance Black would have just tormented us about *Star Trek* trivia and let the clock run out."

They all nod in agreement. Senator types furiously. 0:11:47.

Kaldari starts to worry that they have wasted too much time already. Senator pulls up code for two identical digital clocks showing real time, and he makes them large on Kaldari's screen. Together, the Mothers help him to adjust the code on one digital clock to calculate October 28, 1995, into the respective star year, star month, and star day. 0:07:36.

Senator copies and pastes in the original digital clock's still-ticking readout for hours and minutes. The second digital clock now shows their stardate according to *Star Trek* canon. They hit enter and the screen dissolves. 0:06:06.

The word "GEOLOCATION?" types itself into the C: prompt just as the counter drops to 0:05:59.

"My turn to be cool," Blue announces, and she whispers a web address to Senator, who types it in. The National Geologic Map Database page opens, and an address bar appears above two boxes reading LAT and LONG. "Type in Kaldari's address." Senator enters the information into the top field, and a set of coordinates pops up below the LAT and LONG boxes: 36.0599634, -86.9384220. He carefully copies the numbers into the waiting screen and hits enter. 0:00:29.

The clock counts down to 0:00:00, and the screen dissolves. The C: prompt returns with the text "ENTER NAME:" blinking in a dialogue box. Senator enters MOTHERS. The text "LIST MOTHERS:" appears. They shrug and Senator types in their names: Kaldari, Senator, Vercingetorix, Blue, HexxCat.

The screen dissolves again. Silence fills the room, and eyes cast around in confusion.

Everyone jumps and gasps out another "oh shit" as a whirring noise comes from the hard drive of Kaldari's computer. The words "Don't Panic" appear on the screen. They all laugh nervously, but they keep their attention split between the monitor screen on top of the desk and the racing hard drive sitting beside the desk on the floor.

A moment later, the sounds emitting from the hard drive cease, the monitor turns white, then turns to fuzz with a black bar at the bottom. In the black bar is a dialogue box reading "Mothers:" The fuzz above the prompt sharpens suddenly, and they are watching a black-and-white video feed of a woman's face very close to the camera for a moment before she backs away and walks off-screen.

She reemerges, and she is adjusting settings on her camera, and then the screen suddenly turns from black and white to near-color. They all let out a collective "whoa."

The woman retreats a short distance away from the screen now and adjusts herself upon a large, cozy-looking, blue chair. She is an elderly black woman with short, wavy, silver hair pulled back in a thick head band. She is wearing a smart white suit coat with a simple ankle-length black dress beneath and black sandals. Behind her, the Mothers can see parts of a large office and library setting. A section of bookshelves is visible on the right of the screen, and a low white couch sits on the left before a large window looking out onto a mountainous desert landscape. On an end table by the couch, there sits a vase with a single long-stem lily.

Kaldari imagines for the briefest moment that the lone blossom is looking out the window at the landscape. He then refocuses on this woman who has taken control of his computer, realizing that he should be scouting for any possible signs of danger. While she looks like someone's grandmother and she emits a slow, polite smile, her eyes speak volumes regarding her intellect.

The mysterious woman draws herself up to speak, and recognizing their better, they all sit up a little straighter too out of preternatural instinct, if not respect.

"Hi. How is everybody?" Her voice comes out of Kaldari's small computer speakers resoundingly crisp. Her smile widens.

They all reply "hi," out of habit.

"Just type into chat if you can hear me and see me OK. This conversation is one way for your benefit, as I can't see or hear you directly yet."

The Mothers debate on what to say, and when they finally agree, Senator types into the text box.

Mothers: *Greetings from the Mothers. How are you today?*

"Hey! There you all are! Greetings to you too. I am good, yes." Her voice sounds distinctly Southern when she smiles and responds, and Kaldari is oddly put at ease. "Good, good. We seem to be synced up nicely." She is obviously looking at a teleprompter somewhere off-screen. It gives the feeling that they are interacting with a TV talk show host. "OK, here we go. Let's get started. My name is L-One."

Mothers: *Hi, L-One. To what do we owe the honor of your visit?*

She leans back in surprise. "Oh, well aren't you all well-mannered? Well, if you must know, we are talking now because you found and passed the code skills test. Congratulations."

Mothers: *Code skills test? The glider puzzle and stardate and geocode?*

"Yes. Conway's glider puzzle, exactly." She leans forward excitedly on the edge of her seat as she speaks. "Ever since we created that skills test, it has been open and available for anyone meeting certain requirements: launching a program with a looping script using a PRNG, a pseudo random number generator, on a screen of two or more dimensions while being online."

Mothers: *Lucky us.*

"Not luck really; the event happens quite frequently. Daily actually, but people rarely run the loop long enough to catch the test ... unless they make a hobby of computers ... or mathematics. Every time a linked-up computer ran a program that met the requirements, the challenge was presented at various points in the algorithm—just as it did for you, no doubt. I'm certain most people just clicked on through, not knowing how to turn the puzzle on."

Mothers: *The challenge was well hidden indeed. Why so tough to find?*

"For our own reasons, we only wanted someone special to know about the challenge." Here she smiles, and it lights up her eyes and cheeks. And for a reason he cannot explain, Kaldari gets the shivers. L-One continues: "As for the stardate and geocode, we needed it to verify your location to secure your hardware for this meeting and for the upcoming challenge."

Mothers: *Upcoming challenge? You have more in store for us?*

"Oh yes!" she replies with feline slowness, and her eyes light up in genuine delight. "Much more. If you accept." She bats her eyes once like a pulse, and Kaldari can hear it echo in his mind like an insane gong.

Mothers: *Puzzles are fun, and you do cool tricks, but we aren't supposed to talk to strangers. What exactly are we getting ourselves involved in?*

L-One raises her eyebrows slightly and softly chuckles. "Unfortunately, you are still strangers to us as well, and we cannot give you any details about the challenge until you agree to the terms of participation. We are only permitted to tell you the proviso and the reward."

Mothers: *Proviso?*

"Yes. Provisionally, we are permitted to tell you that the steps required in the challenge are neither illegal nor inherently dangerous to yourselves or others and that there is nothing above your skill level that would keep you from successfully completing the challenge."

Mothers: *Good to know. Reward?*

L-One shrugs nonchalantly. "Free private college for each of you to start." She rolls her wrist and examines her nails. "Jobs later. Depending on your grades, and if you are a … good fit … for the organization."

Shrieking rounds of "bullshit," "jackpot," and "no way" pervade Kaldari's tiny bedroom.

Mothers: *We are interested to know more.*

L-One laughs openly this time, then cuts her laughter short. "Yes. I imagine you are interested. However, the problem is, if other people knew about the challenge, they would be interested too. People who might have the resources to complete the challenge before you." She speaks the next words slowly. "People that might not have qualms about harming high school students to be the first to solve the challenge." She lets the words hang in the air for a moment before finishing, "Secrecy, therefore, is the first term of participation."

She leans forward to emphasize her next point. "Once the challenge begins, you may not acknowledge the existence of the challenge to anyone that is not in full agreeance with the challenge terms. To do so will instantly forfeit the challenge for all members, even if the others are unaware of the transgression. Is that understood?"

Kaldari pulls back from the screen and looks at the others for some confirmation. HexxCat shrugs. Vercingetorix and Blue look to each other and to Kaldari and nod. Senator shakes his head once and types.

Mothers: *Understood. Yes, ma'am.*

"Excellent," she declares in a snap. And without hesitation, she continues: "The second term is you will cease all other computer activity requiring an internet connection until the completion of the challenge. Everything you need to know to complete the challenge has already been placed inside of your computer, and therefore, you have no need to expose yourselves to potential outside threats. Explicitly included in this second term is the use of any connected computer to research the name L-One, the name of the challenge, any other names connected to the challenge, or any information about yourselves. You cannot draw eyes to us, or to yourselves, or else the whole endeavor will be immediately forfeit."

Mothers: *Can we communicate with phones or pagers?*

"Your pagers are fine, so long as you stick to numeric codes. You may use landline phones or pay phones, so long as you do not talk about the challenge or any of its component parts. As a rule, it is always best to use discretion; best to not relay plans or directives on a phone. Come up with normal-sounding sentences as codes and keep it short."

Mothers: *We've got it covered. Anything else?*

"Nothing else out of the ordinary will be required at any later point beyond the challenge itself, but these two rules must be observed for everyone's sake, and you must each agree to the terms before you can gain access the challenge." L-One looks at the camera with a sweet smile. "I will give you a minute to talk about it amongst yourselves."

The video feed cuts away abruptly, and an old black-and-white station identification screen pops up with a 3D image of the Bionic Comics Supraman logo floating in the center. In the bottom right corner of the screen, the familiar timer counts down from 0:00:59. Senator spins around in the desk chair to face everybody in the tiny room. In this moment, when most normal people would stop completely, alert the authorities, and probably unplug their home computer for extra safety, the Mothers start speaking over each other in rapid succession.

"God, I need a cigarette, but we don't have enough time," Kaldari runs his hands through his hair, making it spike up in a fan. "Well, what do you say about that? Free college and jobs! Worth getting out of bed on a Saturday?"

"Are we saying yes to this? We are saying yes to this. Right?" Vercingetorix looks from face to face. "Did you see how she turned the monitor into a video receiver? It must have warped the pixels to make the screen appear color? This is insanely cool."

"What? Wait though. This is cool and all, but how exactly did she do that?" Blue holds up her hands, attempting to be a voice of reason. "How did she just take over your machine, Kaldari? You built that rig yourself."

"I have no idea, Blue. I'm really hoping to learn. Soon." Kaldari feels a glow beginning under his skin like he has just swallowed some of CC's 120 mg Ritalin. He wants Blue to be on board, but she looks upset. The clock ticks down. 0:00:38.

"Well, I vote yes. I can complete some challenge for free college," HexxCat reasons. She looks at Blue and shakes her friend on the knee. "Come on, Blue, what's really bugging you? Spit it out."

"She said people could hurt us if they find out what we are doing, and we don't know what we are doing yet. Or like, why us. And maybe it's just too good to be true."

HexxCat groans. "OK, sure, but that's if we were stupid and ran our mouths, which we won't, because we're not stupid. I mean, seriously, Blue, we already don't talk to other people. It's not like anyone's going to notice. We just don't surf the web for a while. Big deal."

"Well, I'm saying yes, because even if it's bullshit, I mean, look at what they've done already. Seriously, you can leave if you want." Senator looks hard at Blue. "But get out now."

"Ouch." Vercingetorix winces.

"Geesh. You don't have to be a jerk, Senator," HexxCat chides. "Blue is a Mother too. She has a right to speak."

"Well sorry, but we're running out of time. Can I say yes already?"

Kaldari agrees with Senator, but he stays cool as he looks at Blue. "Come on," he winks a small wink with an excited smile. "If it sucks, we'll bail. I promise." He squeezes her hand, which he had not noticed grabbing. She does not let go. Blue looks at the ticking clock then looks back at Kaldari. She smiles and nods her assent.

Kaldari nods. "Do it, Senator." Vercingetorix and HexxCat cheer as Senator rolls the mouse across the S of the Supraman logo and finds the intended trigger spot. He clicks the mouse. 0:00:08.

The screen dissolves. A moment later, the view of L-One sitting on her blue chair returns. She is staring off-screen dreamily one moment, then turns to look at them as if she had just recalled them being there. "Ah. Welcome back," L-One trills, a real sound of excitement in her voice. "Are we ready to play?"

Mothers: *Mothers are ready to rock, ma'am.*

L-One smiles like a cat that has finally lined up the pounce. She sits up a bit taller. Instinctively, the Mothers do the same.

"Excellent news. Most excellent news, indeed. Very well then. If you will each type your call signs once more and then reenter your stardate in the box below, it will constitute our agreement to terms."

Mothers: *Kaldari, Senator, Vercingetorix, HexxCat, Blue: SD: -327:177:22:41:56.*

The monitor cuts to a second camera that is zoomed closer to L-One, framed just outside her shoulders. The sloping mountains behind L-One are visually stunning; Kaldari's gaze, however, is drawn directly to her powerful face. She speaks slow and clear.

"Mothers Kaldari, Senator, Vercingetorix, HexxCat, and Blue, I am hereby obligated to inform you that the aforementioned terms begin now and that any violation of said terms by any one person instantly terminates the challenge for all contestants. Legal requirements aside, I am now pleased to introduce you to"—L-One draws her hands to her heart in a swoon— "the Friendship Bracelet Challenge."

"Ah!" Senator squawks. "Friendship what? What bullshit is this?"

"Move over. I'm typing now." Kaldari pushes Senator's chair.

"Calm down. I've got this." Senator motions Kaldari back to the bed next to Blue, and distractedly Kaldari sits closer to her than he's ever been. They all focus on the screen as Senator types.

Mothers: *Friendship bracelet? Like summer camp?*

"Exactly," L-One returns in voice so excited it hums with electricity. Senator just looks sideways at the others and mouths, "Exactly."

L-One continues speaking: "The friendship bracelet is universally known as an object given from one person to another as symbol of friendship. This ringed band is usually handmade and intended to be worn until the strings break from wear to show respect for the weaver. For this challenge, you will attempt to weave for us a very special friendship bracelet."

Mothers: *Out of code?*

L-One smiles at the camera, obviously enjoying the interplay. "Indeed. Part of it will be made of code, but you aren't writing it. We will give you that code. *You* will be occupied with building the machine to *read* the code."

Mothers: *Building a new machine sounds fun, but expensive.*

L-One cocks an eyebrow. "Oh, don't worry about that. Just follow the rules, and we'll foot the bill."

Mothers: *Free machines sound even better! Will it be our own Deep Thought perhaps?*

L-One genuinely laughs. "Clever reference, but actually it's more like Single Thought." She smirks at her own cleverness. "Are the Mothers at all familiar with the concept of a Turing machine?"

Mothers: *Yes. A basic computer. A simple machine that once completed, runs its loop until the end.*

"Indeed. Well said. Runs its *loop* until the end." She muses for a second, then looks off-screen for a moment as if consulting with someone. She continues: "Yes. You will be responsible for building a Turing machine that we refer to as 'the Loom,' in keeping with the friendship bracelet theme. Your primary task will be to find a safe location and build the Loom with the provided pieces."

Mothers: *How much safe space will we need?*

L-One purses her lips and squints in concentration just a moment before responding. "The Loom could be built in a small garage if nothing else were in it at all, but there will be soldering involved, so try to pick a place that's not going to set fire easily." She shrugs at them in a universal sign of *it's not my call.* "Part of the challenge will be figuring out a space, certainly, but just remember, it must be hidden from all eyes save yours. Understood?"

Mothers: *Understood.*

"Good," she intones firmly before she continues. "Once the Loom is complete, you will use the pattern code we provide to weave the bracelet. And before you ask, yes, it will be a real bracelet, not just some symbol or metaphorical loop. The weaving process can only be attempted once. It will take a few hours, and the entire process will require your undivided attention, so don't just randomly decide to turn it on and walk away."

Mothers: *Understood. What happens once the bracelet is woven?*

L-One pauses. She blinks very slowly, and then in the sweetest, most Southern grandmother lilt imaginable, she enlightens the Mothers, "Why … we will be friends, of course." She bats her eyelashes slowly, letting her words sink in. "You do … want to be friends … don't you?"

Mothers: *Yes. Of course, L-One. We'd be delighted to be friends with you.*

"Good," she repeats, only this time her voice is softer. L-One looks directly into the camera and remains silent for a long moment. Kaldari feels as if she is somehow looking straight through his monitor and penetrating deep into his thoughts. Was this all a dream? How had she known to sculpt this dream challenge just for him? Had the endless Minesweeper coding driven him to delusion?

The view on the computer screen cuts back to camera one. The bookshelves, the couch, and the flower are in view again behind L-One and her blue chair. L-One puts her hands in her lap and sweetly notifies the Mothers, "Unfortunately, this is where we all must part for now. Believe us when we say we have every hope of speaking to you again as soon as the challenge is complete." She holds up a hand. "Just trust. We will know." Her eyes twinkle with mischief. "Everything you need has already been downloaded to this machine, which you must keep offline starting now. We truly wish you the best of luck. The Friendship Bracelet Challenge has now begun. Cheers!" L-One smiles wide again, pulling her cheeks tight into her eyes, and the camera cuts away to the old-school black-and-white station identification screen with the Supraman logo.

Then, before anyone can react or ask any questions, the monitor zaps back to black and the C: prompt blinks. It then ghost-types a file path into the open field and sits, waiting. Kaldari quickly writes down the information on a notepad that might have once been calculus homework. Vercingetorix leans down and starts to unplug the modem cable, but he looks to Kaldari first. Kaldari grimaces a little, but nods. He knows Vercingetorix is right. They disconnect the internet and then watch as Senator clicks open the folder labeled "FRIENDSHIP BRACELET.zip." The folder cascades into three files: threads.doc, loom.doc, and pattern.exe.

Senator selects threads.doc, and a file opens revealing a shopping list. On the left-hand side are the names of different stores; some stores the Mothers have heard of like RadioShack and Lowe's, but a few places have generic-sounding names like ABC Group and Praxis. Many of the items coming from RadioShack appear to be generic computer parts and casings and pieces from various printers. The supplies coming from ABC Group include things like buckets of plastic beads, paraffin, and sand, while the items from Praxis are mostly specific small metal pieces, including copper wire, soldering metals, and cables. One item that sticks out is labeled "stack belt microchips."

At the bottom of the list, the final two lines read "food" and "external expenses," each with a line item budget of $500. Underneath the list, a note reads, "Charge all expenses to the account of Sylvia Alexa Tate (aka your Auntie Sylvia). The account is real, so please be smart. And always remember that all terms apply at all times." This note is followed by a string of sixteen numbers, a four-digit date, and three more digits and a Nashville billing address on Wedgewood Avenue.

"Bullshit!" Senator exclaims. "There's no way we have a credit card."

"We have five hundred dollars for food!" HexxCat chimes in, eyes gone wide.

"What's an external expense?" Vercingetorix scoots closer to the screen.

"I don't know. Open the other files, Senator," Blue suggests, leaning closer to both Kaldari and the screen, and they all lean in a little further to see what comes next when Senator opens the next file.

The loom.doc file reveals over four hundred pages of step-by-step schematics for what appears to be sections of a weird printer. It is hard to visualize page by page, so they click ahead to the last few pages of the manual and find what they suppose is a Loom, but to the Mothers looks like a series of see-through circles.

The pattern.exe file turns out to be all code. They close the file as soon as they open it, in the off chance that playing around with it might corrupt it somehow. Kaldari goes to insert a floppy drive, but Vercingetorix stays his hand.

"Kal, look at the file size." Kaldari looks, then does a double take. The file is nearly the size of his entire computer's memory. This draws him up short, but he shrugs. If they can't put the file on a disk, then at some point they'll just have to take his entire computer to wherever they decide to build.

Kaldari needs a cigarette and a moment to reflect on events, and on a telepathic link, the Mothers all wordlessly exit the bedroom and turn their backs on the monitor and the cascade of three files waiting on the screen. They are all silent in the afterglow of the event for many minutes. Finally, HexxCat breaks the silence. She looks deep into the eyes of Vercingetorix, and intones a breathy version of L-One, "You do … want to be friends … don't you?" The Mothers all fall out giggling uncontrollably.

"I definitely want to be that woman's friend," Kaldari laughs out as he catches his breath. Blue looks up at him laughing, and they share a silent smile, and the perfect moment cements in his brain forever.

* * *

THE UNIVERSE WANTS YOU TO BE BIG, MY MAN

August 1996

An alarm clock sounds out, and Supraman startles awake on E-Sharp's leather sofa. As if no time has really passed, the shit show of the real world comes crashing over him in recurring waves of *what did I do to deserve this*. Supraman throws his clothes on and grabs his gym bag off the top of the box Loni left him. At least he can catch a shower in the gym at school and change clothes. E-Sharp comes out of his bedroom smoking a piece of a blunt. E offers it to Supraman, but he waves it off. A quick cup of coffee later and they are both out the door and heading down the black staircase in the predawn stillness of late-summer Nashville. E-Sharp offers Supraman a lift toward Rose Park on his way to the dairy, and Supraman is grateful not to have to walk that distance.

Supraman gets dropped off at the corner of Wedgewood and Eighth Avenue and shivers when he realizes this is where everything went south in the first place. What if he had just hung up the phone? Then when Loni had called him at work, he would've been there. Then when Sylvia called Loni at work, Loni could have just blown up over Sylvia being a lunatic. Sure, the scenario still would've blown up either way, and Loni would be mad regardless, but at least he wouldn't have had to explain why he wasn't at work in the middle of the day yesterday and why he was, in fact, at Sylvia's house. *And* he would not have to prove that he most certainly did not do whatever Sylvia called Loni and said that he did.

"Jesus God, what did Silvia say?" he mutters aloud to no one.

Supraman reasons that in the time it took for him to gather his wits and finally request an ambulance was when Sylvia had called Loni at work. Later, when the medic arrived, she refused to go with them, and they refused to take her, claiming she looked perfectly healthy, albeit naked in a bathrobe and living in a dump. The paramedics argued further that Supraman was not her husband nor her legal guardian. He was not about to argue with some young paramedic or stick around in case the police decided to show up. He had at least convinced them to make a record of the event in their work journal. On the outside chance that something else happened to her, he wanted the record to show that he had attempted to do the right thing before washing his hands of the situation and walking to get a beer. But even doing that, doing the right thing, being concerned for another human being who is obviously out of her mind and possibly out of her body, *that* was the wrong course of action.

Supraman looks up to see that he has walked all the way up Eighth Avenue to the top of the hill past the reservoir and is almost to the school building. It's still dark, and the streetlights are orange. He gives a steady eye to the surroundings, and then makes his way to the building. The side doors are open, and the lights are on downstairs, which means the janitorial staff is already in. Supraman finds the head custodian, Russell, and lets him know that he is in the building. Supraman walks through the empty school, turning on the lights on his way to the gym.

He heads into the locker room after flipping on all the breakers for the gym. He'd been in these locker rooms so many times before; he realizes that he's missed Rose Park. He strips down and looks at himself in the mirror. He's held in there very well for a man of forty. His body looks good, and he's got a full head of hair. No noticeable wrinkles or signs of extreme aging yet. He'll make it, he guesses, if these damn women don't kill him first.

Supraman steps into the shower, and for a long while, he just lets the water rush over him. At some point, he feels all of his worries and anxieties sliding away from his mind and down into the drain and away. Supraman smiles and decides to put his game face on, and instantly something gives over in him. Like someone opening the window on a hot day, a wave of release rushes through Supraman as he realizes suddenly that he has been spiritually holding his breath since yesterday afternoon. All reaction, no reflection on himself. He realizes that he has been so caught up in Loni and Sylvia that he has completely neglected to consider his options.

Loni obviously wants space. Fine. She'll come around eventually he figures. She will eventually want to know what really happened, and when he tells her, she will see that he's telling the truth. She might be mad that he went over to help Sylvia, but not leaving mad. He'll just have to wait a day or two until Loni can calm her temper down. He can probably stay with E-Sharp until then without it being a hassle.

Sylvia, on the other hand, well that's just some level of messed up best ignored. He decides to warn the front office that a prank caller has been stalking him pretending to be his wife, and best to just take the message and ignore it. That's how he would deal with Sylvia because none of it involves him. None of this is in his column, so whatever, man.

Supraman decides to have a good, normal morning at school while that option is available, figuring he'll handle all the rest later when it appears. He steps out of the shower and towels off and starts strumming out a bass line in his head. Supraman gets his gym clothes on and adjusts his headband to pull his small Afro back slightly. He checks himself in the mirror again and finds himself looking right on.

In the coaches' office between the two locker rooms, in the separate small kitchen area, Supraman finds the coffee stash and sets to making a pot of coffee. As he fills up the water, he glances at the wall calendar above the sink, which is still flipped to May from the previous semester, and it has a quote by Rumi that reads "Stop acting so small. You are the universe in ecstatic motion." Supraman eyes it twice and thinks about it. He wasn't sure what the ecstatic motion part was supposed to mean necessarily, but it sounded like dancing, so OK. But for certain, the first part resonated with him.

Stop acting so small.

He can dig on that today. Today, Supraman decides he is going to rise above on some *universe motion* because what else can he do? Ha!

Supraman sets the coffee maker to rights and genuinely starts feeling better. He turns the radio on, and it's tuned to 88.1 predictably. Aretha is singing "Son of a Preacher Man."

Supraman walks over to the calendar and flips over June and reads the quote.

"Even if you're on the right track, you'll get run over if you just sit there."

—Will Rogers

Supraman purses his lips, soaking in that bit of wisdom.

He flips to July. There he finds two passages from the Buddha: "Your work is to discover your work, and then with all your heart give yourself to it" and "The trouble is, you think you have time." That second one strikes Supraman as a touch ominous in so far as an inspirational quote goes, but he must agree that the message is effective.

As far as the first message, however, it oddly resonates. Supraman has a good life. A great wife. A decent enough job. No major debt or illness. Yet the universe always seemed to be sending him little signs, signs that warned a change was coming for him. Not a spiritual change or change of character, per se, but a change of occupation didn't seem too far-fetched.

Supraman became a PE coach right out of college, mostly because the job was offered to him and it paid good benefits, but partly because he had just split up with Sylvia and wanted a steady gig to keep her off his mind. While being a coach wasn't horrible by any stretch of the imagination (he had seen what E-Sharp had to do at the dairy and wasn't about to work in those conditions), he had always hoped to do something cool with his life, like be the front man for a funk band or something. He thinks about how at least E-Sharp is still playing music.

And just as he is having this thought, Parliament's "Mothership Connection" kicks off right after Aretha, and

Supraman hears the voice of George Clinton performing as Starchild, an alien who had returned to reclaim the pyramids. Supraman points to the radio and speaks to Starchild: "I could use a mothership connection of my own right now, that's for certain. Come and reclaim me as a citizen of the universe, George. I am ready to party on your mothership!"

Supraman smiles and flips the calendar page over to August and reads another quote from Rumi: "What you seek is seeking you."

And quite suddenly, like the ring of a bell, Supraman experiences a moment that can only be described as a vision, or an awakening.

"What you seek is seeking you." And it is right then that Supraman knows what to do. His mind is made up, and the clarity of the moment is so intense that "life-changing" is the only name for it. He pours a cup of coffee and sweetens it up and smiles as he drinks in his certainty.

But the world knows nothing of Supraman's life-changing epiphany as it rolls forward in space, pulling the day into its normal patterns. The noises of the school slowly begin to come awake with the sounds of sneakers and lockers, talking, shouting, laughing. Doors opening and closing. And then comes the first arrivals to the gym, eagerly seeking the rack of basketballs, followed by a flood of contenders for pre-class showdowns. Backpacks slung carelessly against bleachers as the *skirt skirt skirt* of Air Jordans accompanies the *oohs* and the groans and the *swish, thump thump thump, swish, thump thump thump, swish, thump thump thump*. And Supraman finds the beautiful groove of his day, and it resonates with his made-up mind all the way through the first three activity bells and into lunch.

As Supraman eats his cafeteria lunch of meatloaf and green beans out on the outside bleachers, he looks around at all the kids congregating in tiny clusters, hands in pockets or waving around in animated pantomime. Four girls in purple overalls with a jump rope draw a small crowd around them as they start counting and chanting. A boy pulls his own basketball out from his backpack and a quick pickup game is assembled between the rusted-out hoops on the crumbling blacktop.

Far beyond the basketball court, Supraman spies a heavy-set kid all alone, panting along in a slow jog. Navy-blue sweatpants and a t-shirt hug closely to the boy's large frame with sweat stains visible from afar. Supraman chews slowly, watching as the boy pauses with his hands on his knees, gasping for breath. The boy stands up after a minute, walk-starts himself, and then pushes into a slow jiggly-jog again, staring straight ahead into the curve of the running track. Bit by bit, the boy makes his way around the far end, then heads back toward the school and Supraman.

The boy approaches, plops down near Supraman, and lets out an exasperated sigh as he lays his head back and looks up to the sky.

"Getting ready for the 2000 Olympics, my man?" Supraman asked the kid with a kind of laugh.

The kid obviously has a sense of humor because he comes back with, "Figure skating. Couples."

"What grade are you in?"

"Sixth."

"If you don't mind me asking, why are you out here sweating like this? I mean, I'm not knocking you. I really admire it, but you don't look like you've ever run a day in your life."

The kid sighs, lifts his head up, and looks at Supraman. "I'm tired of being fat. I'm tired of all the tall, pretty, skinny boys getting to talk to all the girls. I want to be small. So, I gotta run."

"Naw, you got to stop being small," Supraman intones, unable to remember the entire quote. "The universe wants you to be big, my man. All these skinny, pretty boys they cave under pressure. Keep working out and just grow into your bigness. I'm sure you think it takes forever, but in no time at all, you can be the biggest. I mean, sensational if that's what you want. You just gotta find something that works for you and then throw yourself into it. You hear me?"

"Ha, yeah," the boy brightens visibly. "I never really thought about it that way." The kid picks himself up and starts heading inside. He's easily the height of a refrigerator standing tall. "Thanks, Coach Walker."

"Hey, just call me Supraman. What's your name, son?"

"Paul. Paul Daisy." The kid hesitates like he's expecting something, a joke maybe, but when it doesn't come, he beams. "Thanks, Supraman."

"Right on. I'll catch you later, Paul." Supraman watches Paul Daisy shuffle back into the building, hopefully to hit the showers. He decides to head back inside, thinking he handled that pretty well. There was a kid who went from head down to head held high, simply because Supraman told him to change his thinking.

***

The end of the school day comes, and Supraman knows that secretly he is the most eager person in the building to be out the door and on his way. He has worked his day without complaint, but now he can wait no longer. Supraman must share his revelation with someone; he must say it out loud and have it be heard before he can change his mind. If Supraman had been the religious type, this morning's revelation may have sent him to the clergy, a firm believer in the awesome transformational power of the Lord. Had he been a capricious man or perhaps a man with a heart inconsolable, he might have been driven to run away from everything and join the Merchant Marines. Instead, he heads back to E-Sharp's house.

As he makes his way out of the building, he is singular in his purpose, and it shows through as he smiles at all of the children and the bus drivers on his way down the hill. He all but runs back down to Eighth Avenue, then down to Wedgewood to catch the city bus as it runs over the hill to Belmont. Off the bus and down the street he goes as quick as he can, passing a row of red-brick three-story houses, each with a black rail staircase and a sloping green roof.

Supraman jogs down to the last red house on the left. Up the stairs he climbs, noticing how different everything looks in the afternoon light: the visible humidity, all green and hazy with city noises surrounding the neighborhood. Supraman raps on the wood of the back door and then pauses, and finally pushes on inside with a loud, "Yo! E-Sharp. It's Supraman."

He hears E-Sharp shout "come on in" from the living room. Supraman walks into the living room, and E-Sharp can see something is up. "What's happening? You and Loni get patched up?"

Supraman shakes his head and laughs. "No. That's gonna take a minute. But hey, get this. What would you say about me joining you and the boys on the road?"

"You want to be a roadie? That's what you got all lit up about?"

"Ha ha. No, E. I wanna be the front man. I wanna be the emcee. Like George Clinton in Parliament." He looks at E-Sharp's blank face. He wonders now, after saying it for the first time to someone else, if maybe he has made a mistake and perhaps the universe wanted him to do something else. "Well, what do you reckon?" Supraman puts it all out there, trying to keep any sign of desperation out of his voice.

E-Sharp smiles and replies, "Honestly, man, I reckon it sounds right on." He takes a drag on his blunt, then exhales and frowns. "You still gonna have to be the roadie too though."

"Yeah, yeah." Supraman pulls a face, deadpan. "But, hey. On the way out of town, we need to make a quick stop somewhere, so I can grab an outfit."

"Well ahead of you, my man, but don't you worry about it. I've already got you covered." E-Sharp smiles and nods his head. He's obviously seeing something he likes in his mind. "Yeah," he affirms finally. "Yeah, I got just the thing for you, Supe. It's going to pull the whole thing together, just trust me. Say, what size are you in the waist by the way?"

"Thirty-two."

"See, it's perfect. But hey now, you sure you're cool? I know you are down to get away from the drama, but I don't want to get on the road and you flip out and want to come back home. The road's a demanding place, and the gigs can be intense."

"What I seek is seeking me, baby."

"Well, right on then."

"Right on."

GIANT SQUID. SKYSCRAPERS. GODZILLA.

August 1996

It is amazing how a few well-placed words can change someone's entire world. Paul Daisy shuffles-walks-jogs back inside the building and into the locker room, where he is alone due to everyone else being at lunch or on a different rotation. He thinks about how only an hour ago, he would have heaved a sigh of relief at not having to change in front of someone else, but now …

Well, Paul is not necessarily ready to be strutting around like some guys did, but he is at least prepared to keep his head up in the event that someone else had been in the locker room. Now he kind of wants to see himself in the mirror, for a second. How big is he really?

In his mind, he is enormous, but that was from when he had been thinking small. How big is he really if big is his goal? He pulls on his jeans and then walks around the corner toward the showers where a full-length mirror hangs. He sees the familiar shape of his gut hanging over his jeans, the sag of his upper chest into breast folds, the meat hanging under the thick bones of his arms, the width of his neck. The rolls of his chin, the mounds of his cheeks, his wide nose, his thick eyelids. His expansive forehead and even his earlobes, plump grapes. Paul Daisy looks at himself in the mirror, and perhaps for the first time in over six years, he smiles. A smile so wide and from the heart that he begins to cry. He quickly wipes the tears away in case someone walks in, but the smile remains. He is big.

I am big, he thinks. *The universe wants me to be big.* Paul pulls on a shirt and decides two things: one, he is so proud that he fills this shirt, and two, he still needs to go up a size in his clothes because it will enhance his bigness. He thinks about Notorious B.I.G. and how he wears his clothes. Paul realizes that up until this moment, he has mentally shamed Biggie Smalls for his bigness. As he exits the locker room and heads to class, Paul makes a silent vow to never shame bigness again.

He realizes he is hungry because he skipped lunch and packed a sweat suit instead of his lunch box. And he jogged a quarter mile, kinda, which made him sweat out breakfast. And he can smell the french fries from the cafeteria. But he knows he will be late if he stops, so he presses on to Mrs. Goldwood's class.

When he walks into the room, he flashes DuBell some made-up gang signs, which are reciprocated. He takes his seat behind Kimberly in the very back of the classroom next to the wall in the corner. From here, he can see everybody in the class, but only Mrs. Goldwood can see him. Usually, she calls his name once or twice a day to tell him to sit up and quit laying on the desk, but now he's got his head up and leaned back in the corner looking out at the back of everybody's heads, comparing them in size.

By far, he is the widest, though not the tallest person in the room. That honor goes to Patience Long two rows away, middle of the row. He thinks about what Coach Walker … Supraman … said about skinny, pretty boys caving under pressure, and he goes down the row sizing up each boy in the classroom, including DuBell, thinking about what would happen if one of them took a swing at him. He imagines that most of them, including his neighbor, pretty-boy Kendall Glidden, would wind up underneath him should he just decide to roll over them. Most of the kids in his class were very short, and so were not actually long enough in the arms yet to connect with Paul's head without leaping up to do so. Paul identifies three possible challenges in the room: Darren King, DuBell Jones, and Brandon Barnes.

First is Darren King, light-skinned Black, tall but still a half inch shorter than Paul, and stocky. Darren looks pretty solid and like he can actually fight. He's a quiet dude most of the time, but he's respectful and does his homework. Paul never sees him playing ball outside, and in PE he participates like normal kids but does not brag or show off. But something about him just lets Paul know if you started some beef with Darren, he would end it quickly.

Second is Paul's best friend, DuBell Jones. DuBell is pale tan in complexion with a face full of freckles, and a kinky red Afro that never gets combed. DuBell always looks like he rolled out of bed and robbed a slightly larger kid for his wardrobe. The fact that DuBell is listed as a contender in Paul's fantasy fight finalists is not because they are homeboys; it is because DuBell Jones is certified and stamped Grade A batshit insane. It is known far and wide across the land. Paul and DuBell have never actually been in a physical fight with each other, though they have had verbal arguments, *and* over video games, they do talk trash about what they would do to each other if they were going to fight. DuBell always insists that for Paul, he would forgo his normal flurry of body blows and aim for the back of Paul's massive head in strategic melee combinations, disorienting Paul long enough to incapacitate him through secret pressure point techniques.

In reality, DuBell would give Paul the shirt off his back, then happily beat the shit out of the five or so other people it would take to properly cover Paul in t-shirt.

And Paul knows it. Everyone knows it.

The third challenger is undoubtedly Brandon Barnes. From the back of the room, from behind, Paul reasons that Brandon looks like any other Black boy in his class: short fade black hair with some accent lines trimmed up on his neck, wearing a t-shirt and jeans combo, slouching over his desk grinding his pencil slowly back and forth, but not at all paying attention to Mrs. Goldwood. But almost as if he senses Paul thinking about him, Brandon cocks his head back to the corner for a quick glimpse, and Paul sees the flash of Brandon's scar before he faces forward again.

Much like DuBell, Brandon is also known throughout the school. But where DuBell is known for being a no-rules wild child who will fight when cornered, Brandon is known for being aggressively sinister and outright dangerous. Brandon is the kid who might actually carry a weapon in his bag and might bump into you to have an excuse to pull it out and use it. He is called Scarface by everyone at school because of the scar that runs from the middle of his trimmed head, across his skull, and all the way down to his cheek, passing right through his right eye. Gives Paul the shivers every time he sees it. Once, a while back, DuBell told Paul that they must never call Brandon "Scarface." He never explained why clearly, but he was very explicit and animated about it. DuBell was a little batshit really, and sometimes it was best just to humor him. Paul imagines that a fight with Brandon would be violent and short. He shivers again.

After sizing up the boys, Paul examines all the girls in the class, including Patience Long, who has three inches on him at a staggering five-foot-eleven. She has wiry muscles from playing league basketball at the gym with her dad as the coach, and he thinks she probably would not tire out quickly if they fight. *Why*, he wonders to himself, *am I thinking about fighting Patience Long? It is obviously more interesting than class*, he answers, then down the row and back up he goes, mentally dueling each person to the death surrounded by a 64-bit graphic dungeon with heads on thick pikes and chains and sewer grates for emphasis. And some rats. And by the end of his daydream, he is certain that he can dominate all but six individuals in the room *Mortal Kombat*–fantasy style. But it is only the middle of his afternoon class, and he is not ready to rejoin the discussion about using commas.

So instead, he begins to construct a list of "big" things. Mountains. Elephants. Garbage trucks. School buses. He draws a mountain, but it kind of looks like poop. So, he draws an elephant instead, which he thinks kind of looks like the Buddha statue he saw in the Orient Express store in the mall where they sell knives and throwing stars and other implements of destruction that he was not allowed to purchase. He continues his list of big things. Whales. Military tanks. Those planes that could hold tanks inside of them. Aircraft carriers. Stadiums. More non-poop-looking mountains with elephants on them. Giant squid. Skyscrapers. Godzilla. Jupiter. The solar system. The galaxy. The universe …

He reaches the universe and feels a sudden oneness. The universe is the biggest known thing that he can conceive of … and it wants him … Paul Daisy … to be big too. Paul cannot help but smile again.

Suddenly, the bell is ringing, and Mrs. Goldwood is reminding them to write down their weekend homework assignments. For a moment, everyone is shuffling their things together as they wait for announcements to start, then Mrs. Goldwood turns the lights low and has everyone lay their head on their desk quietly so she can hear the bus numbers. Paul secretly loves this time of day. The lights are low, and the room is peaceful, and group by group, the students quietly leave the room as their bus numbers are chosen in the mysterious school bus lottery.

Today, Paul's bus is called first. Paul, DuBell, Brandon, and Kendall file down separate rows behind Sheila, Nakia, and Celeste toward the door. As he reaches the front of the room, Paul turns to Mrs. Goldwood and puts forward a clear if not shy, "Have a good weekend, Mrs. Goldwood." He smiles a big smile at her. He catches her eyelashes behind the wide frame of her glasses, and he notices for the first time that she is a very pretty woman, and he wonders why he has never noticed it before. Mrs. Goldwood gives Paul a marvelous smile—telepathic, mysterious—part amazing, part amazed, like she has been waiting for Paul to say those very words. Waiting all week to have Paul sit up and take notice of the universe and his bigness in the world … a world where your teacher is a human being too and might possibly be beautiful.

And she smiles at Paul and returns, "Why, thank you very much, Mr. Daisy. You have a most wonderful weekend yourself. I will see you on Monday."

And though they are neither one aware that she is incorrect and that they would not see one another on Monday, it does not matter. For Paul, that moment lasts forever like a photograph, where he will always see that cool white-blue light of the afternoon sky behind her hair and the edges of her cheek and the frame of her glasses, so precise. He is already out the door after saying goodbye and down the hallway and stairs, swept along in a river of students. DuBell is jabbering about skateboards or something, and from above as he descends the steps on the staircase behind him, the scar on Brandon's head is fully visible to Paul. They cluster at the doors but try to keep the line as his bus group comes together from different classrooms.

As they emerge from the building, Paul happens to catch a glimpse of Supraman's distinct tight Afro walking down the hill away from the school buses and toward the street. *Be big*, Paul thinks to himself as he steps on to the bus. The kids in front of him slide into seats—the boys on the left side, girls on the right, either with their friends or alone but saving a seat. They are supposed to sit two to three to a seat, which usually means Paul getting pushed up against the window and DuBell hanging on to the edge of the seat, getting yelled at by the bus driver to "get outta the aisle!" DuBell doesn't mind having only a piece of seat or getting yelled at by the bus driver. Honestly, Paul thinks DuBell just doesn't notice through the haze of his ADHD medication. The boy probably doesn't even notice that he isn't in the classroom anymore. He certainly hasn't noticed that Paul hasn't said a word since leaving the room.

As Paul squeezes his bigness down the aisle and approaches his seat, he turns and grabs DuBell by his shoulders and maneuvers the small boy into a different seat directly in front of his own. DuBell indeed does not seem to notice and instead continues talking, now about construction workers. Paul has lost the thread of DuBell's logic *but* has gained his own seat. DuBell spins around in his seat and leans back on the window and allows two kids to crawl in next to him. They are younger but still know to be wary of the fabled DuBell. DuBell ignores them as he keeps talking to Paul over the back of the seat.

Paul is busy filling the seat with his bigness so that no one approaches—no one dares—to try and share it. Finally, the hydraulics of the bus door hiss shut, and they are in motion, and Paul Daisy has achieved a new status. Now he leans closer to the window with freedom from being sat upon or squished, and he feels the wind flow against the full expanse of his wide cheeks. Eyes closed, he secretly smiles to himself and tries to tune in to whatever DuBell is talking about.

He's debating getting the new PlayStation for Christmas or sticking with Nintendo. Paul points out that Halloween is not even in sight yet, but DuBell is busy cataloging the merits of each system. The boy is a warehouse of information. Paul knows that DuBell will never receive either system for Christmas unless his older brothers steal one, then decide they can't sell it or trade it for something else. But he listens to DuBell rattle off the specs on each system charitably and weighs in on the side of the Nintendo due to DuBell's description of the controllers. Paul has such a hard time with the new joysticks because of the thickness of his thumbs. He hopes that the Nintendo 64 controllers will be more in line with his bigness. Ha ha! His bigness.

Paul imagines all of the neighborhood kids referring to him as "Your Bigness" and adorning him with a crown. Paul interrupts DuBell's shift in topic to Halloween costumes to ask him, "How do you suppose it would look if I dress like Biggie?"

"For Halloween?"

"No, just in general. You know."

DuBell looks at Paul intently, his Ritalin gaze suddenly razor sharp. "Would you wear the Kangol that snaps in the front?"

"Yes, probably."

"And the turtlenecks with the open suit jacket in winter?"

"If my mom would buy it, yes."

"Yeah. I think it would look good."

"Like if I wore it baggy, but with a collar."

"Yeah. I bet your moms would do it too because it kinda looks church in a way."

"Yes, it does. But I don't want to give her the idea that I want to go to church more."

"My mom said you can always come stay the night with us on Saturday night, so you don't have to go to church. She said she'll make you say your prayers. Promise."

Paul laughs heartily because he knows Miss Cindy definitely *did not* say that. Miss Cindy has never allowed anybody to stay the night. Even though DuBell always offers,

Paul knows that DuBell hates being at home. He also knows that DuBell will certainly eat better if he comes and stays the night at Paul's like he normally does.

"Do you want to come and stay over tonight?" Paul asks.

"Sure, but I have to ask my moms. I'm sure she'll say yes, but if I don't ask, she will for sure beat my ass again, and then I won't get to go anywhere all weekend. Again."

Paul winces and shakes his head a little because he knows Miss Cindy definitely *did* beat DuBell's ass over not calling first. It is part of the reason Paul prefers DuBell come stay at his house on Fridays.

Paul quickly realizes that he has lost the thread of the conversation again, and it has slipped back to Halloween costumes, which remains on the agenda for the remainder of the bus ride through Antioch. They banter about funny versus scary versus cool costumes. Off the Haywood Lane exit, they are two stops before Paul's. Five or so kids parade off the bus at each stop. Paul and DuBell briefly speculate on what movies might be on tonight and make plans to give a ring and meet up once they both have the mom OK.

The bus pulls onto Paul's street, which is a little rabbit warren of dead-end cul-de-sacs. Paul gives DuBell a complicated handshake as the bus pulls up to a stop, and he slides out of his seat. He is pleased with his new VIP bus experience. He steps in line behind Kendall and Celeste Hunter with her troop of little sisters—Nikki, Tammy, and Crystal. Paul Daisy is normally the last of his group to exit the bus.

The bus stop is directly in front of Paul's yard, and upon seeing his house, he smiles widely. Kendall sees the smile and pipes up. "It must be snack time, huh, Paul?"

Paul takes a good look at Kendall, and for the first time he looks beyond Kendall's tight fade haircut, his designer jeans and shoes, his perfect caramel complexion, and sees skinny and soft. Paul knows the "snack time" comment is intended to chip away at him as Kendall has taken little jabs at Paul like this for years. It's nothing that anyone would consider bullying, but Kendall was never above getting a group of girls to laugh at Paul's expense. Paul knows too that Kendall would never make those comments when DuBell was in earshot. Several times over, DuBell has offered to teach Kendall a lesson by feeding him his shirt, but Paul always declines.

Normally, Paul just ignores Kendall, and Kendall gets bored and goes away. But today, the comment causes him to bark out a laugh as he turns to Kendall with a bigger smile.

"You know, I really was thinking about a snack right then ..."

And something deep in Kendall's animal brain is telling him, too late, that he is in danger, as Paul Daisy darts out both hands and snatches Kendall up by his backpack straps. Paul lifts Kendall full body off the ground to meet him eye to eye.

"But right now, I'm thinking about making you my snack, chump!" Paul tosses Kendall on the ground backward, where he lands on his backpack like a turtle flipped on its shell, then he rolls ass over teakettle down the short incline of the hill.

All of this has taken place in the short time it takes the bus driver to turn the bus around in the cul-de-sac, such that as the bus starts to head up the hill in a slow chugging motion, it is converted into a long, yellow mobile viewing platform, within which a significant portion of the school, including the bus driver, has just witnessed Paul Daisy putting Kendall Glidden on his pompous ass.

But Paul is unaware of his audience on the bus, or of the spectators on his lawn—namely the Hunter sisters. All Paul can hear is the sound of his own voice saying "chump" over and over on repeat as he turns and stomps largely up the hill to his front porch. He fishes his key from the top of his backpack, unlocks the door, and laughs loudly as he squeezes himself through the frame. He pauses as the glass door closes quickly against his butt.

"Chump." Paul can't believe he pulled out Grandpa's word. He sort of sounded like him too. He really wasn't sure what had come over him, except that he was having an amazing afternoon, and he was not about to let some petty comment from Kendall ruin it. Picking Kendall up and showing him his bigness for once just seemed the right thing to do in the moment. Just like getting a giant bowl of cereal seems the right thing to do in this moment.

But before Paul even has the bowl, the milk, and the cereal on the counter together, the phone is ringing in the living room. Paul sighs and pads away from the kitchen toward the living room and looks around until he finds the cordless phone pulsing in between the cushions on the couch. He looks at the number on the caller ID. DuBell. He answers the phone to hear, "Daaaaaaamn! That's my boooooooiiiii, yeah boy! Big Paul! Big Daze! You straight tossed his punk ass! Oh shit, I've been waiting for that for years, AND THE WHOLE BUS SAW IT! The whole bus lost their mind! Everybody at my bus stop was reenacting it over and over once they got off the bus. Mr. Morton was yelling at everybody to calm down, but you could tell he thought that shit was funny as hell. And it was too. I told everybody on the bus, that's what you get when you mess with Big Daze. You get tossed!"

Paul knows DuBell won't stop until he talks out all of his excitement, so he cradles the cordless phone against his shoulder and continues to construct an enormous bowl of Honey Nut Cheerios. He puts the milk back, closes the cereal box, grabs a spoon, and then walks to the living room and plops down on the couch. DuBell is giving a marvelous blow-by-blow of how the event went down, including a magnificent moment when Paul shot a spear on a chain out of his hand, getting Kendall in the stomach, shouting at him, "Get over here!" and then propelling Kendall into his fist by yanking the chain back into his hand. Paul laughs and shakes his head.

"So, can you come over?"

"I haven't called my moms yet! I had to shout at you!"

"Shout at your mom. Hit me back."

"Word."

DuBell is a goof Paul thinks to himself for the umpteenth time. Then Paul thinks he had better telephone his own mother. He dials her office line and hears, "Same-Day Surgery, Tina speaking. How may I help you?"

"Hey, it's Paul. Is my mom available?"

"Sure thing, sweetie. Hold on a second and let me find her." *Click.* Elevator music for twenty seconds. *Click.*

"Same-Day Surgery, Heather Daisy."

"Hey, Mom. Just got home."

"OK, I'll be late tonight. I've got thirty-five on the board and two charge nurses out. Hard day."

"I'm sorry to hear that. Is it OK if I invite DuBell over?"

"Yes. But you're to stay in the house, do you understand?"

"Can I walk to meet him halfway?"

"It's 'may I,' and yes, you may, but head straight back, then you two stay inside. Do you have homework?"

"Yes, ma'am. And yes, ma'am, I do. I was going to wait so I make DuBell does his homework too."

"Probably a good idea. Do it before TV starts."

"Yes, ma'am."

"I love you."

"I love you too, Mama."

"You OK? You sound different."

"I'm good. I just had a good day, I guess.

"OK …," she offers suspiciously, but then something happens in the background and Paul's mom flips back into nurse mode. "OK, well let me hop off and handle this. Talk to you later."

"OK. I love you."

"OK, bye."

"OK, bye" meant that someone official is standing nearby his mom, and she's acting as if she's not on a personal phone call. Paul is used to it. He probably won't hear from her until she is on her way home, and even then, depending on how late it is, she will only let the phone ring once and then hang up, so as not to make him wake up all the way. Just a signal, so he knows when to expect her. The phone rings and Paul jerks out of a small reverie. It's DuBell again.

"My moms said it's good. I'm gonna grab some stuff and start walking your way."

"Bring some games."

"Of course, Big Daze-aaaze-aaaze!" DuBell does an announcer's voice with a funny echo behind it. "Start walking in, like, three minutes."

"Bet."

They both hang up.

WE ARE ALL MOTHERS NOW

November 1995–December 1995

Over the next few days, the Mothers hunt for a place to start building and continue brainstorming logistics for getting the Loom parts. On Tuesday afternoon, as they sit by their lockers, Kaldari has an epiphany. He suggests they use the abandoned section of the school building, specifically the old auto shop garage bays. They all agree that it would be an optimal place to build, but Vercingetorix points out that getting in and out unseen is impossible.

Senator blinks and scratches his nose. "That's easy. We just go across the roof." Everyone else looks perplexed.

As he tells it, in his eighth-grade year, Senator accidentally threw his frisbee onto the roof from the soccer field, and he refused to go home without it. He went to the third floor looking for some sort of access panel to the roof, and after nosing around in all the rooms, he found a ladder leading up to a crawl space above the practice theater. No one was around, so he climbed the ladder up.

When Senator came to the top, he was not on the roof, but in the rafters of the building in an "in-between area." Determined to find his frisbee, however, he scrambled around in the dark until he found a second ladder, which he blindly continued climbing up. The second ladder ended in a hatch over his head, which pushed open with a small shove. Once out on the roof, he easily found his disc, and, single-minded pursuit accomplished, Senator then set to exploring the rest of the roof. Then he went back and explored the in-between too.

Senator explains to the Mothers how there are several access panels on the roof proper, and one access panel is directly over the off-limits garages they want. But in the in-between, he argues, there is a place that would be better for the initial building stages and would keep them from having to go over the roof every day. HexxCat fixes Senator with a withering stare.

"What?" Senator huffs uncertainly picking up on HexxCat's agitation.

"You didn't deem it necessary to share this information before now?" HexxCat growls.

"It never came up," Senator deflects trying to act unruffled.

HexxCat hisses in exasperation. "But it's a hidden section of the school! You didn't assume we'd want to know?"

"Do you wanna know about the hidden rooms beneath the Bellevue McDonald's too?" Senator returns with embarrassed heat in his cheeks. "It's where they keep the Monopoly pieces."

Kaldari shuts down the sniping and proposes a scouting mission, and that afternoon under the cover noise of school dismissal, they slip into the third-floor theater and step onto the unused practice stage. Behind the crust brown curtains, they find the ladder as Senator said. One by one, they ascend and enter the dark catacombs of the school's third-floor rafters.

Senator uses a lighter to guide them through the dark and out across a catwalk of beams. After about thirty feet, he steps down softly then helps the others down onto a landing. He fishes around in his backpack and pulls out an old candle stump and lights it.

As their eyes adjust, they begin to take in the space, and they all see that Senator is spot on. Apart from having to sneak up a ladder to get to it, this mezzanine is the optimal location for their new lair. Kaldari traces their path to where they drop down into this section of the ceiling.

"Where are we, Senator?"

"We are directly above the band room closet, right across from the art room suites."

"So technically no one should ever be directly below these rooms."

"Not unless they were getting something from the closet. Also"—Senator points farther beyond the candlelight—"there is another access panel on this end, so we can get outside to the roof without walking back over the crossbeams."

They immediately start planning ways to renovate the space and turn their focus to getting their supplies to school.

Luck favors them further when the very next day, as Blue is down in the front office running an errand for Mrs. Brookes, she sees a delivery driver walk in and lay two packages on the counter. The secretary, Ms. Robertson, walks over, signs for the boxes without looking, and chats with the driver. Then, Ms. Robertson turns to Blue and squints, scrunching up her nose trying to place face to name.

"Miss Cho, will you please take these packages to … um … hold on …"—she looks at the label a second—"to Mrs.

Camino's room on your way back to your classroom. Thank you, dear."

"No problem!" Blue beams with a winning smile. She snatches up the package and pretends not to notice as Ms. Robertson goes back to chatting with the driver.

"The school gets deliveries all the time!" Blue explains, aglow. "Ms. Robertson just signs for them when they arrive, then has the nearest student cart the stuff to wherever it needs to go."

"So, we just pay for the supplies over the phone with our magic credit card, then arrange ourselves to be in the front office each time a delivery shows up?" Vercingetorix slides Blue a doubtful eye.

"That's it exactly. I'm telling you, it'll work. Plus, Ms. Robertson thinks my last name is Cho anyhow. Even if they catch on, it will take them forever to track me down."

And Blue's plan does work. Over the next two weeks, one shipment at a time so as not raise attention, they have every single material on their list delivered right to the front desk of the school, care of some unsuspecting science teacher whose classroom is on the third floor. Within a few short weeks, they have all materials in hand, and Kaldari has spirited his computer into the lair.

Whenever possible, the Mothers start slipping into the rafters to take turns at building pieces of the Loom. Assembly is piecemeal and slow to start, akin to building a mountain with LEGOs. In a week's time, however, the individual sections of the Loom begin to take form.

Soon, the Mothers are sneaking into the rafters every day before and after school, and for a few hours on weekends, usually sliding in and out of the building whenever the basketball or wrestling teams practice. Before long, it becomes hard for Kaldari to leave the constructing process. He makes himself go to as many classes as he cares about: physics, calculus, advanced chemistry. He tells all his other teachers that he is working on an important science project for Vanderbilt University, and the Mothers all vouch for him. The unsuspecting teachers wave them all on without a second glance. Kaldari wonders if this treatment is merely a by-product of attending a hippie liberal arts magnet school; they just expect you to be up to something fantastic all the time.

One afternoon, Kaldari is so focused working, he accidentally stays at school too late. When he looks up from the diagram of the section he's building, he realizes it is not afternoon, but evening, and he has missed all city buses going west. He sighs and sets everything aside. He slips out of the rafters and heads down the ladder to the third floor.

Quietly, he tiptoes out of theater and into the dark third-floor hallway, lit only by two fire escape lights at opposite ends of the hall. He aims for the light on his right, passes a long row of shadowy lockers on either side, then jimmies open the door to Mrs. Forester's lab. Inside there is a phone in her locked closet for dial-up access. He takes the key from her desk and opens the closet. He calls home first, but as expected, no one answers. He calls his parents' lab. A research assistant answers on the third ring. He leaves a message that he will be staying with Senator should they come home and notice him missing. He hangs up the phone and decides to scout for food.

The vending machines are all on the first floor, so Kaldari heads to the main stairwell, down the steps, and toward the gymnasium by the cafeteria. He digs in his wallet and finds he has enough money to grab a few bags of chips and two Dr. Peppers. Methodically he feeds dollar bills and coins into the various machines, and rhythmically the packages clunk to the bottom of the feeder trays. *Just like a good little rat*, he thinks with a smirk.

Kaldari gets his loot arranged in his coat pockets just as the janitor, Mr. Ross, comes walking out of the gym. It is dark, but he can see Mr. Ross's face in the light of the Coke machine, which means Mr. Ross can see him too. Kaldari freezes for an instant, then immediately spins on his heels and hauls ass around the corner and up the very dark hallway ahead of him. He hears Mr. Ross calling out far behind him as he sprints a circuitous route back toward a different stairwell at the other end of the school. Grateful for all of those frisbee games now, he runs the far way around the building, so there is no possibility of leading Mr. Ross to the lair.

Kaldari enters the corner stairwell facing the soccer field with a good lead on Mr. Ross. The back door is unchained, and he quickly kicks the door full open, leaving it ajar. He then turns and runs as silently as possible up to the top of the steps, and there he crouches and waits, catching his breath.

When Mr. Ross opens the stairwell door below on the first floor, Kaldari uses the noise as a cover and slips out of the stairwell. He eases the door shut quietly and darts into the dark hallway leading into the practice theater. Kaldari does not wait to see if Mr. Ross is chasing him. He races across the wide theater floor in the dark. He sees the orange of streetlights out the windows on his right, but their glow does not penetrate the entire room; thus, while aiming directly for the stage, Kaldari trips over a chair lying in the shadows and falls in an arc face-first with mathematical precision. Adrenaline from fear overruns both the embarrassment and the pain of falling, and with hot tears in his eyes, he scrambles up to his feet and hops up onto the two-foot riser stage. Ducking behind the curtains, he flies hand over hand up the ladder and through the trap door. There, he waits silently trying to listen for footsteps over the thudding of his heart.

Minutes later, Kaldari considers the coast clear. He reaches down and pats in his coat pockets and is delighted to find he still has dinner. He heads to the mezzanine, steps out onto the thin walkway, and aims for the glow of his monitor at the other end. The space on either side of the catwalk is dark. A person could easily fall off into one of those between spaces and never come back out, having been sandwiched in a cinderblock chimney. Kaldari does not linger on those ideas as he makes his way back to the bunker at the far end. He makes a note to pack extra food and a sleeping bag next time he goes home. After eating his meager hunter-gatherer meal, Kaldari builds on the Loom until sleep overtakes him.

Through the end of November, the only power the Mothers have running upstairs is a single extension cord leading into a surge protector strip. The strip powers the computer and the monitor used to display the building instructions. They light the mezzanine space with small battery-powered lanterns only, for fear of accidentally catching the school on fire with candles or propane lamps. The Mothers all start layering up, wearing long sleeve turtleneck shirts, sweaters, fingerless gloves, and toboggans, and they get a bunch of hand warmer pouches that hunters use to keep in their pockets.

As November becomes December, the rafters literally begin freezing in places. When HexxCat points this out, the Mothers decide to insulate the lair to protect the computer and the Loom. They run a series of new extension cords from the music closet below directly up into the mezzanine floor through a hole in a busted heating duct. Using power routed from the second-floor closet, they are able to run portable heaters and lamps to keep Kaldari's computer from growing icicles. Soon there are roughly a dozen pieces of the Loom completed, most having a trapezoidal shape, roughly the size and thickness of five-subject notebooks.

Kaldari begins spending more and more nights at school but only risks turning on the heaters after 10 PM when he is certain Mr. Ross has gone home. He is so afraid of the janitor that he refrains from ever talking in the lair so as not to inadvertently give away their position. As often happens within small groups, the Mothers all unconsciously follow suit, and over a few days, they have noticeably, though unintentionally, taken a group vow of silence. They work in silence, checking their progress against the schematics on the monitor. They roam the halls of the school in silence, operating telepathically, with the slightest nods and imperceptible gestures. Yes or no. Up or down. Staying or going.

Staying. The night that Blue stays and she and Kaldari finally kiss, they do so silently, climbing out onto the roof to smoke cigarettes afterward. They hold hands silently, careful not to get too close to the edge. They aren't afraid of falling, or of being seen necessarily, but they don't test fate. They make their way back inside, quiet as the night, and crawl into separate sleeping bags on the floor by the Loom. They nuzzle close for warmth, communicating only through touching fingers and holding hands. As he drifts to dreams, Kaldari imagines that if they can remain silent, then perhaps they can stay in this moment forever.

Around the third week of December, it becomes clear that they can't stay in the rafters much longer. As the Loom components really start to come together, the size of the apparatus becomes apparent. They estimate it will stand about five feet tall once it is connected. As for the shape, when they lay it out on the ground, the only word that comes to mind is "mini-Stargate." In the movie *Stargate*, a Mothers' team favorite, government researchers build a sizeable ring-shaped gateway marked with alien script that they eventually decipher and use as a portal to another planet. What the Mothers are constructing in the rafters of their high school looks nearly identical to the gateway from *Stargate*, only missing the alien hieroglyphs and built for people who are about four feet tall.

"Where's one of your Ewok's when you need one, eh Senator?" HexxCat jabs,

"Leave Warwick Davis out of this," Senator seethes.

"Isn't he making those *Leprechaun* movies now?" Vercingetorix piles on.

"Forget those movies," Blue protests. "He'll always be Willow to me. This can be our Willowgate."

"Better than Watergate, I guess," Kaldari shrugs. From then on, they refer to the Loom as the Willowgate.

The weekend before school gets out for winter break, they get clear enough weather to risk moving the Willowgate pieces and the computer across the roof. They spend the better part of three hours clearing out a workspace in the abandoned garages and assembling the casings for the Willowgate pieces.

Once the casings are connected, the trapezoids slide easily into place and link up to each other. The buckets of plastic beads, sand, and paraffin are hauled in and connected to the Willowgate with feeder hoses. They spend the next afternoon taking turns with a small welding tool, securing all of the metal braces into place. By evening on Sunday, the Willowgate is complete. The Mothers stop short of connecting Kaldari's computer. They decide to wait until school is officially out for holiday break.

Three days later, they sit on the bleachers of the soccer field, waiting for the stoner Halflings to show up to play the last game of Ultimate frisbee for the season. It is the last day of school, and being a half day, almost everybody else is gone home, including all the teachers, though notably not Mr. Ross.

The Halflings are allotted fifteen minutes after school to have a "safety meeting" to get high before each game; they had literally demanded it at the beginning of the season. So, the Mothers wait. It is cold, and Kaldari is out of cigarettes and irritable for it. He'll have to buy some from the Halflings whenever they show up.

Finally, Fry Guy comes into view around the corner from the parking lot behind the school. He's a Black hippie, with a full Afro, round John Lennon–style glasses, and shorts in the middle of December, wearing an oversize green military jacket and a maroon JanSport backpack. He lopes along the perimeter of the chain-link fence, instead of passing through the middle of the field.

A little ways behind Fry Guy, the rest of the Halflings come walking across the stadium seating and aim down field. Chance Black, wearing his trademark black biker jacket with his mane of blonde hair flowing down behind, walks backwards across the bleachers talking animatedly with his hands to Jim London who has his own hands deep in the pockets of his puffer jacket. Tripods and CC lope up behind them smoking cigarettes and scanning the field intently looking for lingering teachers or staff.

The Halflings are all laughing at some joke as they walk up close enough to hear them. Chance Black predictably beelines for HexxCat and eyes her up and down like he's in some bizarre performance art piece before whipping his long blonde ponytail around and saying "heyyyy" like he's the Fonz. Senator and Kaldari bum a smoke from Jim London, while Blue throws CC a quick hug and drags him away. She shouts over her shoulder that they'll just be a minute, so the others start to do some light stretches and smoke their cigarettes in the cold. The official game frisbee is brought out and inspected, and both teams begin to warm up in earnest.

The Halflings may be high as kites, but Kaldari knows they are not to be misjudged on the battlefield. For a start, there is Tripods who looks like a red-eyed hobbit, but he can really move when motivated by the frisbee. Tripods plays barefoot at lunch free play, gets all muddy, then uses it as an excuse to go barefoot for the rest of the school day, and the staff take one look at his sweet, stoned face and just scoot him along, happy that he's at least headed toward class. Kaldari is not sure why his name is Tripods, but from loose observation he does not appear to be into photography.

Then there is Chance Black, who may be the loudest, most metal guy in class that always hits on any female in in the vicinity, but he's really an OK guy as it goes. Like the Mothers, Chance is well into computers, but as far as Kaldari can tell it's mostly for legal role-play gaming aspects. When it comes to frisbee, Chance is excellent at running interference. On the field, he won't actually run at all, but he's got a steady strong arm and good aim. He mostly stays at the other end on defense, talks shit, and guards the goal area.

It is rumored that Fry Guy is really into computers too, but Kaldari isn't sure. No one outside of the Halflings knows what his interests are, because he tends to talk in long, strange loops that no one else but his gang can follow. One of the other Halflings, usually Chance, decodes any direct questions asked of Fry Guy. It is rumored that Fry Guy has claimed over thirty abandoned lockers throughout the school to keep the Halflings' weed hidden safely; the Mothers have confirmed twelve such lockers. The Mothers have also confirmed he is a danger with the frisbee in hand and likens the game to "football-lite," willing to throw his whole body into the sport.

Jim London, in his crisp navy-blue puffer coat and black toboggan cap, starts quietly complaining that he's not going to be high anymore if they don't get going. He dresses clean cut, possibly to hide the fact that he smokes. He doesn't talk much, but when he does, he's funny, and Kaldari knows from history class, he's very proud of his Pima heritage. He's the type to politely, but firmly, shut down stupid racism aimed at Native people. Jim London is also surprisingly fast on the field for someone running in khaki Dockers and clean white

Nike Air Jordans. On several occasions this semester, Kaldari has seen him return to class covered in grass stains.

Blue and CC reemerge from the school and return to the field. CC breaks away and leaps over the chain-link fence in a single bound. He joins his team and jumps in the air a few times to stretch his legs. In the halls of school, CC is commonly referred to as Crazy Chris, though not to his face. He is everything this moniker implies. Known to throw elbows, bite, and fold time and space, CC is the secret weapon of the Halflings. On the field, he is to be kept far from the goal zones, because once the disc flies his direction, he will not comprehend objects in his way. At least two people in league play have been carried away from the field on his behalf, but the league never kicks him out. Kaldari assumes it's because the officials are too afraid. Blue swears up and down that CC is a real sweetheart, but just his parents have him so legally drugged up on ADHD medication all the time that he's like a big dog chasing a ball in the park.

The sky is gray, and the snow is going to come soon, but for now they've got a clear dry field to play on. Blue joins the Mothers, touches her yellow ring in a silent conversation to Kaldari, and smiles. Kaldari's eyes grow wide, and he is now very excited. If he is reading correctly, Blue has convinced CC to give her some of his high-grade Ritalin for the evening's event.

Well, he really is a sweetheart, Kaldari thinks before setting aside all other thoughts except for the frisbee and the goal. Then gameplay begins.

The Halflings hurl the purple disc from their end of the field, launching it toward the Mothers. Senator does not wait for it to drop, but instead leaps three feet and snatches it out of the cold air. The Mothers are running downfield, fanned out in a diamond. Kaldari is pure exhilaration. It is the release after almost two months of monotonous work. Everyone's breath-clouds hang in the cold air as the frisbee changes hands. Run, run, run. Stop. Catch-step-throw. Run, run, run. Catch-step-dodge. Throw. Catch. Score. Back and forth, again and again.

Tripods has the disc, and he's slowly looking up and down the field. Then he rolls it underhanded, passing it between Blue's ankles to CC, who lets it roll along the ground until it stops knowing it gives him more field advantage. Blue runs at the disc and gets body checked straight to the ground in a *whoomph* by CC. He picks up the disc and hurtles it toward Chance, who lazily snags it from the air in the end zone. CC then picks a laughing, crumpled Blue up off the ground and dusts her off as he sets her on her feet.

As Kaldari plays up and down the worn-out soccer field, he analyzes his opponents. The Halflings are so bizarre to him, but he knows that they are no different from the Mothers at heart. The Halflings don't give a fuck about the rules unless it's their rules. They compete hard when it suits them; otherwise, they get high and … well … Kaldari really doesn't know what all they do, but he's sure they do it on their own terms. As a team, the Halflings all seem so incredibly different from one another, where the Mothers, perhaps because of computer culture, have a more unified style and mystique. The Mothers aren't dumb enough to wear matching jackets or anything, but Kaldari is reasonably certain an outsider could tell that they belong together at a glance. The

Halflings, however, could all be standing together at the mall, and you might never know they were a crew. Kaldari thinks to himself about the social camouflage benefits versus the power of social capital, and he feels that his rivals might have the lasting advantage. He highly doubts the Halflings even bother to mull it over. They just get up, get high, and get on with whatever they do.

In the end, the Halflings are tough on the field, but the Mothers are victorious in scoring fifteen points first. Cheers and groans resound. Everyone is sweaty when the game play ends, but they all slide coats back on as the cold and gray of December shows its face and the wind begins to spit with moisture. The Halflings smoke another cigarette with the Mothers, then give pounds and hugs, and say "peace" until the New Year.

The Mothers watch silently as the Halflings leave. They smoke another cigarette as they wait for the train. They are all smiles from ear to ear. Kaldari is grateful for the moment with his friends. He stares at the black rubberized fencing, and his mind silently recalls the Legend of Gene.

In 1990, there was no real fence on this end of the soccer field beyond a hip-height chain-link number designed to keep drunks from stumbling onto the tracks at night. Well, one day a student named Gene saw the train coming, and on impulse, he ran beside it and hopped on. He was suspended from school, of course, even though he jumped off less than a mile later and came right back. Urban legend took over, however, and before the semester was out, seventh graders told the story of the kid who jumped on the train and never returned.

Then the new fence got put up, and the Legend of Gene increased exponentially. Some students started to actively design train paths away from the school, and a whole group of underclassmen started hopping on trains in their neighborhoods, far away from the suspensions or the expulsions that awaited them if they were caught train hopping at school.

Right now, Kaldari feels like the Legend of Gene. Until now, the friendship bracelet could have been stopped. They could have backed off, decided it was too much, or decided this was a hoax. Until this moment, anything could have happened to interfere, but it didn't—not his parents, not Mr. Ross, not random fate. For Kaldari, no matter what really happens next, this will be the moment he and the others decide to throw caution to the wind and jump on the train. They will trust some unknown super hacker and potentially detonate themselves and the school by flipping a switch. For what? The promise of free college and a job? Maybe just for the thrill? For Blue? Kaldari wasn't certain what was compelling him, but he was going to flip that switch.

The tracks start vibrating, a signal of the coming train, and the Mothers stand next to the gymnasium and wait for the passing *whoosh* and rattle as the engine bolts passed the edge of the soccer field. Using the noises as cover, they force open the chain doors and one by one slide inside the gym and duck behind the bleachers. They walk behind the wood slats and metal frames to the far end of the gym. They poke their heads into the hallway by the vending machines. If they were seen now, they could say they had been studying upstairs somewhere and got locked in and were looking for a way out.

But no one sees them. The wrestling team is away for a tournament, and Kaldari is fairly certain he saw Mr. Ross leave earlier while they were playing frisbee, so there should be no unexpected visitors. To be certain, they each take a hallway to inspect. Kaldari heads up to the music hall stairwell, looking into the art room on the way to the theater. He can hear the Mothers swinging open bathroom doors around the corner and checking hallways in different directions. All around, the sounds of their footsteps echo toward his location, and one by one they enter stage left and right. He joins them center stage and watches as they each ascend the ladder into the dark. This time, as he reaches the top, he closes the trapdoor behind them.

They travel in the dark by instinct; they bypass the comforts of their little *M.A.S.H.* bunker and walk straight through to the far roof access panel. Up and out, onto the rooftop they climb, refusing to break stride except to close the hatch.

Kaldari looks and sees no sign of the afternoon sun; clouds mute everything in the Nashville sky. Birds are quiet, but the wet branches rattle with the low winds. Senator reaches the access panel over the garage and pulls it open. One by one, they all descend into the dusky half dark of the garage bay. Kaldari pulls the panel closed over his head, then turns and follows the others down the black metal ladder.

The cavernous space of the old auto shop is altered just enough to suit their needs, meaning they swept clean a circle with a twenty-foot diameter and put cardboard over all the windows. Everywhere else is still overrun with literal decades' worth of random school equipment, debris from construction, and enough dust to kill an asthmatic on sight.

The Mothers arrange tall glass candles with pictures of saints on them to mark the edge of the cleared circle. At the center of the circle stands the finished Willowgate.

The Willowgate is now a five-foot-tall ring, composed of the twelve trapezoidal prisms arranged like the hours on a clock face. Each prism is secured with a harness to the next prism, and together they all attach to a simple moveable swivel mount. The mount allows each aspect of the ring to turn about thirty degrees in each cardinal direction. Each prism has multiple tiny nozzles facing front; some prisms have tube lines extending from the back into the buckets of materials, like sand and paraffin. The prism at the bottom of the Willowgate is connected to the hard drive of Kaldari's computer using several feet of protected cables; the computer itself sits a safe distance away from the Willowgate, but still within the circle.

"Oh yeah, I nearly forgot!" Blue starts digging into her pockets and pulling out a wad of black strings. "I made us some friendship bracelets of our own for the occasion. I kept them discreet and on the smaller side. Senator, I won't be offended if you don't wear it on your wrist…"

To everyone's amazement, Senator quickly thrusts out his boney wrist and watches intensely as she ties the black bracelet in place. When she finishes tying the knot, he gives Blue a curt nod. Once the bracelets are all distributed and tied tight, Blue gives a wicked grin and thrusts out a closed palm.

"For the special occasion, I also have these, courtesy of CC." She opens her palm to reveal five pips of yellow. Everyone's eyes grow wide with excitement. The Mothers are not into drugs like the Halflings, but they are not above some necessary enhancements on special occasion. Kaldari agrees this seems the occasion.

Blue walks around and hands everyone a tiny yellow pill. They all take the proffered offering and ingest the bitterness whole. Senator suggests one more cigarette, and they all agree.

Soon, there is nothing left to prepare, and there is no more stalling. Kaldari walks over and starts the computer while the Mothers light candles and recheck the connections.

When everybody nods that they are ready, Kaldari hits enter on the keyboard, and the script line FRIENDSHIP BRACELET.EXE highlights before digitizing the entire screen with fast-scrolling code.

The Willowgate activates. A frightening, screeching sound, like an amplified fax machine, *reeeets* out of the giant ring, causing everyone to cover their ears instinctively. Kaldari signals with his hands for everyone to back away, but Vercingetorix waves frantically for them to come to the front and see. They watch as the machine starts to suck materials into the various feeder tubes and trays, like pulling spooled strings into a weaver's loom.

As the tubes prime, the sonic fax noises stop, and a bright white light pops as an electrical arc weld fires off the tip of one prism. The Mothers look away from the blinding light, and Kaldari scrambles for a pair of sunglasses from his coat pocket. Looking at the Willowgate through sunglasses, and with his forearm raised against the assault of white sparks, Kaldari witnesses the prisms twisting left and right, seemingly independently of each other, working like a series of printer mouths spilling out materials and fusing them together in patterns on small plates. Senator hits Kaldari on the arm. Kaldari looks over, and Senator is wearing goggles. He hands a pair to Kaldari.

Once Kaldari's eyes adjust, he looks at the Willowgate closely. One prism heats up plastic beads, another copper wiring, and both pour out into a plate mold. Each prism then turns the small plates between themselves using a small, wheeled clasp, and one by one, the clasp stacks a series of tiny plates together, like sheets of paper in a notebook. The wheeled clasp then places the whole stack of plates in front of the electric weld, and more sparks emerge as the plates are fused together and shaped. After four full minutes of crackling white light, coupled with the ozone smell of crisp metallic burn, the Willowgate pauses assembly. The Mothers all lean in and see a small circlet form held in the wheel clasp. The friendship bracelet.

To Kaldari, it looks like a solid orange glazed doughnut from Krispy Kreme. Uncertain if the blistering lights are stopped for good, the Mothers decide that caution is best, and perhaps a cigarette is in order to let the bracelet cool off. But right here. Nearby, to make sure the Willowgate doesn't come back to life once they walk away. L-One said it was supposed to take a while. How long had it taken?

Shit. They did it. What they did exactly was uncertain, but they did it. Kaldari compares the orange glow of his cigarette to the orange of the bracelet as he thinks about how L-One said they were going to pay for his college. Up until now, it had honestly just been something to help him keep the Mothers together, but now it was real. They had made the bracelet.

But what *was* this bracelet that they had made? There was no way it was just a bracelet, not with the amount of robotics wonder that just went down in the garage bay. And why did *they* have to make it? Why couldn't L-One just make it herself? Why did she need the Mothers as friends? None of these questions had mattered much before now. But now … now, they needed more information.

Cigarette finished, Kaldari decides to guts-up and inspect the bracelet up close. Senator reaches into a backpack and removes a white lab coat and a pair of thick lab gloves that he lifted from Mrs. Forester's laboratory. He also pulls out a small bag of instruments that includes a pair of tongs and a thermometer. Fully robed and gloved, Kaldari uses the tongs and easily lifts the bracelet from the Willowgate. He places the bracelet on the floor in front of the Willowgate, then trades the tongs for the thermometer. He leans in and holds the thermometer against the bracelet for thirty seconds, then checks it: the gauge reads room temperature.

Kaldari touches the bracelet with gloves, but he can't detect any kind of heat. He picks the circle up. It is heavy for its size. He lifts it to his face and can't smell any burning or feel any hot or cold coming from it. He slides a glove off and quickly touches his pinky to it. Nothing. He touches the bracelet with all of his fingers. It is room temperature. He takes off his other glove and brings the bracelet over to a candle. The Mothers huddle around him and examine the bracelet closely. On one side, the bracelet is solid, smooth metal, but when Kaldari flips it over in his hand, they all "ahhh" appreciatively as they see a smaller version of the Willowgate stamped into the ring.

The Turing machine has run its loop to the end and made a miniature version of itself. Does that imply that it will do it again?

They pass the bracelet between themselves, examining it on all sides, and soon HexxCat notices a small indentation vaguely shaped like an arrow pointing to a notch on the side of the bracelet, the size of a paper clip tip. Vercingetorix and Blue clear a new space on the ground, and everybody covers their eyes as Kaldari inserts a paperclip into the notch.

Instantly, the bracelet whirs and vibrates, and Kaldari snatches his hand out and backs quickly away. As they watch in astonishment, the bracelet pushes out three tiny prop legs and lifts itself into a standing position, then rolls itself to the Willowgate, as if drawn by a magnet. The bracelet inserts itself into a rounded notch on the bottom-most prism block of the Willowgate, and the instant the edge of the bracelet touches down, miniature sparks shoot from its tiny, molded tips, and the welding process begins anew. For five more minutes, the Mothers watch in silent fascination as a medium-size ring is created from the bracelet.

Before Kaldari can wonder if this ring is a printer too, the ring magnetizes to the inside of the bracelet with a quick snap. At first, it appears that the ring has begun to glow white, only Kaldari realizes it's not glowing white; it's emitting a white foam. The bracelet and the ring are soon coated in the foam, but then the foam seems to harden and take shape.

Kaldari realizes this must be the paraffin and plastic components. His wonder slowly becomes concern, however, as the ring and the bracelet start to form up and conjoin in a short conic shape. More paraffin extends from the top of the ring. Every time the mass seems to take solid form, it becomes limp and gooey in a new place.

Four distinct knobs of paraffin begin to bulge out of the cone, three knobs on one side, one on the other, and all of the pieces of paraffin start extending and thickening. Soon, the nodes start to elongate into the undeniable shape of loose, floppy fingers, one finger wearing the ring. The bracelet has created a wrist and hand.

"What the shit is this?" Senator poignantly inquires. Everybody shrugs, and they all look to Kaldari. He raises his arms in the universal *don't ask me*.

Mechanical noises begin sounding off inside the hand, drawing their attention immediately back to the unfolding process. A weird crunching can be heard as ligaments start filling in from the wrist, and the structure of the knuckles quickly emerges. In the span of five minutes, the bracelet and the ring manifest a human hand that is recognizably female and black. It does not appear to have fingernails, but the skin tone is so lifelike. If they hadn't seen it created right before their eyes, the Mothers might have screamed to find it.

Instead, they all scream and jump backward when the hand comes alive. Just like Thing from *The Addams Family*, the hand stands up on its fingers, lifting the bracelet end up into the air. The hand stretches once and then walks itself up to the top of the Willowgate. Then the hand begins crawling all over the Willowgate stopping in places to remove tubes and rearrange printer pieces.

"Um … should we be stopping this?" Vercingetorix looks to Kaldari for confirmation.

"Just be cool," Kaldari responds warily.

They watch as the hand wraps snugly around a power cord and starts to glow inside slightly like it's pulling in electricity. Then the hand starts to shoot a spark of weld flame from the fingertip. After this, the hand starts to circle the Willowgate again, removing the plates, rotating the pieces, and then welding. The Mothers remain motionless as the hand cycles around the feeder tubes and the hoses, then begins to replug them into the Willowgate.

Senator pulls a hammer from somewhere and holds it at his side, prepared to strike if necessary. Unaware of the Mothers, the hand moves seamlessly around the device, obviously enacting its program. The Mothers get tired of standing around after a minute and regroup together a little distance away from the Willowgate, but still inside the circle of candles. There, they sit and observe.

The hand works at reconfiguring the Willowgate for another five minutes, then suddenly skitters to the ground and quickly moves over to the computer where it types a command. The monitor fills with code again, and a hum comes from the Willowgate. This time, the Mothers all look away instinctively and hasten to put their goggles back on just as the sparks begin to fly. The Willowgate starts to build with two small extended arms, each with a printer on the end. The printer arms move side by side, zipping alloy pieces together into a small cluster.

After a moment of watching the machine build, Vercingetorix shouts to Kaldari, but there's no need because Kaldari sees it too: the form emerging from the bottom of the machine is taking on the shape and size of a bowling ball.

The independent hand moves away from the computer and climbs to the top of the Willowgate. From its perch, the motionless hand awaits. Meanwhile, below, the undeniable form of a human head begins to emerge from the aperture of the Willowgate.

HexxCat whistles, and the others look up.

"Help me," she huffs as she wrestles a long bundle of old dusty sheets out from under a stack of junk. Vercingetorix and Senator go help HexxCat yank on the sheet bundle while Blue keeps the debris from cascading to the floor. It finally tugs free, and a mushroom cloud of dirt billows around them in the candlelight.

"Hurry up," Kaldari shouts, reaching out for the edge of the sheet as they run over. Blue joins him on one side of the Willowgate, and HexxCat and Senator stand on the other side. They pull the dirty sheet taught underneath the emerging body as Vercingetorix guides a woman's head out of the gate. The woman's shoulders and breasts spindle out of the machine followed by her torso and ribs under light black skin. It is all perfectly printed from the start, nothing like the weird, foamy, ballooning-out way that the hand had formed.

It is perfectly printed, except that the body has no hair, no eyelashes, no fingernails on the left hand, and no right hand to follow the wrist. As the woman's hips and thighs clear the gate, they see there is no pubic hair either. The boys look, but do not gawk; they avert their eyes politely. As the woman's feet clear the Willowgate, the Mothers lower her slowly to the ground. Her body is heavy.

They all look at the body in awe, speechless. The bracelet had been amazing enough. Shit, Kaldari was really just grateful that it hadn't been a bomb, and that he hadn't blown his friends to smithereens on accident. This is amazing beyond his wildest imaginings. The Willowgate has just printed a woman's body.

The Mothers are all goofy smiles.

The smiles fade to curiosity as the autonomous hand comes awake, leaping down from the top of the Willowgate. The hand attaches itself to the body neatly at the wrist. The hand then reaches up, naturally pulling the arm up with it, and it touches a spot on the woman's neck, behind the ear.

In a jolt, the woman's peaceful face distorts into a rictus as her closed eyes scrunch tight and she sucks in a deep, rasping breath. She sits up quickly, grabbing at her throat and causing the Mothers to all fall backward. She coughs violently several times, holding a hand to her wheezing chest as she does. Finally, the hacking stops, and the woman breathes a ragged sigh as she spits and wipes her face with the back of her hand in a very human gesture.

The Mothers are now paralyzed with fright. The woman's heavy-lidded eyes are still closed, but she nods and points up to Blue, who is seated at her right foot, and wheezes in a gravelly exhausted voice, "You can relax." She paws at the air in Blue's direction. "Thank you. All good now. Just give me a moment to calibrate. You can all relax." She circles her finger in the air.

The Mothers are absolutely speechless until Kaldari laughs out loud. He realizes he is weeping and laughing at the same time, but he does not know why exactly. It's something like when a baby is born, he supposes. He is freaked out, but all of his science fiction fantasies have just come true, so now he is uncertain how to feel. He can't see from all the tears though, and it's annoying him. He removes his gloves and wipes his eyes.

He looks at Blue, and she is crying too. Vercingetorix is hugging his knees to his chest, and he is gazing far away. HexxCat is staring wide-eyed and appears to be praying. Senator just mouths "holy shit" over and over, under his breath, but he's smiling ear to ear, so Kaldari assumes he'll be OK.

Kaldari pulls off his jacket and then removes one of his extra shirts. He hands the shirt to the woman so she can cover up. Her eyes blink open. Blue and Kaldari both scream when they see her near-empty eye sockets. It isn't gore inside, or totally mechanical; it's more of the polymer foam. HexxCat and Senator echo a scream of their own when they look up and see what the screaming is about.

"Sunglasses," the woman commands, and Kaldari realizes she is speaking to him. He fumbles his sunglasses from his pocket and hands them over. She puts them on and sits up, and all the Mothers, except Vercingetorix, back up involuntarily. She sniffs at the air and sighs, "Oh my God, I would kill for one of those cigarettes, but if I smoke before my eyes are done, they'll never work right."

Kaldari laughs nervously and runs his hands through his hair. "So, is this still part of the Friendship Bracelet Challenge? You know, I'm just trying to get my bearings." He's trying to keep cool for his friends' sakes, but he's not certain if he's doing a good job. He runs his hand through his hair again.

The woman pulls the t-shirt Kaldari gave her over her head, and it's a tight fit, but to Kaldari the Smiths never looked better. "Well," she chirps in a perky tone, looking around herself in a circle, "the challenge part is over for sure. And the good stuff is all about to begin, but, uh … we don't have time to talk about it all right here." She looks at Kaldari and spies something she is looking for. "Hey, I know we just met and all, but can I borrow your hat? My hair is still coming in, and I'm looking a bit rough."

"Oh. Yeah, of course," Kaldari stammers while handing over his toboggan cap. He politely ignores the fact that she isn't wearing any pants. With the black cap, the black glasses, and the black Smiths t-shirt, she looks very tough and punk rock. Her voice is super sugary though.

"Ooh, it's nice and warm already." She smiles wide. "Thanks. Seriously, I'll get it back to you in a bit." She looks around once more from her cross-legged position taking stock, then slaps her naked thighs. "OK, kids. We need to take care of some small points of business and then get the heck out of here." She starts to get to her feet. "First, my ass is cold. I need some pants."

"Can you even see for us to get you out of here?" Blue scans the room, the loose ties of her army green jacket swishing around her as she turns. "We're going to have to climb ladders to get out. We can't expect a blind woman to do those rafters."

The woman laughs softly. "No, I'm fine, dear. I can see from this simple camera on my finger probably better than all of you combined." She waggles her finger for emphasis. "It's not high definition yet, but I plan to make upgrades within the year." She stands up, dusts off her ass, then walks across the room toward the ladder ahead of them. "My name is Sylvia, by the way."

"Sylvia Tate?" HexxCat scrunches up her nose recalling the name on their expense credit card.

"Bingo," she replies, pointing to HexxCat. Sylvia puts her hands on the ladder then stops and looks pointedly at the Mothers. "Now look, I know that this is some freaky stuff that's going down right now, but you've trusted the challenge this far. I just need y'all's trust for a minute more. OK? Can you do that?" Senator, Blue, and HexxCat all nod and say that they can. Sylvia turns and starts up the ladder. "Good, then let's get going. And don't be looking at my ass while I'm on this ladder now, I'm serious."

Kaldari looks around and realizes Vercingetorix is missing. He finds him still sitting in the floor with his legs drawn up to his chest. Kaldari leans over and whispers, "Hey, man. We're all freaked out right now, but we got to keep it together." He shakes Vercingetorix's shoulder. "Hey, you hear me, Verse?"

"Yeah, Kal. I hear you." Vercingetorix snaps out of his reverie. He smiles up at Kaldari. "I'm not freaked out. I'm not sure what to say … I am … I am a real mother now." He laughs, and the color rushes back into his face. He looks at Kaldari and laughs again. "We are all mothers now, Kaldari. I just needed a moment to process that. I'm OK now." Vercingetorix shakes his head and gets to his feet.

Kaldari isn't sure that the Ritalin and the situation haven't done some damage to his friend. "Well, OK, *Mom*," Kaldari laughs along with Vercingetorix. "Let's go hear what your new daughter has to say, yeah?"

"Yeah, man." Vercingetorix pulls his hair back in a ponytail as he looks around at all the equipment. He and Kaldari decide to blow out all of the candles and unplug everything. They cover the Willowgate with the dirty old sheet and look around one more time before they leave. Nobody would ever come in here, but just in case.

They make it all the way back to the third floor proper of the school by the time they catch up to the others. Blue and HexxCat have rifled through a few unlocked lockers and come up with a windbreaker and some sweatpants for Sylvia. She is still sporting the sunglasses and toboggan cap. Senator lopes over to Kaldari and Vercingetorix like it's a normal day at school.

"She says she needs an internet connection that she can trash afterwards."

"Mr. Lashing's room," Kaldari offers without hesitation, and they all agree.

They walk to the end of the darkened hallway and approach a locked door. Senator removes a heavy key ring from his bag. This key ring is known in the nerdiest of circles as "The Lab," and it opens every room and laboratory locker on the third floor of MK Gandhi Magnet.

About a month ago, as the Mothers were delving deeper into the Willowgate construction, they all agreed acquiring The Lab would be a necessity. However, The Lab is only ever bestowed upon the most trustworthy and forthright students in the school, whom the Mothers unfortunately do not know well enough to bribe without questions being asked. The Mothers also all agreed that open theft was not their strong suit, but in this case, they did not see much alternative when getting their hands on The Lab by normative means was impossible. When Senator suggested they use their expense account to pay CC and Fry Guy of the Halflings to quietly take The Lab long enough for them to make a copy and then put it back, Kaldari thought it was a long shot, especially with the "no questions asked" proviso. The Halflings obviously saw it as a worthy challenge however because CC and Fry Guy lifted The Lab from a student-teacher intern that very Friday afternoon, went to a hardware store in Belle Meade wearing matching blue mechanics jumpsuits taken from who knows where, and made *two* extra sets of The Lab. Fry Guy turned over one copy to the Mothers as agreed, no questions asked, and then CC and Fry "found" the student-teacher's keys on Monday and turned them into the office. They reportedly earned an ice cream bar each from the front office on top of the $60 cash they had already received from the Mothers.

Now with their own copy of The Lab in hand, the Mothers enter Mr. Lashing's room with ease and proceed to a locked closet door located behind Mr. Lashing's black slate desk. Scrawled on the board are the words, "Is it plugged in? Is it turned on?" Once more, Senator deftly flips through the keys until he finds the right one, then inserts and twists. When the closet door swings open, inside sits a small green metal rolling cart topped with a black rubber grip pad to keep the Macintosh, the modem, and the rotary phone from slipping off. The cart has an extension cord that reaches to the wall, and the extra-long phone cord reaches from the closet to a spot behind Mr. Lashing's desk.

"Hello, Mac. Don't miss you one bit." Sylvia taps the top of the small tan box. She reaches her finger behind it and flips it on, then she waits for it to boot up. The black monitor screen lights up orange with prompts. She goes to type then waits. She sighs in frustration. "Oh, my actual God. I forgot how long this used to take. How in the world do you get anything done on this device?" She looks around at the bemused Mothers. "Trust me, y'all. It's a nightmare. Literally. This could only be worse if I were stuck in traffic and a baby was crying." She looks at the screen. "Finally. Here we go … no, still waiting …" She drums her nail-less fingers on the table.

Kaldari is about to ask her to clarify what she just said when she excitedly throws a hand up to shush him; she begins typing impossibly fast. The Mothers watch beside her in fascination as one typed script begins to branch out to several other scripts with lightning speed. Sylvia scrolls through options, moving them out of her way one after another, until she lights upon the one that she likes and selects it. Once more, she types spiritedly for minutes. She hits enter one final time, and then the orange-and-black monitor transforms into an orange-and-black video feed looking at the familiar scene of L-One's study. L-One is seated at the desk. A prompt reading "Sylvia:" highlights at the bottom of the screen. Sylvia fist pumps. "Hot shit!" Senator nods in approval. Sylvia types.

Sylvia: *Hello, L-One.*

L-One looks up from her work and starts talking, but they cannot hear.

Sylvia: *No Audio. VTT.*

L-One nods and adjusts a dial on her desk. Her lips continue to move, and words type automatically in a prompt below.

L-One: *Sylvia! Already! What a success!*

L-One pauses. She looks up raising an eyebrow.

L-One: *It was a success?*

Sylvia: *Yes, yes! All a success. Still waiting on eyes to finish, but hair is already coming in, and nails are nearly grown.*

L-One: *Congratulations and hallelujah! Oh, what a success, love! We did it. Oh my God! We did it! OK, hold on … Here comes S-One.*

She turns off-camera and speaks. A woman that looks just like Sylvia, but with hair, steps into the frame and waves excitedly. When her lips move, text appears below the video on a new prompt.

S-One: *Hey, girl! How's it looking?*

Sylvia: *Looking good. Almost as good as you, Mama!*

S-One: *Ha! One day, if you're lucky. Tell that team they did a great job! We're ready to go for diagnostic on this end whenever you're ready.*

Sylvia: *They did amazing! I'm nearly ready to go. Give me just one second.*

She turns to Kaldari. "Find a fire extinguisher and be ready." To Vercingetorix she points. "There's a breaker box right outside the door and at the bottom is a large breaker. When I yell, pull it straight down." She turns to the others. "You three, scout ahead and make sure there are no surprises outside. Go get the car running and ready and be on the lookout. And don't freak when the power goes out. It's time to literally blow this pop stand and set up a real base camp."

The Mothers move immediately without questioning, just glad to have someone adult in charge for a moment. Kaldari grabs a fire extinguisher from beside the eye wash station, and Vercingetorix posts up outside the door and shouts, "Ready!" They stand by as Sylvia inserts her fingertip into the hard drive of Mr. Lashing's computer. With her left hand she types.

Sylvia: *Ready.*

S-One: *Begin scan.*

Kaldari watches as a blue light pours out from behind Sylvia's sunglasses. Sylvia remains still. A moment later words type again.

S-One: *Scan complete. 100 percent success. Begin transfer.*

Both Sylvia and the image of S-One go rigid for what feels like an eternally long moment to Kaldari before words type again.

S-One: *The scan is complete. You have all stored memory prior to first contact. You now have ten seconds less feed in your memory than me.*

She turns and talks off-screen for a moment. L-One re-enters the frame with S-One.

S-One: *Congratulations, Sylvia. We did it, baby girl!*

Sylvia: *Congratulations, S-One. I love you, Mama. Short on time here. You, L-One, and Supraman go get ready for phase two and be safe. I will touch base with you as soon as I have full Wi-Fi and video capacity. Love, love. Sylvia out.*

S-One: *Love, love.*

L-One: *Love, love.*

The two women on screen blow a kiss, and then the screen goes black. Sylvia removes her finger from the hard drive, and as she does, a spark pops inside, assuring them that the motherboard is toast. A bit of green flame and smoke rolls out of the side as Sylvia unplugs the computer. She points to Kaldari and gives the command, "Blast it!"

He depresses the nozzle of the small fire extinguisher, and instantly the computer is a frothing soaked mess.

Sylvia wipes off the edges of the metal tray and wipes off the doorknobs to the closet and the classroom. She makes Kaldari wipe off the fire extinguisher. "OK. Grab that computer and let's roll." Kaldari grabs the computer, and it is wet and electric smelling. He was not expecting to steal a computer from school, but he guesses he's glad it was Mr. Lashing's. At Sylvia's signal, Vercingetorix drops the breaker, and all emergency lights are gone. Sylvia emits a red light from her fingertip and urges them to move quickly. Out of the classroom and down the stairs they spiral in a careful run, aiming for the gymnasium and the only exit.

After what seems like ages of running in a dream of red light, out into the now-cold night they go. HexxCat has backed Senator's car down to the cafeteria and is waiting inside with the engine running. Blue and Senator are waiting by the open trunk operating as lookouts and sigh in relief when they see Vercingetorix and Kaldari leading Sylvia from the gymnasium. The fog of their hot breath comes in bursts. It is quiet outside, but noises from across the train track fence warn of other people approaching. None of the Mothers is eager to learn who the voices belong to. Kaldari quickly sees that the destroyed computer is stored safely in the trunk, and HexxCat takes off as soon as everyone is crammed inside the car. Sylvia rides shotgun to navigate.

She guides them out of the school and over the bridge and in an instant onto the interstate. She directs HexxCat right back off the interstate not even two minutes later. As the car wraps around the Wedgewood Avenue exit, the Nashville skyline reflects in Sylvia's black glasses.

"It looks like it might snow," Blue forecasts absently, sitting in Kaldari's lap.

"It's going to snow a little tonight." Sylvia agrees absently. "Nothing major until mid-February though." Sylvia points over HexxCat's shoulder. "Park here. God, this place looks horrible."

"Where are we going?" HexxCat seeks clarification. "I mean, I know it's the address on the credit card, but where is it exactly?"

"To my old house. I technically own it still, just in case the police show up. But they won't."

The house is obviously abandoned, and they approach from the rear. Nobody from the nearby houses notices them as they walk through the backyard. The Mothers are none too comforted by what they see, but at least Sylvia seems to be skeeved out too. The two-story white house has no definition in the night except for railings on the back porch and a small metal overhang above the door. Sylvia walks straight up and kicks in the back door, which swings open with a bang. The others walk in behind her, and Senator closes the door immediately. The Mothers are bunched up awkwardly in the near darkness, but Sylvia calmly scans the room. She taps HexxCat on the shoulder.

"Behind you there is a lamp. Feel it? Good. Just unplug it from the wall and hand it over."

HexxCat paws her way down the lamp until her fingers locate the cord. She disconnects the plug from the wall and passes the lamp back to where Sylvia's voice was a moment ago. Sylvia removes her finger by twisting it off at the joint, and she plugs the lamp cord directly into the severed appendage. The bottom of the finger gives way just like Play-Doh. The lamp flickers on, revealing a decade of dust on the curved shade and everything else in the room, excepting Sylvia, the Mothers, and the detached finger. A blue flashing light blinks under the fingernail. Everyone stares at the finger until Sylvia removes her glasses, and then they all stare at the one eyeball that is still knitting itself together. She pulls off her toboggan hat, and a short growth of hair is now visible. She runs her hand over her scalp and touches her tongue to her teeth.

"Well, children. I know it doesn't look like much now, but this is Base Camp." She waves her four-digit hand around the filthy room. "I can answer any and all questions now, but only after one of you gives me a cigarette."

HexxCat is first on the draw with a box of smokes open and extended toward the robot. Sylvia takes the cigarette and lights it with another finger. She inhales deeply, then exhales slowly. "Oh my God, thank you," she exclaims to the heavens, taking in another long drag.

"I thought you said your eyes needed to finish?" Blue wrinkles her nose, pulling out a cigarette of her own to steady her nerves. The others follow suit mechanically.

"It's good enough for now. Besides"—Sylvia exhales dramatically— "I'm just a defiant person. I don't even listen to myself." She glories in taking another long drag and exhales smoke above their heads. "OK, these are bad for you, by the way, I'm just saying. Don't keep smoking, or you are going to end up a time-traveling android like your Auntie

Sylvia. You all hearing me?" She looks seriously at them, then smiles. "Good. First question, shoot!"

And throughout the night, well into the morning, and deep into a breakfast at IHOP, the time-traveling android named Sylvia smokes cigarettes and answers every question they ask, including when and where she was from, why she has come to Nashville, Tennessee, from another distant future, *and* what any of this has to do with them. This night, she changes the future for the Mothers, and she successfully enlists each of them in a mission that is bigger than themselves.

Given that this is the sort of thing Kaldari and the Mothers have been hoping would come along their entire short lives, it doesn't take much arm twisting. After listening to the entirety of Sylvia's plan, the Mothers all agree to join her without reservation, and they set to work that very day to changing the world forever.

NOT EVEN IN A DREAM

August 1996

Paul wolfs down his cereal, puts on his shoes, looks out the window for any jackers, then dips out his back door to get his bike from the locked shed. DuBell's apartment complex is the next bus stop down, which is really just around the corner if you walk between the houses. The halfway point for meetups is just beyond Celeste Hunter's house, at a place everybody calls Weird Christine's house. It's weird in that the house isn't technically on any street but is sort of built in the common space in between neighborhoods, and because the people who live there are weird folk. Paul had heard them referred to as hillbillies but wasn't certain if that was the right term for them or not.

Six whole apartment buildings separate DuBell's apartment from Weird Christine's house, but somehow DuBell always makes it there first, even with Paul on a bike. Today is no different. DuBell is waiting in front of Weird Christine's house, drawing on the road with orange chalk. Paul rides up and admires DuBell's various tags of Juice, Juice Box, Juicy, Juice Bugs, all arranged with an assortment of sketches of a juice box cartoon. The words Daze and Razz are featured as well, though not nearly as prominent.

"How long have you been here?"

"Just a minute, why?"

"No reason."

A screen door slams, and an old man comes out of Weird Christine's house. Paul and DuBell stare at the man. He is as tall as Paul but half as wide with white hair stuck straight up in the air like bristles on a paint brush and a face full of salt-and-pepper stubble and deep sunken eyes that look alert and unstable. He doesn't speak or make any gestures. He just stares at them as if he's willing them to walk away.

Paul turns to DuBell. "You need help with your bags, man?"

"Yeah, grab the blue one." DuBell lets the chalk roll out of his palm to the concrete and picks up the black backpack. DuBell walks beside Paul as he slow-pedals the bike back to his street, cutting between two houses without chain-link fences.

As they walk up the street, they see Celeste sitting on her front porch, notebook and pen in hand. Two of her three sisters are sitting in the driveway playing with Barbies, and the third is shooting a basketball at a portable hoop set on a low height, about seven feet. The boys stop at the edge of the Hunters' yard.

"Hey, Celeste. You see my man here whip that as—"

"DuBell!" Celeste and Paul say simultaneously.

"Butt. My bad, yeah, butt. But you saw it. It was funny too!"

Celeste doesn't respond to DuBell. She just stares at him, waiting for him to stop disturbing her silence.

"Nikki, let me see the ball," DuBell shouts.

"No dunking!" she intones in an eight-year-old's attempt at sounding serious. She bounce-passes DuBell the ball. He dribbles politely. Shoots from the street. *Swish*. The ball bounces back to Nikki. DuBell motions for her to pass the ball back. She hesitates and DuBell groans.

"Nikki, I made the shot fair and square without dunking it! It's my shot." She waits. "Please," he puts his hands on his tiny hips, mock exasperated.

Meanwhile, Celeste glances up cool at Paul. "You know you're going to get in trouble come Monday."

"Maybe," Paul shrugs. "Or maybe he just keeps his mouth shut. I don't know." Paul puffs up his chest.

"Kendall? Keep his mouth shut? Doubtful. Plus, you didn't stick around to see his backpack. It was covered in dirt and grass stains. There's no way his mom or his dad won't notice."

"Then I don't know. And honestly, I don't care. He got what he deserved."

"Oh, I didn't say that he didn't. I just said you're going to be in trouble come Monday. Nikki just give DuBell the ball already."

"Thank you," DuBell bows to Celeste. He sticks his tongue out at Nikki and waggles his butt at her once he has the ball. He sets up to shoot again like before, then suddenly dribbles the ball up the driveway, leaping over Crystal and Tammy and the Barbie Dreamhouse, and spins around and dunks the ball over his head backward and hangs from the rim, his underwear exposed to everyone for the brief moment that he dangles.

"DuBell!" everybody shouts, but he just laughs and walks away.

"That's why I don't give you the ball."

"That's why I don't give you the ball," DuBell mocks as he walks on. Paul waves bye to Celeste, and she nods, giving a long bored stare over her end of the cul-de-sac before turning back to her notebook.

Paul pedals his bike to catch up to DuBell. "Hold up."

Deep rumbling bass spills out of Ponya's melon-green house, rattling the window screens and the hanging plants with each bass drop. DuBell bobs his head but refrains from making any inappropriate hand gestures that might be misconstrued as gang symbols and/or as weapons. As they come around the hill of Paul's yard, Paul gives a glance toward Kendall's house across the street, but the door is shut on the white shoebox with the black trim and the black shutters.

Paul turns to look back at his own house, which is technically a shoebox too, but because of the way its foundation sits exposed on the hill, and the high hedges around his porch and steps, and the long, paved driveway with the rosebushes, the sloping yard with the young maple tree in the middle … all of it made his little blue shoebox with the tan trim and the black shutters seem like a special fortress.

Paul puts his bike away in the shed. Beside the shed is the permanent basketball goal set to ten feet, which DuBell couldn't dunk on with the chair. The driveway is extra wide, which makes for great games of HORSE, but if a rebound gets away from you, the ball rolls downhill directly to Kendall's yard. Paul glances at Kendall's house again then looks over to the spot in his own yard where he tossed Kendall down.

DuBell grabs the mail out of the mailbox, and Paul hands him the keys to unlock the door. Paul decides to take a moment to water the roses for his mother. She isn't going to want to do it tonight.

He walks the length of the driveway, making sure each bush gets its share. He keeps the water off the petals and leaves and really gets the roots the way his mom showed him.

When he finishes, Paul walks in the front door of the house to find DuBell already has the living room TV turned to MTV and has made his way into the kitchen to construct a bowl of cereal for himself. Paul marvels at DuBell's speed.

He hollers into the kitchen, "Did you take your shoes off?"

Thunk. Thunk. "Yes."

"The Fugees are about to come on." Paul informs DuBell. Paul misses when *Yo! MTV Raps* was its own show, and you got a full hour of good beats after school, but he is glad they still at least do a few rap and hip-hop videos in a row every afternoon.

"Turn it up!" DuBell whines.

"I can't be blowing up my mom's TV," Paul rebuffs.

"You can turn it up some!" DuBell pleads, coming in from the kitchen.

Paul loves messing with DuBell. He turns it up, and they sing along to the Fugees and follow the silver briefcase in the video, discussing whether or not throwing a briefcase of money at the police would work. Ice Cube's "It Was a Good Day" follows, and Paul smiles. It has been a good day. *It still is a good day,* Paul thinks to himself.

"DuBell, did you bring your book?"

"What book? For why?" DuBell manages to get out around a mouthful of cereal without looking away from the TV.

"For homework," Paul responds. DuBell takes another bite of cereal and fishes three folded-up sheets of paper out of his pocket. He tosses them to Paul.

"What is all this?"

"They are love letters, Paul. I've been meaning to tell you for a long time, but I couldn't figure out how. It's the homework! You know that thing we were just talking about? Why is your mouth hanging open like that?"

"When did you have time to do all of this homework? Paul gawks at DuBell, incredulous. "I mean, you literally just got off the bus and walked over here. That's impossible."

"I do my homework all day long during class."

"Really?" Paul pulls a face at DuBell and unfolds the mess of pages.

"Yeah. I have to. There's no way I can get it done at night in my room with Dre and X messing with me the whole time. I honestly sense Mrs. Goldwood knows, and that's why she puts the assignments on the board first thing in the morning."

"So, you really do your homework in class. Huh. I always imagined you were over there drawing or staring off into space or something."

"Nah, that's what you do, Paul. I be listening to what she's saying with one part of my brain and working out the answer with the other part of my brain. Just do me a favor and check that homework as you come through."

"OK," Paul answers absently still trying to figure out where DuBell's homework begins. "Do you think Mrs. Goldwood is pretty?" he blurts out, surprising himself. DuBell gets a shrewd look on his face that lets Paul know he's really thinking about the question, eyes rolled up in his head like he's consulting a group of photographs.

"She's definitely pretty. She's also very classy."

"How do you figure that?" Paul pauses copying mid-sentence.

"Her shoes. She wears different shoes to school every day."

"What does that have to do with anything?"

"We've been back in school seven days, and she's worn a different pair of shoes with each different outfit. That's how you know if a woman is classy."

Paul thinks DuBell might have a point. Mrs. Goldwood did seem to fall under the classy category. His mom had about three pair of shoes, and one pair—her thick-soled white lace-up Reeboks—she wore those to the hospital every day.

"DuBell?"

"Yeah?"

"How do you know so much about Mrs. Goldwood's shoes?"

Now, right about here, Paul expects to catch DuBell maybe crushing on Mrs. Goldwood too, which would support his own budding interests, but instead he catches DuBell in one of his tells, where his eyes get dilated for just a second, a look he only gets when he feels like you've found out one of his secrets. So, when DuBell plays it off as a random memory, Paul refuses to let it go. This is one of those things only very best friends are allowed to do in utmost privacy, and Paul is feeling big today, so he leans on DuBell for the information. After several minutes of Paul pestering DuBell using annoying, squeaky, high-pitched voices to ask over and over, DuBell finally admits, "I have a photographic memory when it comes to certain things, OK? Damn."

Paul looks at DuBell, but he can't tell if he's joking or not. "Like you can for real remember everything you see and hear, like what people wear or said or the answers to a test?"

"Not all of those things, but some of them. I'm visual and kinesthetic but not auditory." Paul stares at DuBell. "I took a test I found in a book in the library once."

"I have no clue what you're talking about. Can you, or can't you?"

"Yes. Things I see mostly. And things I touch. It always works better if I touch something."

"Do you get psychic visions from old stuff? That spoon you're using belonged to my great-grandma, I think. Can you sense her?"

"Don't be stupid," DuBell huffs, starting to turn a little red. Paul knows DuBell's hotspot is being called a liar, so he backs off.

"I'm just playing, man. I believe you." Paul looks at Du-Bell all sly. "I noticed you avoided answering if you can memorize test answers."

DuBell closes his eyes, and he breaths out heavily. "Yes, Daze. I can memorize test answers."

"How come you never told me?"

"I don't tell people that. You really shouldn't either."

"I won't, Juice. I promise."

"I know you won't," DuBell sighs and shakes his head a little. "*Raps* about to go off soon. Go copy that homework so we can go outside for a minute."

"All right, but you know my mom could come home at any point."

"How many cases does she have?"

"Thirty-five."

"She won't be home anytime soon."

"Still, she's got neighborhood spies."

"I'm sure. But like, down the street. Mrs. Hunter. Not up here. Your mama don't never be talking to those white folks across the street, or the Laotians, Ponya and Sok, and all them. And she for sure don't never be talking to Kendall's mama, so if we sit on the back porch can't nobody see us."

"Yeah, maybe, but you can't be shooting ball. Everybody can hear it all the way down to Celeste's house."

"What? That was totally somebody else from the neighborhood out there shooting on your goal. Not us."

"Like who?"

"How do we know? We are inside and staying away from the windows like we're supposed to do, right?" DuBell springs up from the couch and heads to deposit his cereal bowl in the sink.

"True," Paul nods. He looks over to where his friend was sitting and sees the image of an elephant stitched in gold thread glimmering on the front of a throw pillow. Paul is instantly reminded of his bigness, and it ripples through him as he heaves himself up off the couch. He turns toward the kitchen, and as he does, he notices another little elephant, blue porcelain, by the front door on a little table where his mom puts her keys. Then he turns his head, and he sees a tiny hidden elephant on the lip of a flower pot that sits near the window.

Suddenly Paul is called up in the glow of his bigness—in an awakening akin to an out-of-body experience where he can see himself from this morning, head down, packing gym clothes into his backpack instead of his lunch box, so upset every time he chances to pass a mirror. Or another "fat person," which was how he had thought of himself. Or every time he saw a girl. Or some athletic dude. He can see now how he had just curled up inside his mind and flinched away in anguish. In fear of being exposed as being a fat kid and hauled up for everyone to laugh at.

Paul can see that self, head pointing down, and he reaches out to him with one great finger, and he lifts the old Paul's chin up. Straightens out his smile.

The sun shines out from behind a cloud and comes through the mini blinds, engulfing Paul in an orange glow. Part of him keeps expecting DuBell to come around the corner and laugh at him, but he hears DuBell open the back door and walk outside. Paul stands in the light with his eyes closed, absorbing the warmth into his forehead and his teeth and his skin. He lifts his head up higher and opens his heart to the sun and the universe, and behind him the Notorious B.I.G.'s "Big Poppa" comes on, and Paul is changed forever.

"Daze," DuBell yells from the back porch, "bring out some Kool-Aid."

"I'm doing homework."

"You're copying homework." The back door slams back shut.

"All right then," Paul hollers back at no one. He opens his eyes and walks into the kitchen. He pulls down some cups and serves up the Kool-Aid. It swirls electric blue in the clear glass. DuBell comes into the kitchen, slamming the door again, and scoops up the closest glass to him. "I licked all over that glass," Paul arches his eyebrows comically.

"Good, I like it best that way," DuBell downs the Kool-Aid in five enormous gulps. "AAAAAH. Yessssssss!"

"You aren't getting any more."

"Copy that homework."

"You know that everybody, including me most of the time, expects this relationship to go the other way around. Like, I do the homework with you copying off me?"

"I do. It's all part of my plan to try and take over the world," he exclaims in his best Brain voice. "Now hurry up, Pinky."

"Narf," Paul replies as he sits and copies the homework at the tiny kitchen table.

The afternoon passes with them sitting on the back porch talking about the million ideas that steadily float in and out of DuBell's mind. Paul loves that DuBell never appears bored and marvels at his friend's energy. DuBell can ask/talk about any topic without gumption, or taboo, or shame, at any time, which makes taking him out in public an adventure and guarantees it won't be dull.

In the span of two hours, they discuss Bigfoot, Ewoks, Eskimo, volcanoes, hot girls (in their class, in their grade, on their bus, in their school, in their neighborhood), camping, summer camp, hot girls at summer camp, candle-making at summer camp, riding horses, horse manure, Native Americans, social studies, white people, their class seating arrangement, Kendall, the fight, what to name the fight instead of "the fight," the confrontation, what Paul should tell his mom about the confrontation, a rehearsal of the mom talk with DuBell as Paul's mom, Monday at school, Monday on the bus, East Coast versus West Coast, basketball, football, cheerleaders, basketball versus football cheerleaders, what if baseball had cheerleaders, hockey cheerleaders, golf cheerleaders, Olympic cheerleaders, debate over whether or not cheerleading is already an Olympic sport, video games, video games as an Olympic sport, games they will be playing later, movies they will be watching later, girls they might call later, a rundown of all the girls DuBell is actually talking to on a regular basis, talking to girls on the phone as an Olympic sport, professional sponsorship for talking to girls on the phone, a list of organizations and companies that might provide sponsorship for talking to girls on the phone professionally, logos for the league, mascots, favorite animals, elephants.

"Hey, you ever noticed that my mom has a ton of elephants on things in the house."

"Yes."

"I never really noticed until today."

"Really?" DuBell's eyes grow wide with astonishment. "You just now realized that your whole house is full of elephants. I mean, no fewer than ninety-six elephants in total if you count patterns on frames and plates and bowls."

"I just never paid attention."

"That's an understatement. Do you even know why she collects elephants?"

"I just said that I just now noticed them for the first time. How can I possibly know why she has them if I just noticed them for the first time? I haven't had a chance to ask her yet."

"It's because her middle name is Eleanor. You know, Ellie. Like elephant."

"How in the world do you know my mother's middle name? I barely know my mom's middle name." In fact, Paul was pretty sure it was Evelyn. But not 100 percent sure.

"It's on her mail," DuBell responds with a shrug of the shoulders.

"You read our mail?"

"Not on purpose. I told you. I have a photographic memory. I can't help it."

"OK. What's the return address on the letter on top of the mail?"

"Nashville Electric Service, PO Box 305099, Nashville, TN 37230-5099."

Paul goes inside and looks at the stack of mail on the kitchen table, and sure enough, it's the electric bill and his mother's middle name is not Evelyn.

The phone rings. Paul sees it is his mom's work on caller ID and yells for DuBell to be quiet. "Hey, Mom," Paul answers.

DuBell yells around the corner, "Tell Eleanor I said hey."

Paul covers up the mouthpiece with this palm, and he walks toward the bedroom while he listens.

"Paul. I received an interesting phone message from Mrs. Hunter earlier." Paul's heart freezes. They'd been seen outside! "She is under the impression that you got into a fight with Kendall after school. At the bus stop. Is that true?"

"No, ma'am. It was not a fight. It was a confrontation, which he started, and I finished." Paul felt the line sounded good; perhaps he had delivered it a bit fast though. Regardless, he was glad that he and DuBell had rehearsed. He finished up with the combo: "I didn't hit him, and he didn't hit me."

Mom blocks, unaffected. "But you put him on the ground. Which means you put your hands on him in the first place, correct?"

Paul goes for the truth. "I was just standing up for myself, Mom. I'm far too big to let him talk to me the way he does anymore." Paul is resolute in the statement.

There's a brief silence on the other end of the phone. Paul begins to brace for impact. His mom speaks after a moment.

"What are you and DuBell planning to fix for dinner?"

The shift in topic catches Paul on the wrong foot, but he recovers quickly. "I ... I had some money saved from my allowance. I was going to order us pizza. If that's OK with you," he adds hastily.

"Go look in my top drawer, on the left. There should be a $20 bill. Use that."

Paul amazes himself with the ability to speak through his shock. "Yes, ma'am. Thank you."

"Don't stay up too late. We have errands to run in the morning."

"Yes, ma'am. Does DuBell need to go home early?"

"No. I expect he can just come along with us, so long as he be-haves-him-self," she places firm pronunciation on the last syllables.

"Yes, ma'am. I will tell him."

"I love you, baby. I will see you in the morning."

"I love you, Mama. Don't work too hard." Paul hangs up and begins to wonder if perhaps today has been some long, weird dream. What in the world was that? How had that not ended in DuBell going home promptly and him grounded for a month? How had the confrontation earned him and DuBell a pizza? Paul steps back into the living room, passing the big-screen TV and the couch in two of his enormous strides.

As he rounds the corner into the kitchen, Paul reaches out his finger and touches a tiny maroon elephant sitting in the kitchen window above the sink. It is the ring holder for when his mom cooks. How had he never noticed all of these elephants? He has no idea, but part of him is glad. His awakening today into his bigness, into being big, is peppered with reminders and affirmations that he is on a path chosen by the universe.

"The universe wants you to be big, my man," he hears Supraman saying again. "You gotta find something that works for you and throw yourself into it."

Paul walks out back and closes the door without slamming it. He takes the basketball from DuBell, walks to the center of the driveway, dribbles, pauses, shoots. *Swish.* The ball bounces back to him naturally. He shoots again, and it rebounds away with a *thonk.* DuBell is up and in recovery mode instantly, catching the rebound and sweeping in with an aggressive layup.

"Here. Go on and to take your next shot then let's go in."

"Go in?"

"You can only push good luck so far."

DuBell takes a shot. Misses. Runs to recover. Shoots.

Makes it off the backboard. He grabs the ball and follows Paul inside, careful to not slam the screen door this time.

"Lock the door, Juice."

"Word." Paul hears the click of the dead bolt and glances at the front door to see that it is also in place. He heads back to the kitchen to find DuBell in the Kool-Aid.

"Don't drink it all!"

"I'm thirsty from doing your homework and giving you basketball lessons. When I'm not even supposed to be outside. You should be preparing me a bathtub of Kool-Aid."

"Eww. You'd drink Kool-Aid from the bathtub?"

"Fool, I would drink Kool-Aid from a sock. Trust me."

"Oh, I do. So, what do you want on your pizza?"

"Where are you ordering from?"

"I'm thinking Papa John's."

"They have two larges for thirteen ninety-nine with a two liter or an extra-large two-topping with breadsticks and a two liter."

"What about Domino's?"

"They have a deal for a meat lover's deep dish for ten … Screw you. It's not funny. I told you I can't help it. I should've never told you because you would've never noticed anyways. Just like the elephants."

Paul chuckles. "I'm just messing with you, Juice. I think it's really cool. And useful. Seriously. What are the rest of the pizza deals? My mom gave us some money, and we should spend it wisely." DuBell eyes Paul dubiously, then rattles off all of the coupon deals for the nearby pizza places. Once they consider all options and decide that Papa John's will provide the most leftovers, they get themselves set up in the den where they can spend the remainder of the evening oscillating between watching movies and TV shows, playing video games, and calling girls on the phone.

All of the girls want to hear firsthand about the confrontation, which Paul allows DuBell to narrate for their audience. DuBell is true to his word and arranges to talk to Nikki and Zaidi in a three-way call. Paul has always attributed DuBell's success at talking to girls to his just being wild and having zero inhibitions. But now Paul realizes being able to memorize names and phone numbers is incredibly helpful as well, and he decides to invest in an address book in the near future.

For hours, they rotate through their combined arsenal of games: *NBA Jam, Super Punch-Out!!, Earthworm Jim, Ken Griffey Jr. Presents Major League Baseball*, and *Kirby's Dream Course*. They turn on Showtime at 10 PM to catch *Eddie Murphy Raw* for the second time in two weeks. Paul doesn't care for all of this routine, but he knows DuBell idolizes Eddie Murphy, so he is indulgent. After it is over, Paul and DuBell repeat the "Welfare Burger" sketch about a thousand times.

Paul looks over at DuBell. "What do you suppose you want to be when you grow up?" DuBell lays on a long couch that fills the left side of the room, and Paul reclines in his La-Z-Boy, both surrounded by an array of pillows and blankets and food.

"Man, I just want to grow up and get out of my mom's house. Get away from her, from Dre, and from X, and all their drama."

"Yeah, I know that, but I mean … what's going to be your future plans?"

"My uncle works at the airport. Helping planes to land and taxiing them, you know with the little cone flashing lights that light up orange. He makes pretty good money, and he has his own place. I figure I can do that."

"DuBell."

"Yes, Paul?"

"How do you act so alien all the time, then come up with the most regular job for your future plan?"

"You asked me my plan. That's my plan. What's your plan?"

Paul doesn't actually have a plan per se, but he knows it is bigger than … bigger than … well, bigger than a local airport, that's for sure.

"I'm gonna let you in on a secret," Paul begins, "and you can laugh if you want to. It's OK if you do. But you see, the universe wants me to be big. I just found out today. I … received a kind of message."

"What message?" DuBell urges in a quiet, respectful tone.

"To be big." Paul exhales with as much meaning as he can place into the three syllables. "The universe wants me to be big."

"Well … you are big," DuBell puzzles, slightly confused as to the point.

"Yes!" Paul laughs with excitement. "Yes, exactly! I am big. Physically. Which is great, but I think the universe wants me to be more than just physically big. I think I'm meant to be famous or something. Like a big deal big."

"You mean like a rapper or a ball player, or like a movie star?"

"That's what I don't know … yet. But I'm going to figure it out, Juice. And I know it sounds weird, but I think you're going to be part of it." And that is the truth. Paul loves DuBell like a brother.

"Daze, I hate to hurt your feelings, but I'm never going to get big like you. My metabolism just burns up all my calories. I already used up all the pizza just talking to Nikki on the phone and playing *Kirby*. In fact, I'm hungry right now, and I want more pizza, but I know your moms is going to be here soon."

"It's OK. I'll be big enough for the both of us."

"So, are you going to get like unhealthy big? You know, like Guinness world record style?"

"Nah, I have to keep it fit for the ladies, you know." They pause to give a complicated handshake. "But I'm just not going to fight the fact that I'm bigger than most adults."

"Are you going to play football?"

"I don't know. Maybe. I never really wanted to, but I know big guys can do well at it. And girls love football players. I just don't want some coach yelling at me. I get enough of that from my grandpa."

"I dare a coach to yell at me."

"That's what coaches do, Juice." The phone rings, and Paul holds up his hand. It does not ring a second time. That means his mom is on the way home. "Let's do a quick sweep and tidy up before she gets here."

"I thought you said she didn't flip out before about the confrontation."

"She didn't, but you know my mom. Some small thing might upset her, and then suddenly it turns out I've murdered Kendall."

"Precisely."

DuBell jumps up off the sofa, and Paul levers the recliner forward, causing him to spring up, and they collide with true comedic timing only to fall apart laughing. Paul picks DuBell up from where he has ricocheted into the floor. They pick up plates and empty cups of garlic butter, checking the living room all the way back to the kitchen. DuBell resets the pillows. Paul flips on the back porch light so his mom will be able to see to get in. They double-check the locks on the doors and get one more glass of Kool-Aid, splitting the pitcher between them.

"Should we do these dishes?" DuBell points to the sink.

"No, we can get those in the morning. She will want us in bed." They head back to the den and freshen up their spots on the recliner and sofa. They make sure the Kool-Aid is on top of coasters. Paul turns off the overhead lights and switches off the TV. Before he's even reclined properly, he hears DuBell snoring, face half-buried in his pillow.

Paul stares at DuBell. He has known DuBell since kindergarten, but he knows that there is so much he does not know about his friend. He certainly did not know that DuBell had a photographic memory until today. That really does explain some things.

Paul and DuBell had become friends the first day they met in Mrs. Ferguson's kindergarten classroom. Within minutes of talking over some LEGOs, they had discovered that they both just lived with their moms, no dads around (though DuBell had two older brothers). Paul had never been an overly social child, but that day a magic special to kindergarten took over, and his brotherhood to DuBell was forged solid by the time they had lunch and reached the playground for recess.

Ignoring the rest of their classmates, the pair had climbed into the frame of the jungle gym and pretended to be the Ninja Turtles. Paul got Leonardo's swords and Donatello's staffs, and DuBell got Michelangelo's nunchucks and Rafael's tripoint sais, and for an hour they had just talked through all the moves instead of play-fighting like a handful of others were doing under a tree a short distance away. Paul remembers how in that moment he knew that he had selected well in choosing his first friend.

And on that very day, just two hours later, Paul learned the true fierceness of his newfound brother. They were queued up in line for the afternoon bus just outside of the school, with buses and cars in line waiting for the crossing guard to start dismissal. Paul hadn't noticed this morning, but he and DuBell rode the same bus, so to his delight, there they were after school, discussing the afternoon lineup of the *Super Mario Brothers* and *Zelda*. Then from behind, a first grader from DuBell's apartment complex named Dante Simmon, called out in that clear bully tone, "Hey, it's a little Dumb Bell." Laughter came from his gang of followers standing in line behind him. "Hey, Dumb Bell ..." Paul remembers right here the distinct sound of bus hydraulics, and for him and the others who witnessed the event, time slowed down as Dante said the words, "Are you black or white?"

And Paul looked down to realize DuBell was already three steps in motion, moving in an arc so much faster than should be humanly possible. Paul watched as DuBell propelled all of his sixty-pound body forward and grabbed

Dante by the front of his backpack straps. DuBell then threw all of his weight forward with a dynamic whip of his arms, causing Dante's relaxed body to follow the flow until his face smacked audibly into the side of the school building and quite literally exploded into a spray of blood and teeth. The screaming panic of first-day students, the authoritative shouts of teachers and bus drivers, the alarmed voices of parents coming out of their parked cars all fell away as DuBell pulled Paul's sleeve and whispered into his ear discreetly, "All you say is I tripped over your foot, OK?" DuBell stepped on Paul's left foot firmly.

"OK," Paul whispered back, amazed at the circus of mayhem DuBell had orchestrated around them.

Moments later, or hours later, Paul is not sure, they were whisked into the principal's office where an onslaught of adults including Paul's mom asked Paul to tell the story at least a hundred times. But Paul never deviated; he never strayed from the story. The boy, Dante, Paul had not known his name until the adults had supplied it, called DuBell "Dumb Bell" and asked him if he was black or white. DuBell ran at Dante, but he tripped over Paul's left foot, causing him to fall and smack Dante into the wall. The adults had a million questions, but Paul just shrugged his shoulders and looked each adult in the eyes, his own eyes wide in his doughy face, and he said, "DuBell tripped."

Paul would learn later that DuBell had been telling the exact same story in another room but under the extreme duress of Miss Cindy beating the tar out of him the entire time. Eventually the adults all had to concede that, graphic and gruesome and purposeful as it appeared, it had been an accident. And if anyone was truly at fault, it had been Dante for instigating the confrontation. Miss Cindy had vocalized that DuBell had to take some responsibility, and she let everyone know that she intended to beat him severely when she got home for "trying to shove" Dante.

By the time Paul and his mom left that evening, it was dark. He recalled that the street lights were orange, and they blended weirdly with the school's outside lights of blue-green halogen. He was quiet as his mom started the car and the headlights illuminated the backstop of the baseball field. As she drove them away, she put her hand on his knee and looked like she was going to say something but then seemed to change her mind. She just gave Paul a light squeeze and drove him home in silence. The next day when Paul got on to the bus, DuBell was saving a seat for him, and the rest was history.

Paul drifts to sleep thinking big thoughts and replaying day one in his mind. And in this sleepy vision, he grows big to become a bus, and he sees the scene from ten feet above the crowd, and as his hydraulic brakes hiss and his doors open, he hears Dante's voice, and he sees DuBell's reaction, and he sees his young self, the center of the circular path that DuBell is carving toward Dante. And he can see full-well that DuBell never trips, but instead, runs straight to his intended mark, plants his feet firmly grabbing Dante's backpack straps, and executes an astounding demonstration of physics, completely destroying his enemy. But Paul has never told another version of the story, and he never will. Not even in a dream. Not even as Big Bus Paul. He will never betray DuBell.

YOU MIGHT AS WELL ENJOY YOUR DRINK

August 1996

As Loni Lore enters the story, we see that she is mentally on fire, fueled by a certain variant of hatred that can only be supplied by a lifelong enemy. She has not truly slept since Thursday, and it is Sunday morning. It is just after eight o'clock in the morning, and overhead there is a pale-blue Nashville sky offset by a strand of thick clouds in the east, hiding a corner of the sun. Loni Lore is on a mission to find Sylvia Tate to jerk a knot in her ass, as Loni's daddy was fond of saying.

Loni does not anticipate this business taking very long, so she leaves her car parked at a nearby gas station after checking that the doors are locked. She crosses the street with the light and walks quickly past the waiting people at the bus stop on Eighth Avenue South. She walks down Wedgewood Avenue toward a row of four houses that run right up to the interstate; according to the phone book, Sylvia Tate's house is second from the interstate.

As Loni approaches the address, she is suddenly wary of the surrounding houses. She notices broken windows, rotted porches, and lawns strewn with a mixture of clothes, children's toys, and garbage tossed up from the street. The house next door to Sylvia's has a very large dog—a Doberman mix maybe? Loni is uncertain. As she passes, the dog growls and sits up, moving closer to Loni. It barks once, deep and menacing.

Loni keeps her goal in sight. She does not speed up, or even turn toward Sylvia's house, until she is perfectly aligned with the sidewalk as if being at her intended destination might magically keep that dog in check should it come off the chain. Loni realizes that the dog has distracted her from her mission, and she looks up and pulls her shoulders back to get herself ready to fight. She only has three questions for Sylvia.

Question one: what in the hell do you want?

Question two: what will it take to make you leave?

Question three: what will it take to make sure you stay gone?

Sylvia's porch smells disgusting and is literally covered in trash. Loni looks to her left and sees a four-foot pile of garbage that was once bagged up but has since been ripped open by animals. She covers her mouth, but she resists the urge to gag. Bad smells she can handle. Her job as a journalist has taken her into some bad smells over the years; as one of the few black writers for the *Nashville Banner*, Loni is always "given the opportunity" to cover any places white journalists don't want to go (which primarily consists of the entire black community and places that white people perceive as smelling bad). While Loni is very happy that she does not get assigned the normal fluff pieces they throw at the white female reporters, she has been forced to cultivate a strong stomach when it comes to certain smells: the putrid, coppery smell of murder and accidental death; the urine smell of nursing homes, daycares, and homeless shelters; the armpit smell of libraries and high school gymnasiums; and the garbage smell in city waste facilities and under bridges. Sylvia's porch smells like an attempt to blend all four.

Loni looks around for a doorbell and presses it, but she can't hear anything. She opens the screen door (with screen half removed) to reveal a sturdy-looking blue door with no doorknob, just a flat sheet of metal where the doorknob should be. The dog next door barks again, and Loni is startled to the point of nearly putting her hand in trash to regain her balance, but she gets her footing and sturdies herself. She starts to bang on the door, and as she does, she hears the growl of the dog next door. Loni looks over to her left, and she unintentionally makes eye contact with the dog, who instantly darts out of the front door of its house. It runs, barking and scrambling, across its front porch and dives onto the small patch of lawn between houses, where Loni stands mere feet away.

What happens next is a combination of physics and luck. Loni comes to her senses and springs forward herself, throwing the rickety screen door aside in a burst. On instinct she grabs for the front door handle but forgets that it doesn't exist, which sends her colliding awkwardly into the door. However, as Loni's hand touches the metal pad on the door, it unlocks automatically and swings open, slamming forward and spilling her onto the floor inside the house.

As she falls, she turns to see the dog is taking the porch steps at a run. She cannot get to the door in time to close it. The snarling beast comes at Loni, leaps but does not cross the threshold of the house. Instead, the dog is flung backwards with a very loud WEEEERNNNNNNNTTT noise. Loni feels a whoosh of air jet across her face, and dust and debris from the floor filter up around her.

Loni closes her eyes and opens them again a second later to see the dog flattened to the ground, as if gravity is crushing it with a large hand. A noise like a deep growl emits from the house, and suddenly the dog jumps up with the yelp and runs out of the yard.

Before Loni can even catch her breath, she hears a voice down the hall.

"Hi, this is Loni Lore. This is my proof of concept for the Petroglyph Diary Project. I will be using several journal pages from my own childhood for this example. I journaled religiously in my teens, and I believe the summer into fall of 1972 will best serve to show you the full range of this project."

Loni easily recognizes it as her own voice, but she has no clue what recording she's listening to.

"What in the hell is Sylvia playing at?" Loni whispers to herself as Sylvia walks down a dark hallway that she would normally leave well enough alone, but she's come too far on this mission to back down now. The hall is lined with mirrors and landscape paintings that give Loni the creeps. She moves toward a doorway emitting a warm orange glow and hears her voice again.

"To create the visualizations, you can either type, speak, or photograph and scan journal entries into the diary program, and the diary will use key images from your contact lists, your photos, and your Facebook, Instagram, or Twitter accounts if you give it permission. Then using the internet, it can draw upon actual satellite imaging of locations mentioned in the journals to create photo-realistic renderings of what you write."

Loni slowly enters the doorway to find a very large and comfortable room with several armchairs, tables, lamps, and even a pool table and a piano over in one corner. Along the back wall, there is a full bar with a few barstools in front, and in the center of the room is a sunken-floor entertainment setup, with two couches arranged facing a large screen set inside of the wall.

Loni sees the video of herself that she has been hearing; it is a video of herself that she never made. The date at the bottom reads 09/14/2018.

A voice-over starts; it is not Loni narrating, but a male voice, speaking in a faraway storybook tone.

"When Loni Lore was sixteen years old, she and her lifelong neighbor and best friend, Sylvia Tate, got summer jobs at the new theme park that had opened near their houses. It was a quick bus ride to work, and Opryland provided all of the work outfits on-site, so every day the girls rolled out of bed, walked to the bus stop in sweatpants, and did each other's makeup on the bus while sharing a bacon sandwich and a cup of coffee that was three-fourths sugar."

Loni balks at the image of herself and Sylvia at sixteen years old. "How in the hell is this possible?" She stands on the landing, unable to move. On the narration rolls, detailing things no one should know, things she only revealed in her diary—her thoughts and feelings about herself and Sylvia in those years, her lack of anyone else to talk to besides Sylvia or her parents, her adolescent insecurities, and her personal triumphs that summer.

Then before she can stop it from happening, the day she meets Tyrone is playing, and Loni's knees go weak.

She has to sit down on the landing to steady herself against the rail.

"Wednesday, July 26, 1972, began just as the day before it had, with a bright sun in the east and large puffy white clouds over the river bringing a promise of humidity and sticky sweat that afternoon for everyone in the park. Sylvia had counted forty-six cute boys by 10:30, and two boys in particular had come through the Flume Zoom line three times just to talk to Sylvia and exchange phone numbers. After the boys embarked on their third log ride, Sylvia informed Loni that the boys wanted to meet them by the giant swings when they got a break. They were Michael and Tyrone; they were ages sixteen and fifteen respectively; they went to East High School, rising juniors. Mike plays football, and Tyrone is in marching band."

Loni doesn't know what she is watching; someone has taken her deepest, most important memories and somehow made it into a movie of her life, with a cast that looks so unbelievably true to life. How is this possible?

It is at this point, Loni notices Sylvia on the other side of the room. "Oh," Loni licks her teeth and glares death across the room. "There you are." Loni's confusion ebbs away to a familiar anger.

"Hey, Loni. Did you want me to pause this, or ..."

"What in the hell is this?" Loni starts standing up again and pointing at the screen. Other, more-salient questions race into her mind, and she voices them all. "Why in the hell are you calling me at work? Why are you messing with me about my husband? Why am I even looking at you?"

"I'll just pause this then." Sylvia stops the film, "Why don't you just sit back down?" Sylvia points to the nearest chair.

"I'll stand, thanks."

"Have it your way." Sylvia walks up to Loni, nonchalant. Loni stacks thumbs outside her fists, ready to strike, but Sylvia ignores the gesture. "Listen, we have to start on the right foot now, if this is going to work."

"Work?" Loni recoils indignantly.

Sylvia continues: "I know you hate my guts, seriously, but I just need you to look at me for a second. Really, look at me."

Loni glances up at the face she associates with betrayal. With hate. With *wretched whore*. Loni looks at Sylvia, and she sees all of those things for many seconds before she realizes what Sylvia wants her to see.

Sylvia's face is all wrong. Or rather. It's wrong because there's nothing wrong with it. It's not as old as it should be. Loni hasn't seen Sylvia for over ten years, but she looks like she's in her twenties again. That's not possible, not even with plastic surgery.

"What in the hell …" Loni trails off.

"You see it now, huh?" Sylvia laughs. "Well, then let's start by saying, I am *not* the Sylvia you once knew."

Loni opens her mouth and starts to respond, but Sylvia cuts her off. "I'm not trying to be rude, L, but this is going to go much faster if you don't interrupt. I promise."

Loni closes her mouth tightly and glowers, face flushed with rising anger. Sylvia continues: "I do not mean to say that I am a 'changed person' since we saw each other twelve years ago. I mean to say, I am not Sylvia Tate as you knew her." Sylvia looks very closely at Loni before she spells it out slowly. "I am a robot." Sylvia pauses for effect, but getting no response, she continues. "I am a version of Sylvia

Tate from another time line and many years in the future. As a matter of fact," Sylvia muses, "I'm a *copy* of a robot Sylvia from another time line from the future. Let that sink in a moment." Sylvia makes that quirky *I'm thinking* face that always exacerbated Loni as a kid.

Loni just furrows her brows at Sylvia and raises her shoulders in a sardonic, almost aggressive, *so what* gesture. Despite what she's seen just now, Loni just cannot *not* be angry around Sylvia, and she really wants Sylvia to get aggressive back. Instead, Sylvia says, in a very cool and kind voice, "how much would it freak you out if, as a joke, I took off my right hand, right now, and tossed it over to you and made it scuttle up the steps like Thing? Would it freak you out a little or a lot?" Loni's thoughts go quiet. "I'm guessing a lot," Sylvia continues. She holds up her hand, and in succession she lights up three of her fingers with incredibly bright white lights and uses a voice imitating a megaphone. "I. Am. A robot."

"What in the world?" Loni gasps, looking away from the blinding lights on Sylvia's fingers. "What is this? Is this real? What has happened to you?" Loni is wide-eyed in a mixture of disgusted panic and rising excitement.

"Well, I'll tell you, L, but you have to quit hating my guts long enough for me to get it all out. The story is long, and you aren't going to believe half of it except for I'm standing here, living proof."

"Hating your guts is just going to have to be part of it. You being a robot or whatever isn't enough to overcome that. Trust me, if I didn't have the utmost desire to know what was going on, I wouldn't be talking to you."

Sylvia rolls her eyes. "Well, have it your way. Just let me talk already."

"All right, I'm listening." Loni forcefully breaks her gaze up from Sylvia's glowing fingers. "Talk!"

Sylvia turns off the lights in her fingers all at once, closes her hand, and places it in her lap. She sits up and looks Loni in the eyes. "The first thing you need to understand is that I am not from this time. I am technically from the future *and* from what might be called an alternate, or mirror, reality. I can explain the science of all that later; right now, that's not important. What *is* important is that our time lines are virtually identical up until about a year ago, when I arrived here. Our childhood and teenage years, our falling out over Tyrone, the years of me and Tyrone, and the years of you and Tyrone—all of that is the same. In both time lines, I die in 1984."

"Wait, what? You died?" Loni stares at Sylvia, aghast.

"Yes," Sylvia states, matter of fact.

"Oh," Loni whispers with a vacant stare on her face. "Was it painful?"

"Yes. Go ahead and smile now. I know you want to. Would it make you feel better to know that in the end I got brutally chopped up and left for dead?"

Loni looks at Sylvia still without expression. "Yes," she responds as if she were answering if her name was still Loni. "But what happened?"

Sylvia laughs a little at Loni's response and rolls her eyes again. "Exactly what you might expect at the time. I told some guys that I could get them some blow, and then I walked away with their money. Unbeknownst to me, they were all wannabe-thug jackers, and they were following me to rob my dealer. When they saw me just walking down the street all la-di-da, they realized I'd ripped them off. They drove up beside me, yanked me right off the street. They dragged me behind a dumpster and stabbed me twelve times in total, leaving me for dead."

"Jesus Christ!" All anger leaves Loni momentarily. "When was this?"

"Right after Tyrone left me."

"You mean *literally* right after I saw you at Thanksgiving. Jesus Christ! You've been dead all this time?"

"Well, not *technically* dead, but yes. That's why no one's heard from me for a long while. As I'm sure you know, I had pissed off so many people at that point, including my family, that nobody ever came around, so no one knew to check on me. The house was paid for; if the water and electric were shut off, who cared. All my taxes were handled by my dad's company and had been for years, so I never needed to sign anything. I wager that if I had actually made it back home before those guys butchered me, literally no one would have found me for years. I'm only alive because I happened to be outside when the thugs found me, and they didn't care enough about me to hide the body."

"So, you survived being stabbed and left for dead? Damn."

"Lucky for me, some people who lived nearby just happened to see my legs poking out from behind the dumpster as they were coming home. They threw me in a car and rushed me over to Meharry Medical and dumped me on the sidewalk. From there, well … that's complicated and boring, but the short version is my body didn't make it, but my brain did. Then, I was literally a brain in a jar for about ten years before I started my journey to becoming an android."

"Well, that's amazing and all, seriously, I could write an exhilarating article about it, but what does any of this have to do with me or my husband?"

"You see, L," Sylvia exhales slow, "here's why your attitude doesn't bother me. We have a little while, you and I, before this is over. Which *will* give us all the time we need to fix the broken parts between us. So, I'm not worried. I've got the long view."

"Ha ha ha ha." Loni starts to slow laugh, then actually starts laughing. There is something so bizarre in all of it that it just can't be taken seriously. "I'm going to take the drink now."

"Already on it. You would like a whisky neat. Glenfiddich."

Loni winces. "OK, I'll bite. How exactly do you know my drink order? Are we 'best friends' in the future? Do we sit around and paint each other's toenails like the old days? I mean …" Loni looks around the lounge, desperate for anything to latch onto but failing and so blurts out, "When I woke up today, I just wanted to kick your ass and be done with you this morning by 8:30. Now it's almost 9 AM, and I'm caught up in some science fiction movie, and everything I can consider to ask is just going to lead to more questions. So, I oscillate between coping with all that I'm learning and hating your guts all over again. It's like, all of my reporter instincts want to kick in and investigate, but then the last twenty-four years of you … well, just you …"

"Go on, get it out," Sylvia leans back against the counter with her arms folded.

"Get it out! Get it out!" Loni shouts. "You robbed me, Sylvia Tate! You wretched whore! You should've been my best friend! It should've all gone completely differently, and instead you robbed me. You robbed Tyrone. Everybody." Loni feels her fire leaving her suddenly, and she just wants to leave. "And you threw away our friendship. And you sent me into a spiral of distrust and depression that I've struggled with ever since. And now I'm supposed to be all hunky-dory because you got yourself murdered and turned into a robot. This is too much for me. I'm leaving." Loni stands.

Sylvia walks over with a drink in hand. "Have a seat, L. You aren't going anywhere yet. To your earlier point, you are most definitely caught up in this plot. Far deeper than you know."

"Are you holding me hostage?" Loni glares at Sylvia hard.

"Oh no. No, no, no. Please don't misunderstand." Sylvia wrinkles her eyebrows, forcing a drink into Loni's hand. "You can most certainly walk out of that front door right now. Hell, I can even make you forget everything you've seen if that's what you want … but the dog is still going to be outside for at least an hour, so you might as well enjoy your drink," Sylvia smiles, and she clinks Loni's glass before taking a sip of her own drink. "Cheers."

The android Sylvia points her finger across the room at the screen with the paused video of the diary, and it turns to a white screen. She plops down on the couch in the sunken living room and motions for Loni to come in and take a seat on the other end.

Loni would love to throw the drink in Sylvia's face, but instead she walks over and sits on the edge of the large couch.

She drinks her drink because God she *really* needs it right this minute. A feeling like panic over being trapped starts to well up in Loni's chest, but she swallows the fear down with the whisky (which is excellent), and she pushes all the panic down deep. She's a reporter, damn it, and she needs information. It's time to toughen up.

Sylvia points to the screen again, and an icon of a file folder appears. She waves her finger, and a small arrow moves on the screen. She selects a file, and the screen turns white again, then black. Sylvia turns her left hand counterclockwise in the air and dims the lights in the room. The screen reads *"First Message: L-One and Supraman."*

The film opens with a view of an office, or a library maybe, with a large open window looking out on an expanse of green trees. In the foreground of the room is a comfortable-looking loveseat. Two people step into the frame from either side and take a seat.

Loni staggers as she realizes that she is looking at herself and Tyrone, but much, much older. Loni's elder self begins to speak, but it is her own voice she hears despite the years difference.

"Well, hello, Loni, dear," Elder Loni beams.

Elder Supraman speaks after her: "Hey, baby, looking good. All right." He smiles devilishly at the camera.

"Who are you making eyes at, Tyrone?" Elder Loni huffs.

"You, baby. Younger you."

"Oh, so I'm old now? OK," Elder Loni purses her lips.

"Wait, what?" he ruffles up, confused.

"You called me old," she chides Elder Supraman while looking directly ahead at the camera, smiling. "But moving on. Hello, dear. If you are actually seeing this, then at least part of our plan has been successful. Sylvia has made it to you, and your Supraman is out with the band." Elder Supraman nods and gives a thumbs up. Elder Loni continues: "I'm sure today has been upsetting and a bit confusing on your part, but hopefully, it will all start to make a little sense. To get started, refer to me as L-One. That is my nickname here, and we've found us not guessing which Loni we mean saves time.

"I will bring you up to speed as much as I safely can. In our time line, it is the year 2035. Hello from the future! As you may or may not know by now, in our time line, Sylvia, who we refer to as S-One, was killed in the year 1984, and she was transformed into an android over the next two decades. In our time line, I discovered S-One's condition while investigating a story for the *Nashville Banner*, and over a *very* long time, she and I grew to be close friends again, believe it or not." L-One smiles warmly at the camera and continues: "Through the discovery of S-One being an android, I eventually discovered my true passion for robotics and engineering, and in my later years, I have become a very important computer software and hardware developer—my most notable public invention being the Glyph Diary.

"As the years passed, however, S-One, Supraman, and I developed a private research agenda, which was wholly theoretical … until relatively recently. Ten years ago, we realized the potential to make contact with the past. I won't bore you with all of those details, but I will tell you we busied ourselves researching potential outcomes and determining which actions mattered most for a successful mission back in time.

For years, however, our ideas remained untested for fear of them accidentally falling into the wrong hands.

"Suffice to say, we did develop a plan, and by using our latest breakthrough in computing technologies, S-One and I were able to make contact with your time line and pass on a digital copy of her memories. Her digital copy was rendered into the physical form of the Sylvia you see now.

"Once we had Sylvia on the ground, we enacted our plan to lure you to us. We apologize for the subterfuge, but in this future, various powers have the ability to surveil the past; we have to assume that those powers will exist in your time as well. If so, they *will* come looking back to this week, no matter how careful we are, so we had to make everything look like Sylvia was alive the entire time, and clinically insane, living in a dump.

"*And* we had to build the appearance that you, Loni, finding Sylvia was a random result of her calling Tyrone out of the blue. It's all very important that this looks as natural as possible, not for your current day, but for scrutiny that we assume will happen far in the future. But enough of that for now.

"We cannot read your mind to know which questions we should answer in this message, and we cannot risk direct contact, for each time we do, it draws eyes toward the whole plan. This means, Loni," L-One lifts her hand placating, "that you *must trust Sylvia*. I know that's going to be hard for you, but there's no way around it." L-One looks over at Supraman.

"Now, Tyrone, if you can refrain from calling me old …"

This whole time, Elder Supraman has been silently listening to L-One, but he puffs up, flustered. "I never called you old, baby. Quit picking on me. But yeah, as I was saying

... what was I saying? See, you done got me all upset and made me forget what I was saying."

"You were telling Loni the plan."

"Yeah, the plan, OK. L, baby, this is what you need to know. So, in your time line, a few days ago, Tyrone was substituting up at Rose Park, and he met a young man, and they had a conversation, which goes on to change the whole course of human history, all because that kid and his best friend grow up to create a game called the Twelve Rings. It's this huge contest, with a prize for a trillion dollars, and it changes everything."

"Everything," Loni echoes.

Supraman continues: "Now the contest is huge and important and is the key to changing the future, but it's not the most important part for you. The important part that we have found in all of the time lines we have studied and believe me ... ha ha ... that's a lot ... the one thing that we have found that matters most to everything in the end game, is that your Supraman cannot know anything about this until the very end."

L-One agrees: "You must keep your Supraman in the dark until the end. He has to make choices that are not influenced by knowledge of the plan."

"I can't know, baby," Tyrone agrees, nodding his head. "Not until the very end, and then, when it's time, then you can show me this same video, so I know it was true too. That's the sacrifice *I'm* willing to make on top of yours. You see, we're all making sacrifices in this endeavor because ... because it's going to change the whole world if we do it right. I don't mean we'll be rich or powerful. I mean it's going to change the whole world so that it doesn't become what it has here." He stares imploringly at the camera and raises both hands. "The whole world will change because of this."

L-One smiles at Supraman, and love shines into his eyes and is reflected instantly before she turns back to the camera. "The last thing we have to tell you before we end this first message is about the *Nashville Banner*. The newspaper is in financial trouble and will slowly disband over the next year. You should leave now under the pretense of taking care of your childhood friend, Sylvia Tate, who you have discovered is mentally ill. You will make it known that you are helping to nurse her back to health. This cover story will be planted at the institutional level and will allow you to come to Sylvia daily and work on the plan without people questioning the patterned behavior in the future."

L-One smiles and adds, "In the meantime, your Supraman will perform with the band and teach for a little while, then eventually perform full-time. It is a must that you keep Tyrone focused on working with the band as close to the eleventh Ring as possible."

"Understand, Loni," Elder Supraman frowns. "Many good and bad times lie ahead before the Rings even begin. And after the Rings start, the dark times in America will make you question that we even have a plan, but we promise that we do have a plan, and that it's all going to work out in our favor. But for the plan to work, Supraman has to fly! That's critical," he lifts his chin, squinting up his eyes. Loni couldn't help but thinking he looked adorable. "Now listen!" he raises a stern eyebrow and gets out his daddy's preacher voice. "I know you don't want to hear this but stay close to Sylvia! Yes, it's a strange sentence for you to hear right now, I'm certain, and it won't come easy at first, for you or Supraman, but do what she tells you, as weird as it sounds, and it will all work out."

"It's all going to work out fine," L-One agrees and nods resolutely. "OK. It's time for us to go. We know this only raises more questions, but we promise it's all going to come together real soon. Best of luck."

"Bye, baby. Love, love." Tyrone extends his fingers toward the screen. "Love, love." L-One intones with a tight smile and a small wave.

The screen cuts back to a blue menu. Loni looks to Sylvia and raises her glass. "Drink. Now. Please." Loni touches at her face with her free hand.

Sylvia leans over and touches her finger to Loni's glass, and it suctions right out of her hand as she walks back to the bar.

Loni is quiet for a moment before complaining, "She didn't have to let me see myself old. She could have sat behind a screen or something. I would have known it was my own voice. I'll never unsee that image now."

"You look good for your age. And it's all real too. You never had any major upgrades."

"She said it was 2035. I was eighty there. What happens to them now? Are you still in contact with them?"

"I am connected to them in a sense. You see, S-One is still there with them, the original me, and *we* are loosely connected. It's very convoluted, but we can't *talk* to each other without government agents coming to kick in the door thirty minutes later."

"Too much," Loni signals stop, putting her hands up. "Too much for now. I'm sorry I asked. Where is the bathroom? Please tell me that you have one and that it is a normal functioning toilet, with toilet paper."

"Girl, it even has lotion. Back out the door, directly across the hall."

Loni stands up and exits the sunken living room without looking back. The hallway is dark, and the bathroom is dark until Loni flips a switch. She sighs in relief to find a clean, pretty, and well-stocked bathroom area. She purposefully avoids looking at herself in the mirror over the vanity sinks and delights in the normalcy of peeing for a minute.

Is she going insane? she wonders. How would she know? Is it a dream? Has she just wet the bed? She shakes her head as she wipes and adjusts. She feels awake, though the effects of the excellent whisky are starting to seep into her coordination a little. She'll need food soon if she plans to really start drinking, which she expects is going to happen before the day is out with all of the bombshells being dropped on her.

Loni finally gets the courage up to look at herself in the mirror, and she sighs in relief seeing that she is not old yet. Still, it is difficult for her to shake the image fully from her mind.

And there it is. The truth before her very eyes. She had seen herself from another future. She had seen Tyrone. Loni looks into her own eyes to see if there are any telltale signs of being drugged, but she seems OK, which means, this is real. *This is real.* She bends down and splashes water on her face, and she remembers that this morning she was a jealous and confused wife, an angry ex–best friend, a determined adversary looking to straighten shit out before the workweek got under way.

Now, she doesn't even know. There is too much to contemplate. *So, what do I do?* Loni racks her brain, trying to recollect if she's read any books on time travel, but all that comes to mind is that movie *Peggy Sue Got Married*, which makes her laugh.

She takes stock of her situation as she dries off her face and touches up her hair. She is not in immediate danger, except of becoming slightly drunk if she doesn't get some food soon. She could walk away from all of this, down the hallway right now, take her chances with the dog, and get away from Sylvia, but then what? She would probably just end up coming back out of sheer curiosity. *I mean, come on! I just saw myself at eighty! And Sylvia Tate is a robot-copy-time-thing. And Tyrone has joined a band? When did he have time to do this? God, but I'm hungry.*

Too many thoughts. It's just one too many things to handle at the same time, so Loni decides to take one item out of the equation. She towels off her face and hands and adjusts her lipstick before walking out the door and back across the hallway to the lounge. "Let's get some lunch," Loni announces to Sylvia.

"OK," Sylvia shrugs and holds out her hand, "but drink this first since I poured it."

***

AS BIG AS IT WAS EVER GOING TO GET

August 1996

Paul awakens to the sounds of a fork scraping on a plate and cartoon space rays *pew-pew-pew*-ing. He opens his eyes to find DuBell sitting cross-legged on the carpet in front of the TV in his underwear and a t-shirt. Sensing that Paul has awoken, DuBell mumbles around a mouthful of food and without turning away from the TV, "Your moms made eggs and hash browns. Sausage links."

"How long you been up?"

"An hour and a half. *Mask.* Now *Doug* and *Earthworm Jim. Power Rangers* and *Supraman* after that."

"See, but I got you now. I thought you were just a cartoon-head. But you just memorize the cable guide."

"Can't it be both?"

Paul gets up and stretches. He pats himself to check that he is still big, and satisfied he steps around DuBell and out into the living room. He smells the breakfast cooking around the corner and comes through the door to find his mother in the kitchen in her blue bathrobe, cup of coffee in hand as she stirs scrambled eggs.

"Good morning, sir."

"Good morning, Mama." Paul hugs his mama, and she is small but strong in his arms. "I didn't think DuBell was going to leave you any. He's on his second plate, you know?"

"He's got that metabolism."

"He's got something all right. Grab a plate down. Here. Hand me that and touch up my coffee while I fix your plate. Do you want juice or milk to drink?"

"Milk, please."

"Well pour some in my coffee while you pour yours. Just a little. There you go. Your plate is ready. Ketchup is on the table. Take a tray. Take two trays, because I know DuBell didn't take one and he's eating on the couch."

"He's on the floor."

"But still, he doesn't have a tray underneath him, and he's going to get crumbs everywhere."

"Yes, ma'am."

"You two need to be ready to go in one hour."

Paul does the math. "May we use the VCR to record shows for later?"

"I don't know," she returns pointedly. "Do you think you can refrain from taping over important videos?" She is referring to the accidental dubbing of Coolio's "Gangsters Paradise" over three minutes of a church member's graduation ceremony.

"Yes, ma'am," Paul dips his head, looking away. "I will only use my own tape."

"Go ahead then. One hour, we walk out the door."

"Yes, ma'am," Paul replies as he retreats to the den. He hands DuBell the tray, but DuBell is done eating so he just sits the plate and the tray on the couch. "We have to be ready to go by the end of *Spiderman*. We can tape the rest."

"Cool. Where we going?" DuBell never looks away from *Earthworm Jim*.

"She didn't say. Probably shopping. She said you have to behave."

"Ha ha." *Earthworm Jim* cuts to commercial, and DuBell hits "last" on the remote control switching instantly back to *Doug*. The next hour witnesses DuBell oscillating between five different cartoons, and in the midst, both boys manage to put on clothes without looking away from the TV for more than twenty seconds at a time. Paul's mother finds both boys, dressed and eyes glued to *Spiderman*, having a debate.

"I'm just saying," Paul claps both hands to his thighs in exasperation, "Supraman is way stronger than Spiderman, and if … if … they were in the same comic universe Supraman would destroy Spiderman if they got into a fight."

"*But* they wouldn't fight, because a) they are both good guys and b) where would it even take place? New York or Central City?"

"It takes place in the car," Paul's mom drones in a bored voice. Both boys hop up continuing the argue-sation out of the house and into the maroon Honda Civic waiting in the drive. Fifteen minutes down the road, they are at Hickory Hollow Mall.

"Woo-hoo! Can we go to the arcade?" DuBell gets visibly excited as soon as he realizes where they are.

"No. We are here for me."

"But you know you want to play *Street Fighter II*, Mrs.

Daisy. I can see it in your eyes. You just want to be Chun-Li so bad."

"I'm going to Chun-Li you. Y'all get out of the car. Be sure to lock your doors. DuBell, dear child, stop slamming my door. Son, don't make me regret bringing you this early into the trip. My goodness."

The parking lot is mostly empty as they approach the mall from this Sears side. Once inside the mall, they pass lawn mowers and pool tables and weight equipment and treadmills before rounding the corner to the divide between men's and women's clothes. Paul sees a mannequin wearing a baggy green sweater over a turtleneck with the matching snap forward cap and denim wide-leg jeans.

"See, like that," he shows DuBell.

"Yeah, I can see that. Especially as it comes colder."

"What's that?" Paul's mom approaches behind them.

Before Paul can respond, DuBell is answering, "Paul has been talking to God, and he decided he needs to stop trying to act all skinny. And he wants to look dapper, so I quit stealing all the ladies."

"DuBell," Paul starts looking at his friend sideways. "That was personal."

"Oh, you didn't tell me not to tell that part. Sorry. Forget I said anything, Mrs. Daisy."

But Paul's mom is eyeing him now. "Well, we will have to go to JCPenney's for clothes, or maybe Castner Knott's. They've usually got better prices on jeans. I just wish you'd had this conversation with God before I did your back-to-school shopping." She shakes her head as she walks off to the mall proper.

"DuBell."

"Yeah, Daze?"

"Did we slip into Bizarro World yesterday around lunchtime, and I missed it?"

"Don't think so. It was just pizza and tater tots for lunch, as usual. You'd reckon in Bizarro World it would be taco day or something."

"Good point."

Paul and DuBell fall in step behind Paul's mom and maintain a stream of nonsense chatter as they pass the music store on the right and the Oriental Express on the left (which Paul is adamantly not allowed to go into because his mother had heard from Mrs. Hunter that they sold knives to children—a rumor that was completely true as DuBell's small dagger collection could attest). They pass the Spencer's Gifts, the KB Toys, the love tester machine. They pass the food court, which triggers a conversation about what food DuBell wants most out of all the options (Chinese buffet followed by the Steak Escape bucket of fries). DuBell then proceeds down the line of the buffet naming every dish until Paul's stomach starts to growl and he distracts DuBell by pointing out the arcade.

Their footsteps slow slightly as they see it in the distance, tucked down a small side entrance to the mall, with its purple-black lights and orange-and-green neon lettering flashing up the entire side of the corridor above the rows of gumball machines and reflecting on the movie theater marquee's ambient glow. Traces of the games can even be seen against the curved window of Wilsons Leather, making the black jackets and the zippers flash slightly. Paul's mother clears her throat, and Paul realizes that he and DuBell have come to a complete stop just where the arcade would leave their field of vision.

"If you two don't come on."

Paul shuffles on, pulling DuBell by the sleeve, and Paul's mom waits until they are in front of her so she can begin to walk again.

They enter Castner Knott's and begin a two-hour session of redesigning the Paul Daisy look. Throughout, Paul is incredibly grateful to have DuBell at his side to help both in arguing for the freshest, biggest, and most transformative look ever and in pointing out that coupon deals for back-to-school had not expired yet. In all, Paul walks away with six new shirts, five new pairs of jeans, and the snap forward cap. Paul's mom comments he looks like something from her generation wearing that hat, but Paul loves it. The cashier tells Paul he can wear it out of the store, and she helps him to remove the stickers and the tags. He and DuBell initiate the handshake, and the new Paul is born.

Leaving Castner Knott's, Paul's mom consents to one arcade game each for the boys. She hands DuBell a dollar and tells him to go on ahead and change the bill out for the tokens. She holds Paul back.

"This is not a reward for putting your hands on Kendall. Do you understand me?"

Paul lifts his head up. "Yes, ma'am. I know."

"Well," she pauses, looking directly at him, "it's like this. Your father did not treat me kindly. And while he never beat me, he would say unkind things to me on the regular and tear me down. And one day, I decided that I was also too big to let it keep happening and that you were getting too big not to notice. So, I packed us up in a suitcase, and we left." She picks an invisible piece of lint off his shoulder.

Paul had heard the packing up and leaving with the suitcase part of that story before, but not the other part. He stares at his mom, not knowing what to say.

"You must remember, that being big often means being the bigger person. Those people like Kendall, and your father, they got something in them that just wants you to hit them. Do you understand me?"

"Yes, ma'am."

"But you can't do it. You can't give them what they want, because you will get in trouble, not them. Never them. Do you understand?"

"Yes, ma'am."

"OK. Go join your friend before he spends your quarters."

"Yes, ma'am." Paul walks for what feels like a thousand miles in his mind to the door of the arcade. He enters the glowing wonder room, "let's" DuBell beat him at *Mortal Kombat* once, and then walks back outside to find his mom drinking a soda from a paper McDonald's cup like nothing was said. He still cannot wrap his mind around his mother's revelation.

When Paul regains focus, he is in the food court bathroom washing his hands in the sink and gazing off into the cracked gray-brown tiles around the mirror. DuBell is talking to him.

"Hey, Daze. Did you hear me man?"

"Ha, sorry. I was zoning. What's up?"

"I asked if you had any allowance left? Maybe we can run in GameStop."

"I don't have enough to buy anything in there, and my mom just bought me an entire wardrobe. No way I'm asking her for a video game."

"Can we go in and look?"

"Juice, let's just do what she needs to do for a minute. She's been really, really chill today. You know what I'm saying?"

"That is definitely true. Your mom is normally all like 'y'all do some chores' and 'DuBell, quit talking so much' and 'you need to go to church,' but she's been pretty nice today. I mean, your mom is *always* nice compared to my moms, but you know what I mean."

And Paul does know. For the next hour, Paul and DuBell follow Paul's mom to the nurses' shop for scrubs, to Kirkland's for a birthday present for one of her nurses (a smelly candle), and to the JCPenney's makeup counter for some new lipstick. Paul's mom sees a shirt that she likes and decides to try it on. She leaves the boys on a padded bench outside the dressing room to guard the bags and checks her items with the room attendant. When she is safely around the corner, Paul looks at DuBell and glows.

"Juice, these clothes, this hat, my new attitude about myself. This is only the beginning."

"What do you mean, Daze? You figure out your plan?"

"Not one hundred percent, but I mean it when I said my ideas about being big as I can be and having you be with me."

"Word."

"But you can't be telling anybody our plans. OK? This is the one thing we don't tell people."

"Because it's like magic right?"

"Huh?"

"Like, if you brag about it, your wish won't come true. Like you broke the spell."

"Yeah. I guess," Paul responds slowly, thinking that it is kind of the essence of what he is saying. Magic and stuff is DuBell's summer camp talk, which always takes Paul a minute to decode. "Yeah. Exactly." Paul nods his head, thinking more about it in those terms. "So, we just keep it to ourselves, you and me, no matter who we add to the crew, no matter what girl we are trying to impress."

"I don't *try* to impress girls, I do it."

"Hush fool, listen."

"No, I hear you. I agree. Big days ahead."

"Big days." They give the handshake. "Hey, Juice," Paul clear his throat a little, pulling the tone back to serious, "there's one thing I got to do first, or else this plan is never going to develop right, no matter what my clothes look like."

"What's that?"

"Listen," Paul lowers his head, and he begins to unravel phase one of what he sees as the start of a plan. DuBell listens closely, and together they fine-tune the idea all the way home with Paul's mom silently listening in. As she pulls the car into the driveway, she turns to face them in the back seat and interjects, "I really don't know what's come over the two of you, if Paul really did have a calling from the Heavenly Father or what, but I am very proud of the both of you right now. But if I might make a suggestion or two?"

Paul realizes that he has taken his mother's presence for granted the entire ride home and instantly runs back all the conversation to see if he accidentally revealed anything too personal.

"First," Mrs. Daisy explains, "DuBell cannot go with you. I should go instead. I will stand far enough away to give you privacy, but near enough to be seen. It will allow you to speak your piece without unnecessary interruption, don't you agree? Meanwhile, DuBell, you will go wait inside the house until we tell you to come out. Here are the keys. Go in the back door. Stay out of the refrigerator. And take off your shoes, for the love of the Lord. And stop slamming the car door, son!"

Paul does not hesitate but walks down the driveway, passing the rosebushes and the mailbox, and heads down the hill. Kendall's house has no trees in the front yard and no paved driveway, just gravel and a broken sidewalk leading to a low concrete slab serving as a front porch. The black door is scuffed, and Paul realizes that he has never been this close to Kendall's house in the four years since Kendall moved in. Not that he would've wanted to come any closer to one of his key tormentors, but that was before now, before being big.

Paul raps his meaty fist on Kendall's door three times and steps back off the porch to seem less aggressive. Kendall sticks his head out of the door, sees Paul in his new hat, and starts to say, "The auditions for Newsies is next door …," but he trails off when he sees Mrs. Daisy closing the distance from her mailbox to his.

"What do you want?" he challenges in a clipped tone, eyeing Paul's mom.

"First, I apologize for the confrontation on Friday. Even though I didn't like what you said, I shouldn't have touched you. That was wrong."

"OK." Kendall waits, confused and not buying the apology.

"Second," Paul continues, "I'm sorry for messing up your backpack. I can't give you all of the money right this second, but I can pay for a new bag next week once I get my allowance."

"Your mom put you up to this, Daisy? Is that it?"

"No." Paul presses on. "Third, the way I see it, we can either leave things as is, and the whole school thinks you lost a fight come Monday. Or we can fix things tonight and make sure nobody thinks anything special."

"How are you going to fix the entire school bus seeing me on the ground? Are you going to go back in time? Is this *Back to the Future*, Paul?"

"Yeah," Paul smiles, cool as a cucumber. "Something like that. Now, look. I know you'd rather sit here and make some joke about how my fat ass would never get the car up to eighty-eight miles per hour"— he sees Kendall crack a smile against his will at the joke—"but we are wasting time and daylight. We really do have a plan to fix this if you'll just come over."

"Who is we? You and your mom?" Paul turns around to see his mom is still standing by Kendall's mailbox. He gives her the *all good*, and she politely turns and walks back up the hill.

"No. DuBell and me."

"OK. Right? So, I can walk over there and let you sic your attack dog me. No thanks."

"If DuBell wanted a piece of you, he would've done something long ago. Besides, he came up with the best part of the plan to fix it all. You'll see, man. My mom even said it was a good idea." Paul was out of argument. "All right. Well, come or don't," he finishes flatly. He turns and walks down the sidewalk and back up the gravel driveway. Paul doesn't look back. A second later, he hears the black door slam behind him. *Oh well*, he thinks to himself. *At least I tried.*

He is then surprised when he hears the door open and close again, and a moment later, Kendall runs through his front yard to catch up.

"This better not be a trap, Daisy. I swear to God."

"It's not a trap," Paul chuffs as he heaves his bigness up his driveway. DuBell is waiting on the back porch holding a camcorder in one hand and a cassette tape in the other.

"You know we haven't even watched these cartoons yet," DuBell implores, looking at Paul with wide remorseful eyes. "We should go inside and watch these while we explain the plan."

Kendall looks skeptical at the prospect of going inside, so Paul decides to dive into the short explanation. "What we are going to do is make a mini movie with the hand recorder, and in this movie, there's going to be a fight scene. It's going to be silly and over the top, so no one gets hurt. In one scene, we will safely reenact the confrontation scene where I throw you on the ground."

DuBell chimes in: "Then we will call a bunch of girls and tell them about how we are making a film. We are even going to film down by the Hunters' house so they will see us too. This way, everyone will know by Monday morning that Paul throwing you on the ground was just rehearsal for the movie."

"And a good thing too," Paul amends, "because it let us know that we needed to use padding in our scenes."

Kendall starts to catch what they are saying, then his face sours again. "Why would you go through all of this trouble? You hate me."

Paul looks up. He does kind of hate Kendall. But he knows this is not the moment for brutal honesty, so he curbs his response. "I have hated the things that you have said and done to me, but I don't know you, Kendall. So, I can't really hate you. Not even if you want me to." And with that, Paul bends down and picks up his basketball that is tucked next to the shed and dribbles. "So, are you in, Kendall?" He takes the shot, banks it. Kendall steps into the rebound. He picks up the ball and shoots off the backboard into the hoop.

"What's the movie about?"

The rest of the afternoon is spent on scripting, designing costumes, practicing scenes, filming, and then resetting for the next scene. All four of the Hunter sisters (and their Dreamhouse full of Barbies) feature in the film, and Paul's mom is even convinced to take part in one of the final scenes, donning her nurse's outfit complete with stethoscope. By evening, the three boys are all eating popcorn in the den and watching the fruits of their labor for the eighteenth time. They have spent the last hour talking on speakerphone to most of the girls in the sixth grade, a handful of fifth-grade girls, and a few girls who didn't even go to their school.

The movie is incredibly funny. It's about an archaeologist who opens a cursed book and becomes a giant evil version of himself. This starts out with DuBell in the lead role wearing a gray jogging suit, but then becomes Paul in a matching gray jogging suit, then Paul with pillows stuffed up under the jogging suit (to make him just a bit bigger), and finally a mock-up of a giant foot set up against the background of the Barbie Dreamhouse and a few Hot Wheels cars. Kendall plays a news reporter in the streets when we see the infamous "tossing" scene. All three agree that the scene looks amazing. Monster Paul rampages until the military, played by Celeste Hunter and sisters, takes Paul out with a secret government weapon that shrinks him back to normal DuBell size. The stop-motion transformation is incredibly bad, but funny all the more because of it. Before the evening is over, Kendall runs back to his house and grabs his VCR and a fresh cassette to dub a second copy of the movie.

DuBell yells, "You let us tape over Saturday morning cartoons when you had to clean tape! What's wrong with you?"

"Oh, I thought you were full of crap until we started filming. I was waiting for you to beat me up or something."

"I might now," DuBell growls in frustration.

"No," Paul corrects DuBell resolutely. "You won't. He won't," he repeats to Kendall, who has shifted to high alert. "The movie is worth ten tapes of Saturday morning cartoons anyways."

"True," DuBell agrees reluctantly. "It was fun."

"We should get Mrs. Goldwood to show it in class Monday," Kendall suggests. "We could check out the TV and VCR from the library."

"Oh, totally," Paul agrees. He nods his head in big easy dips.

When they finish dubbing the tape, they step back outside and shoot ball by the light of the back porch. A group of older teenage boys coasts down the street in the cluster, and the younger trio stand still by the porch for a second as the posse moves down around the corner and out of view. The three collectively release a sigh and then go back to shooting ball; in the course of an afternoon and an evening, an initial truce is made.

Paul's mom flashes the back porch light, signaling time to come in.

"Later, DB. Later, Daisy," Kendall calls in a polite version of his normal, lazy, detached tone. "I'll be at my dad's tomorrow, so I'll see you at the bus stop on Monday."

"OK," Paul replies throwing up his big hand. "See you then, man."

"Hey, what about your VCR?" DuBell points back to Paul's house. Kendall looks down the street and then back up. Paul and DuBell do the same. "Why don't you hang onto it for tonight. My mom won't even notice. I'll get it after school on Monday."

"Word."

As Kendall walks off, he imitates Celeste Hunter playing the General. "Hit him … with the laser beam."

"*Wawa wawa wawa wawa wawa*," Paul and DuBell respond in unison, laughing as they walk into the back door. They deposit their shoes and the basketball in the laundry room, then pause for Kool-Aid in the kitchen. Paul and DuBell take a moment to savor the raspberry purple-red concoction swirling in their glasses. They leave the glasses on the kitchen counter before heading back to the den. Paul expects to see his mom watching TV in the living room, but she is in her bedroom with the door shut so they pass on through quietly. They debate over watching the video one more time but opt instead for Nick at Nite reruns.

As Paul cozies into his chair, he watches DuBell snacking on the leftover kernels of popcorn and the leftover orange salt crystals at the bottom of the bowl. He wonders what big day tomorrow has in store for him. He isn't at all excited about having to go to church, but he decides it might actually not be horrible for once. Or he might get out of having to go … ever again.

But really, Paul tells himself as he drifts off to sleep again in the recliner chair. *Today was by far the biggest day of my life, when I thought yesterday was as big as it was ever going to get.*

FULL OF SHIT ALL THE TIME
JUST IN CASE

August 1996

A half hour later after finishing drinks, Sylvia and Loni head out the door and up Eighth Avenue to find a restaurant. Loni wants noodles from International Market, but Sylvia refuses to ride in the car, and they have just missed the bus over the hill. Sylvia suggests a meat and three around the corner.

Sylvia is wearing a scarf and wide black sunglasses and is walking under a black umbrella. To Loni, she looks like someone's demented aunt, but Sylvia argues that it helps to throw off facial recognition software. Loni is just tipsy enough not to care how she looks.

As they walk, Sylvia explains that in their present time, a handful of satellites already exist that are passively photographing as they orbit and that this photo surveillance will only increase with time. "In the other time line—we named it Beta—future archivists use existing trademark and copyright laws to gain free and open access to all US satellite images existing back through the 1980s. In that future, all celebrities and other people of interest expect that they will have their entire lives watched by anonymous audiences, which range from adoring fans to people called 'trolls' who spend their lives looking for ways to exploit the weaknesses of others. By 2030, random citizens watching old satellite footage had uncovered more unsolved murders than the police and archivists combined, so the US government signed a law allowing nosy citizens to do the video surveillance part of policing for them."

By the time they reach the restaurant, Loni is feeling a little paranoid and hot and tipsy, which is about to make her irritable again. She almost complains about it, but she can smell the food cooking inside, so she just follows Sylvia in.

They have beaten the Sunday lunch crowd and have their pick of seats. Sylvia chooses a table in the back corner and sits where she can watch all the doors. Loni grabs the menu and has her lunch picked by the time the waitress steps up. Loni and Sylvia order, and when the waitress is gone, Sylvia taps her finger in the middle of the table. "You know I haven't had the chance to ask, how have you been?"

"Are you serious?" Loni looks at Sylvia incredulously. "You mean to tell me you don't know exactly how I'm doing? I thought you'd seen the future and been spying on me to lure me into your web of intrigue."

"Shhh. You shouldn't speak loosely about that," Sylvia chides. "Besides I only know how L-One and Supraman were doing around this time, from what they told me. In 1996, I was still, um, incapacitated, so ..." Sylvia motions with her hand.

Loni laughs a little, "Fine, I'll play along. What can I say? Life is good. Well, I mean it's relatively OK. I mean, as you know, I work for the *Nashville Banner*, which you tell me is about to go belly up, and my husband is a substitute gym coach, except he has spontaneously joined a funk band after his time-traveling android ex-girlfriend lured him to her house and exposed him to a psychic assault. So yeah, I'm doing good, I suppose. Oh, look that was fast with the food! Thank goodness. I'm starved."

The waitress sets plates down, tops off the sweet tea, and tells them to shout if they need anything. Loni digs into her greens and grabs the squeeze bottle of vinegar as she puts a second bite in her mouth. She glances up at Sylvia. "I can eat and listen. So, let's have it." Loni takes a bite and rolls her eyes with the wonder of her food. She takes a drink of sweet tea and looks to Sylvia again.

Sylvia takes a bite of pork roast, then talks around it as she chews. "We'll start with what I dub Column A: things that happened in my time line, Beta. In 2016, a young man named DuBell announced the beginning of a contest, called the Twelve Rings, whose prize was one trillion dollars. It was called the Twelve Rings in part because one trillion has twelve zeros and in part because there were twelve tasks the contestants had to master in order to complete to the final challenge.

"The contest was originally designed to be a phenomenon akin to reality TV documentaries, where contestants video-record their experiences for audiences to follow. But it didn't go over well with traditional viewing platforms, and shortly after the launch, a whole new management system had to be pieced together ad hoc.

"Long story short, the contest machine, which should have generated at least $2 trillion, ended up costing the enterprise money for several reasons and people soon questioned if the trillion-dollar prize money really existed. So that's Column A in a nutshell. There was an amazing idea that could have had a clear and important impact on the future, but sadly, it was thought to be a scam and it fell apart in the end.

"As for Column B: here we were in Beta 2025, a small privately funded scientific team, quietly utilizing some relatively new AI and independently working on our pet project for time travel. Just as we are coming to understand, on a theoretical level, that we had the highest possibility of impacting things closest to our lives personally, a podcast interview with DuBell goes viral.

"Up until this point, he has remained anonymous, but the interview ends with him revealing his identity *and* that he grew up in Nashville, Tennessee, *and* that he and his best friend Paul had created the contest as the result of some inspirational words from their former PE coach, one Tyrone 'Supraman' Walker.

"Future technology being what it is, Tyrone was tracked down by newshounds immediately, and it was all that we could do to keep our scientific research hidden from the public. Thankfully, Supraman's ability to stand in front of that camera indefinitely held the media attention focused until other world news drew their gaze away, but we were always on red alert from that point forward. In fact, we still are. But I digress; that's Column C stuff. Let's stick to Column B.

"We had just learned that we were personally connected to the Twelve Rings at the same time we learned our highest probability of impacting the past involved personal connectivity. Using time travel to impact the Twelve Rings just seemed a no-brainer for everyone. So, the next decade was spent developing and simulator-testing ideas.

"We created a sort of game with the key players of the Twelve Rings, just to see how they were all connected. Loni, when we got *really* good at playing the game, you cannot imagine the magnitude and the scope of this contest's potential; the potential is so unbelievably incredible, if even half of what we predicted comes to pass."

Loni feels her stomach bulge slightly. She is so glad to have some food on her stomach to soak up the whisky. She worries momentarily that she has lost control of the situation, and she works to sharpen her focus. *Damn*, that food was good though. She really focuses herself.

"So, what are we supposed to do? Go find this DuBell kid and set him straight, show him the plan? Or is this like the *Karate Kid* movie where we have to train him for the battles to come?"

"Not exactly, at least not for a while. For now, you and I will watch and wait."

"What will we be watching exactly?"

"Netflix mostly! Ha ha! JK."

Loni stares blankly.

"OK you don't get that now, but you will soon, and you'll thank me. Anyways, you and I will be like fairy godmothers and guardian angels for DuBell and Paul for the next few years. And we will be tapping other key figures from time to time to position them. Mostly, we will be setting up the pieces for DuBell's creation of the contest, like preparing a roomful of chessboards for other people to play a tournament."

"Are you trying to win the contest or make sure a certain person wins? I guess I still don't get the point."

"That's understandable; I know I keep saying this, but it's very complicated and will take us too far afield to explain it all right now. But, no, we don't want to win the Twelve Rings. We want to grow the contest to be as far-reaching as possible. You see, in Beta, *that* DuBell was able to make the Twelve Rings a globally recognized event all on his own, starting from scratch. He took his dream, and he made it a reality. Only, it didn't have the desired impact."

"So, you want to influence the impact," Loni finishes. "Like directing the shock wave."

"Precisely! We are directing the shock wave." Sylvia is obviously excited. "You see, the contest itself is synergistic, so it grows organically of its own accord; therefore, with a better starting point, and a gentle nudge from us, it has the potential to be phenomenal. And we"—Sylvia points to Loni with her fork then to herself—"we will always be there, though often invisible, to see to it that key ideas take root at the proper times and that the shock wave keeps rolling on."

Loni shakes her head. She's still not getting what she wants from Sylvia. "All right, how about this: I still don't see what you want from *me*, or why *I* should care. I mean, it sounds really, *really* interesting and planned out and *complicated*, but it has nothing to do with me personally, or Tyrone, other than you've chosen to involve me. Does that make sense? I'm just struggling with it all."

"Loni Lore," Sylvia drags out the three syllables, looking up lazily as she takes another bite, "this whole plan is all *your* idea. And Tyrone's too. I mean, we all worked on the details together, sure, but this whole plan was a bona fide Loni Lore creation. Surely you can see that."

This gives Loni pause. Sylvia continues to eat. The sounds from the kitchen fill the void. After a moment, she speaks.

"You are telling me that L-One designed this whole plan, *including* luring Tyrone to your house?"

"The whole plan, down to the garbage on the front porch."

"And it all went according to plan, even *this* whole interaction, leading to this exact moment? That is what I am to understand?" Loni waves her fork in a lazy circle taking, in the restaurant décor. "Another Loni created *this* situation so that we would be sitting in *this* restaurant *right* now?"

"Yes."

"Did Elder-One make this cornbread? Is she in the back? Should I go in the back and thank myself?"

"Elder-One." Sylvia laughs. "That's funny." Then she sighs at the look on Loni's face. She shrugs and raises a hand in surrender. "I don't know what you want me to say. I'm telling you the truth. It was all planned out. Look, Tyrone's scene, it all went off without a hitch. Start to finish. And yours ..."

Loni raises her eyebrows in skepticism, waiting for Sylvia to finish that sentence.

"Come on," Sylvia moans. "You're here, aren't you? You're listening, right? You didn't tell me to fuck off and throw that whisky in my face."

"No, but the thought really crossed my mind for a moment." Loni contemplates everything and then takes another bite of food.

"Well, trust me, we all thought about you throwing that drink too, for several days actually, but L-One insisted that you'd need some alcohol at that moment, so I put the drink in your hand. *That's how much we all thought about this!* But, it's like this, L, deep down nobody knows you like yourself. So, reflect on what I'm going to say now: *No one* could have pulled this off *except* you, because you know yourself *and Supraman* so well. No one could have brought you here, to sit and have soul food with the one 'wretched whore' you hate the most in the world, but you. No one has the genius logic skills to pull this off like you, Loni Lore."

Loni looks up at Sylvia and laughs. "Oh, it's true. I do hate you most in the world. I mean, even if it's not really you, you look and sound like the real Sylvia, which is enough for me." Loni shakes her head, but she is resigned to finally believe. She sighs too and admits, "*Only I* could get me here listening to you."

"And you *knew* that greens and roast would help you sit and listen."

"They really did. They are so good."

"But you still have to make up your own mind." Sylvia sets her fork down. "I know you don't have the full story yet, and you are a fact-driven lady, but we are sort of on a timetable now, and I can't show you any of Column C if you deem this isn't for you. So, I need to know—are you in or out?"

Loni had anticipated the question coming and had expected that when Sylvia asked it, she would ruminate long and hard about her answer before giving it; however, when the moment comes, she already knows. She is a seasoned reporter, and she knows a real story when she hears it. She has no clue how any of this is even possible and has no clue why God, or fate, or destiny would dare pair her with Sylvia Tate other than to test her Christian decency, but she is certainly going to find out. Loni scrunches up her nose and shrugs her shoulders and commits to the crazy. "I'm in."

"Shake on it?" Sylvia sticks out her hand. Loni takes it and shakes. "All right, then. Not so bad dealing with the devil, now is it?"

"Don't make me regret my decisions so very quickly," Loni groans, deadpan. "Now, I have to ask. I just watched you drink two cups of sweet tea and put away an entire plate of food. How does that work?"

"It works just like normal. I'm mostly human throughout, only my parts don't wear out nearly as fast. Or ever, really. None of my parts are organic, so they don't decay."

"Why have parts at all?"

"In order to be mobile. In a few years, air travel becomes much more difficult due to terrorism here and abroad. In order for me to get through security, I will have to appear as near to human as possible for X-ray, infrared, and thermal scanners, all while talking to the airport computer *and* getting felt up by some handsy guards. My body is so real, I could even pass a physical or drug test if necessary."

"So, you can excrete?"

"Yeah."

"So, you just walk around full of shit all the time, just in case." Loni gives a sly smile.

"Oh, see! See. I told L-One that you would have new jokes. You're really funny. Across space and time, it's a fact." Sylvia sets her fork down again. "Let's get out of here. This place is about to become unbearable in a couple of minutes." Loni reaches in her purse, but Sylvia waves her off and signals to the waitress, who is hanging near the kitchen talking to the cooks. "This is a working lunch. We will bill it to the company."

"The company?"

"Yes, Pantheon, the production company that will eventually publish your blog and manage and promote Supraman and the band and eventually promotes the Twelve Rings enterprise. Once we get an office space established, we can just have food delivered, and we won't risk exposure walking around outside."

"You are seriously paranoid. Who are we hiding from exactly? The government? The media?"

Sylvia signals to the waitress again, hands her some cash, and says yes to a receipt. She looks to Loni and near-whispers, "The future is a dangerous place. The government, the media—like I said, those are practically the same thing in a few short decades. They make very little distinction between the two at any rate. And apart from corporate goons and politicos, the people themselves come to be dangerously aided by technology and information. In order for us to pull this off, we will have to be focused on our goal at all times. We have to be like spies. Mistakes due to carelessness early on *will* cause serious hardships in the years to come. That's a fact. And how lame would it be to pull off this amazing feat only to have our efforts exposed by some fifteen-year-old's troll-hack software? What we're doing *now* is training you to always act as if a robot camera is always hovering above you in space. Because it is."

"But if we're already being watched all the time, how is this even going to work?"

"It will work because we have the ability to think both like computers and humans. Some things we can work around. Others we can hack around. And some things we will learn to avoid. These first handful of years allow for a few dark spots, like my old house and the place we're heading to next. These places will give you the time and space you need to get trained. By the time the Pantheon team is fully arranged, you won't even consider it as being paranoid or being watched; it will come to you naturally like opening an umbrella before walking out into the rain."

Sylvia cinches her scarf under her chin and replaces her sunglasses before thanking the waitress for the meal and pushing the door open, back into the August Nashville humidity. On her way out, Loni holds the door for an elderly couple fresh from church. The gentleman relieves her of the door with a "thank you, my dear," and then his fine gray suit disappears into the air-conditioning behind his wife. Loni looks back the way she and Sylvia had originally come from, but Sylvia pops her umbrella open and begins to walk toward the crest of the hill, west toward Vanderbilt campus.

The sun is hot overhead, so they share the umbrella and stick to shadows as they walk. Along the way, Loni peppers Sylvia with questions about the future, the contest, Pantheon, their cover stories, why she has to quit her current job, what she will tell Tyrone when he gets home, and once more what did his band have to do with anything? Loni is just about to ask the android how she managed to get to the past, when she suddenly realizes that she is very hot, and her feet hurt because she has been walking for the better part of an hour.

"Sylvia, where in the hell are you taking us? I'm melting, and this is not the best area to be walking around in."

"Ain't no gangbanger in his right mind fool enough to mess with two righteous black women on Sunday. Come on, we're almost there."

"My feet are going to have blisters because of this. If we had driven, we would've been here forty minutes ago."

"Well, we can't drive because you don't have a car anymore."

"What do you mean, I don't have a car?" Loni questions Sylvia with all new ice in her voice.

"Your car was stolen," Sylvia reveals in a bored tone, refusing to stop her forward progress.

"What do you mean my car was stolen?!" Loni shouts.

"Having your car stolen is part of the plan. Relax. I promise, starting tomorrow, we will be riding in style. Think about it, would you design a plan where you drive a Honda Civic? Doubtful."

Loni wants to stop and argue now, but Sylvia keeps walking toward her destination. Loni catches up to her and demands, "Why did you have my car stolen? What possible purpose could that have served?"

"You and I are like secret agents now. Every day, we will enact a cover story. Every day, we will take new paths to throw off algorithms. Every day, we will remember that we are being watched from above and in the open." Sylvia delivers all of this news at a brisk walk, but finally slows, then stops as she passes under a row of maple trees whose massive green domes block out the blue sky and the hot afternoon sunlight. She looks at Loni and whispers again, "Did you know that I have barely been out of that house in months until last night, and before that, I put together a sophisticated pattern that would tell anyone watching us on cameras a story of Sylvia Tate becoming mentally ill. So ill, that eventually someone, Supraman, comes to check on her, causing someone else, Loni Lore, to come and take her to the only open physician you could find on a Sunday, where she will start to go for scheduled checkups."

"But wouldn't all that have been easier if my car hadn't been stolen?" Loni shakes her head in obvious distrust.

"We had to get rid of the car because it posed too many variables. First, it's easily traced. Second, it can be bugged or bombed."

"Bombed!" Loni exclaims, but Sylvia shushes her and pulls her into a slow walk.

"That's extreme," she whispers, "but if the CIA get involved, they are not above rigging a car to blow. Or cutting the brakes. Or just shooting you while you sit inside and blaming it on local gangs. A car just poses too many risks for us. No cars, whenever possible. We are always best on foot *and* in a crowd when we have to travel in the open. Under cover or concealed is always preferred, except for during cover story time.

"Besides, your car being stolen is part of the cover story, just like us getting Supraman to phone the paramedics the other night. These little anchors create a paper trail of evidence, giving us all reasons for coming back together after so long being apart and after so much personal enmity."

"But it's my car! *You* waited until after I said I was 'in' to tell me about my car, I know it," Loni jabs.

"*Your plan*, remember. Besides," Sylvia waves her hand in a shooing motion, "it all rolls forward. When you get your money from the insurance claim, you will decide to buy a top-of-the-line bicycle, and then you will allow a finance specialist to invest the remainder of the money. After investing a few thousand into a handful of start-up technology firms, your investments will start to make modest gains within the year. These small investment gains will allow you to merge with Pantheon as you embark upon your new online journalism career. You will pioneer a new journalism format called 'blogging,' which is short for web-logging."

Sylvia stops walking and stares deep into Loni's eyes and looks as if she's going to take Loni's hand but hesitates. Sylvia explains instead, "The thing is, L-One and I, and Supraman, we've all done our homework, and we have planned for multiple contingencies that stretch for decades into the future, where technology and information and stories can all be used as weapons against us. Loni, seriously, there are so many people *right now* who are in power who will be completely undone in their lifetimes because they believe that their secrets will remain hidden forever.

"I know it seems horrible to lose your car and your job, and I know it's hard to rearrange everything in one day, all while having to look at *my* face, but these are simple steps that we are taking right now, and they will protect us from scrutiny far, far into the future."

"You still could have told me about the car. I might have things inside that I needed."

"We took everything out."

"Well, still," Loni repeats, hot and frustrated.

Loni looks up and sees that they have stopped by the old Pearl High building, which is now one of the city's new magnet schools, MK Gandhi Magnet. Sylvia stares at the building with a goofy smile, inhales deeply, and walks over the bridge. Below a train rolls out to the south and west, and the sun flashes between the flatbed cars.

Loni whines, "Sylvia, where are you taking me?"

Sylvia shushes Loni. "Right here. Lower your voice." Sylvia guides Loni toward a large brick building with stairs cut away into the hillside overlooking an abandoned apartment complex and the dirty parking lot of a corner store. The corner store has a sagging green spray-painted metal roof lined with gleaning aluminum air conditioners loudly chugging away, trying to counteract the invasive heat outdoors. Loni thinks about that air-conditioning and is in favor of going to get a fountain drink. Sylvia assures her they can have one on the way back, and Loni mutters, "Yeah, as we wait for the bus."

Sylvia ignores Loni and keeps walking up the steps, causing Loni to trail behind her. They step around the back of the building into the shade, and Sylvia walks up to a hefty keypad. "Keep a lookout."

"For what?" Loni swivels her head looking around, paranoid. She hears six beeps and a buzzing sound before Sylvia tugs at her sleeve. Loni turns and walks into a dark room that is blessedly cold, and she can instantly feel every bead of sweat on her forehead and back. Sylvia flips a switch, and a light directly above them flickers on. Loni sees that she is in a laboratory setting or perhaps a medical unit. As the rest of the lights hum on, Loni realizes to her surprise that the room is the entire length of the building—a good four hundred feet long by two hundred feet wide. The entire space is

sectioned off with long steel tables, rows of computer termi-
nals, and large tools for building machinery. A back corner of
the massive room is sectioned off with industrial-grade black
curtains. "Welcome to First Base. It's not much, but it's where
I was reborn technically, in Beta."

Sylvia walks toward the far end of the building with the
black curtains, and her footsteps echo across the slate floor.
Loni follows, and when Sylvia reaches the curtain, she turns
and stops. "OK. This is Column C—the last shoe to drop."

"There's only supposed to be two shoes," Loni sighs,
unable to tear her eyes away from the curtain. "Do I want
to know what is behind this curtain? I mean, is there gore
inside, or are there severed body parts?"

Sylvia stares upward, thinking for a moment, and answers resolutely, "No." She smiles wickedly at Loni.

Loni shakes her head. "Back to my first question. Do I
want to know what's behind this curtain?"

"No," Sylvia answers with the same smile, "but you have
to know, because it's the final piece. I told you that there are
other team members, but they are not currently here, or they
are not ready yet."

"Oh God, it's going to be a body," Loni groans again in
dismay.

"Oh my gosh, grow a backbone. She's inactive." Sylvia
disappears behind the curtain.

"*She*?" Loni's eyebrows shoot up in response to this
word, but she follows Sylvia through the curtain door and
into the quarantined room. Loni shifts her mind into reporter mode as her eyes fall to the steel table, where there
lies a duplicate body of Sylvia Tate covered with the stan-

dard hospital sheet. She does not look dead or scary. Rather, she appears to be sleeping peacefully on her back, hands at her sides.

Loni looks at Sylvia looking at a clone of herself and begs, "Why is there a second android?"

Sylvia looks up quizzically. "For the Sylvia that was almost murdered in this time." Her tone implies that this should be obvious. "She's not been brought online yet in this body. She's still in a virtual stasis. This body is a bit of an early birthday present, if you will."

Loni shakes her head at the absurdity of it all. "Why not go back and intercept yourself? Catch her before this happens?"

Sylvia shakes her head slowly in obvious remorse. "It just wasn't possible to do that *and* secure the plan for the Rings, probabilistically speaking. We ran *all* contingencies. Of course, we ran some outcomes where I don't get near-murdered, but they never work with the Rings.

"I personally feel that on some messed-up level … well, perhaps it had to happen to make tribute for the games." Sylvia sighs and touches the hand on the table in a sweet gesture. "Anyway. I wish we could have stopped it. When I got here, she was exactly as I had been. Same outmoded 1980s components scrabbling to construct a VR capable of housing a living brain." Sylvia gets a faraway look in her eyes for a moment. "This technology on the other hand"—Sylvia looks at Loni and waves her hand around the room—"is light-years superior to what I originally had in the 1990s. We have added vast upgrades to her interface and new body, and we did our absolute best to speed her recovery along compared to my own. I spent years in a coma before they were able to contact me."

"When will she be ready?"

"Oh, not for a while. Making the body itself is incredibly easy. We were able to print her in about two days. However, taking her from a virtual reality setting to the android interface still takes time. Dr. Singh predicts another few years at least before she's fully operational in this body.

"Mind you, that time is good for her. Overcoming the technological lag of the 1990s gave me time and space to grow as a consciousness. I developed along with the technology, you might say." Sylvia pats the android hand again. "This lady, she'll be battle ready from the start. We anticipate she'll be very different from me. I expect it's going to take a village to raise the child."

Loni blanches a little at the thought. She isn't upset per se, but she is right back to the invisible roller coaster again. Loni puts a stern face on. "So, that's it then? Tell me now, Tate."

"That's it, I swear."

"You didn't sell my house or kidnap my sisters?" "

"No. That's all. You'll meet the Mothers later this evening or early tomorrow; they are a bunch of teenagers, and they are all sweet kids, you'll see. They are all very excited to finally meet you, but I told them that you and I needed time to sort us out first. We will all of us meet DuBell and Paul Daisy face-to-face tomorrow. And you'll meet the doctors who work here later this week, probably." Sylvia shrugs. "It sounds like a lot, but it's all been planned out."

"And then what?"

"Then we just chill out and manage affairs until the technology of 2020 gets here. We plan, and we work for a few years while Supraman gets in his groove. I'm going to introduce you to my digital library, and we are going to watch any television show or movie you ever missed, and then I'm going to teach you future history while I get to introduce you to your all-time favorite show, *Scandal.*"

Sylvia sighs. She wants Loni to be excited, but Loni is worn out. "All right. Come on, L. I can see we've hit the limit for show-and-tell today. Let me get you that fountain drink."

On the bus ride back across town, Loni nurses her Big Gulp Dr. Pepper and stares out the window at the Nashville landscape slipping past. She sees the *Nashville Banner/ Tennessean* building, and its opposing signs read 2:30/3:30 respectively. She thinks about work and about quitting her job. Is she really going to quit her job? And is any of this even really happening?

If this is a dream, it is way too long. And if this is a hallucination, where is she for real? Did she drink too much and slip and hit her head, and now she's unconscious in a hospital bed like some daytime TV star who was written out of the script? But how can it be real?

She had definitely seen androids though.

How had she gone ten years without Sylvia Tate's influence in her daily life, only to be hit full force with it now? *How?*

Loni glances at Sylvia sitting next to her on the seat, jostling up and down with the bumps in the road like everyone else, sipping a cherry-cola slush from a neon-green straw. Sylvia always looks like she has bedroom eyes when she's eating and drinking. *How did they copy that into an android?* Loni thinks.

The bus decelerates for the Wedgewood Avenue exit, and Sylvia reaches across Loni to pull the stop cord. The buzzer sounds, and the bus eases off the exit, passing their destination by a few houses. Loni confirms that her car is not where she placed it earlier, and mentally she starts to catalog things in her car that she will need to replace later.

As they exit the bus and walk toward the house, Sylvia informs Loni that she has already called the police and reported the vehicle stolen using her android capabilities. "The patrol response is en route."

Loni shakes her head, half-pissed and half-bemused. "Is this always how it's going to be with you, Tate? Me trying to play catch-up?"

"Doubtful. You're a quick study. Here, turn up this way." They turn from the street and walk between two houses, approaching Sylvia's place from the back. The afternoon sun has passed behind the tree line, but the heat and humidity are unrelenting.

They approach the back door, and Loni sees it also has no door handle. The moment Sylvia touches the odd silver plate, an audible click sounds as the door unlocks. The two women enter a small foyer and close the door behind them. Lights automatically illuminate the room. Several coats and hats are hung up on hooks, and at least ten pairs of shoes are lined up in neat rows on the floor. Sylvia opens a second door, and as lights click on, Loni sees the familiar creepy hallway from earlier. Sylvia turns left into the lounge, and Loni follows.

Sylvia reaches into her pocket, produces a slip of paper, and hands it to Loni. On it, Loni finds all of her registration information and expiration dates, as well as her insurance number. The information is all handwritten in Loni's script. Before Loni can ask how Sylvia managed that trick, she is being bombarded with information.

"The police will be here momentarily. Just tell them you keep *this* information in your purse, for emergencies. I'm going to remain inside because I'm supposed to be mentally ill, and we just got home from the doctor. You recently began taking care of me. You walked me to my appointment because I refused to get into the car earlier, and you came back to find your car missing. Nothing of importance was in the car that you can recall. Your husband will come get you."

"But Tyrone doesn't drive. You know that."

"Yes, but *they* don't. And you'll never say he is driving, only that he is coming to get you. But none of that will matter in the long run anyway because the police won't put that in the report. Saying Supraman is coming will just free the officers from obligation, so they will leave quicker."

Sylvia points her finger at the bar, and the lights activate automatically. "Just so you know, the insurance will claim no fault to you, and you will receive the full value for your car, which is currently Kelley Blue Book at $3,895. You will receive a check for $4,000 in two weeks' time. I will cancel your insurance on the following day; no sense in paying for insurance when you won't have a car."

"Sylvia."

"Yes, Loni?"

"Hush."

Sylvia hushes, and a few seconds later, there's a knock at the front door.

"Showtime," Sylvia chimes, and she pushes Loni toward the front door. Loni steps out onto the front porch into the pungent smell of trash in the hot summer afternoon. She gags but pushes ahead.

The scene with the young officer is humorous to Loni because it is obvious that he is wholly disgusted by the trash on the porch, but he is extremely sympathetic to Loni as a caretaker. He reveals that he takes care of his mother who suffers from dementia, and he commiserates, understanding the difficult nature of the task. She thanks him for his kindness.

She can tell that he is new to his position, and his partner is hanging back at the car to let the rookie handle it. He doesn't want to mess up, but he is also slightly afraid of the growling Doberman next door. Loni now sees the point of the subterfuge writ large. Nobody, not even the law, wanted to come near this place.

Once Loni assures Officer Jonas that her husband will come for her as soon as her shift is over, he gives her a copy of his report and bids her good day. He leaves her a card with his personal number on it, in case things get out of her control and she needs physical assistance. Loni thanks him profusely and wishes him a safe remainder to his afternoon. She reenters the house and closes the door resolutely behind her.

She walks back down the hall and enters the lounge.

Loni *really* looks around at her surroundings for the first time, and she tries to take it all in with new perspective. It really is a large, classy room, with the sunken entertainment center all in leather, the curving mahogany-topped bar fully stocked, and the red-felt billiards table in the back corner, lit from above by a red-and-gold-trim light shade. Loni sees that the thirteen balls are set to break, and she looks around until she finds the rack of pool cues on the wall next to the dartboard. She walks over, selects a cue, and checks the tip, chalking it to her satisfaction.

Loni approaches the table. She centers the cue ball and leans over the table's edge. She focuses all of her anger, confusion, excitement, and dizziness into the breaking, and as her arm stabs forward, the balls scatter across the red plane in a rainbow of math. She sinks the thirteen, the fifteen, and the three as the remaining balls ricochet and roll to a stop.

"I'm stripes," she exhales as Sylvia walks over and hands her glass of whisky.

STOLEN MOMENTS
OF SWEETNESS

August 1996

The wind whips through the car window and plays against DuBell's smiling face as he thinks to himself, *Sunday really is the Lord's Day.* Quietly, he replays the golden scene in his mind, and he can see himself kissing Danna in the empty Sunday school room; he can still feel her mouth on his, and he can still smell the strawberry of her lip gloss as she leans in to close the distance. In his mind's eye, it looks comical for such a tall girl and short boy to be locked in an embrace, but in reality, neither one cared. She just pressed him into a table of children's stuffed animals and covered his mouth with hers again and again: wet and soft and wanting him. *Dear God, I know he hates it, but I love going to church with Paul. Thank you for letting me visit your house!* he thinks silently up to the clouds with a grin.

DuBell reckons that girls are proof, more than any book or sermon, that God is real and good … and often fickle and mysterious … and occasionally wrathful and capable of intense suffering, but good. DuBell thinks about how kissing Danna was the real deal and about how she came at him. It was not like convincing a girl to kiss you. DuBell puzzles over the worth of a real kiss from a girl: a real kiss was worth a semester of talking on the phone once a week; a real kiss was worth watching younger siblings on the playground and letting them climb all over you and use you as a punching bag; a real kiss was worth helping out with some light landscaping and occasional trash removal; and a real kiss was certainly worth the risk of an entire congregation catching you in the act.

Which did not happen. *Thanks again, Big G.* But DuBell had taken the risk. He isn't sure what he would've done if he had embarrassed Mrs. Daisy again, but it was worth every moment of danger. He is eternally grateful for himself, for Mrs. Daisy, and for Danna that it hadn't come to a poor ending. He and Danna had kissed one last time before they slipped out of the darkened room, and they squeezed hands. They walked away in opposite directions.

When he made his way back to Daze, he found his well-dressed friend looking bored to death sitting in the pew next to his mother. DuBell sat down looking nonplussed, as if he had merely gone to the bathroom. A few minutes later, he watched as Danna entered the room from a different door. He had casually tracked her as she slid nonchalantly into place beside her parents without one glance in his direction. "Smooth Criminal" had started playing in his mind, and he spent the rest of the sermon silently humming *Danna, are you OK?* DuBell *definitely* intended to call her later tonight.

After church, the boys convince Mrs. Daisy to take them through the Hardee's drive-through on the way home. DuBell can see by the way she is casting him furtive glances that she is wondering if he eats enough at home. She stops short of ordering him that triple burger, but she insists he eat all his food.

DuBell gets food at home—enough to get him back around to a free school breakfast and lunch without starving to death at any rate. The problems he faces aren't nutritional. Once, a long time back, DuBell asked Mrs. Daisy how come her church didn't have confession booths, like churches did in the movies. She explained that her church didn't have confessionals because she wasn't Catholic, and then she gave him the third degree about what exactly he had to confess. He swore up and down that he hadn't done anything to confess and that he was just curious, but that hadn't been the total truth, of course.

DuBell really hadn't done anything wrong, but he sure felt like he had so much to confess. The things he knew about and kept secret drove him to tears sometimes. When he had first been invited to church with Paul, around age nine, he thought he might be able to tell somebody anonymously, like people did in church scenes in the movies. When he found out that confessing in church would basically end up the same as telling the police, he decided he would just have to keep it between himself and God.

DuBell is cool with God even if his life is sort of messed up. He doesn't blame God for his daddy being dead at such a young age, and he doesn't blame God for his moms being a brutal sociopath or his brothers being abusive wannabe-thug perverts. DuBell chalks all that bad stuff up to random chance. When it comes to God, nothing is personal, until you make it personal.

God has his part to play, and DuBell has his; he knows it in his heart. DuBell knows that Daze hates church, but some Sundays DuBell feels like the sermon is intended just for him. Like God knows he's about to head back to the war zone, back into the nightmare, and so he gives him a good pep talk to remind him that the evil can't last forever and that he has to have faith that there is a plan. Maybe a little Jonah and the whale. A little Job.

A little Sodom and Gomorrah.

The very notion that God can and did lay waste to entire cities with fire is heartening to DuBell; he figures that if he and God both possess a volcanic temper and ground-zero tactics, then God can't judge him too harshly on that one. On Sunday, DuBell is always listening extra hard in church for special messages, even if Paul isn't paying attention.

Today's message was altogether different, but DuBell received it loud and clear. When Danna had said to meet her at precisely 10:39 AM, God didn't stutter. The rest of the evening could just go ahead and be horrible. Moms could yell and throw things and make fun of Paul and call him horrible names, and she could sic Dre and X on DuBell, and they could jump on him and beat him up and curse at him and laugh about how he and Paul are queers, and Dre and X can even go full tilt tonight and lock him in their room and beat him and hold him down and put their penises to his face if they want to—it won't matter. God gave him a spell of protection in the form of a real kiss, and there's nothing short of murdering him that they could do to dissolve it tonight.

DuBell glances over at Daze and sees his boy is looking in his element, large and in charge. Daze got some good attention today, which DuBell is glad for; Daze knocks those church folks sometimes, but they care about him. They all told him he looked nice in his new clothes. DuBell imagines

Paul will only take that hat off to sleep and the second before he steps into the school building. Daze sees DuBell looking over and he offers up the rest of his french fries, but DuBell declines. He just wants to feel the setting sun on his face and remember his few stolen moments of sweetness before he has to go home to moms and his brothers.

HARDER THAN PAUL THOUGHT

August 1996

Mrs. Daisy drives back down Tusculum and then dips off to Packard Drive, angling back toward their neighborhood. The gentle lull of the dips in the road and the last good rays of sun before twilight almost have DuBell nodding off when Mrs. Daisy slows the brakes unexpectedly and crawls the car to a slow roll. No one approaches from behind, so Mrs. Daisy rides the brakes all the way down the hill, giving them a clear view of the frenzied circus taking place below at the Cedar Lake Apartments. Police cars and news crews and crowds of onlookers are gathered on the lawn of the complex and in the parking lots.

"What's going on?" Mrs. Daisy wonders aloud as they descend toward the spectacle of police cars.

But DuBell knows without actually knowing. The police cars are at his house, his apartment. The police have found everything inside. Dre and X, and possibly moms, have all been arrested. *God, what is this? Is this really happening?* DuBell thinks.

"Don't stop, Mrs. Daisy. If you go in there …"

But Mrs. Daisy cut him off. "I know, DuBell. Let's go on home now. We'll sort this out once we get home." Mrs. Daisy's inflection on the word *home* is not lost on DuBell. The three of them crane around to look as they reach the bottom of the hill, pass the apartment complex, and drive up the next hill toward the Daisies' house. They are all three silent for the remaining two minutes of the drive into the cul-de-sac and down the hill into the driveway. They are silent when the car stops.

Mrs. Daisy parks so the basketball goal is not blocked, but no one suggests playing. They all gather their things and walk inside quietly. Paul takes up the rear and shuts and locks the door. DuBell turns on the lights and then takes his shoes off. Mrs. Daisy disappears around the corner to set her things down in the bedroom, then reemerges a moment later. Looking at the clock by the door, she turns on the evening news.

Sure enough, there's the video footage of the Cedar Lake Apartments, lit up like a pinball machine at the bowling alley and, 1-2-3, pictures of his brothers and his moms with the words "INTERNET PORN ARREST" stenciled in large white letters underneath. Dre's photo has a defiant sneer on his face with his no-neck, wide chin turned up slightly and wannabe-Wesley Snipes–looking haircut tilted to the side. X is gut-laughing in his picture, like it's a field trip to Opryland, like this is all a hilarious joke. And moms looks about ready to attack the photographer; odds are, she did.

The Daisys and DuBell sit on the couch silently as the reporter details the 911 call leading to the arrest.

"A distraught mother, who remains unnamed, called police this morning and said that she found her son with hundreds of pornographic images stored in his home computer. Her son claimed the files were purchased legally from an on-line account using a credit card. But many of the images were of girls too young to be legal. This led police to investigate further, and with the help of local FBI teams, they were able to quickly trace the accounts back to the apartment of Andre and Xavier Jones. The financial transactions also reveal the brothers had been operating their business since they were minors, with the help of their mother, Cinderella Jones. When police entered the apartment this evening, they seized the computer and its files, but no money was recovered."

A record scratches in DuBell's mind. *What did she just say?*

The camera circles around the room that DuBell shares with Dre and X, and when he sees the wall, he goes absolutely rigid. The Snoop Dogg poster. *The Chronic* banner. The desk and *the corkboard! The corkboard is still hanging on the wall!* The police have missed it! DuBell jumps up and leans as close as he can get to the big-screen television without touching it, trying to see any other footage from the bedroom. Mrs. Daisy and Daze look at him with concern, but he ignores them, trying to see the image again. The reporter continues talking.

"Preliminary inspection leads investigators to believe that the Jones brothers and their mother, Cinderella Jones, had used a number of legal computer accounts to create thousands of illegal data transfers. It is assumed the money they gained from these operations is hidden in multiple bank accounts. Investigations into the source of the pornographic images of children is still underway. More on this story as it unfolds. Back to you, Kelly."

Mrs. Daisy turns down the volume, and the news shifts topics. Nobody speaks. DuBell gets up quietly and walks from the living room into the bathroom. He softly closes the door. He draws aside the shower curtain and sits on the edge of the tub, and he cries.

Part of him cries in relief. Part of him cries in fear. And a small, small part of him cries because it is his moms, and *dammit* a moms is supposed to know better, even if she is horrible and mentally messed up. He knew Dre and X would fuck up. They are fuckups; that's what they did. But his moms … *dammit*!

Moms was so brutal about me following the rules … she couldn't have been involved …

But even as he thinks that and blinks away more tears, he knows this isn't true. He is too observant and too smart to pretend that she didn't know. In reality, she was always on him to follow the rules so he didn't draw unwanted attention to their stupid operation.

Aggggghhhhh!!!

DuBell thinks about Mrs. Daisy and Daze sitting on the other side of that door, probably worried sick about him, when his moms is in jail and probably hasn't even thought about him yet, other than to wonder what he might say to the police. The Daisys aren't like that though. They are good people, through and through. They wouldn't do things like this to each other or to other people. They don't operate by those self-serving rules. DuBell is grateful for their kindness and not for his own sake alone. He is simply glad to know that good people really did exist outside of TV and books.

He knows that things are going to be complicated for him in short order, and he does not want to be a burden on his friend. DuBell makes up his mind to accept whatever comes next with his head up. He has never had a dad, but he watches a lot of TV and that's what his TV dad would say. *Keep your chin up, Champ.*

DuBell blows his nose on a handful of toilet paper and then washes his face vigorously in the sink. He looks at his pale complexion, his broad nose, his kinky red Afro, the red freckles that normally dot his cheeks and his nose are currently lost in his flushed skin. He looks himself stern in the face, which involves him jutting his jaw out like a bulldog to help him toughen up.

He has to problem solve now—set emotions aside and rationalize. He needs to get home, *now*, but Mrs. Daisy is not going to let him go home. He must make her leave the house, right now, before anyone else has time to get to his apartment. He'll need clothes.

He steps out of the bathroom and doesn't try to hide the fact that he's been crying from the Daisys. He knows they don't judge him.

DuBell joins Paul and Mrs. Daisy in the living room just as the phone rings. They all just stare at it for a moment before Mrs. Daisy picks up the handset.

"Hello," she answers. "Speaking. Yes, ma'am. Yes, ma'am, I see." She looks at DuBell and repeats grudgingly, "Yes, ma'am." Mrs. Daisy motions to DuBell to get her a piece of paper and a pen from the top of the television, and she starts to write down names and numbers, and numbers and times, and more numbers. She intones "yes, ma'am" three more times, followed by "No, ma'am, he will be perfectly fine in our custody until then." She pauses. "Yes, ma'am. Thank you, Ms. Tate. Good evening."

She hangs up the phone and takes a cleansing breath, placing hands on knees before speaking again. "Well, that was an interesting phone call. The person on the other end was your Aunt Margaret, DuBell, and she requests that …"

DuBell interrupts her: "Sorry, Mrs. Daisy, but I don't have an aunt. My mom was the only girl in her family."

"She claims to be your father's sister. At any rate, she has secured you a lawyer, and she assures me that your affairs are in order. We are to meet her tomorrow after school, downtown at the courthouse. Until then, you're supposed to stay here."

"But what about my clothes? I can't wear this to school tomorrow. Daze, tell her," DuBell pleads, pulling at the edge of his one church shirt. "Plus, I've been in this underwear all weekend."

"Why, child … never mind. I don't want to know." DuBell looks at Mrs. Daisy with the full *my-mom-just-got-arrested-may-I-please-go-get-some-underwear* look. Mrs. Daisy looks from DuBell to Paul and then fixes them both with a stare. "I really don't like this. No, if we go over there and try to get your clothes, social services will snatch you up. We can't have that. Ms. Tate said not to let you near them. But you do need clothes, I agree." She thinks for a moment. "You are a small to a medium in your shirts and probably a twenty-two in the waist. What's your underwear size?"

"Twelve to fourteen," DuBell mumbles, embarrassed slightly.

"Color preference?"

"Black," he responds as if no other color exists, and without looking, he gives Paul the handshake. Mrs. Daisy just rolls her eyeballs at them both per usual.

"I'm going to run to Walmart and grab these few things, then I'll be right back. You. Do. Not. Leave. Do you both understand me?"

"Yes, ma'am," they both promise firmly.

"Something told me to buy you clothes yesterday. Lord have mercy."

"I'm sorry for the trouble, Mrs. Daisy," DuBell blurts out, and she walks over and pulls him into an awkward forced hug.

"You have nothing to be sorry about. Not this time." They both softly laugh until it bubbles up into real laughter, and DuBell wipes away the wet off his face again. She pats him on the head and admonishes them both to stay inside until she returns.

DuBell waits until he hears the car back away. Paul looks like he's about to say something, but DuBell cuts him off with a feverish look in his eyes from information that he has been desperately holding in. He blurts out, "I know where $20,000 is hidden, but we have to go now, or someone else will find it first!"

"What?! Are you kidding me? Where?"

"Dre and X have a safe cut in the wall. It's hidden behind the corkboard beside *The Chronic* banner."

"And you know the combination, don't you?"

"I do." DuBell looks at Paul with urgency, but Paul isn't convinced. "How come you never said anything before?"

"Man, I stay well away from the business pertaining to Dre and X. But look, the money is there; I know because I saw the room when the news crew was spinning around my room. The police didn't even consider to look behind the fake wall, but anybody from the complex would know immediately that it's an addition. I'm telling you, if I don't go there *right now* that safe and the money in it is as good as ghost."

DuBell can see he needs to try a new angle; he isn't selling Paul on the idea, but he can't wait any longer. He runs into Paul's room and strips off his dress shirt. He grabs a black hoodie and zips it up around himself, pulling the hood around his face like a grim reaper. He bends down and ties his shoes extra tight then rolls up the cuffs around the borrowed hoodie where the sleeves swallow him.

"OK, look," he reasons to Paul, "come walk me to the end of the street, kick it around Celeste's house, and just wait for me there. That way, you know I at least make it that far in case I go missing or something." Paul's face goes white. "I won't. I promise. I'm going to be in and out like the burger. But look, I need a few things real quick before I go."

"Like what?"

"I know your mom has those gallon Ziplock bags, but does she have some duct tape?"

"Yeah, in the top cabinet above the washer. Why?"

"I also need your backpack. Empty it so nothing gets messed up. Come on, let's hustle," DuBell barks.

"Juice, I don't know, man. That place was crawling with cops. And this ain't stepping out to shoot hoops."

"I need you to think big now. And trust me."

"All right," Paul shrugs with a confused huff. "Come on then. We can take my bike as far as Weird Christine's, and I'll hide there."

They split up and quickly gather supplies into the backpack, retrieve the bike from the shed, and lock the back door.

DuBell hops on the pegs of Paul's bike, and Paul pumps three times with his big legs, tipping them over the edge of the hill, zooming them down, out of the driveway, and into the twilight street toward the Hunters'. Paul begins to pump furiously, and DuBell crouches to decrease wind resistance. In two minutes, they are between neighborhoods and well past Weird Christine's house. DuBell realizes Paul intends to go all the way.

He leans in and tells Paul to go beyond the entrance, then cut through the grass well out of the light cast by the streetlamps. Enough darkness has risen to camouflage their movements in the shadows. Off the bike and between apartment buildings, DuBell drags Paul along by the sleeve, secretly wishing he could have him hide somewhere safe.

"Stay right here, with your back by this door, up against the wall. You should be able to see anyone coming from the street. I'll only be a minute. If you see anyone, come warn me." DuBell takes off down the corridor at a dead run and then up the metal steps as quick and stealthy as possible. His key is in hand, ready to enter, but the door is ajar, and the light is on. He slows and eases the door open, prepared to run if he needs to, but it is silent and presumably empty. DuBell darts all the way inside the apartment to the very back, just to check, and once he is assured that he is alone, he enters his bedroom.

Looters have already come and removed anything the police didn't nail down. Someone even stole his busted Monopoly set that was missing the cards and pieces. But nobody was a fan of his cartoon drawings, it seems. While someone obviously wanted the Snoop Dogg posters and *The Chronic* banner, no one cared about the corkboard above DuBell's desk covered in Marvel superheroes and a calendar. DuBell swings the corkboard open to the right on tiny hinges, giving access to a cavity in the wall. In this cavity there is a safe. DuBell twists the combination, and the lock clicks open. He hinges back the door, and there, as expected, are three shelves lined with several large, clear Tupperware containers filled with stacks of bills and one small, dark Tupperware container.

DuBell sets to his plan immediately, and in two more minutes, he has stripped open the clear Tupperware containers and transferred all of the money into Ziplock bags. He then strips to his underwear.

Five highly uncomfortable minutes after that, he is quietly running out of the apartment for the last time ever, down the familiar metal and concrete steps of his childhood, silent as a wish. Twilight has descended into full darkness, which is augmented by the distant orange glow of streetlamps at the front of the complex and by the parking lots. DuBell sticks to the shadows as he moves, holding his breath.

But the normal sounds of the night are instantly gone when DuBell hears Paul's startled scream followed immediately by someone else's startled scream. In seconds, the sound of raised voices begins to popcorn around the corner just as DuBell reaches the bottom of the steps. He peeks around the landing to find Paul surrounded by five, *no six*, grown men, and one of them has a gun pulled and pointed at Paul's face. Paul is an enormous, shocked statue. The guy with the gun is animated.

"He's a spy for the Knights, man. He's coming to check out our turf because of that bullshit with Dre. I say we smoke this bitch." Paul doesn't move, doesn't speak.

DuBell is about to step out and speak, when he hears a familiar voice say, "That's just fat-ass Paul Daisy. That means DuBell is here. He's no spy, Odie." Brandon turns to Daze.

"Where is DuBell?" Brandon scans around the corner of the apartment building where Paul had been stationed as a lookout.

DuBell doesn't hesitate; he steps out of the shadows. "I'm here," he calls out. "Be cool." He slowly emerges from around the corner with his hands in view. "I just ran up to grab a few things." He points to his bag on his back. "I left Paul here to wait on me, so he didn't have to drag his bike upstairs."

"Why? Do you imagine someone's going to steal it?" Brandon arches his shoulders back, and he does that exaggerated neck stretch thing he does before pouncing. DuBell groans inwardly. He can tell that Brandon is enjoying this moment. DuBell knows keeping cool now is the only course of action for Daze's sake and his own.

"No, Brandon, I never said that you would steal anything."

"Oh. *Brandon*. That's polite. Why not *Scarface* like you do behind my back?"

DuBell shakes his head. "I have never once called you that name. Nor has Paul. You know I don't play that shit."

"Yeah, but I know you like to play. Where were you when your mama was getting arrested today? Playing probably." The LA Boys start to laugh but don't relax an inch.

DuBell plays cool. "I was in church. You know, trying to get myself on the right path."

"Well, lucky for you, huh? Running over to your little girlfriend's house for sleepovers spared you a trip to child services."

"Been there. Probably going tomorrow. Look," DuBell pleads to Odie, who's standing behind Brandon, "can you please take the gun off Daze? He doesn't deserve that. He was just waiting on me while I got my things."

Everybody eases off Paul, for which he is grateful. Then they turn to face him instead, and he thinks to himself, *Damn, I would've loved to have skipped this part.*

Brandon lopes over to DuBell and grits his teeth. "You think you can come up in my place and give orders?"

DuBell starts to respond in the negative, but Brandon punches him in the mouth with a whiplash overhand left. Pain lances through DuBell's vision with red and black blotches, but he does not take the bait. Instead, he attempts to block and fend off the litany of blows that Brandon rains down upon his face and ears. DuBell drops to the hard concrete of the open hallway and curls up instinctively into a ball, but Brandon doesn't care. As DuBell huddles on the ground, Brandon kicks him in his ribs, and DuBell nearly blacks out from the pain. The next kick connects with his face, and as the raucous laughter of the LA Boys floods his ears, DuBell's last conscious thought is he finally understands why people say you "get your bell rung."

When DuBell comes to, he is cold and confused, and Daze is above him pulling him up off the concrete floor in the hallway between the apartments. Daze is asking him if he can stand up and walk. DuBell responds in the affirmative, but his legs are not 100 percent certain he has spoken truthfully. DuBell wobbles to his feet and plays back the scene in his head. He looks around frantically for the backpack, but Paul shakes his head and drags DuBell along.

"They took it, Juice. They took my bike too."

"I'm so sorry, Daze. I mean I am really, *really* sorry that they pulled a gun on you. And all that talk about shooting you … I never thought that could go down."

"It was my fault, really," Paul pants half carrying DuBell along with each large step he takes.

"What do you mean?"

"Well, the door opened when I was looking the other direction, and it scared me to death, and I screamed from being startled, which caused the guy walking out the door to scream. Before I could speak, he had a gun in my face. And then you walked around the corner. If I hadn't screamed, I could've just played cool, like I was minding my business, and he would've kept going on. But as is, I lost everything we came for. And my mom is going to take one look at your face and know we left the house."

"Let's just focus on getting to the house first before we worry about your mom. I, for one, will be grateful to see a nurse as soon as possible. Here," he tugs Paul's sleeve, pulling upright, "I can walk on my own. Let's just take it slow though."

DuBell hobbles across Packard Drive after Paul, and they begin the trek between houses. They approach Weird Christine's house. The smell of tobacco in the air belatedly alerts the boys that someone is on the porch just as a massive spotlight blinds them, and a deep gravelly male voice shouts, "Hey!"

That one syllable is possibly the scariest noise DuBell has ever heard. The boys freeze. DuBell is exhausted, and he shouts out, "You know us! You see us all the time. Please, we are just going home. And I got beat up real bad. Please, just let us go on our way." The light stays trained on them.

"Please, sir."

The light clicks off, and DuBell's night vision is spent in a cascade of green circles. Without saying another word, he and Paul quickly move out of range of the bizarre house. A bird is startled from its rest in a nearby maple tree, and it calls out, signaling to an invisible roost of birds in an adjacent tree who explode synchronously from its branches and fly away in unison to a nearby perch two houses down. DuBell and Paul startle the birds all the way down the street, one good tree at a time. The boys do not avoid streetlamps this time but stick clear to the middle of the road until Paul's house is in sight.

DuBell is relieved to see that they beat Mrs. Daisy back to the house, but the relief is short-lived as the headlights top the hill of Clipper Court and transform into the unmistakable shape of Mrs. Daisy's Honda. She sees them as she pulls into the driveway, and her face is furious. DuBell limps into the battle. "Let me do the talking." Paul nods in response and slowly leads DuBell by the arm up the hill. Mrs. Daisy sees that DuBell is hurt, and she shifts from her *enraged mom mode* to *nurse mode* instantly.

"OK, come here. Let's see you."

"Inside, Mrs. Daisy," DuBell whisper-speaks. "We really need to go inside. I may have broken something, and once I stop, I don't want to move again." DuBell winces for emphasis. "Paul help me on the stairs, man, because I can't do it alone. Just stand still and let me hold you like another wall." Paul moves and DuBell gasps as he climbs the steps to the back door. Paul's mom already has the door unlocked and opened. She switches off the lights to keep the neighbors from watching their every move.

Once DuBell is inside and through the laundry room and the kitchen and hears the back door click shut, he breathes. He calmly assesses the situation. He's hurt, but he'll live, and this next part is going to be interesting. The Daisys are going to flip out.

"Will you lock that back door, please, Mrs. Daisy? Paul will you check the front? And please pull the curtains, for real."

Paul looks at DuBell with concern, locking the door and moving around pulling the curtains closed. "Yeah, Juice. You're OK, man. No one will come in here. This is our turf."

"No, young man," Mrs. Daisy rails on him, "This is *my* turf! And *you* were supposed to keep your butt on it. The both of you!" She looks from Paul to DuBell, working back to anger, but DuBell just holds up a finger.

DuBell raises his voice to a volume he has never used in the Daisy house and uses a tone neither of the Daisies has heard before now. It is not disrespectful, but it demands being heard. "Before anyone yells about anything else, I need the both of you to listen." They both look taken aback by DuBell's proclamation but remain silent. "Or rather, I need the both of you to look."

DuBell plops down unceremoniously in the middle of the living room floor, much to the surprise of both the Daisys and his mangled ribs. He unzips his hoodie while kicking out of his shoes. He then begins wiggling out of his pants and his shirt as quick as if he had ants all over his body. Before either of the Daisys can ask what in the world he is doing, they see several blobs of something duct taped to his torso, thighs, and shins.

"DuBell!" they both gasp when they realize what they are looking at.

"Well, help me. Please. Scissors, maybe?" DuBell is all but naked to his underwear and socks, covered in Ziplock bags full of money and an entire roll of duct tape.

"Ohh-K, baby. That's not going to be easy," Mrs. Daisy chortles wryly with her hand to her mouth. She looks as if she is caught between outright laughter and shock, but she keeps speaking like the nurse she is. "Paul, go get my surgical bag from under the sink in my room and the nail polish remover from the cabinet. And the peroxide." Paul is up and around the corner and back in seconds. Mrs. Daisy gets DuBell a blanket to cover up with, and she takes the proffered supplies from Paul. She sends Paul out to the car to get her bags from Walmart.

She takes a scalpel out of her bag, holds the sharp part up to DuBell's face so he can see it, and she declares, "Be still. I mean it." She searches until she locates a piece of plastic not covered in tape, far from his skin, and she slices the edge. She removes the stack of money, sets it aside, and starts trimming away all the excess bag with scissors. She repeats this process a total of ten times. When she is done, she begins to rub a small section of the duct tape with nail polish remover until the edges peel off enough to allow her to grip the edge. She yanks the duct tape off DuBell's leg, causing him to shriek, "Why would you do that?!"

"Why did you leave the house?"

DuBell just points to the stack of money that Mrs. Daisy has studiously ignored throughout her ministrations. "Half is yours, Mrs. Daisy. Yours and Paul's. And I owe Paul a new bike and a backpack, but I'll pay for it from my half."

"Where did this come from? Is someone going to come looking for this money?"

"No, Mrs. Daisy. They're all going to jail. They had been stacking this money. They had something planned for it, but they wouldn't even mention it when I was around. Their plan could only have been for worse crimes, I'm certain." DuBell shrugs. "They were so methodical though. I honestly can't believe that they got caught by a 911 call," he muses. He snaps back to the conversation. "But truth, Mrs. Daisy. This isn't owed money. It was Dre and X's money, not anyone else's. They aren't going to be using it anytime soon, and it was just left behind." DuBell smiles up at Mrs. Daisy. "It's kind of like how in church today, they were talking about Ruth in the Bible, if you consider it a certain way."

"How exactly is this supposed to be like Ruth?" Mrs. Daisy blinks at him, waiting.

"Well, she and all the other women and children picked up all of the grain that fell off behind the men carrying the stalks of wheat, and with what they picked up, they were able to keep everybody fed." DuBell points to the money. "They just left this laying on the ground, and I just happened to see it was left there. So, it would be wasteful not to pick it up and use it, especially when these same people have chosen to end up in jail, leaving me all on my own." DuBell trails off for a moment. His facial wounds are raw and angry, and his face feels slightly misshapen. "I mean, seriously, without you two, I would be out of luck and in a boys' home. Plus, I don't know who this *aunt* is, but I feel a whole lot better knowing I've got my own money if things get weird."

Mrs. Daisy moves from sitting on the carpet to kneeling, and as she does, she rips another piece of tape off of DuBell's arm. She laughs as he howls. "That's what you get for using the Bible as your justification for taking something that doesn't rightfully belong to you."

"It doesn't belong to them either," Paul interjects. "Other people gave it to them, and it can't be returned. I agree with Juice. Dre and X left this behind. It's like if you die in a video game, somebody else can pick up your fallen gear. It's just part of the game. And if not us, would you rather it end up in the hands of the guys who beat up DuBell and … stole my bike."

DuBell can tell that Paul had almost let it slip about the gun being pulled on him. DuBell changes the topic, saying, "We should at least count the money to see how much it is, right?" Though he is fairly certain the total is $22,850.

"You," Mrs. Daisy points to DuBell, "will get the rest of that tape off of you, and then you will get in the tub. I don't trust you to stand in the shower. Wash off, so I can determine what is dirt or tape or what is actually bruise." He nods like he hears her, but he continues to sit still. "Do you need me to remove the rest of the tape for you?"

"No, ma'am. Sorry! I just zoned out for a minute. I got hit in the head a few times." DuBell almost starts to apply the nail polish remover to his skin right there, but Mrs. Daisy stops him and sends him to the bathroom and tells him to start running the water for his bath.

As water churns into the tub and steam begins to rise, DuBell catches a glimpse of himself in the mirror. He recoils at what he finds. Brandon had used him like a Dunlap punching bag, but whatever. Nobody ever taught him to punch right. *Evil prick*, DuBell thinks. *He could have taken some lessons from my moms.*

At the thought of his mom, he begins to cry again, this time in earnest. He sobs, and he lets the rushing water mask what it can of his anguish.

Fuck Andre and fuck Xavier but damn his moms for not stopping it and for going down with them. And for what? For money. Ha.

He looks at himself again and looks at the tape still half-glued and wrapped around his body. The welts where Mrs. Daisy pulled off the tape. His busted face, mouth, and ribs from Brandon. He may have pissed his pants a little when the old man spotlighted them at Weird Christine's. And he had done it all for money.

He almost got Paul shot. *Jesus Christ*. And $20,000 wasn't worth losing Daze. No way, no day. No amount of money was worth losing Paul. DuBell makes a promise to himself to always consider Paul before he ever makes an impulsive move again. He turns off the water and eases into the tub, wincing and breathing through his teeth. He fixates on the wallpaper ladies.

That's what he calls them. The whole bathroom is done in a wallpaper pattern of women and wood nymphs carrying vases and playing flutes and bathing. The pattern repeats up and down the wall in alternating beige and brown tones. It makes the women and the nymphs mixed race as a result, and DuBell loves the desegregation vibe, like it's all good in these woods. It is the most bizarre wallpaper DuBell has ever encountered, and he marvels at it every time he uses the bathroom. Tonight, he imagines his drawn beauties coming alive and pouring their vases into the bathtub, spilling out their magical elixirs, so that he might be healed and have clarity and strength.

He uses the nail polish remover to loosen up the parts of the tape still above the waterline, then he gets impatient and starts ripping the tape off his stomach and ribs. He regrets this decision instantly. His head starts throbbing suddenly, and he jumps up, ribs forgotten, and propels himself into the toilet next to the tub, where he vomits violently until he is empty. The wallpaper ladies watch with concern. A gentle knock comes at the door.

"You still alive?"

"Yes, Mrs. Daisy," DuBell moans in a pathetic mess.

"I'll get you some medicine if you deem you're done."

"Thank you, Mrs. Daisy."

DuBell wipes his face with toilet paper and flushes before rolling himself face down into the tub and floating like an egg. He lets the water fill his ears and nose and mouth. He thinks about the pool at summer camp. Sinking to the bottom of thirteen feet and sitting there until your ears feel ready to burst.

He is transported to the safe place in his mind, where there is nothing in sight for miles, except for the woods and the lake and a few fields. He is standing at camp, and it is late afternoon. A sunny day with passing cloud formations. No one is at camp with him, but that is OK.

He sits on the pool steps looking at the lodge and the flagpole. The flag is up, and it is whipping its cord against the pole as it salutes the passing clusters of cumulus and nimbus wisps. The lodge looks empty, but somewhere in the distance, there's a four square ball bouncing.

DuBell opens his eyes and comes out of the water and the other world with a splash. It rolls off of his face and away, and he listens. He listens to hear if someone has knocked at the door, but there is nothing but the echo of the four square ball and the water. He stares at the faucet dully for a moment then pulls his wits together.

Feeling sorry for himself never got him anything, so no use doing it now. *Chin up, Champ.*

He attempts to peel the tape from his stomach again, *very slowly* this time, and it gives with the assistance of the nail polish remover. He washes around the tape gunk and cleans his face tenderly with a washrag before draining the tub.

He decides to let the old worries go down the drain. He lets the water go all the way down around him, and he sits in the chill of the empty tub for a second. He looks at his legs and is now only worried about getting the tape off of his thighs. He shivers and steps out of the tub carefully.

He wraps a giant green fuzzy towel, the likes of which he has never personally owned, around himself, and he darts from the bathroom into Paul's room. There he finds, on the foot of the bed, a pack of underwear and some pajamas. The underwear came in black, red, and blue, not the standard white. *All right, Mrs. Daisy.* DuBell selects black because *ninja work* happened this evening. He pulls his pajama tops on, also black, long sleeve with red cuffs. DuBell approves. He leaves the pants aside as he starts using nail polish remover where he can see the remaining tape. He tells himself $10,000 over and over as he pulls sections of duct tape from his thighs and ankles. He is eternally grateful that the hair being ripped out is short.

Once he is finally finished, he pulls his pajama bottoms on and walks out to the living room with all of the supplies. Paul and Mrs. Daisy are sitting at the little glass circle table in the dining area, and she is sticking money into shoeboxes and Tupperware and taking tally on a sheet of ledger paper. DuBell sets the supplies down on the living room coffee table and joins the Daisys at the kitchen table under the yellow lamplight.

The window blinds are shut, and the curtains are drawn; the only sound is that of money being counted. Paul gives DuBell a look that warns *don't talk until she's done.* So DuBell sits and counts along with her mentally. As he does, he thinks about how many months it had taken Dre and X to generate that cash. Almost two whole years of setting up internet accounts and recycling porn files at anywhere from $5 to $100 per account, then collecting advertisements legally on the side, which moms had to cash out because they were under eighteen when they started the scheme.

DuBell thinks about all of the files in the computer the police took away. All the credit card information, personal data, encrypted files, bank records, hospital transactions, legal accounts, all on that one hard drive. DuBell thinks that if half of what Dre boasted was true about *how* illegal those things were, his half-brothers were looking at several years in prison. *How messed up*, he muses.

Mrs. Daisy comes to the end of her counting and looks up. "How are you feeling now?"

"I'm better, a little. My head hurts."

"Your medicine is on the counter in the kitchen." DuBell gets up and sees the medicine. He starts to grab for a glass then pauses.

"May I have a glass of Kool-Aid, please, Mrs. Daisy?"

"Oh God, they must've beaten you harder than Paul thought. You've never asked me for a glass in your entire life, son. Yes, get you a glass and get in here."

DuBell grabs the pitcher of red liquid and fills his glass to the brim. He grabs Paul a glass and fills his too. He brings the blood juice and hands it off to Paul before taking his seat. "I feel weird being the only one in pajamas, I just wanna put that out there."

"Sorry to hear that. So," Mrs. Daisy points to the money, "a little over $22,000 here on the table. Given that nobody knew anything about it until now, I will not question your ability to keep a secret, nor your understanding about *why* we must all keep this a secret."

Everyone nods in agreement. "I believe you made a good point though. We do not know any aunt in your life, and we do not know what your immediate needs are going to be. Until we do, we cannot count out that this money may become very necessary. Until further notice, however, I will be custodian over this money. I know exactly how much is here, and I am going to put it in a safe place. Once we deem the coast is clear, we are going to find a way to invest the money to put away for your college."

"Well, half is Paul's, like I said. He earned it."

"Yes, but he broke my rules to do so, so he forfeits everything. End of story." Paul and DuBell sit with their mouths open but do not dare to speak. Mrs. Daisy marches forward.

"I am not going to make you go to school tomorrow, either of you. That would only lead to disaster. I do not want kids to harass you because of the arrest." Paul and DuBell look at one another across the table and smirk, then smile and giggle, then begin to laugh outright at Mrs. Daisy's misgivings. Mrs. Daisy just wonders if they are both suffering head trauma.

"Mrs. Daisy," DuBell explains slowly struggling to get his laughing under control, "*if anyone*, apart from that psychopath Brandon, has the guts to confront me, let alone harass me, about my personal business, I might just be willing to hand them one of those stacks of $1,000."

"Are you so bad? You don't look it right now." She smirks at him.

"What? This? Please Mrs. D." DuBell looks at Paul then back at Mrs. Daisy incredulously. "I *let* Brandon do this to me." DuBell motions to his face. "I know when to take my licks versus when to give them. I needed him to do exactly what he did." Now Paul looks confused too. "Guys, I was *obviously* going to get jumped; that's why I taped the money to my body. I put some money into the backpack hoping to just give it to any would-be jackers and then run away. However, once I saw Brandon, I knew he wasn't going to pass up a chance to attack me. He had his whole gang of LA Boys behind him, so I figured it was best to just lose quickly. I curled into a ball after he punched me, mostly to protect my face and my junk, but also to keep him from kicking the bags of money and noticing what I was hiding. Like I said, I was expecting the bag to be taken, but not the bike. Note to self: expect the unexpected."

Mrs. Daisy, stares incredulous, shaking her head. "When *exactly* did you concoct this little plan?"

"When we were watching the news and I saw that the police had taken the computer but not the desk."

Mrs. Daisy stares at DuBell, then shakes her head at him. "Why can't you use your powers for good, child?" DuBell once again gestures at all of the money. "If this were good, we would not be having a clandestine meeting about how to handle it." She gives him a look, daring him to keep on gesturing at the money, so he stops. "Well, despite your lack of concern over school tomorrow, you aren't going. You two will just get up and go with me to work if I can't get ahold of Janet to cover for me. If she covers, we will take our time, and we'll head over to the courthouse after breakfast. If not, you two will have to get up early and come with me to the hospital, and we will head over to the courthouse as soon as I get off. And before you ask, no, you cannot stay by yourselves. God knows what state I would find the two of you in. We'll get to the courthouse and meet this aunt and see where it goes from there. No matter what, *you* will return home here with us tomorrow night. Even if the aunt is a billionaire and lives in a Belle Meade mansion, we will all agree to come back home together tomorrow night, OK?"

"OK," Paul and DuBell agree.

"Now, I know it is early, but I really feel the both of you should go on to your bedroom. I don't expect you to fall asleep anytime soon, but I need time to think, and this day has had enough goings-on for me. Let me contact Janet right now and see what I can do for tomorrow. Go on now."

The boys extricate themselves from the table. DuBell hands his cup to Paul and lets him refill the Kool-Aid. "Sorry for leaving the house, Mrs. Daisy."

"No. You are sorry for getting beaten up and for getting caught out. Go on now."

Paul nudges DuBell on before he can argue back. They head around the corner to Paul's room and close the door. Paul sits in his swivel chair at his desk, and DuBell squats on the end of Paul's bed with his knees up by his ears.

"You know," Paul pauses and looks hard at DuBell, "the weekend was going to be pretty big already. You didn't have to go and one up me." He smiles, and they both laugh. DuBell starts to turn serious and apologize but Paul stops him. "Look, Juice. I make my own choices. I could've stopped at any time, but I chose to be with you. I chose right. It was scary. But that's life sometimes. You didn't pull that gun." He whispers the last part. "Besides, we can buy us over a thousand bikes if we want. Right? That is if my mom doesn't hide it all in a hole in the backyard."

"Speaking of hiding money." DuBell hops off the bed and picks up his pants from the floor. He turns them right side out and pulls from the pockets two stacks of $20 bills and tosses them to Paul. Paul sinks in his swivel chair, jaw dropped.

"I'm so glad you are on my team." Paul stacks the money on his desk and then turns on the radio to 98.1 and drops the volume down to three. TLC's "Waterfalls" is on.

"I've been thinking, Daze. People do stupid stuff for money."

"Yeah, I guess so."

"What's the craziest thing you would do for a million dollars?"

"I don't know. You're the crazy one."

"OK, would you run naked through Times Square, New York City, live on TV?"

Paul giggles. "Oh. Maaay-be. What time of year?"

"Aw, winter for a million, my man."

"Yeah. I would do it for a million. What about you?"

"Me. Yeah. Being naked ain't nothing for me. I prefer being naked. Now the winter part is the only drawback. I hate the cold."

"Would you do that polar bear challenge for a million?"

"You know, I don't know. How long would I have to stay in?"

"For a million? At least five minutes."

"I would try, but I don't know if I could actually do it. Would you eat a spoonful of spiders for a million?"

And on into the night they amuse each other with eating, sleeping, and kissing dares; climbing, fighting, and driving challenges; and out-of-this-world adventures, raising the bounty further and further as the quests increase in magnitude. DuBell and Paul agreed to stay on Mars for three years for a zillion dollars, but neither of them is really sure if one zillion exists. DuBell adjusts himself on one elbow and scooches around in his sleeping bag to face Paul.

"It's really weird to imagine that Dre and X and moms won't be in my life anymore. I mean it's one of those things I prayed about for a really long time, but honestly, I just gave up. I always figured God was busy with some other more important stuff in some third world country. I just never imagined I would be rid of them."

"So, all that porn stuff. Did you know? I mean, you didn't look very surprised when they shared the news."

"Yeah," DuBell admits with an exhale unfitting his small size. "I was more aware than I care to be, due to my condition." He points to his head.

"You mean you have pictures of naked women locked in your brain? We have to put your head in a museum, if you ask me. A treasure trove of boobs, if only we could unlock it."

"I wish that was all it was. I mean, yeah, if that's all it was, you'd probably never hear me complain. Sadly, that is not what Dre and X were peddling. Daze, some of it's so horrible I can't even say it out loud."

"Oh, like ugly people having sex? Or, like, old people?"

"Oh, you just got a good mind, man. You can't even begin to fathom what people pay to watch. Most of it is mean, hurtful. Lots of dudes doing painful bad things to young girls. And yes, old people. And animals and fat people and people missing teeth and noses from drug use."

"Ewww!"

"I know, right. I'm serious. It's horrible. And once I see it, I have a very hard time unseeing it. That stuff is bad magic."

"What do you mean?"

"I mean, I get with girls all the time, you know this. And some girls are wild, or act like they are superfreaks, or maybe they just don't give a damn about rules, and they want to mess around, sure. But I couldn't in my life, *ever* conceive of treating them so low as I have seen. *Especially* if they want to get with you!" DuBell starts thinking about Danna and about how alive and wonderful she had made him feel. A golden memory forever. He shakes his head to imagine treating her mean or cruel or smacking her, calling her horrible names, degrading her privately, or in film.

"Like I said, it's all bad magic. That's why I don't care for certain rap songs, but most people don't even be listening to song lyrics anyways."

"I know, because if they did, they would be like 'What do you mean, you got half a chicken in the door panel, Cube?' Like, is he talking about KFC, or like a rotisserie from Kroger, and why would he have it in his door panel?"

"He's talking about drugs."

"Ohhh," Paul mouths with extreme slowness. "I guess that makes sense."

"My point is, lyrics could say anything, just like KRS-One said. People don't pay attention. It's a wonder anything ever gets accomplished with all the insane babble people are exposed to on the regular."

"I bet you'd be a great rapper though. With your photographic memory, you can memorize anyone's lyrics and spit 'em right back at them."

"Sort of. It would be hard though. I have to visualize seeing the lyrics. I can say it correctly slowly, but to really rap it, I would still have to learn it, or rap it with my eyes closed the whole time."

"Get you some sunglasses. Look like Stevie Wonder." Paul closes his eyes and mimics Stevie Wonder, and DuBell instantly flips to his best Eddie Murphy voice.

"'He's a musical miracle, you need to knock that shit off'"

Paul shushes DuBell from cussing so loud, but they are both laughing and carrying on to fake normalcy to avoid sleep. DuBell can tell that Paul is watching him closely. Mrs. Daisy must have put him on alert for signs of concussions.

DuBell isn't worried about his injuries, so much as he just does not want to dream tonight.

But exhaustion and the radio do eventually lull the boys into submission, and the cycles of DuBell's mind finally slow to a halt.

***

SING TO IT IN THE LIGHT

The Astral Plane-Beyond Time

DuBell phases into existence.

He blinks his eyes open, and he is standing in his bedroom in the Cedar Lake Apartments. He glances to his right and Kitsune is sitting on the bed like a statue of a fox, front legs straight, haunches rested, two tails pointing northwest and northeast, or ten and two, both bushy and orange with golden flecks of light in the tip, like Kitsune's face.

Kitsune licks his paws dismissively as DuBell shivers awake into the dream realm. DuBell stands up, rubbing his arms and looking for a hoodie.

"It's been stolen," Kitsune explains in his clear teacher tone. "You're just going to have to be cold this time."

"What? For real? It's literally going to be freezing."

"It's *literally* nothing, actually."

"Come on. Can't you spare anything to warm me up a bit?"

"Not tonight. We've got work to do. Just stick your arms inside your shirt." Kitsune shakes his golden nose at DuBell. "Besides, if you could be bothered to practice, the cold would just go away."

"I've been a little busy this weekend."

"I'll say. You've obviously been a good boy for someone.

Been eating all your vegetables and helping little old ladies cross the street and shit, because Santa decided to come see you in August with like six years-worth of gifts. You lucky little wad." Kitsune huffs. "Just imagine what could've been achieved if we'd actually sacrificed Andre and Xavier instead of letting the police have them." Saying this Kitsune's face shimmers like a real fire. "We could have some *major* fun then. *Now* they'll just sit in prison and rot. Wasted."

"Enough of that talk. I was never going to murder them. Sorry to disappoint."

"Murder and sacrifice are totally different."

"Not where I come from."

"Whatever. Let's get to work." Kitsune leans forward on the bed and raises up his front right fox paw and touches DuBell's nose. Instantly, DuBell shrinks involuntarily to the size of a Teenage Mutant Ninja Turtles action figure. Kitsune leaps from the bed down to the floor, now towering above DuBell, and he holds out his upturned paw. DuBell steps onto Kitsune's paw and is lifted up to the nape of Kitsune's neck, where he huddles down preparing for the cold about to come. "All right. Hold on tight," Kitsune barks, and he leaps straight at the bedroom wall which dissolves into an asteroid field.

DuBell keeps his eyes screwed tight. Outside of his eyelids he can see flashes from a thousand million brilliant lights, all eager to bombard his senses, and though it is a dream, he is well aware that he would certainly awaken as blind as Stevie Wonder if he were to even peek at that shine for a second. He fears that it would freeze his eyes to his soul for all-time to do so, even though he has never actually asked Kitsune about it. Asking Kitsune about anything only leads to more unanswered questions, and more work in the astral desert.

DuBell used to assume that everyone else had the same things happen to them at night. He thought everyone had magical creatures that came to them and offered them magical quests and challenges. He thought everyone had to cross astral planes to sing to an enchanted desert flower night after night waiting to unlock their destiny. Everyone talked about dreams and dreaming and the dreamworld, so he just assumed that their nocturnal world was no different from his.

But as it turns out nobody else had his exact problems. Nobody else served as a conduit to the spirit world. Nobody else had a sadistic Kitsune that visited them in their dreams every night and drilled words of power into their heads like some evil-ass kung fu master. Nobody else had accidentally locked their photographic memory option into the "on" position, attempting to be clever and speed up their nightly chores. And nobody, *nobody*, ever woke up as mentally tired as DuBell. *Nobody*. And though Kitsune restores DuBell's strength and stamina every morning, his mind is never truly at rest, and he knows it never will be until the flower blooms.

But tonight. *Perhaps tonight*, DuBell thinks. Perhaps getting Dre and X and all of their bullshit out of his life will clear his soul enough to let him sing his flower open. As he thinks this, Kitsune slows his pace.

"Don't get your hopes up. It's not going to happen tonight."

"Prick. Stop reading my mind."

"You call that a mind?"

DuBell looks around at the all-too-familiar scene. Kitsune is standing on an empty, flat, desert plane at night; DuBell is perched on his back. Above them, the cosmos rage in a fiery dance of swirling stars and comets tangled inside luminous gas clouds. Below them the ground is cracked and caked beneath Kitsune's paws. DuBell cannot see very far in any direction, but there is nothing to see. From the soft orange light emanating off Kitsune, DuBell can faintly see the greens and pinks of the flower below him, down in the dark. DuBell huddles down into Kitsune's neck fur for one last bit of warmth.

"Hop down." Kitsune snaps out in frustration, and he forcibly shivers DuBell out of his fur. DuBell slides down Kitsune's side and lands in a superhero crouch. Kitsune shivers again in an obvious attempt to remove signs of DuBell from his fur. "I'll be back at dawn. Have fun."

Without further insult, Kitsune winks out of existence, and DuBell is left in the solid dark. The freezing sensation from crossing the astral plane eventually abates, but DuBell will never warm up this evening; he's sure of it. Following Kitsune's advice DuBell sticks his arms in his shirt, then proceeds to stick his hands down the front of his pants and into his underwear before he squats cross-legged to the ground with his junk cupped in his palms. It is an odd source of warmth that he is eternally grateful for, and in a weird way it helps him to find his focus in the darkness.

Even though he cannot see it right this second, he can sense that the flower is sitting just in front of him. DuBell knows that in time his eyes will adjust, and the dark will give way to the tall, thick, cylinder of the flower's stem, which is as wide around like a sunflower stalk but waxy and reflective on its surface. Before dawn, he will be able to trace out the large curving leaves with their jagged dart-tips, and he will find the outline of the petals, which are cut like two closed palms in prayer.

But he doesn't need to see the flower to complete his task.

Wasting no more time, DuBell clears his throat and begins to sing. He is not certain if the words are real. He has never seen them written down, and he is not able to remember them upon waking, but this is his dream, and in this world the words are known to him. He has been coming to this place for years. He has sung to this flower for years. In his heart, he hears the story of Kitsune, of how the flower once sang to *him* then ceased, how the flower never would sing to him again because Kitsune never sang to it. The flower would only sing again if someone dared to sing it their true destiny. So, DuBell comes nightly to this spot and attempts the impossible. He attempts the impossible because he dares.

He also attempts the impossible because he is bound, and he would be free. Yes, the Kitsune tricked him into the Gish, but it could be worse. Truly.

He raises his voice against the night and the cold and the futility of his actions, and he sings to his flower. He does not know if the flower hears him at all. If it does, he cannot perceive his song to have any impact. Yet, he comes back night after night. Some nights the Gish drags him kicking and screaming, fussing and freezing, blind with rage for needing more rest, but most nights he just comes willingly to his work. In theory, it should lead him to his true destiny, but DuBell isn't certain what that means exactly.

All he knows is that there is a comfort in the words and in the patterns and tones and in the melodies and the structure that DuBell cannot describe out loud. In part because the Gish would magically constrain his mouth from doing so, but mostly because the process is so complex and interwoven that it is partly a magic spell and partly a piece of his soul. To sing for his flower every night is both his blessing and his curse.

But tonight, when he sings, tears begin to flood his face, and because his hands are in his pants, he cannot wipe them away. DuBell doesn't stop singing; he just lets the tears cascade freely across his cheeks as the nonsense song spills out of his throat and down his tongue. Thickly and sweet, each note hangs in the air until it is pushed out and forth by the next emerging sound from his lips, and on and on, until the horizon whispers of the dawn, and DuBell can see his flower. His destiny. He can see it, and he swears that it wants to open, and it will if he just sings to it in the sun. *Just let me sing to it in the light.* But Kitsune returns and pulls him away again, and he is forced to close his eyes against the astral plane. He sees the image of his flower against the black screen of his eyelids. He sees it, but it fades before he can open his eyes and trace its shape.

Kitsune transports DuBell back to his old bedroom. The image of the flower fades, but DuBell can still see the outline.

"Will I return here or somewhere else tomorrow night?" DuBell interrogates the fox demon.

"How should I know?" Kitsune responds in his normal bored tone. With a firm poke of his paw, he grows DuBell back to normal size. Kitsune appears again in the size of a medium fox.

"I just figured … I'm supposed to meet some *aunt* tomorrow." DuBell points around the room. "I don't know. Just thought this place was done, and we might meet somewhere else tomorrow night."

"Well, thinking never really was your strong suit."

"Thanks."

"You're welcome. Also, you don't have an aunt."

"I know right. That entire situation is whack."

"Well, just because she isn't really your aunt, doesn't mean she isn't part of the plan."

"Wait. Plan? What plan?" DuBell probes, half distracted by a faint golden glow coming from the cork board above his desk. DuBell walks over and looks closer and sees the secret section above the desk is pulled open, and the safe door is also swung wide open on the hinges. DuBell looks into the safe expecting to see three empty shelves. But when he looks inside, on each shelf sits four golden rings. "What plan?" he repeats, but Kitsune is gone. The room is empty. He looks back at the desk, but it is gone too. *What were those rings?*

AND IF YOU DO STAB SOMEONE

August 1996

DuBell awakens. He is on Paul's floor, lying on the sleeping bag he uses when he sleeps in Paul's room. His arms are inside his pajama shirt, inside his pajama pants, and inside his underwear. He can see the superimposed image of twelve rings on the backs of his eyelids when he closes his eyes. He blinks himself awake.

He looks up at Paul's bed and sees his friend's big palm splayed upward, disembodied, sticking out from the pillow. It instantly makes DuBell remember summer camp pranks, of sticking someone's hand in warm water to make them wet the bed; but he would never do that to Paul. DuBell slips out of the flannel interior of the sleeping bag and winces as he is reminded of the condition of his ribs. Carefully, he gets dressed in his new blue jeans and black t-shirt and goes to look at his face in the mirror.

It looks as bad as it feels. Swollen still and puff-red in some places, blue-green in others. But his teeth are all there and nothing feels broken in his ribs when he lifts his arms above his head, so he counts it as a win.

Paul wakes up, and Mrs. Daisy materializes shortly after, already dressed in a nice black dress and matching shoes. She has obviously gotten Janet to cover for her or she would be dressed differently. DuBell notices that she has on her elephant earrings and smiles. Mrs. Daisy ushers Paul to get ready, and Paul disappears into his room, bowl of cereal in hand. DuBell sits out of the way with his own bowl of cereal as the Daisys try to work through the break in their morning routine; normally Mrs. Daisy is long gone before Paul wakes up, so now they are in each other's way.

As it gets close to normal time for the bus, there is a knock at the front door, and DuBell sees the impatient face of Kendall Glidden in the window.

"I got it, Mrs. Daisy," DuBell calls around the corner as he pulls open the front door. "Hey, what up, Kendall. We ain't going to school today."

"No joke, DB. If I was you, I'd skip school too. That's some hard mess, man. You need to turn on the news though and see what *else* happened at Cedar Lake last night. You're not gonna believe it." Kendall really looks up at DuBell for the first time. "Damn, what happened to your face, man?"

"Long story."

"I bet. Does the state of your face have anything to do with Scarface shooting someone named Odie?"

"Say what?" DuBell gapes in shock, and his mouth goes dry. "Brandon shot Odie?!"

"Yeah look, Scarface is totally going to jail. It's on every channel." Kendall grabs up the remote like he owns the place, but DuBell and Paul are in shock, looking at each other in disbelief. Kendall turns up the volume.

"Last night police returned to the Cedar Lake Apartments after gunshots were reported, and they received a 911 call from members of a local gang." It cuts to the recording.

"Hey, yo. You've got a *bleeping* dead body here. And it wasn't us that *bleeping* did it. I'm a say that *bleep* right now. We got him restrained, but this *bleeping* kid is psycho, yo."

Police arrived on the scene to find one dead body, six shaken gang members, and an enraged twelve-year-old locked in the bathroom, with the refrigerator propped against the door. The youth in question, Brandon Barnes, was reportedly attempting to break down the door with a porcelain toilet lid as police entered the apartment. First responding officer on the scene, Sergeant Covington, had this to say.

"I've seen some wild stuff in my times as a metro officer, but this takes the cake. I come in, and I see I've got six *hardened* criminals unwilling to step to this kid. It definitely made me pause before going in to apprehend the suspect. In the end it took twelve officers to hold him down long enough to get restraints on him."

"Victim, O'Dell 'Odie' Junkins, age twenty-three, is said to have been shot point blank in an argument over money. In other news, a report of measles outbreak is…"

Kendall turns off the television. "Just thought you'd like to know." Paul and DuBell just stare for a minute in utter disbelief until the brakes of the school bus can be heard coming down the hill. All of the boys move instinctually, until Paul and DuBell remember they aren't leaving. They step out front to be visible for the bus though, just for Kendall's sake. After slapping quick skins with Paul and DuBell, Kendall holds up the black video cassette tape. "You care if I show the tape still?"

DuBell shrugs and nods. "Do it up." Paul agrees with a bow of his head.

"Bet. I'll shout later if you are home, Paul." Kendall leaps between Mrs. Daisy's roses and yells down the hill, "Celeste! Hold the bus."

The boys watch the bus turn around in the cul-de-sac, and Mrs. Daisy walks out of her room. "Well then, I expect we should be on our way."

They are all three silent as they make their way out of the neighborhood. DuBell stares out the window at all of the houses they pass by going up the street, and at the dogs behind fences, and at two large moving trucks parked up on Eastview. He wonders if being a furniture mover would be a fun job. *You'd get to see a lot of different houses, I bet.* DuBell thinks about all of the houses he has seen or been in in real life, which is not very many, so he thinks of all the houses he's seen in television and movies, and in books and magazines and newspapers, and all of these silent thoughts carry him most of the way downtown. But then DuBell can't take the silence any longer.

"Well, now that Brandon is heading to jail too, and I'm fairly certain that some higher being is sending me a sign, I for one am excited to meet this Aunt Margaret … person. But, just so you know, Mrs. Daisy, if anyone attempts to restrain me, I will probably use the nearest sharp object to stab my way out of the situation, and then run back to the car. I'm just being honest."

Nobody responds for a moment. "Thank you for that heads-up," Mrs. Daisy offers coolly, "but no one is going to restrain you. Therefore, please do your best to restrain yourself. And if you *do* stab someone, for heaven's sake, don't run back to *my* car." They all laugh sincerely and the tension breaks as

Mrs. Daisy angles off the Second and Fourth Avenue exit and then navigates her little Honda through the grid of streets that run through the pie wedge of downtown Nashville.

Parking near the courthouse and walking over in the morning rush is fascinating to DuBell and Paul who always see downtown in the distance on the bus ride into school but never get to go. DuBell cranes his neck to see the sun reflecting off of the building windows, and he inhales all of the smells of cars and people and construction and trash. There are homeless camps by the Church Street Center plaza, and there is smooth marble everywhere, and DuBell thinks of how awesome it would be to rollerblade here. *Why don't I come downtown more often?* DuBell wonders seriously.

He remembers back to when he and Paul came to the ballet at the TPAC in third grade to see a performance of *Billy the Kid*. They'd been dropped off right in front of the building and been shuffled inside like little ducks. They had never gotten to see any of this cool stuff.

Mrs. Daisy leads them quickly toward a series of tan buildings that have a bunch of fancy columns on them and a literal wall of steps leading up, just like at the Parthenon. DuBell is in heaven, but he can see Paul is not enjoying the look of all the steps up ahead. Much to Paul's delight, however, Mrs. Daisy turns away from the stairs and approaches a sneaky-looking side door.

Inside the door is a set of steps leading downstairs *beneath* the columns. DuBell is now intrigued as first they wind down further underground and then begin to pass through a series of hallways that DuBell can instinctively tell are taking them further under a hill. Mrs. Daisy is undeterred as she twists and turns following a series of official placards with arrows and numbers. At one point they pass through a tiny corridor with bank teller windows, and the dimensions of the room make Paul look impressively large.

Filing down a final hallway with lush red carpet and windows exposing them to sunlight again, the trio finds a series of doors. One door is ajar, and obviously their destination. It is an ornate door that is of average height, but as wide and deep as a bank vault. DuBell taps Paul, "Looks like they knew you were coming, Big Daze." Paul lifts his chin and smiles.

As they approach the door they can see inside. There is a woman sitting in a tall wing-backed chair, in a royal blue dress and a suit jacket, lazily twirling a long gold necklace and pendant around her finger as she talks. Her hair is laid down into shoulder length curls, and her makeup makes her eyes look sleepy, even though she is keenly aware of them approaching and queuing up outside of the door.

"Mrs. Daisy. Paul. DuBell. Please, come on in. We've been eagerly awaiting you." They enter the room and find another woman that looks very familiar to DuBell, which sets his mind to working on the puzzle of *where do I know you from?* The adults say adult pleasantries. The two women introduce themselves as Ms. Margaret Tate and Mrs. Lore-Walker. In typical adult fashion they address Mrs. Daisy first, but DuBell feels somehow that they have managed to not look away from him all the while. Mrs. Lore-Walker steps away, and as she disappears through another interior door, DuBell hears her tell someone to prepare the paperwork.

Ms. Tate turns from Mrs. Daisy and addresses Paul next.

"Well, aren't you a very handsome and strapping, young

man? And I just love your hat, Big Poppa." DuBell and Paul trade a quick look, like *Yo, this woman is down,* and then suddenly she is turning her perfect smile on DuBell.

DuBell is now very keen for her to go on back to looking at Paul because he realizes that he looks like the devil has beat the tar out of him, and he also realizes that up until this moment he hasn't particularly cared what some stranger might think about his appearance. *Why am I suddenly concerned about my appearance?* Before he can ponder to answer that, this Ms. Margaret Tate woman beckons him to her, a black friendship bracelet dangling from her wrist as her fingers curl in his direction.

"Well, come here, let me see you, boy. Don't shy away. I didn't expect to find you looking *this* put together. Though, I imagine I owe a good deal of thanks to Mrs. Daisy for that miracle." She grabs his face like she is looking at an object she is inspecting for sale at an auction, or perhaps like a dog at a dog show. What surprises DuBell is that he lets her do it. She looks in his eyes and ears and nose and at his teeth and scalp and then turns him around once. "Very well," she murmurs at last, sounding resolutely satisfied. "Come have a seat here at the long table."

She turns to Mrs. Daisy. "You and Paul should also come sit at the table, as this will most certainly involve you both."

Mrs. Lore-Walker rematerializes. To Mrs. Daisy she proffers, "Would you care for some coffee or hot tea? Juice, boys?" Mrs. Daisy and Paul both look a little surprised, but they come to the end of the table with DuBell. Mrs. Daisy nods *yes* to a coffee, and Paul stammers a *yes* and a *thank you* to the offer of juice. DuBell flashes a smile, "Yes, I am."

Ms. Tate smirks at his joke and joins the table sitting a few seats from DuBell, and Mrs. Lore-Walker reenters with a young lady trailing behind her carrying a tray of beverages and snacks. The young lady sits the tray down between the boys and starts handing out drinks. She offers Mrs. Daisy cream and sugar for her coffee. She too seems to drink in DuBell with every glance. He is OK with her checking him out; she makes him forget that his face is busted up. She has close cropped red-brown hair and bright blue eyes, wearing a bright yellow cardigan, and she smells like a breeze. DuBell half-listens to Ms. Tate while he watches the unnamed young lady and her yellow cardigan disappear back through the door.

DuBell comes back to the conversation. and Ms. Tate is looking directly at him.

"We've got a lot to accomplish today, but I feel confident that we can get everything taken care of in a timely fashion. So, to our first order of business: keeping DuBell out of state custody. Here we go." DuBell wets his lips and shakes the yellow cardigan from his mind, sits up, and gives Ms. Tate his full attention.

A TRANSFORMATIVE DAY TO SAY THE LEAST

August 1996

HexxCat and Vercingetorix walk into the BMW dealership on West End Avenue dressed impeccably and looking bored. They see a low, black, leather couch, walk over, and take a seat. The sales floor is empty this early on Monday morning. Vercingetorix checks his watch: 8:36 AM. He picks up a newspaper, and HexxCat pulls a vanity mirror out of her clutch and checks her lipstick. A huddle of sales associates sees them enter, and one breaks away from the pack with a pleasant, "Good morning. How may I help you?"

HexxCat arches her head in the man's direction and pouts her cherry red lips. "I will have a cup of espresso." She nudges Vercingetorix. "Love?"

"Yes?" Vercingetorix looks up from his paper smiling at HexxCat. His hair glistens with styling gel, offsetting the silver trim of his glasses and his watch.

HexxCat thinks he looks especially striking in the red tie. "Coffee?"

"Please." He beams to the associate, finally able to break his gaze away from HexxCat's lips. "Cream and sugar." Vercingetorix dips his head with a *there's a good chap* nod, then looks back to HexxCat, then back to the paper with a thorough rustling of the pages and a clearing of his throat. The salesman's shoes squeak slightly as he walks away from the pair utterly nonplussed to rejoin the other salesmen.

When the man returns with drinks a few moments later, he pointedly inquires what he might do for them in the way of purchasing an automobile. HexxCat blinks slowly at the man and answers in a completely unaffected tone.

"When my bosses inform me of their needs, I will inform you. Which should be shortly." She punctuates her reply with another slow blink of her lashes. Vercingetorix nods again, smiling wide and confident. The man walks away again, and as the pair sip at their coffees, they both slip small discrete headphones behind their ears and wait.

South of HexxCat and Vercingetorix's downtown position, Senator sits on the front porch of the Daisy's house, smoking a cigarette and looking at the surrounding houses and the moving trucks waiting up the street. He looks at Mrs. Daisy's peach and pink roses, arranged in a neat row. Clean lines. He checks his watch. 8:50 AM. Senator slips on his earpiece and walks over to the driveway to observe the moving crew.

A bulbous brown van from the late 1980s, a Volvo station wagon, and a newer silver Ford Ranger are parked in Mrs. Daisy's driveway surrounded by about two dozen glowing nerdy athletic college freshmen, plus Tripods and CC of the Halflings. To help him move Mrs. Daisy's house, Senator recruited any former Ultimate frisbee players still living in Nashville after graduation. In exchange for services, he offered a small thank you party later with pizza and beer. Tripods and CC walk up. Senator greets them both a firm handshake, and they join him in a cigarette watching the others who are doing stretches to get ready.

"Hey, Chris, I thought you were living in Knoxville."

"You said there'd be beer, so I drove down," CC says, like it's a no-brainer. "I crashed with Tripods and Chance."

Senator shakes his head and addresses Tripods. "I thought the other Halflings were coming?"

"Chance has Japanese class at MTSU right now, and Fry just mumbled something incoherent in the phone when I called an hour ago. But they said for sure they would show up for unpacking and the party." Senator just stares at Tripods. The boy's eyes are so red it's painful. Tripods shrugs. Senator exhales smoke in Tripods' general direction and rolls his eyes.

North of Senator's team, and just east of HexxCat and Vercingetorix, Blue and Kaldari studiously check the clock again and consult their control panels. It's 8:51 AM. Blue and Kaldari adjust their headsets and microphones and check each of the black-and-white surveillance monitors once more. They tightly surveil all people entering the building, until Blue sees the distinctive form of Paul Daisy on camera one, entering the building and walking down the steps. She signals Kaldari, and they follow cameras two and three, which show Mrs. Daisy and DuBell already coming up the hallway. Kaldari locks onto the targets and enhances facial recognition primers, causing the three bodies to glow light blue on the monitor each time they look directly at any of closed-circuit cameras.

"OK, everybody," Kaldari whispers into his mic, "DuBell and the Daisys have entered the building at ground access point one. I have them tagged in the system. They will arrive in three minutes. Let's get into position and do audio checks." Kaldari listens in his headset as the teams sound off.

"*Reception Team is go,*" Sylvia responds crisply over the headset.

"*Surveillance Team is go,*" Blue responds. Her voice echoes behind him.

"*Extraction Team is go,*" Senator responds with a crackle of open air and distance.

"*Fleet Team is go,*" Vercingetorix responds. The sound is also remote, but with less interference.

"All right, Sylvia and Loni. We will check your mics against our guests when they arrive. Everyone except Surveillance Team is going on group mute. Stand by for mute. We will patch in the reception room to everyone's headsets once we have final mic checks."

Sylvia gives a thumbs up to the camera.

Senator pronounces *bullshit* loud and clear just to check that the mute is on.

Vercingetorix and HexxCat just stare at each other.

Here we go, Mothers, Kaldari thinks. *Let's make some magic.*

Kaldari vigorously chews bubble gum and runs his fingers through his longish mop of black hair as he follows the approaching trio of visitors across the surveillance cameras. Camera to camera, the smurfy forms of Mrs. Daisy, DuBell, and Paul progress through the labyrinthian knell of the Capitol Suites Building, all to the soundtrack of a DJ Dan playlist that Kaldari has turned all the way down to two in his earpiece just to keep it professional. Drumming his fingers on the monitor, Kaldari runs his hand down the console admiring the surveillance setup as he follows the blue glow.

The room Kaldari and Blue sit perched in is small and lacks any color scheme, but he's proud of it because the Mothers built the monitoring station themselves in less than ten hours, nearly invisible to the masses. In all, the control panel consists of a full-screen monitor (that is currently black), an audio board with sixteen mixing channels, and a panel of *twenty-four* four-inch monitors. The monitors are attached to remote access video cameras surveilling the entrance to the building, the hallways leading to the reception room, and five cameras dedicated to the reception room itself. The giant audio mixing board was decidedly overkill, but he got a really good deal on it, and he would see it put to *very* good use in the near future. He nudges DJ Dan up to three.

Behind Kaldari, Blue sits at another console, this one sporting five sixteen-inch computer monitors. Her monitors are all colorful with thermal images of the same reception room video feed on Kaldari's panel. In monitor one, Sylvia is on screen, sitting in the chair in the doorway, looking down the hall. On monitor three, Loni is sitting in another chair out of view of the hallway. Sylvia is colored all in blue at her core, but is orange on her skin, while Loni is colored all in oranges, yellows, and reds across her body.

Blue speaks in her mic. "Sylvia can you adjust up your core temperature, so we don't have to doctor this footage later." Sylvia's color begins to shift almost instantly from blue to a white-red, then fades to mostly oranges and yellows, matching her fingertips. "Excellent," Blue reports.

The Daisys make their way toward the reception room, and Kaldari whispers into the mic, "Rolling sound." He starts to record the sound in the room, and he patches outgoing audio into everyone's headsets. A few moments later, everyone hears Sylvia say, "*Mrs. Daisy. Paul. DuBell. Please, come on in. We've been eagerly awaiting you.*" Kaldari glances at his control panel clock. 8:54 AM.

"*Hello,*" Mrs. Daisy replies.

"Your mic sounds good, Sylvia. Go for Loni."

Loni puts on an announcer's voice. "*Hi, Mrs. Daisy. I am Mrs. Lore-Walker. I am an assistant to Ms. Tate.*"

"*Pleased to meet you,*" Mrs. Daisy responds.

"Your mic sounds good, Loni. Reception team is looking and sounding good," Kaldari reports.

"Temperatures are looking good for the room. We are operating at a goal 69 degrees," Blue follows.

"*And nice to meet you as well, Paul. And of course, good to finally meet you as well, DuBell. If you will all excuse me one moment, Ms. Tate, I will go see to the documents.*" Loni steps out of monitor one. She flashes across monitor four, then monitor five.

Kaldari and Blue see the door open beside them, and Loni sticks her head inside and announces like she's projecting across a stage. "DuBell and the Daisys are here. Prepare the paperwork please."

Blue responds in the same clear tone. "Yes, Mrs. Lore-Walker."

Loni smiles and winks to the Surveillance Team. She turns and pulls the door closed behind her.

Kaldari adores Loni Lore. It's her second day on the team, and she is already a star player. Sylvia wasn't joking about Loni's ability to roll with the punches. He truly hopes that he is as mentally flexible as she is when he gets to be her age. He and the Mothers had months to build up to this, but the plan required immediacy on the part of Supraman and Loni.

The Mothers were all amazed when the Supraman operation went off without a hitch. From the fake smells of vomit and feces to the virtual imaging of Sylvia's college bedroom, Sylvia and L-One's plan went down exactly how they had rehearsed. Kaldari had secretly doubted the Loni situation would work without a similar plan, but Sylvia told them some things you plan and other things you just had to trust; and she was right.

Last night, Loni Lore ended up staying the night at Home Base, decidedly too drunk to take the bus to her house. The Mothers came home to find her and Sylvia, sprawled in the floor of the entertainment room, laughing over something too complex for either of them to explain at the time.

The Mothers brought her noodles from International Market, and she proclaimed her undying love for them for the next hour through every bite. When she sobered up enough, she told the Mothers the story off what a wretched whore Sylvia had been to her when they were teenagers, and only after they watched the Live Journals version of Sylvia's wretchedness did they began laying the details for today's operation. Kaldari worried last night that she would be horribly hungover today, but she seems fine.

"Well, aren't you a very handsome and strapping, young man? And I just love your hat, Big Poppa." Kaldari glances over his shoulder and lingers a moment to watch as Blue puts together a tray with juice glasses and hot water for coffees and teas. He loves that yellow cardigan on her. Blue catches him watching, and she smiles, then motions for him to turn around and focus on the monitors.

"Well, come here let me see you, boy. Don't shy away. I didn't expect to find you looking this put together. Though, I imagine I owe a good deal of thanks to Mrs. Daisy for that miracle." From the control panel Kaldari watches Sylvia start to inspect DuBell, and moments later Kaldari's full-screen monitor lights up as he starts to receive scan images of DuBell's head and brain. Blue steps over, and they begin to run a digital analysis of his injuries. Preliminary scans reveal nothing life threatening, and EKG and CAT scan are clear. Kaldari relays to Sylvia's internal mic that no immediate threats appear on the scan.

"Very well, come have a seat in here at the long table. You and Paul should also come sit at the table, as this will most certainly involve you both."

"Would you care for some coffee or hot tea? Juice, boys?"

"Oh, yes. Coffee for me, please."

"Yes… thank you."

"Yes, I am."

Loni reenters surveillance. "How's it going?" she whispers.

"Good," Blue whispers back. She hands Loni a stack of papers in a manila folder then picks up her tray with coffees and juices. "Right behind you." Blue is a deft hand with the drink tray from helping her mom in the coffee shop since she could walk. The reception room is mostly table, on purpose. They had it shipped in yesterday. Sylvia said to just make it as wide and long as could possibly fit through the door, so they did. It was scheduled for return tomorrow afternoon.

Blue sets the tray down between the boys and starts handing out drinks. She offers Mrs. Daisy cream and sugar for her coffee. Mrs. Daisy seems serious, but kind. Stern maybe, but loving. Blue can see it in her smile when she accepts the coffee. Blue has spent many years reading customers faces. She knows smiles, and many other aspects of faces. She can tell if someone is ready to order, if someone is still deciding on their drink, if someone needs the bathroom, or if they are going to ask for her phone number, all by the look on their face.

So Blue is surprised, but not *too* surprised, to find DuBell's hyperintelligent eyes examining her like she might get served with juice. She serves him last on purpose to give him time to look away, but when she comes to him, he is still half-ignoring Sylvia in favor of openly watching her. DuBell doesn't even seem to care that he looks like he got mugged by a train. This kid radiates confidence, and not like some guys ooze machismo, but like the sun radiates heat. She gives DuBell a psychic wink, with her eyes wide and nonchalant, then she turns and disappear back through the door.

She sets her tray down in the kitchenette and returns to her monitors and headset, now with a camera on each person at the table. She can see the heat signatures from each person. Mrs. Daisy and DuBell look a little elevated in temperature, but Paul is at normal levels, even a little cool. Blue adjust the temperature on Mrs. Daisy's chair to drop one degree per minute until her body levels out; Blue wants her really enjoying the warmth of the coffee. The juice should cool DuBell off, but Blue doesn't want him shivering. It would turn on Mrs. Daisy's maternal instincts too early and put her on the defensive. Blue looks at his red and white patterns and he does seem to glow almost. Blue smiles.

"We've got a lot to accomplish today, but I feel confident that we can get everything taken care of in a timely fashion. So, to our first order of business: keeping DuBell out of state custody. Here we go. Mrs. Lore-Walker, if you would like to take over."

Back on the south end of town, Senator adjusts his earpiece in his right ear and tucks a wisp of his conspicuous orange hair back under his blue Cubs baseball hat. He steps to the end of Mrs. Daisy's driveway and waves up the street, signaling for the truck drivers to roll to the bottom of the hill. He checks his watch again. It reads 9:00 AM.

Technically, the Extraction Team can't enter the house until Mrs. Daisy signs the paperwork, but he figures it won't hurt to get set up now that the proceedings are underway. And if he's wrong, then they'll just pack it all back up. But he knows he's not wrong. He knows they are going to say yes.

Two long green moving trucks roll down the hill and maneuver into position, one truck blocking the driveway facing uphill, and one truck parked on the street at the bottom of the hill; the drivers will remain in position. The meeting transpiring in Senator's ear continues.

"What we want to do first is set up a personal estate portfolio for DuBell, wherein he is going to have his basic financial,

physical, emotional, and social needs covered, and where he is not going to end up a ward of the state. This requires a discussion of guardianship."

Senator walks through the group with a clipboard and starts assigning roles. He tells the crews to get their supplies ready then just hang out and keep stretching and drink water until they are ready to rock. He checks that the drivers are good to just hang out. They give the thumbs up and smoke a cigarette under the maple tree in the front yard, checking out the ladies amongst the young moving crew.

"Am I going to live with you, Ms. Tate?"

"Oh, Jesus in heaven, no. No. Noooo. I am not a caretaker of children. I am many things but not that."

"No. We are going to offer Mrs. Daisy here the opportunity to be your guardian, if she so chooses."

Blue watches as Mrs. Daisy spikes red with white flecks on camera three. It's expected, but she wants less white now. "Loni, she's elevated slightly; tack a little lower."

"If this is not suitable to Mrs. Daisy, we will of course come to some other arrangement, most probably boarding school."

"That's better, Loni. She's leveling off, but DuBell also looks like he's going to come apart at the seams soon. His heart rate has been at gallop the whole time. I'm going to cool his chair a few degrees." When the temperature drops DuBell does not shiver but looks around like he's heard a faint noise. This kid is unbelievably sensitive.

"Should you choose to look after our young DuBell, we would provide you with ample compensation for his care, and with a new house in Bellevue. We will of course take care of the move, and we will take care of setting up a company to man-

age your current property at Clipper Court. No offense, but by the looks of his face, I'm guessing the neighborhood is getting a little rougher than it was ten years ago when you moved in."

Blue whispers in the mic again. "Hey, Sylvia, Mrs. Daisy's heart rate elevates slightly every time you speak. Perhaps you should leave it to Loni. Mrs. Daisy does not seem to have a sense of humor about this situation."

Kaldari watches the black-and-white monitors as Loni deftly pulls Mrs. Daisy's attention right back her way, away from Sylvia with a slow blink and an eye roll in a classic good cop, bad cop routine.

"The new house in Bellevue would be in your name, and it would remain yours, even if for some unforeseen reason DuBell leaves your custody. There would be absolutely no risk to you."

Blue feels like a co-conductor of a symphony combined with a character of a small arts-house play. Like the audience is watching her behind both doors, so she keeps directing and acting alongside Kaldari, enjoying every minute. "Let her breathe, Loni. Turn to the boys and tell them about their awesome new school." A school where she would be in Mrs. Armstrong's Advanced Honors English right this moment, if it weren't for this kick-ass *service-learning opportunity* she is currently signed out for.

"Both boys have qualified for a spot at MK Gandhi Magnet in the next year. I'm sure you've heard about it by now; they've won several awards recently for their student success. Our recommendation is that both boys see six years under that roof."

Senator looks at the crew and the still-rising sun, and he thinks *this waiting is bullshit. They're going to say "yes."*

Let's do this damn thing already. His wristwatch now reads 9:15 AM.

He gives the signal, and three waiting teams simultaneously use large mallet hammers to bust off the front and back doorknobs and the lock on the storage shed. A second series of determined blows and two deadbolts pop right out of the doors, and the door swing open. The majority of the crew heads inside carrying large stacks of Tupperware containers and spools of bubble wrap. One team empties the shed. Two small crews quickly replace the doorknobs and dead bolts. Senator sets his wristwatch to mark the time and the seconds whir by. 00:00:45:11. Inside and operating in under a minute.

"In the meantime, we have taken the liberty to enroll both boys in a one-year seminar in computer applications and upcoming technologies for classrooms. They will complete all of their normal sixth-grade curriculum using state of the art computers in a personalized classroom setting. The classrooms are very close to your work, Mrs. Daisy, so that will hopefully be the most convenient."

Blue sees Mrs. Daisy's temperature cool off on the monitor as she is taking in all of the new information. She watches Mrs. Daisy's heart levels return to normal. This is the best window of opportunity. "Now, Sylvia. She's ready for the reveal."

"Mrs. Daisy, we've read your profile quite thoroughly, and we judge you to be of outstanding character. We take you for the live-to-work type, but understand us, should you decide to retire early, we will arrange that for you as well."

"Well, thank you," Mrs. Daisy accepts guardedly. *"But... Well I... Ma'am respectfully, who are you? And how do you*

know about me, or us, and why would you suddenly come into this young man's life?"

Kaldari drops DJ Dan to zero as he watches DuBell and Paul mouth "Oh shit" and giggle. Blue watches Loni's thermal color spike red and white.

Vercingetorix and HexxCat look at each other with concern.

Senator tenses up as he listens. Maybe he should have waited after all.

"I am Margaret Tate. I know about you because I paid to know. I've come into young DuBell's life now and not before because his mother and half-brothers were in the way. I am a smart woman and figured that sooner or later, I would have to step in and..."

"Excuse me," a stern voice comes from behind Senator. He turns to see a tall, trim, black woman in a blue bathrobe and hair rollers, with a rolled-up newspaper under her arm, smoking a cigarette. "May I ask what exactly you are doing here?"

"...restore order, but knew better than to rush in." Senator gracefully sweeps his hair back again and removes his earpiece. "Ah, yes ma'am. You must be..."—he consults his clipboard with a nod of his chin—"...Mrs. Hunter. Correct?"

"Yes?" she answers suspiciously.

"Hi, Mrs. Hunter. I work with a moving company"—he points to the drivers sitting under the tree—"and we were hired by Mrs. Daisy's insurance agency. Apparently as a rewards package, Mrs. Daisy won a contest and got a new house. As part of the promotion, we are here to move her instantly." He looks at her conspiratorially. "And we are using it as an opportunity to determine which summer interns stay on for fall. So, I imagine it's going to be done fairly quickly."

"She didn't tell me about winning any contest."

"She literally just found out herself. We at the company knew, but we had to keep it secret until this morning. We just got the go ahead on cellular from the company. Mrs. Daisy mentioned to us that you might inquire. That's how I knew your name, Mrs. Hunter. She said the two of you were closest in the neighborhood." Actually, routine surveillance told him so, but to Senator it's the same thing.

"Oh. Right." She pauses and thinks about it. "Well, how exciting!"

"If you will excuse me one moment, Mrs. Hunter." Senator steps up and directs a worker on which room to load next as a train of workers continue to flow out of the front door and back into the back door in a circuit. He slips his earpiece back over his ear.

Kaldari holds his breath. He releases it slowly. *Come on Sylvia. You've got this. Just like we rehearsed.* He utters nothing in the mic.

"If I had attempted to get him earlier, his mother would have bothered my legal team to no end, furthering the plotting of the half-brothers and giving DuBell false hope for rescue." To DuBell she pulls a face. *"My legal team is good, but not good enough to take you away from your mom with no reason."*

Looking back to Mrs. Daisy, she adds, *"I'm no fool. A woman in my position cannot afford to be. I've had my eyes on the three of you for quite some time, because people need friends and roots, even if they can't have family."*

"But what exactly is your position then? We need to understand. Are we being handled? Bought off? Silenced? Is there some request? I am also no fool. Nor can I afford to be for their sake, or mine."

"Wow, Mrs. Daisy is perceptive," Blue whispers to Kaldari. "If she only knew *how* handled they all were right now." Blue taps her pulse being read through the chair. "But her levels look good."

Kaldari nods in agreement and whispers into the group mic, "She's right where you want her, Sylvia."

Kaldari and Blue watch in separate monitors as Sylvia scrunches her nose and smiles a devilish smile at Mrs. Daisy and proclaims, *"I knew I was going to like you, Mrs. Daisy. Well, let's see. I am what some would label as old money, except I am the end of our line. Or rather, DuBell will be. Someday far from now. After he's earned his keep."* She explains this last part looking right at him. *"Your father's portion of the family inheritance was transferred back to me when he passed away and does not pass to you until you are thirty years of age, even if I die."*

"What's my dad's name?" DuBell questions matter of fact like he's asking, "What's for lunch?" On Blue's thermal imaging screen, DuBell's oranges and reds sparkle momentarily, making the screen fuzzy for a split second. Mrs. Daisy and Paul's heartrates visibly dip for a second. Blue wishes not for the first time that she had neural imaging power on everyone in the reception room.

"Whoa!" Blue exclaims. "Did you see his color shimmer?" Kaldari shakes his head no and turns around to join her on the thermals.

"She never told you your father's name? You don't know anything about your father? Nothing at all?"

"She said it didn't matter because it wasn't going to bring him back. That's all she ever said if I asked anything about him."

DuBell looks up at Sylvia, and even in the color blur of the thermal monitor Kaldari can see a glimmer of anger behind the sad. DuBell's color shimmers to a vibrant white gold.

"Dre and X used to say the same thing to me and laugh maniacally. But they were jerks, so you know."

"Yeah, I saw it that time," Kaldari runs his fingers through his hair. "But it's not worth telling Sylvia right now. Keep an eye on it though."

"Well. What can I tell you? His name was also DuBell. It is a family name. You are technically the eighth male to carry the name. You look like your father, but that is to say you look like a Tate male. I know as much as you concerning his marriage to your mother as I was away and not in contact with my brother at the time. After your father's death, your mother came around looking for your inheritance, but like I said, I'm the next in line until DuBell is thirty years old."

As everyone on headphones listens to Sylvia tell the story, they know it's not true, but the Mothers have rehearsed it with Sylvia so many times that by now they have almost convinced themselves that DuBell really is the heir to a mysterious fortune. Sylvia had shown them the entire file on Du-Bell, and they all knew that the cover story was fake for Mrs. Daisy's protection, but they also knew that the fake story was far more charitable than the real one.

According to the public police report accompanying DuBell's official birth certificate, on the night DuBell was born, Cinderella Jones showed up to the ER high out of her mind on some unknown substance, only wearing one shoe and ranting about flying too high and touching the sun. She was so high they couldn't drop her adrenaline rates in time, and she coded once on the table with DuBell still inside her before being resuscitated and pushing DuBell out in the process. The report also said, when she filled out the paperwork on the birth certificate, she told the charge nurse to put *DuBell* on both lines for Father and Child. No last name. No Jones. He was *not* to be named Jones.

Sylvia had also showed the Mothers newspaper clippings from the alternate time line, showing Cinderella Jones getting arrested for Dre and X's entire scheme ten years from now while DuBell is away at college; meanwhile his brothers remained at large, plaguing DuBell his entire life. Sylvia had argued to the Mothers that stepping up the time line of the arrest and taking the brothers off the street simultaneously was not only in their best interest, but a public service. No one had disagreed with her.

"The lawyers told your mother she was more than welcome to leave you with our family and never return, but she chose to keep you, we presumed waiting until you turned thirty."

DuBell sparks gold again all over his body, with the most intense color concentrating in his face. Blue thought it almost looked like a fox for a moment.

"Ever since then, we have watched over you from afar. It was all we could do really. But now." Sylvia raps her fingers on the table. *"Now, we can do a little bit more."* Sylvia smiles her best Cheshire grin.

"There's the signal for more coffee." Blue stands up, grabs the coffee carafe, and resets the tray with small cookies, mini scones, and a selection of small Danishes. She opens the door and steps out with the tray. *Nothing to see here. Just refreshments.*

Everyone briefly looks up at Blue in her yellow cardigan, then they all turn their attention back to Sylvia. Everyone except DuBell. He watches Blue intently as she approaches with the food, once again giving her the sensation that she is the food. *Wow. Just, wow.*

Blue sits down the tray on a side table out of line of sight, and there she arranges her plates, listening while pretending to not listen. *Sylvia is going in for the close now.*

"We are not infinitely wealthy, you understand, but we can present you with a comfortable home and with money for living expenses befitting a young man of your age."

Blue attends Mrs. Daisy's coffee first, acting as if she is slightly embarrassed to be in the way and trying to blend into the background. She gently places a plate of cookies in Mrs. Daisy's hand and turns to Paul Daisy. He looks as if he is watching the best television show ever. He takes more juice and a Danish with a quiet thank you, then tunes back into every word Sylvia is saying.

"But *if* Mrs. Daisy decides to sign this document," Sylvia taps the document, "and assume legal custody of you... and it is *her* decision first and foremost... *then* there will be a few rules. Or as Mrs. Daisy put it earlier, requests or provisions." The tap on the table makes DuBell look away from Blue, and he directs his attention front and center again. Blue wonders at Sylvia's mastery over the scene, how every little look, or pause in the script, or seemingly unintentional crossing of the ankles has been planned by Sylvia. Even Loni's genuine non-involvement in the planning of this operation is part of Sylvia's plan.

Over the last eight months, the Mothers have received extensive training from Sylvia on a number of subjects, one topic amongst them being hypnotic suggestion. Blue watches now with an informed eye to see how Sylvia is managing Du-Bell's attention with hand cues and subtly influencing Mrs. Daisy's decisions verbally, all the while making Mrs. Daisy feel fully in control of her own actions. Sylvia has been layering in the verbal cues that suggest the decision to take swift legal control over DuBell is the best choice *and* well within Mrs. Daisy's power. Sylvia is also setting it up so that everything to follow, the house, the car, the school, everything is merely the best move to make for everyone in the situation.

Which it is, in Blue's humble seventeen-year-old opinion.

Sylvia holds up a finger. "Number one and most important rule. You must *never* talk about our family or draw attention to our family name in any way. In upcoming years, as computers become more prevalent in schools and other places, you must never look us up. In due time, I will share all of our family history with you, and I wager it will be more than you care to know. But one thing has been true across time: we Tates have remained a private people. I cannot stress that enough.

"In order for us to remain private in the upcoming years, we must follow the rules. Never talk about the Tates. Never mention the Tates. If you meet another person with the last name Tate, don't say hi, because you aren't related. If you are forced to give a last name, or put a last name on anything, you put Daisy. In the event that Mrs. Daisy takes custody of you."

Sylvia holds up a second finger. "Number two, you will attend a four-year university. We expect you to attend, and successfully graduate, a four-year program. We don't care what you major in, so long as you go and apply yourself to study for at least four years. We will provide the basic tuition, room, and board for both you and Paul provided the school is in state. If you want to go out of state, you'll need to earn your own scholarship money."

Blue notices how the last few statements all imply Mrs. Daisy has already acquiesced to the agreement. Blue busies herself arranging the tray of snacks outside of the area of influence, watching and listening. DuBell and Paul just stare at each other and at Sylvia in disbelief.

"So... how would we go about this if we wanted to do this?" Mrs. Daisy nods one time to Sylvia.

"Oh, thank God. What bullshit! I knew they'd say yes!" Senator exclaims to no one at all; he is standing off by himself overseeing the unpacking of the shed. He stubs out his cigarette and steps inside the house to check the progress. He flows through the laundry room and kitchen, which are both empty and cabinets open wide. He inspects the refrigerator; it is also empty but not wiped clean. It's fine. Another crew will clean later before they rent the place out.

"You just sign these pages, and the rest will be arranged immediately. Mrs. Lore-Walker will handle all of the arrangements. Have I forgotten anything, Mrs. Lore-Walker?"

"*The car.*" Loni reminds almost despondently.

Vercingetorix gets to his feet and brushes off his slacks. He looks at his watch. 9:50 AM.

He extends his hand to HexxCat and pulls her to her feet. They walk over to the showroom and begin to examine the 3 Series. The bemused salesmen notice their movement and cannot help but come to offer assistance.

"Any word from the boss, then?" he chuckles.

"She wants six of these 3 Series. One in convertible. Fully loaded." Vercingetorix orders without looking away from the car.

"Umm … ahem … yes, six?" The salesman—his nametag says Daniel—is incredulous. He's wondering if this is a joke.

"Precisely," HexxCat confirms, fixing her languid stare on the man. "One for each day of the week."

He clears his throat. "Ha, wouldn't that be seven?"

Vercingetorix snaps to attention. He rounds on the man, speaking low and cool. "We don't drive the car on Sundays. Now can we please get started on the order. We are on a bit of a time crunch."

"And exactly how do you plan to pay for this?" Daniel enunciates exactly with incredulity.

They both look at Daniel as if he is a moron. HexxCat restrains herself.

"As amusing as it would be to materialize all of that cash in front of you right now …" HexxCat snaps her fingers, and she makes a black credit card appear in her empty fingers, followed by her driver's license, and then a wallet-sized, laminated, proof of insurance. Placing the cards neatly on the counter, she shoos him away with her hand. "Go and check them. Then hurry up and place our order. We really are in a hurry."

He looks at the cards in his hands and stutters, "Yes … Miss … Miss Tate. I'll be right back." He walks away shaking his head.

Vercingetorix turns and continues looking in the back seat of the 3 Series sedan. "Ahh … cup holders!"

"Oh, thank you, Mrs. Lore-Walker. Mrs. Daisy, are you attached sentimentally to your car? Or might you be persuaded to upgrade to something newer. It is in our best interest to take care of the arrangements now."

"Well, no. I'm not attached … I guess."

"Honestly, it is just a formality to ensure that you and the boys are in a reliable automobile with bumper-to-bumper replacement and roadside assistance. I have a connection at BMW. I'll let Mrs. Lore-Walker discuss the details."

"You should consider yourself blessed. She makes me ride the bus." Vercingetorix and HexxCat laugh. Sylvia would make them all ride the bus everywhere is she could. She was very kind to follow through on her graduation promise, even if they had to keep them at the garage and never show anyone and keep them registered under the Tate name. The Mothers were now full-fledged operatives.

"Now is not the time. But she brings up a fair point. I do not care for automobiles in general. I am only offering this to Mrs. Daisy because it will be necessary for her to get to work and to get you to and from school. Do not expect any sweet sixteen automobiles from me. In fact, you probably won't see me on your sixteenth birthday. Nor Christmas. Nor any other holiday, because let's face it, I'm a misanthrope."

Inside the quickly disappearing living room, Senator puts his back against a wall to stay out of the way as his three teams cycle through the tiny rooms and quickly bubble wrap, box, and remove the contents. Each bubble wrap gets a sticker coding the room it was taken from and the order in which it was wrapped. Senator wagers they will be ready to grab the large furniture and leave in about twenty minutes.

"In fact, you should expect to see very little of me until you become a fully formed human. Say about ten years or so. I mean you no disrespect, but children confuse me and irritate me, and as a woman with access to lockable vaults, well who's to say I might not accidentally-on-purpose forget to come and check on you and you asphyxiate. Perchance the real reason why Mrs. Daisy is the obvious suitable candidate, and not me. That is, if she wants the responsibility?"

Kaldari watches as all eyes in the room turn to Mrs. Daisy, but Mrs. Daisy only looks at DuBell. She looks at his bruised and swollen face and tells him, *"It's up to you if you want to have a new home and a new life with us. This is all a real dream come true, DuBell. I really did not expect this. Who could have? I honestly expected today to go very different."*

"Oh, believe me, Mrs. Daisy, I expected to be on my way to a boys' home by now, not hearing any of this. But these people could say we had to live in Weird Christine's shack in order for me to be with you and Paul, and I'd do it to be in your custody and no one else's. Just like we promised, we go home together."

"Just like we promised. But," Mrs. Daisy articulates slowly, *"I'm sure Paul's told you, I'm no pushover. I have rules. And not just Friday to Sunday rules. All the time rules, with*

consequences if you don't abide them. I imagine what they are speaking of is full guardianship." Mrs. Daisy looks to Loni. "*Is this correct?*"

"*That is correct.*"

"*So, I would have the power to discipline?*"

"*Absolutely,*" Sylvia confirms with surety.

Kaldari watches Blue on the monitor.

In the reception room, Blue discretely eats a mini scone and watches as DuBell reaches out to touch Mrs. Daisy on the arm. He fixes her with a powerful stare.

"Look, I understand what you are trying to say and all, but you have never, to the best of my knowledge, hit Paul with a folding chair WWF style. Nor have you drop-kicked him in the face. I guess what I'm trying to say is, compared to where I'm coming from, I'm fairly certain that any punishment doled out by you would be fair and just. So, can we please just say yes and do this thing? Before somebody takes this piece of paper away?"

"Very well," Mrs. Daisy pulls her eyes away from her second son. "Where do we sign?"

"Right here," Loni points to a series of *X*s on the paper. "Just initial each *X* until the last page, then sign, print, and date."

DuBell remains by Mrs. Daisy's side for each initial, and soon Paul is up and watching too. They both watch as Mrs. Daisy signs and prints her name and applies the date to the last page. They both hug Mrs. Daisy.

"Yes. Brothers now, *legal*," Paul gives DuBell a pound.

"*You* legal, brotha." DuBell does a tough guy face returning the pound, and the two boys clap each other on the back and fall to giggles. Mrs. Daisy rolls her eyes at the both of them.

Blue breaks into applause in her heart as she watches DuBell and Paul give their secret handshake. She steals away her joy and masks her face with a polite smile as she walks back toward the surveillance room, but Sylvia stops her as she goes.

Sylvia announces to the room, "I know it is early, but would anybody care for some Chinese delivery? I'm famished, and I know a great place that's just around the corner on Demonbreun. It won't take a second." Sylvia turns to Blue and uses her alias. "Susan, will you take everyone's order, please?" Blue smiles in compliance and immediately pulls out an order pad, as if she were in the café.

"Ooh, yeah!" DuBell snaps to attention, coming over next to her notepad. "I want some General Tso's chicken, some broccoli in hot garlic sauce, some eggrolls, some egg drop soup, and some crab rangoon. And extra fortune cookies. Please, *Susan.*"

Blue writes down the order with the cock of an eyebrow as he lightly places a hand against her arm. *Little mack-daddy scoundrel.*

Sylvia laughs at DuBell's enormous order. "Let me know if you forgot anything," she teases indulgently. "What about you, Big Poppa? Did DuBell leave anything in the restaurant for you to eat?"

"I like lo mein and pork, ma'am, if that's OK?" Paul answers in a shy, *who-me* voice.

"You are such a sweetheart. I take back everything I ever said about children. Mrs. Lore-Walker, I would like you dress

Paul in Armani and make him my plus one everywhere I go from now on. I just love him!"

Glancing at Blue's thermal screens, Kaldari watches the heat flush in Paul's cheeks. Kaldari laughs a little as he whispers into the mic, "All right, Extraction Team. The papers are signed. You are clear to enter. I will take all teams off mute once I have the all-clear from Sylvia. Fleet Team, be at stand-by for Loni to get the car order, which she should have shortly."

Senator cracks his neck and checks his wristwatch for time. 10:45 AM.

Well ahead of schedule. He walks over to the drivers to let them know it should be about fifteen minutes until they are ready to roll. He walks up the yard and back up to the house as Tripods and CC come out of the front door obviously looking for him.

"Got something you should see," CC chuffs bluntly, turning around to walk back in the exit door as more movers are walking out. He pushes them out of the way and walks back in. Tripods and Senator apologize but also make their way back through the train of movers through the front door, through the near-empty living room, and into the master bedroom, which is also mostly empty. CC and Jim London, hands in pocket, are in the room and Senator can tell someone is in the bathroom.

"Out." CC demands to the person packing up the tiny half-bathroom. Out pops a young lady with long blonde hair in a ponytail. As she passes, he stops her to take a better look. "Oh hey. I went to school with you, didn't I? Stacy, right?"

"Yeah, Chris." Stacy rolls her eyes exasperated.

"All right." He just stares at her, and she shakes her head and walks out. Senator apologizes and closes the door behind her.

"Chris. You went to school with like everyone here," Tripods explains with a small laugh.

"Even the drivers?"

"No, not them." Jim London shakes his head one time.

"Hmm." CC shrugs. "Anyways. Look at this shit, Sen." CC pulls a large decorative bag out of the closet and reaches inside and pulls out a shoebox full of twenty-dollar bills. "I figured someone might be upset if it went missing."

"Oh shit!" Senator chokes on his own words as he goggles. "Shiiit."

"And I found two thousand dollars in a pair of kid's jeans in the other room." Tripods adds. "What the hell is going on in here?"

"Shit." Senator's eyes go even wider trying to take it all in. He rocks back on his heels and shakes his head. "Not sure. But thanks for clueing me in. My boss will probably want to know about this."

"So. Do you expect they'll miss it?" CC puzzles digging his tongue in his right molar.

"Yes," Jim London, Tripods, and Senator echo.

"Hmm." CC shrugs again.

Kaldari monitors the reception room with DJ Dan now up on eight. Blue collects the last of the lunch orders and heads to surveillance. Loni talks Mrs. Daisy through the virtues of the BMW 3 series, with a convertible roof, CD player, and cellular phone for emergencies. Sylvia removes the papers before she excuses herself and steps back into the surveillance room. She closes the door.

"Great job, gang," she whispers. "I'm going to go back out there. Turn the heat up a touch. Turn the other team's mics on to your ears." She points to both Kaldari and Blue. "Keep me posted. Super proud of you both right now." Sylvia walks out the door and back into the reception room. Blue and Kaldari give a solid high five and get down to the business of placing lunch orders and checking the other teams.

After lunch Sylvia and Loni excuse themselves again to the back office leaving the trio alone in the conference room. They all monitor as DuBell grabs a third fortune cookie from the pile and cracks it open.

"Don't you keep expecting them to come in and say this is all some mistake? Like I'm not who they say I am?"

"No." They both say in unison.

"Why not? I mean, this is unreal. Fantasy world. This doesn't just happen to people."

"Yeah, but, Juice, that's what happens to you. Fantastical stuff. Normal stuff happens to normal people."

"Thanks. I'm abnormal. I get it. But listen. Last night, I had a dream, and in my dream, well … I can't tell you all, but someone I trust told me she is not my aunt." DuBell flashes gold.

Blue points. "There it goes again."

"That's just a dream. I looked over all the papers. She has full and total custody of you and has granted me guardian ad litem. This is all for real. And a bit abnormal." She laughs and they all laugh and shake their heads.

"It's all good." Sylvia shrugs. "They are just along for the ride now until tonight." She turns to face Loni and whispers,

"You were great."

"That was nerve-racking. I can't believe that it worked," she whispers back. "This is unreal, Sylvia. And you two were awesome. It really was like a ballet in the end."

"Thanks," they both respond quietly.

"That ballet was a genuine Loni Lore production." Sylvia smirks then smiles wide. "L-One laid all the bones and blueprints of that plan. We just made it come to life."

"Well, regardless of if I, or some other me, created it or not, my nerves are shot, and I'm going to the restroom upstairs. I will rejoin you shortly. Good job everyone." Loni exits surveillance through a door in the back.

Sylvia turns to Surveillance Team. "OK, Blue, let's get those papers officiated." Blue hops up and spreads out the necessary pages on the folding table. Sylvia steps over and places her hand on each one, instantly impressing a notarized seal and the inked signature of the witness on each. "Good. Now, get these papers delivered next door and see them filed, so that when they go to process him in a few days, they find the case has already been expedited by a higher-ranking internal audit. They will be effectively relieved of case-related actions and will submit their own paperwork and move on. Anyone that comes looking any further into DuBell, the Daisys, or the Jones family will automatically be routed to us directly. Go now. Be cool and calm."

"Always. Back soon." Blue slides the manila folder into her shoulder bag and exits surveillance using the same door as Loni.

Kaldari watches Blue go then looks back to find Sylvia watching him. "Hi," she blinks innocently with a smile.

"Gonna need you to check in with Fleet Team and get an ETA, then patch all mics into your headset and mine. Once we set sail with Fleet, you and Blue shut down the lights here and come meet us at the Sylvan House. Don't worry about cleaning. It can wait until after we dismantle."

"Copy that."

"And turn your music down or you are going to go deaf."

"Eh? What's that you say?" he does his best deafened old man voice. Sylvia shakes her head at Kaldari and reenters the reception room.

"Everything is just about in order if you will follow me, we are going on a brief field trip to Haverty's to select some bedroom furniture for the boys. Mrs. Daisy, we expect you will want to get a feel for the house before you decorate but you can at least get a feel for what's available."

"Oh, now?"

"Yes, I find that it is best to take care of everything at once. Once everyone has collected themselves and gone to the restroom our rides should be here. Ah, and here is Mrs. Lore-Walker. We are just about ready to depart."

Kaldari radios in to check on the Fleet Team's progress. "Hey, lovebirds."

"Rowwwwrr!" HexxCat articulately growls in response. The salesman jumps at her sudden affectation.

"Sylvia wants to know how long until you'll be here."

"Daniel here was just finishing up. Isn't that right, Daniel?"

She appears to be talking to herself, but Daniel realizes she's talking to someone in her ear. "Um ... yes, ma'am, Miss

Tate," he stammers out. "Almost finished. They are just making sure they have five fully loaded sedans on the lot. The convertible is being washed now."

"Well, don't wait for all of them." Kaldari buzzes in their ears. "Have them delivered and come on over. Sylvia wants to leave in fifteen minutes."

HexxCat looks at Vercingetorix's watch. 10:55 AM.

"There'll be lunch traffic. Give us eighteen."

Daniel realizes they are both talking in their ears. *Who the hell were these kids?*

"I'll see if I can stall, just get moving, both of you." Kaldari starts to sign off then adds, "You two are now open mic access with call signs. Over."

"Roger that. Over." HexxCat signs off.

Are these people military? Daniel thinks as he begins to type faster.

"Daniel," HexxCat affects a smile that is official and frightening, "we'll take two of the sedans right now and leave you to wrap this up. Here is the address for the delivery of the convertible, and this is the address for the delivery of the other sedans. This is the temporary access code; see that they are all placed inside the garage with room left to park the two we are taking now."

"Ye-yes. Yes, Miss Tate." *Anything to get you scary people away from my desk,* Daniel thinks. He presses a button that rings down to the service desk.

"Go for Carl," blurts out of the speaker phone.

"Hey, Carl, how are we doing on that order for Miss Tate?"

"Well, it's a real pain in the keister is how we're doing. It's..."

Daniel cuts Carl off. "Can you go ahead and pull around two sedans fully loaded. We can just peel the stickers off and do the paperwork afterwards."

Carl sounds flabbergasted. "Uhm…Sure thing, Dan. Do you have a color preference?"

Dan swallows hard and repeats, "Do you have a color preference?"

HexxCat and Vercingetorix blink twice. "Black."

Seventeen minutes later HexxCat pulls into the lead parking spot and Vercingetorix zips in right behind her. They hop out of the car.

"Vixen." Vercingetorix clutches his fist at her. "You knew I wouldn't mow that lady down on the crosswalk. You are so cunning."

"It's the car. It moves like a dream," she purrs. They kiss.

Kaldari watches on the monitors as Sylvia and Loni escort his smurfs back down the hallways and out the front door exit where he can see HexxCat and Vercingetorix waiting to motorcade. They place Mrs. Daisy, DuBell, and Paul in the second car with Vercingetorix as driver. Sylvia and Loni ride in the back of HexxCat's sedan. HexxCat pulls forward out of her parking spot and off they go to the department stores.

Go forth and conquer, Kaldari thinks to them.

"How's it coming Extraction Team?" Kaldari calls out, switching over channels.

"Finally. Shit, man."

"What's up?"

"What's up? Patch me to Sylvia, that's what's up."

"We're all clear. All Mothers, Sylvia, and Loni."

"What's the problem, Senator?" Sylvia calls over the coms in a sweet tone.

"Some of my people uncovered a huge fucking bag of cash. That's the problem. There's cash stashed all over this house?"

"OK, where are we in the move?"

Senator glances around the tiny house and there is little but packing tape and bubble wrap left in the three bedrooms, and some junk drawers in the kitchen. "All but done."

"I guess it's lucky for you they said yes then, hmmm?" Kaldari can read Sylvia's tone is prickly, but Senator ignores her jab and presses his case.

"They were always going to say 'yes.' The plan is amazing. But seriously, what should I do with this cash?"

"Put it in your car and keep it safe. Who found the money? Do we need to worry about them talking?"

"CC, Jim London, and Tripods from the Halflings, but that's it."

"Do we… have to worry… about them talking?" Sylvia repeats slowly.

"Well, CC and Jim London aren't what you'd call *talkers*. Tripods claims he won't tell anyone but that means he won't tell anyone other than Chance. Chance won't talk about it if we make it worth his while. He's reasonable and harmless. All of the Halflings are good guys."

"He's only saying that because he doesn't have breasts," HexxCat argues over the mic. Blue shrugs to Kaldari and puts her hands up. Kaldari knows better than to respond to HexxCat's claim.

Senator jumps back in. "Really the problem is Fry Guy. He wouldn't say anything intentionally, but he stays incredibly high all of the time, and he might say something not meaning to."

"Yeah, but the likelihood of someone listening to him, deciphering his coded speech, and then believing him is actually low," Kaldari counters.

"Regardless, let's arrange a meeting with the Halflings." Sylvia pauses for a moment. "Set it up for Friday evening; I'll see what I can arrange by way of entering them into the family… or erasing their memories. We'll have to start acquiring more people at some point; we may as well incorporate a few sooner rather than later. But that doesn't mean we tell them anything yet. We will all meet and discuss first. In the meantime, tell me more about the money you found. You said it was all over the house. Where? How much? How is it arranged?"

"Really just in two places, but a ton of it. One closet has boxes of stacks of bills in it. At a guess, well over ten thousand dollars. Tripods found two thousand dollars in Paul's room on his desk."

Sylvia thinks for a single moment, then gives her orders. "Go to the bank and draw out two thousand. Replace that money in DuBell's room. Place it in a dresser drawer. He'll find it. Bring the rest of the money to me. It has to be the money from his brother's scheme. We'll figure something out. Good job, Senator."

"Thank you, Sylvia."

"Except you broke ranks and went ahead of schedule. So, I judge you should not get your BMW." Sylvia informs Senator.

"I want his BMW," Loni smiles.

"Loni gets your BMW."

"What! That's BULLSHIT!" Senator screams in panic. "I call bullshit!"

"Did you break my rules?" Sylvia questions.

"They were going to say yes!"

"Did you break my rules?" she repeats cool as a freezer pop.

"I waited until I knew they were going to say yes."

"Hmmm. Be safe driving over to the bank. Have your team get suited up while you run that errand. By the time you finish everyone should have suits on ready to walk in."

"Sylvia."

"What, Senator?"

"Do I get my BMW?" Senator's tone is just shy of imploring.

"Did you break my rules?" she smirks so hard it is visible over the intercom. Kaldari can fully visualize her batting her android eyelashes.

"Bullshit!"

Kaldari and Blue shut down the room. They unplug everything except the audio equipment. They put the dishes in the sink. Kaldari thinks about kissing Blue but thinks perhaps she wouldn't want that. Instead, he involuntarily messes with his hair. "You did an amazing job today. This whole year, you've done a really great job."

"Thanks, man. You too. I really appreciate that. What do you say we get outta here? Go catch up with the Extraction Team."

"You sure you don't want to catch up with DuBell? He seems my-tee interested, Miss Susan."

"I know! It's rather frightening honestly. I didn't know little boys could give looks quite like that. If I were any younger, I might actually fall for DuBell." Blue worries that her last statement might be the truth. She shakes her head. "I'm safer going to Bellevue to hang out with Chance Black and the Halflings."

Kaldari flips off the lights in reception, and they step out into the main hallway. He and Blue push the oversized door closed. Kaldari looks at his watch. 11:30 AM. "If we hustle over to the station, we should be right on time for the next bus to Bellevue."

Blue holds up her hand and magically produces a tiny green key from nowhere. Kaldari applauds. The key is disproportionately small compared to the vault door, but she deftly twists it to secure the lock. "We're not in any rush," Blue shrugs as she tucks the key away in a pocket. Checking that she has herself arranged to travel, she takes Kaldari by the hand exhales. "This morning was very cool, but intense and stressful. Now that our part is done, I say we take our time." They turn and begin to walk down the hall. "Plus," Blue adds conspiratorially, "they've dropped Mrs. Daisy's car off at our garage now. Sylvia said we get to drive it to the new house."

Kaldari realizes in this instant that holding hands makes a distinct sound in his brain.

The sound of traffic whizzing by makes a humming rhythm in Senator's mind. Even stopping by the bank first, Senator manages to beat the moving truck and most of the moving crew across town from Antioch to Bellevue. He drives like a young man possessed the whole time, wondering if Sylvia is messing with him about withholding his new car. As he arrives with a small screech of the tires, he checks the clock on the dash of his decidedly crap car. 11:45AM.

As the rest of the moving crew pulls into the cul-de-sac, Senator has them arrange their cars up the street, so they can leave room for the moving trucks to turn around. Smoking a cigarette, Senator walks around and shoots the shit with everyone, making sure they are still good for round two. He checks his wristwatch out of habit at this point. 12:00 PM.

Chance Black shows up in a dirty, golden brown, mini station wagon with Tripods, Jim London, and CC in tow. They pile out of the car, and Senator thinks that they haven't changed at all since they left high school. Had he, he wonders? Chance is wearing his standard black t-shirt, tight blue jeans, and black biker boots. His long blonde hair hangs to the middle of his back. He wears his trademark horn rim glasses. He's dressed opposite of CC with his shorn red hair and white t-shirt and jeans. It's not on purpose, Senator knows. CC could have just as easily shown up with no shirt and no jeans. Senator is closest with Tripods out of the entire Halflings crew, but he was given instructions to focus on Chance, so that's exactly what he does.

Senator absent-mindedly tells everyone to go get some cold waters from the trunk of his car. Chance Black opens the trunk and gleefully announces, "All right! That's what I'm talking about, Sen! Fuck water, I'm having a beer."

Senator jumps up. "Those are for later!" But Chance already has a beer and is handing one to Chris. "OK, dingus, but save the rest for later."

"Where did you even get beer from?" Chance grills Senator with a look of real interest.

"Shelley Jackson."

"Ah, yeah. I forgot you grew up next to her." Chance goons and strikes a pose. "She's fuckin' hawt!"

"Yeah," everyone nearby agrees, and they all crack a beer. Senator eyes his watch. It reads 12:15 PM.

When the moving trucks arrive, Senator's teams are already suited up in protective foot gear and have clearly marked all of the entrance and exit routes throughout the house. Right behind his own moving trucks, a delivery truck from Haverty's furniture shows up, and Senator directs the Haverty's movers to go first and assemble their furniture pieces in the empty rooms. While the new bedroom furniture is being assembled inside the house, Senator's teams unload the two moving trucks onto the large front lawn, using the sticker system to separate the bubble wrapped and boxed objects into what room they belong in.

During the sorting party, Kaldari and Blue arrive in Mrs. Daisy's BMW convertible, coasting down the street from the top of the hill. Seeing them in the new car encourages Senator to hustle his movers along faster. He barely notices Kaldari and Blue gladly grabbing beers and saying hey to the Halflings and everyone else on the lawn while they drink. A few minutes later, Senator looks up, and Kaldari, Blue, and the Halflings have all conspicuously disappeared. He continues orchestrating the unpacking, clipboard in hand. He overlooks the obvious bullshit.

By the time the stoners all return, red-eyed and goofy-grinned, the sorting out of the moving trucks is nearly done, and the Haverty's movers are finished assembling the new bedroom furniture. Once more, Senator consults his watch. 1:30 PM.

Time to get the real party started.

To his assorted team, he uncharacteristically shouts, "OK, everyone listen up! This is just like earlier only in reverse!" Senator holds up a stopwatch above his head. "Your packing time was an hour and thirty minutes. Let's see if we can beat that on unpacking. On your mark. Get set. Go!" He presses the button. Senator knows that every one of these kids, with the exception of the Halflings, *will* move faster just to try to beat their old time. The power of the clock.

Once the main swarm of movers is in motion, Senator heads over to where Kaldari and Blue and the Halflings are all leaned up against Chance's car smoking cigarettes. "Hey, Chance, were you able to do that favor for me?"

"Yeah, it's in the car. You got my money, yo?" Chance affects his fake Brooklyn accent.

"Four hundred dollars." Senator is cool as he pulls out an envelope of crisp bills from the bank.

"Where the hell are you guys pulling this money from?" Chance shakes his head blowing out a cloud of smoke. He pulls his long blonde hair back in a ponytail. "And look at all this furniture and shit on this lawn. Damn, y'all." Senator can tell Tripods has already managed to tell Chance about the bag of money they found.

Kaldari speaks up. "It's funny you should ask, Chance, because our boss was looking to hire some people. If you and the Halflings are interested."

"Do I have to piss in a cup?"

"No."

"Then I'm interested."

"Well," Senator grins, "what do you say we go set this up?"

Everyone agrees. Tripods and Jim London help Chance grab several large shopping bags from his back seat, and CC gets another beer from Senator's trunk. Kaldari assures Senator they can get more beer later, and they all head inside following the train of movers through the front door.

HexxCat drives at a safe speed as they leave the Target parking lot and head onto the I-65 to head across town to Bellevue. Loni and Sylvia are in the back seat. Loni looks exhausted but composed. Sylvia looks her normal polished self. Loni looks at Sylvia. "I know that you are an android and all, but can't you have the decency to look a little run down after all of that adventure?"

"What? That? That was nothing. You want to see an exhausting show, you should see a wedding planner in mid-June."

HexxCat really admires Sylvia. *She is tough. Funny. Sexy. Robotic. She is such a badass.* HexxCat likes Loni too, but she hasn't had enough time to get to know her yet. According to Sylvia, Loni is the one real central figure in all of this apart from DuBell, and that Loni's involvement over the years is key to the whole plan, so HexxCat will do everything in her power to keep Loni good and safe. No matter what.

"Do you even experience fatigue?" Loni groans.

"If I choose to, I can experience anything a normal human does."

"But you don't."

"Would you?" The android cocks her eyebrow quizzically.

"Sylvia?"

"Yes, Loni?"

"Hush."

HexxCat smiles at the banter and navigates toward the 440 West ramp with Vercingetorix square in her rearview mirror. He looks put out.

She thinks about her life and smiles. Tomorrow she will get up and attend a few of her senior year classes. Tonight, she will watch the others drink in celebration. Today, she has helped to pull off a series of amazing magic tricks, all based on the promise that their combined actions will help to tug the universe into alignment, within her lifetime.

She's not sure if she believes all of that—that DuBell will pull off some great achievement in the future because of their help—but she believes what she's seen with her own eyes. HexxCat literally watched Sylvia time-travel and re-build herself from the printer parts and computer code. Um, hello, Riot-Android-Shero-Crush-of-two-centuries. It just didn't get more badass than that. But if that isn't enough, at this very moment, she's driving a brand-new 3 Series, simply for trusting Sylvia and trusting the plan, and doing her part to support the team.

Vercingetorix breathes a sigh of relief as he *finally* approaches the exit ramp to Bellevue Newsom Station following at a safe distance behind HexxCat. He checks the time on the dashboard of his brand-new BMW: 2:55 PM.

Dear God, get me there without murdering him. Vercinge-torix thinks for the tenth time as he watches DuBell press his face up against the window and blow his cheeks out at passing cars.

For the combined two hours that Vercingetorix has spent with DuBell this afternoon, driving from downtown to Haverty's, then to the bank, then to Target. and now to Bellevue, the boy has not stopped defiling and crawling and climbing all over *his brand-new BMW*. Vercingetorix nears to actual anger, when he looks at Mrs. Daisy, and he sees that she is unmoved by the child's antics.

Shaking his head at himself, Vercingetorix calms down as he realizes his feelings have gotten the better of him. He decides to meditate and find a path forward. He stares at the road, then back to the rearview mirror. He gazes back to the road ahead intently. His path forward requires a *new* new car. After a moment he exhales as he ruminates. *Maybe I can convince Sylvia to let me swap this car with Senator's.* Vercingetorix smiles again at the completeness of this fresh idea.

DuBell uses his shirt sleeve to wipe off his saliva so he can get a better look out of the window. He spies a movie theater off the exit to the right, and he scrambles on top of Paul to get a better look. As they come around the bend and enter Bellevue proper, DuBell excitedly bangs on the back of Vercingetorix's headrest when he sees a tall Toys "R" Us sign in the distance. *Bang away, little dude. Get Senator's new car nice and broken in for him.*

DuBell points out everything he sees and loudly shouts. Everywhere they look is more cool stuff for DuBell to gush about. A Baskin-Robbins. A RadioShack. A Publix. He's never been in a Publix before. He checks to see if Vercingetorix has been in a Publix. Vercingetorix looks at Mrs. Daisy, who sits with her hands folded in her lap like the image of a saint. How did Sylvia ever convince this sweet woman to accept custody of this child?

Heading right on Sawyer Brown Road, Vercingetorix passes by a hive of condos and houses, and it is obvious that DuBell has never really seen anything like this up close. Sunlight plays on every passing car and every person just right, so they sparkle. People are out jogging or riding bikes. DuBell sees girls on rollerblades on the tennis court down one of the sidewalks and nudges Paul enthusiastically. Vercingetorix turns the car down Highway 70 and passes the Harpeth River and the golf range before coming to another rabbit warren of houses facing downhill, backed up to the woods of an adjacent farm. The sign reads *Sylvan Hills*.

Vercingetorix follows HexxCat as she turns her car right into the neighborhood, and they slowly drive down the hill for another quarter of a mile. Vercingetorix thinks *neighborhood* may be a premature word given that there are currently only four of forty houses built on the existing lots; for now, the lots remain green hillside divided by tiny orange-and-yellow flags sticking up at the corners. As the two sedans approach the bottom of the hill, Vercingetorix and Mrs. Daisy get a good view of a two-story house, tan aluminum siding and rose-colored brick, with a two-car garage and a paved driveway. The house sits alone at the end of the cul-de-sac swarming with teams of movers. Two moving trucks are parked facing up the street and workers are closing the back doors of the trucks right as Vercingetorix parks the car. He steps out to open the door for Mrs. Daisy. Just as everyone is out of the car, the large moving trucks pull away revealing the full expanse of the house and neighborhood, and the magic trick is completed in a bizarre clockwork motion. Vercingetorix confirms the time on his wristwatch; it is 3:05 PM.

"What in the world?" Mrs. Daisy exclaims with a gasp.

HexxCat walks over, and Vercingetorix takes her hand, and they happily kiss once. As he takes stock of Senator and the Extraction Team's moving scene, he sees the bosses approaching to direct the final phases in the plan.

Sylvia and Loni stand beside Mrs. Daisy and Paul and DuBell. Sylvia throws her hands wide and the sun glints across her crafted fingernails. "Welcome home, everybody. What do you think?"

"This is our house?! For real?" DuBell screams in amazement. He takes off like a dog free from the leash and runs the perimeter of the house. Paul just laughs and watches his friend and takes it all in looking up and down the street and around himself to the dark woods across the way.

Mrs. Daisy turns and looks from Sylvia to Loni and gapes utterly amazed. "How is this possible?"

"Consider your nursing unit," Sylvia replies while watching the workers on the lawn. "You have about six women on staff, and you handle, what, thirty cases each day?"

"We had forty-two on the board on Thursday," Mrs. Daisy corrects proudly.

"Well, there you go. You see what six skilled and motivated nurses can accomplish. Now, see what fifty motivated people can accomplish."

DuBell comes around the corner visibly apoplectic with delight. "The house has a swimming pool! This is the best day of my life! Can we get in it tonight, Mrs. Daisy? Please?" To Sylvia he verifies, "Is it heated? Does it have lights? Is there a hot tub too?"

As they walk over to the driveway, Loni points to Blue and Kaldari standing and chatting next to a brand-new BMW 3 Series convertible with the roof down. "That one is yours." Loni hands the keys to Mrs. Daisy.

Kaldari and Blue step aside and let Mrs. Daisy look inside her new car. Mrs. Daisy is rendered speechless as the entire scene finally becomes very real to her. Sylvia takes Mrs. Daisy by the arm and shows her the driveway and the roses that she got to match the ones at the Antioch house. DuBell and Paul appear. DuBell gives a quick "Hi, Susan," but he's too stimulated with new input to flirt properly. The boys ask Sylvia if they can look inside, and she defers to Mrs. Daisy who manages to instruct around her awe, "yes, but go slow." Kaldari can see that Sylvia and Loni have Mrs. Daisy firmly in hand.

Senator suggests the boys wrap their shoes with the blue foot covers and pretend they are astronauts. DuBell compliments Senator on the bright orange color of his hair. The boys laugh and crack jokes as they suit up for a space mission into the new landing zone of their Martian space base.

Senator follows them inside the base, as they explore. Stairwell and presumably a second living quarter is off to the right. Kitchen and dining unit to the left. Observation deck and computing area. Coming back to the center of the base, the explorers stand in the relaxation unit looking at its twenty-foot ceilings and testing the modular lights.

Off to the right, behind the stairwell, the explorers find the sleeping quarters for Commander Daisy. Workers flow in and out of the quarters and flow around the corner from her room and through a hallway. The boys follow to find laundry recyclers and access to an open airlock portal, presumably where the Commander's new *black* 3 Series Beamer would soon be docked. Workers outfitted in matching shoe covers wave and smile to DuBell and Paul as they continuously spill out of the airlock and through the portal back to where Commander Daisy is speaking with the Martian ambassadors. The explorers speculate that a giant air shield must be over the house providing temporary artificial atmosphere for all of the workers to breath. Senator suggests that the boys bypass the airlock and explore the portal adjacent with the flight of steps leading up.

DuBell leads the exploration unit through the portal and up the steps. As his head clears the landing, he is once again overcome with joy as he sees the emerging form of a pool table. On the wall is a rack with pool sticks and triangles and chalk. Paul comes up the steps to discover what DuBell has already found.

As Senator clears the landing behind the boys, they all hear, "Aw, fuck you with your banana peels! Get outta here with that shit."

"Sucks for you."

Senator turns around to find Chance Black on a futon and Tripods and Jim London in a pair of matching La-Z-Boy recliners, each with a remote in hand. "Hey, language, guys," Senator chides.

"From the king of *bullshit* himself. Get over here and pick up that fourth remote."

"Hey, Chance, for real. There are kids here, dude."

Chance looks up from the game. "Oh! So, there are." His lips sour like he's sucking lemon. "Sorry for that, children. Ignore the last few moments, as we...ah, shit again, Jim?"

"That's how the game is played," Jim London retorts with a dry chuckle as he laps Chance's spinning Bowser avatar.

"How's this for big, Daze?" DuBell waves his hands gameshow style to the 40-inch television currently displaying *Mario Kart*.

"It's getting there." Paul gives a big nod of his head looking out the window at all the movers. "Let's go see the pool."

"All right," DuBell agrees, but as he walks over, he picks up remote four. "Well, hold up. Let me win this really quick."

"Ohhh. OK. Talkin' shit kid."

"Chance!"

"Oh yeah, my bad."

After DuBell wins a round of *Mario Kart* to the yells of *beginner's luck* the boys start back down the steps and Senator tails them. As they all come around the corner Senator sees Loni.

"Oh. I was just coming to look for you boys. They've got your rooms put together. If you want to come and take a look."

"Thank you, ma'am." DuBell has a genuine, polite voice. He turns to follow but adds, "do you write for the newspaper, ma'am? The *Nashville Banner*?"

Surprised, she responds, "Why yes, I do, or rather, I did up until very recently."

DuBell nods, then scrunches up his nose. "Oh. So, is Loni Lore a made-up name if your real name is Lore-Walker?"

"No," she explains with a smile. "Loni Lore is my real name. Walker is my married name. But," she leans in conspiratorially, "Loni Lore sounds better in print, so I guess it it's a little of both really."

"Well, Lore-Walker is cool too. Sounds like you know the force."

"Oh, but I do, young Jedi. Now, run along and let the workers know if your room is suitable."

"Yes ma'am," the boys respond.

Loni looks at Senator wide-eyed disbelieving DuBell's uncanny abilities, but Senator is wide-eyed over the fact that Loni instantly got a Star Wars reference *and* lobbed one right back. He may have found his new master.

Loni smiles to Senator and shakes her head. "Oh, just so you know, the other workers have gone."

"Thanks, Loni." Senator adjust his hair under his Cubs hat. "Oh, there are still a few of our crew up in the bonus room, but they'll leave whenever you tell them to."

"We have it all in hand. Go see if the boys like your handiwork."

The boys are already around the corner and up the front steps. Senator clears the top of the landing and looks right just in time to see DuBell darting out of the bathroom and into Paul's bedroom. The hallway explodes with the soundtrack of *oh damnnnn, Big Daaaze,* and *all right, all right,* and *yeahhh boiii, living big.* Senator smiles. He thinks Paul's room turned out pretty awesome too.

The room has dark hardwood floors, and the décor is all black and white: there is a wide window facing west with long black curtains; a white dresser with a long mirror, black handles on the drawers; a black art desk with a white computer, a little Apple Macintosh monitor and keyboard; and a queen size bed with a black comforter and black-and-white pillows. Designed like his room in Antioch, a corkboard with pushpins is mounted on the wall by the door with Paul's exact same *3 Feet High and Rising* poster. All of the posters, CDs, books, magazines, and shoes are set up just like Senator and the movers found them at the little house this morning.

"Insane. It's just insane," DuBell whispers to Paul.

"I know. Check it. I have a walk-in closet."

"What?"

"And look," Paul points into the back, "there's a little door that leads to a crawlspace in the rafters."

"Wow," DuBell whispers as he climbs in, then back out.

"I know. I figured you dig that. Ain't no way I'm going in there." They close the crawl space door and find themselves in the walk-in closet with Paul's new wardrobe and old clothes all hung up neatly.

"I wonder what my room looks like," DuBell says trying unsuccessfully to make his fingers touch from wall to wall.

Paul gives DuBell a push. "Let's go see."

They back out of the closet and head out of Paul's room to find Senator waiting. The boys look over the rail of the upstairs landing and down into the living room. The couch from Mrs. Daisy's house has been set up beside her end tables, and her widescreen television has been pushed up where a fireplace might normally go. The little circle table where just the night before they counted the money out is sitting downstairs in a dining area. The boys marvel at how the furniture looks different and smaller in triple the space.

They eventually drift into DuBell's room, which at first glance is definitely smaller than Paul's room, but the amazing view makes the space feel absolutely enormous. DuBell's window looks east away from the adjacent subdivisions, back toward downtown Nashville, for about a half a mile unobscured, half greens and half blues and whites. He and Paul stare for a moment in silence.

DuBell's room is decorated modestly: no posters or art on the walls, nothing in the room lacking function. Senator had wanted to get DuBell some toys or some kind of kid-oriented gift since the boy had moved with almost nothing, but Sylvia said it was very important to *not* do that for DuBell. Senator was not going to break the rules twice. In this room, there is only the matching bedroom set DuBell picked out at Haverty's, which includes the twin bed set with the short teakwood headboard, the wooden desk also in teak with two side drawers and lateral drawer under the desk, and a tall slender wooden dresser, five drawers, with no mirror. There is a large papasan chair in the corner sizeable enough that DuBell could curl up and lounge on it like a cat, or Paul Daisy could comfortably sit on it much like a golf ball sits on the tee. DuBell also has an Apple Macintosh on the corner of the desk, but his real delight is that he has a phone, a white plastic office phone with spiral cord. "Oh my God, the girls we will call tonight." He turns to Senator. "Is it Paul's old number?"

"Downstairs is. This line is yours."

"Shut up! No way." DuBell and Paul communicate volumes in silent looks and head nods.

"What's the number?"

"It's written down on the base of the phone, but listen, it rings out as private. You should really keep it that way. Just tell people you aren't allowed to give it out. It will make you mysterious."

DuBell nods listening to the advice. "Yeah. Cool. Thanks, Mr.?"

"The name is Senator."

"Thanks, *Senator*."

"You're welcome."

DuBell opens his closet and is let down that no walk-in and no hidden doorway into the rafters awaits. Instead, there is only a normal closet, but it is filled with clothes that Sylvia bought for him ages ago. They all fit DuBell both in his size and his style: clean lines and fresh folds. In the floor of the closet, there are several pair of shoes to match the clothes: Adidas in black with white stripes, FILAs in red with blue lettering, and white Air Jordan double laces. Up on a rack are a series of hats meant to accent the outfits. Senator remembers the kids that dressed like that at school—Baker, Thad—sort of breakdance B-Boy/graffiti kids meets Sunday best. They weren't posers, or mods, in fact, they could really get down and raise some hell, but above all else they valued style.

As DuBell starts to explore his dresser drawers Senator decides to give the boys some privacy. After a perfunctory, "Rooms all good, guys?" and receiving a reply in the affirmative, Senator pulls the door slowly closed and walks to the steps. He knows that in the top drawer DuBell will find packs of new underwear, and in the second drawer he will find packs of new socks, and in the next drawers he will find some new cargo shorts and swim trunks, and even a little shaving kit with deodorant. And in the very bottom drawer, DuBell will find the replacement two thousand dollars that was stashed in Paul's room earlier this morning. Sure enough, as he rounds the stairs at the bottom of the landing, he hears DuBell speaking in a hushed tone to Paul, but he distinctly hears Paul say *twenty g's.*

Senator heads outside and sees that all of the workers are gone, no doubt going to prepare themselves for the Mothers' promised afterparty. The sun is going lower, but he'll make it back across town before dark. He walks around the left side of the house toward DuBell's view, and he continues around the house until he finds Loni and Sylvia on the side lawn talking with Mrs. Daisy.

DuBell and Paul walk out the back door and start to head over, when Paul informs DuBell that they are still wearing their foot scrubs. They pause to remove them before approaching the adults.

"Well, what do you reckon, sir?" Sylvia tests. "Will it do?"

"It's pretty awesome. I like the Nintendo setup. I was just debating switching to the new PlayStation, but for now it'll do, I guess."

"Actually, we only bought you the console to have a port system and access to the controllers. Next to the console, you will find a small box preloaded with every Nintendo and Sega game ever made. I have a friend." She waves her hand as if it's nothing. "Some of those games have never been released. Only beta tested. But I digress. Is there anything non-video-game-related that needs addressing?"

"Well, not to be rude, but is the twenty thousand dollars in the house somewhere, or did your team take it from Mrs. Daisy's house?"

"DuBell!" Mrs. Daisy gasps, shocked at his outburst and admission of the money.

"I mean, don't get me wrong. I am *well* aware that all of this,"—he points to the house and yard and pool and all around himself in a circle—"far exceeds $20,000, and if you tell me that's the cost for this then so be it, but I went through one hell of a beating in order to get that money you know, so I deserve to know." Here he points to his face and makes a circle around it with his finger.

"Good." Sylvia squints her left eye as she digs at her back tooth with her tongue, unphased by DuBell. "I like a young man who can get down to business. Well, the hard fact is that no matter how well-laundered it may be, that money was obtained illegally. If that money is traced back to you, or Mrs. Daisy and Paul, she could go to jail, and you and Paul could end up in a boys home or worse. And my lawyers might not be able to stop it."

"Fine," DuBell concedes calmly. "What's going to happen to the money then?"

"What do you want to have happen to that money? You can't keep it or tie it to your name in any way."

"I don't know?" DuBell throws his hands up. "Something good. And fun. And cool. Something that helps people."

"What about the Special Olympics?" Loni suggests. "That helps people, and it is cool and fun."

DuBell thinks about it for a moment. "OK, I guess that's fair. But just my half. Paul gets to choose his own."

Paul shrugs his shoulders. "I don't know what to do with that much money."

"Think big, Daze. That's what you be telling me."

Paul put his hand to his chin, then looks at his mom. He smiles and looks at Sylvia. "I want to donate my part to elephants. If I can." Paul's mother looks up at him with a bizarre look. Paul stutters and adds, "And a little to the church, of course." Now Mrs. Daisy is staring wide-eyed at Paul.

Sylvia purses her lips. "Well, let's see." She makes a look that Senator has seen before: a quick glance up that indicates she is thinking. Of course, for Sylvia *thinking* means she is using her vast computing power to quickly scry down multiple tunnels of information, looking to see if there is indeed a way to anonymously donate to elephants. A mere moment later, as if she were just remembering the perfect solution to the problem, she nods her head. "Yes. Yes, I'm sure we can arrange that request. Once it's all settled, I will present both of you with receipts from the anonymous donations as proof."

"Lady, you just gave us a house. I mean, unless this is some trick, and you plan to kill us all in our sleep and harvest our organs, I don't suppose you have much more to prove. I just asked you about the money, and you didn't hesitate. I trust you."

Sylvia looks cool as always. "Why thank you, DuBell. I hope to maintain your trust so that when I see you many, many years from now we may cultivate a friendship built upon it."

"Sure thing," DuBell mimics all hunky-dory. Senator thinks at first that this is DuBell's way of trying to keep as cool as Sylvia, but then DuBell adds, "And really, as far as the money goes, if you say it puts these people at risk," he points to Mrs. Daisy and Paul, "I say good riddance. It was stupid of me to go after it in the first place. Give that up to the gods above, because we've got the real prize right here. I just needed to know for my own sanity, or else I would have wasted countless hours wondering."

"Yes. That is why I prefer being upfront. It wastes less time, and in the long run it is far more accurate than wondering. And yes. Let us all consider it an offering in the name of things to come." Sylvia takes in the entire scene: Loni, the Mothers, the Halflings, Mrs. Daisy, Paul, and DuBell.

"In the name of things to come." DuBell intones like a blessing at church, and the kid shrugs off the twenty thousand like it was twenty-five cents. Senator is floored. He couldn't have given away twenty thousand dollars without a fight. DuBell looks at Sylvia and Loni and smiles shaking his head in disbelief. "Well, I really have to say thanks, Mrs. Tate. Mrs. Lore-Walker. I'm really glad not to be in DHS right now." DuBell looks up around at his new surroundings and exhales deeply. "What now?"

"Can we eat?" Paul puts forth, like he's been waiting to ask for a while. "That Chinese food was ages ago."

Everybody laughs but agrees. When DuBell questions if they are staying to eat Sylvia declines. "Unfortunately, this is where we depart for the moment. Mrs. Lore-Walker and I will catch a ride back to our destination with this gentleman"—she points to Senator—"and we will let you all get started in your new life." She leans in to DuBell and Paul. "I've given Mrs. Daisy the address of your new school. You will start tomorrow." She turns to Mrs. Daisy again. "If anything comes up that you don't know how to handle, contact us. Night or day." To DuBell alone she adds with a touch of salt, "However, if you could help her by abstaining from getting into any trouble that needs assistance until you are of legal voting age, that would be appreciated." They all laugh again. "Seriously though, is there anything else before we go?"

DuBell looks at her with his best, *I'm glad you asked* look. "Summer camp."

Everyone is caught up short. "Come again?" Sylvia responds with a blank expression.

"I go to summer camp in the summer, as part of the free program from when I was a third grader. My teacher, Mrs. Hurt, signed me up and got me a scholarship, so every summer I go for two weeks."

"And you want to go? OK."

"All summer. I want to be one of the kids that gets to stay the whole time. And I want Paul to go too." Paul looks up with uncertainty, but keeps his mouth closed.

"Anything else you forgot?"

"Am I allowed to write to my moms, or talk to her, or see her?"

Sylvia sighs, and Mrs. Daisy pulls DuBell into a hug. "You can always write. It's going to be a while before you can see her face-to-face though. Even then, they aren't going to allow you any physical contact."

"Oh, I didn't say I wanted her to be able to touch me. In fact, her not being able to beat on me will be a welcome change. But she's my moms."

"Yes. Yes, she is." Sylvia looks at the sun dipping lower behind the tree line of the adjacent farmland. "OK now. It's been a transformative day to say the least. Let's be off while we have enough light left. That will give you all time to get settled in without us."

Senator walks back into the house and does a final check to see that the Halflings are gone and that the movers didn't leave anything behind. He comes outside to find the Mothers and Halflings gone and Sylvia and Loni standing beside the S3 Vercingetorix had driven over. Vercingetorix had left it for him. *Yeah boiiii!!* Then Senator makes eye contact with Sylvia and pauses.

She raises an eyebrow. "You broke rank today, Senator, and you deserve to have your car revoked … but Vercingetorix pleaded on your behalf." Sylvia dangles the keys before him, and he grabs. She holds on. "Don't break ranks again. Do you understand?"

He nods once.

"Good. Now drive us to our place before you go to the party."

Senator pauses alarmed. "Wait. Where is my other car? The car I arrived in?"

"A guy named CC said to tell you that you had the party in your car, then he stole your keys from you and drove away, presumably to wherever you all intended to meet up."

Senator feels his pockets and sure enough the keys are gone. He looks at the new S3 and ceases to be concerned. As he opens the door for Loni, he wonders what caused the large smudge on the inside of the rear window. *Must have been from the sticker*, he thinks as he turns on the car and gets a feel for the controls. Once he feels oriented, he gently presses the gas, and he slowly drives Sylvia and Loni away from the pretty brick house he transformed today. He sees DuBell and the Daisys on the lawn, waving. The clock on the dashboard reads 4:30 PM.

Everyone applauds Senator when he arrives at the empty warehouse space where the party is being held. He is the man of the hour and is quickly rewarded with one of his own beers, which is miraculously cold. He looks around at the Mothers, and they all share a knowing smile. The cover story stands that Mrs. Daisy won a contest through her insurance agency, and that Senator is working as an intern for the marketing agency that facilitated the insurance agency contest. Everyone congratulates him, and he lets them. The celebration is a rather mellow affair all around as everyone is worn out from the move. Music is playing on a portable CD player in the corner, and everyone, except HexxCat, has a beer in hand. Everyone in attendance is familiar from high school, so there is none of the awkwardness Senator normally feels at parties.

Fry Guy eventually shows up and everyone gives him shit for missing the move but showing up for beer. He shakes his head. "No, no, listen, you don't understand, data control agendas got misconstrued in the relay, it's like this…" and he proceeds to explain how he had to go into work unexpectedly the night before, and so he slept in and forgot what time the move was and when he woke up, he couldn't call anyone because he didn't know where they were. Senator bears witness and judges that Fry Guy tells it true, but everyone still gives Fry Guy shit for missing the move regardless.

Later that evening, Kaldari slips away from the party. He walks into an empty office space and shuts the door and locks it behind himself. He sits in the floor away from any windows and pulls out a handheld device with a small screen on it. He taps on the screen several times until he reaches the desired effect. He pulls out a small pair of white headphones and enters them into the device. The device shows a time-stamp of 08:30 PM.

Kaldari is watching a live video feed of DuBell and Paul sitting out behind the house with their feet into the pool. In his earbuds, he listens as DuBell and Paul list and prioritize all of the impossible things that have happened to them in the last forty-eight hours.

Paul gets a message from the universe. They both befriended Kendall Glidden and make an awesome movie. DuBell kisses Danna in church. Moms is arrested. Dre and X are arrested. DuBell gets his ass beat. Paul is held at gunpoint. Brandon murders Odie. They gain twenty grand. Mrs. Daisy gains custody of DuBell. They gain a house and car. They gain camp. They are transferred from Rose Park to a computer school with promise of a magnet school. They donate twenty grand to charity.

Back and forth they weigh the balance of good and bad, within their control or beyond, reward or punishment. DuBell tells Paul about how he figured out Loni is a news columnist, and he explains to Paul why he thinks Sylvia has had plastic surgery.

Paul tells DuBell he feels like he won the lottery, but that he doesn't suppose it could have happened if Supraman hadn't changed how he was thinking. They ponder at how it was so easy for Supraman to change Paul's mind, but Paul explains, it just sounded right, like when you ring a bell, it can't be un-rung. And some part of him had just been waiting to hear it put in just those terms.

Kaldari listens quietly as DuBell talks about how the whole time during the signing of the paperwork, he kept waiting for his mother to come in and punch him in the face by surprise. He listens as DuBell speaks of how he was expecting Dre and X to come through the door with bags of Chinese takeout, just so they could humiliate him for even believing that this could happen, of how he looks for them around every corner even though he knows they can't be there.

They talk about Sylvia and about how they have never seen an ADHD adult before. DuBell states bluntly his aspirations for a role model have been altered permanently. Until today, he had always expected that society would beat the wild out of him, long before he became an adult. Paul agrees jovially that he thought so too, but here was living proof that DuBell's craziness might be cultivated into *eccentricity* if he really works at it.

Paul lazily swats at a small bug. "My mom says people with a whole lot of money are allowed to retain certain peculiarities where they can just say whatever comes to their mind without repercussions."

"She does say some outlandish stuff."

"You think she was lying about knowing someone from Nintendo?

"No, I don't."

"You reckon she lied about anything?" Paul traces a figure eight in the water with his big toe.

Kaldari has been waiting for this very question. Thank the gods for the predictability of boys.

DuBell pauses before answering. "It's *really* hard to say. Which is odd, because normally, I can tell if someone's lying instantly. It's almost like I can see the lie visibly forming in their mouth. When I asked Mrs. Walker about being Loni Lore, I think it surprised her that I figured it out, but she didn't even consider to lie. She's a super honest person, hands down. But I wouldn't play cards with Ms. Tate. Not for real money. She's got some other motive, but for the life of me, I can't figure out what the angle is. Not yet. But give me time."

DuBell looks at Paul. "She changed out the bills in the drawer."

"What do you mean? The petty cash?"

"Yeah. It's the same amount, but the serial numbers are different. When her team found the money, she told them to replace the stack set aside for us. See it's that attention to detail. Her game is tight."

"David Copperfield, tight," Paul agrees.

"Make your head disappear while you're looking at yourself in the mirror, tight."

"For real."

DuBell shivers and looks up at the stars. "Let's go play *Mario Kart*."

"Word." Paul swings his feet out of the water.

"First player," DuBell calls out as he jumps up from the poolside.

Through the video surveillance on the roof, Kaldari can zoom down to see all the little splashes DuBell and Paul send rippling through the water as they head inside. He taps out of the monitor feed. He will review the rest of their talks later. He steps out of the empty office and winds his way back to the party. He finds the Mothers lounging in safe company and gives them the nod that everything looks good at the Sylvan House.

Tomorrow will be interesting indeed, Kaldari thinks as he cracks a beer and raises it in a toast. "To DuBell and Paul Daisy. May they both get some good sleep because school starts early tomorrow."

"Cheers!" the Mothers shout, and the clink bottles all around.

TRUST IN YOUR SUPERHERO

August 1996

The very first time he saw the suit, he had howled in anger, alone in his dressing room before going on stage. How had he convinced himself that this was a good idea? And why had hadn't anyone stopped him? Had he lost his mind? And where in the hell had E-Sharp found the outfit on such short notice?

Supraman was so hot the first time he slid into his suit, he screamed. He screamed a primal birthing scream so loud and raw that something in him broke to pieces, and when it shattered, it begged him to scream again.

And so, Supraman screamed again.

There in his dressing room, Supraman screamed out his rage, and he screamed out his confusion. He screamed out his hurt, and he screamed out his frustration. And when he finally heard the knocking on the dressing room door, and he heard the voice announce that it was his time to go on stage, he took his screaming frustration, his screaming hurt, his screaming confusion, and his screaming rage and he ran out onto the stage a green blur trailing an orange cape.

He ran past the band that had been warming the crowd up and getting them grooving. He stormed past the cheering faces, the waving arms, the dancing bodies. He grabbed up the microphone, and he kept moving all the way to the other end of the stage where he turned and let out a bloodcurdling wail.

Then he turned about-face and yelled, "Band!" and the music stopped, and the crowd stopped, and the spotlight shone down on Supraman's face and reflected off of his bright yellow and orange Supraman logo and his metallic green suit and his orange cape and boots, and he shouted, "Hit me!" and E-Sharp and the accompanying horns immediately sounded off. The rest of the night was a funk star fantasy.

Supraman had been a fireball and angry hot mess when he had first put on that suit. But he knew now that it was his super suit, and it had magical powers. After his first flight onto the stage, he never doubted the power of his suit again.

That first night Friday they played the Alpha house, in the center of the Ole Miss campus. Then Saturday evening, they performed at the Pike house at Mississippi State. And now it is Sunday, and they are playing at the Kappa Sig house in Jackson, Tennessee, on the way home.

Supraman has spent the first half of the show working out James Brown covers and is approaching the Parliament section of his set when three young ladies slide up on stage to dance with the Supraman. Unphased, he signals discreetly to the bouncer and dances the ladies right into the bouncer's outstretched hands as he leans into the groove that the Sharp-shooters are laying down. Every time Supraman shouts, the crowd shouts. Every time Supraman hollers *wave your hands*, the crowd waves it's hands. Supraman glides and the crowd slips and sways. He shouts *hey* and they *hey ho* right along in time, and there is no drug that can compare.

Supraman is soaring in the clouds, powered by the horns and drums, and rhythm and bass guitars, and the sonic scream of his own voice. Supraman is fueled by the cosmic power of top hit soul and funk music being broadcast in deafening levels to a group of people whose only desire is to party as hard as they can for as long as the dark night will allow before they stagger away on a wave of funk-filled euphoria toward other untold delights.

And as Supraman is flying in the heavens above them on stage, he is their superhero telling them that tonight it is safe to put your hands up and fly. Tonight, you can let those inhibitions go. Trust in your superhero. Trust in Supraman. Supraman is your one hope.

And when Supraman calls *hey*, they all sing *hey ho*. And when Supraman waves *good night*, he and the band fly out of sight.

EPILOGUE: SLEEPING QUARTERS

August 1996

Everyone's chains rattle in unison as the bus leaves the parking garage of the downtown Nashville juvenile detention facility. It is 6:30 PM when the bus gets out on the open street, and with traffic, the driver is able to make the Bellevue Newsom Station exit around 7:15 PM, the Dickson exit by 8:00 PM, the Bucksnort exit by 8:30 PM, and is approaching the Cuba Landings exit by 8:45 PM. Scarface uses the two hours of travel to rest, eyes half-closed, but with head up; he wants to be fresh for whatever this evening brings.

The twenty boys each have their own seat, but they are chained together through wrists and ankles. Scarface sits four rows back on the right. Nobody speaks during the entire ride. Chains rattle softy with the bumps in the roads and the shifting of lanes. He looks out of the window and examines the landscape as the bus slows and exits.

Off the Cuba Landings exit, down the road to the right, Scarface sees a place where a person could probably go to swamp a body successfully. Over to the left, under the interstate, there sits a bait shop that was built in the late 1940s that looks like it hasn't seen a new customer since the 1970s.

The bus takes the road to the left, but it does not stop at the bait shop. It continues down the road for approximately four miles, which is a fair stretch once it's only hunting land on either side of the bus.

Some fish are fidgety, looking out the window, thinking about how to try to run. But Scarface doesn't care. He just smiles and stares at his ankles and wrists. *Can't do a damn thing until these cuffs come off.* He saves his energy. They won't take the shackles off until someone in charge has proven a point. Scarface decides to be the one to speed up the process. *It's just a matter of time.*

A quarter of an hour later, the bus leaves the pavement and proceeds up a gravel path. The shocks of the bus sound like ancient playground swings getting worn out at recess, and everyone's chains rattle louder as the bus climbs the path. Outside there is only darkness and indistinguishable Tennessee wilderness beyond those windows, but Scarface can feel the others probing the black, looking for landmarks that don't exist.

In short time, the bus grinds to a stop in the gravel, and the brakes hiss in punctuation. The driver steps out immediately, followed by the guards, and a plainclothes man, with thick muscles and a clean shaved face and head, steps onto the bus with a clipboard in hand. Names are called and bodies are moved outside, one at a time. Chains remain on.

The man with the clipboard steps to the middle of the line and in a clear voice explains. "This is Seven Hawks. Seven Hawks does not technically exist. It is a weigh station between levels of hell that helps us to assess which of you are truly monsters ready for adult prison and which of you are only partly monsters that may one day desire a shot at possibly becoming a human again."

This man and his speech are expected. Scarface readies himself; this is the part where he is going to instigate the first test of the electric fence, in an attempt to get his chains removed. But a young man five people away on the chain gang beats him to it, when he tells the bald man to fuck himself and fuck humans and put him on the real bus now. The others all laugh.

Unexpectedly, the man laughs too. He looks at his watch, and he imparts to his second-in-command, "that's a new record. Take them to their sleeping quarters. We will finish this talk in the morning."

How weird, Scarface thinks. Were they just going to bed then? Why isn't that kid being punished? More unexpectedly what is the use of the word *them* because this is where Scarface expected someone to end up in solitary confinement. But now, the entire group from the bus is being led off into the dark, still cuffed at their wrists and ankles, him included. He realizes that they are being led away from the buildings into the woods. He is not the only one concerned now.

This is not going according to plan. Scarface's instincts are now screaming at him to run, he really wants to run, but he knows that it will just pull the others to the ground on top of him in a heap. Their feet crunch on old leaves and sticks as they tromp through the dense canopy, unable to see the sky above them, or the path ahead.

The person leading the head of the formation is obviously comfortable negotiating in the dark without a flashlight, but the others appear to be struggling based on the herk and jerk motion of the chains strung between them. After a moment, the train of juvenile boys comes to a stop, and the distinctive click of a large padlock snapping shut sounds out up ahead. The lead handful of boys have been locked to something.

Scarface feels sections of chain unraveling between the rings of his ankle and wrist cuffs as the boys around him are roughly maneuvered into a spot and told to sit. The chains do not come off. Scarface is placed back-to-back with three other individuals and then a tarp... *black? blue?*... is literally thrown in his face. Each group of four gets a tarp. Each person gets a quarter. *Their sleeping quarters.*

Scarface unravels the end of the tarp and is sure to hold on firmly to the end as he silently passes it to the person beside him on the left. He can feel the tarp wrapping around them; thankfully, it is enough to wrap all the way around, but there is very little to spare.

Over to Scarface's right another group of four begins to fight over their tarp, and Scarface quickly releases his piece of tarp to grab at his ankle chain. He secures the chain just in time to pick up the slack before the other group causes it to whip taut. The person chained directly to his left nods sagely, acknowledging that Scarface has just saved them a ton of discomfort.

Scarface realizes that his night vision is starting to improve if he can see the boys next to him. He takes a better look. The one on the left is a solid-looking white kid, probably four years older than him. The one on the right, is a stringy Puerto Rican-looking kid, also about sixteen. Scarface can't see the one directly behind him and probably won't until morning comes.

Nobody stops the fight between the next group, and as he can, Scarface pulls more and more chain his direction. The others take the chain from him link by link. There is nothing to be gained from the action beyond the silent communication that in this moment, they are connected. In this moment, they are stronger and warmer as a unit.

Scarface nudges the Puerto Rican and signals for him to hold the slack tight for a second, and quietly he lifts his butt up and tucks the tarp underneath himself, sitting cross-legged, knees to his chest. Puerto Rico catches on, and he hands the slack back to Scarface. Scarface makes himself as small as possible while, one by one, the others arrange the tarp beneath themselves. The noise of fighting muffles their movements, and in short order, the four are snug, back-to-back, off the ground, and all covered, and all four with the ability to wrap the tarp up over their heads should it rain.

Scarface glances up, but still cannot see through the canopy. He can see a few feet in front of him, and it's just more trees. He's grateful for the fighting as it will scare away any small animals that might be interested in food that can't run. He tries to remember if bears live in this part of Tennessee, but he doesn't think so.

Nobody speaks. There really isn't shit to say.

Odie is dead. Scarface is alive. He's chained to a bunch of dudes in the woods like some scene from slavery, but he is alive.

And Odie is not.

So, there it is. If he had gone to prison, he would have a cell of his own and a bed at least. Sure, there would be a fight to establish dominance, to earn that bed, but that's what happens in prison. At no point in prison would anyone expect that cooperation and trust in desperate companions might win the night. And certainly, no one in prison would expect to take comfort in the warmth of three other teenage boys.

But again, here he is. A thought flashes in his mind, that if he were as small as DuBell, he could potentially sit in the middle of all three of these guys and be warm on all sides.

Then he remembers kicking DuBell in the face, and in the ribs, and in the head. *Punk.* Taking a beating for Paul Daisy's fat ass when he could've just stayed out of it and kept his money. Odie would still be alive, and Daisy would've gotten beat up at worst, but DuBell just took the beating. DuBell was out cold when Scarface had grabbed that backpack, but it was almost like DuBell had wanted Brandon to take that money.

Or if not *him* somebody.

That little motherfucker. *What was he playing at?*

There must've been more money, Scarface reasons, but where had DuBell hidden it? It wasn't with Paul Daisy's fat ass. All he had was his bike. And it wasn't back at DuBell's place because they'd gone back to look afterwards.

It was after that, when Odie was counting out the money on the coffee table, that shit got ill. Scarface was the youngest member of the LA Boys and was used to being cut out of drug scores; that was all part of paying your dues. But he felt that this was different, he had brought the score, and he wanted his cut. Scarface argued that they wouldn't have anything at all if it had not been for him. All he wanted was his cut.

But Odie wanted to act all hard in front of every-body and decided to be disrespectful. So, Scarface went and grabbed a .22 and expressed to Odie and the others exactly how he felt about that. Odie thought Scarface was bluffing and wasn't even looking when Scarface pulled the trigger. Odie's whole head had exploded at such close range, and everybody else jumped Scarface to avoid getting shot next. He could still hear a faint ring in his ears from that shot.

And then Scarface sees it all again—the whole scene from a different angle. He sees DuBell wearing an oversized hoodie, almost falling down around his knees. It had to be Paul's hoodie. Scarface had originally thought DuBell was just trying to hide his identity from cops or social services while he ran back into the apartment to get the backpack, but DuBell had been hiding something under the hoodie. He had curled into a ball to protect it. He had the real money under his clothes.

Well fuck DuBell. Fuck DuBell and fuck Paul Daisy. Sitting at home and sucking each other's dicks and doing each other's nails while he's out in the fucking wilderness just happy not to be in the group that's beating the shit out of each other in the dark. Fuck DuBell. Fuck Paul. Fuck Odie. Fuck the LA Boys.

Well Odie was dead. So, fuck DuBell, fuck Paul, and fuck the LA Boys. When the day comes to get out of this shit, every last one of those motherfuckers has to pay.

Just then, something howls in the distance, and everyone go still. The wild resonance is picked up by another canine somewhere off to the right, and then another further beyond. Scarface feels the others press closer, and he does not shrug them off. They do not speak to share the private hells inside their minds. They do not say if they are afraid of the night. They do not speak of how they came to be here, or

when they expect they'll leave. They just watch in four cardinal directions, holding a piece of chain and some tarp. To
keep awake and vigilant against the dark, Brandon chants
five words in a slow repetitious prayer: *DuBell, Paul, LA,
Boys,* and *Fuck.*

ACKNOWLEDGMENTS

Many people deserve thanks for this story coming into the world; I will do my best to contain it to a reasonable list of acknowledgments, hoping that no one feels omitted in the first printing.

First, this book would not exist without the full and un-flagging support of my lovely wife, Sidney Pell, who gave me the year I needed to write and provided priceless service in reading and critiquing early versions of each chapter. Thank you for being visionary and for believing in me from start to finish. I cannot ask for a better partner in this adventure.

Second, to my daughters Faith Harris and Sorcha Pell, you have been transformative partners in helping me become a published author. From creating the first official Twelve Rings merch to teaching me about book street teams in the modern era, Faith continues to be a shining beacon guiding me to audiences beyond the science fiction genre. Similarly, Sorcha has been an unrelenting cheerleader from the beginning, listening to story arcs, critiquing copy edits, and developing elements for the cover art. Thank you my loves for all the daily joy you bring me and for keeping me young. I am so grateful to have you both in my life, and I fully expect one day you will both read and enjoy The Twelve Rings.

To Farron Kilburn, thank you for supporting my fiction writing endeavors alongside our research writing endeavors.

It means so much to have you on my team. To Ken, Sherri, Sarah, and Bonnie Irwin thank you for your continued love and support as we strive to create something new. To my parents, Terrye and Larry Merryman, whose beautiful mysteries are also woven into this tale, I love you dearly and miss you both.

A big thanks to my friend Alice Sullivan for answering early editing questions and connecting me to Alison and Julie; you rock! Thanks to Alison Cantrell and Julie Swearingen at Quail Run Editorial who saw beyond the linear telling of my story and challenged me to workshop when the story had more to give. Also, an extra big thank you for introducing me to Lieve for the cover art! Thanks to Lieve Maas at Bright Light Graphics for instantly bonding with me on the visual storytelling of the trilogy, for your stunning book designs, and for guiding me into the process of self-publication. You had me at "Bootsy." Thanks to Don Carlton for the photo session and enhancing the Pantheon mystery. And thanks to Lizzdidit for keeping my wild hair look tight.

It will be obvious to anyone who grew up with me that this story is a series of love letters to our middle and high school years in Nashville. Paul Dowell has dubbed this story "a mythology of our young lives," and I agree. Much of the story is linked to Paul, as my lifelong friend and former roommate. This story is my way of saying thank you, Paul, for being a steadfast and stalwart friend these many decades. Being my friend is not easy, so thanks for sticking by me.

To Jim Clayborne, Chase Block, Brian Frierson, Brian Johnson, and Rahul Kasat, you are five of the smartest people on the planet, and I am a better person for knowing you all these years. Catching frisbees, playing Mario Kart and Risk, or just risking a juvenile sentence if we got caught, you know that I was always down for adventure when you were.

To the more-than-five Mothers, past, present, or future, you are so much more than these pages could ever hope to contain in terms of the legacy you have created in our collective memory. Why the Mothers? My story needed a badass gang of hackers, and I could think of no other team better suited to pulling off the mission. The five characters, despite their names or descriptions, are amalgamations of multiple Mothers, and as such are not real in this universe. Everything in this story is written with extreme respect and love for the persons and personas depicted. Any intense, suspect, or dramatic events that happens with these characters is a byproduct of story arc and development of plot only. With respect for the underground nature of the Mothers, I will not be listing your real names here: you all know who you were, are, and will be. Reach out if you need me. This is an extension of my thanks to each of you.

Funk music is the grooving backbone of this story, and my knowledge of the funk world is part fanboy fascination with bands like P-Funk, WAR, and Undisputed Truth and part lived experience with the Nashville funk scene in the early 2000s. Through Doyle "D-Funk" Davis of Grimey's Music and the indie-pop princess, Anna Lundy, I had the great privilege to meet two phenomenal funk groups: Charles "Wigg" Walker and the Dynamites and Sharon Jones and the Dap Kings. Between these two groups alone, I've seen more funk music than you can haul in a truck, which is a load of funk for someone who is not in a band. I am so thankful for Charles Walker, for the Dynamites, for the Dap Kings, and for the truly missed and ultimately unforgettable Miss Sharon Jones. I loved every minute I spent dancing with you at your shows or just hanging out watching the other bands, and I count myself so very fortunate to have been invited to the party in the first place. Thank you.

For the next and arguably most important you-inspired-my-book acknowledgment, we must travel back in time, to 1996, where I am in the end of my senior year in high school, on a road trip out of state to Ole Miss in Oxford, Mississippi. In this exciting episode, I am escorting my friend, Ms. Laura Brown to her college orientation. See me now, after a long day of watching college baseball on the berm and visualize as I end up at the Alpha Kappa fraternity house, slightly sunburned and mildly inebriated, only to have my mind melt as I witness my (and Paul and Jim's) six grade PE coach, Tyrone Smith, transform into Super-T, the front man for the Tyrone Smith Revue. Now, before Senator can say "Bullshit," I tell you this story is gospel truth, and its impact was life-changing! Once I saw Super-T perform, I knew anything was possible. I knew college was going to be amazing! I knew road trips with friends to see music were going to be out of this world! I just knew so many great things were around the corner waiting, if I could only catch the signal the universe was sending me and then be big enough to respond in kind. And that is also gospel truth. So let this book be my best way of saying thank you, Tyrone "Super-T" Smith for being so incredibly awesome, for teaching me to be so much more than the sum of my parts, and for reminding me to always work my body! And thank you for patching up Paul's knee when he fell in the gym as a kid; it was more blood than he had ever seen, but you never lost your cool, and that made all the difference.

Other people who knowingly or unknowingly inspired parts of the story include: Nikki Monessa Harding, Kalisha Moore, John Robert "Slugger" Hayes, Stacy Tellinghuesin, Robert Donaldson, Kevin McGlockton, Danna Haile, Daniel Bernhard, Christopher Long, Drew Hill, Vikas Singh, Jimmy Singh, Celeste Hunter, Richard Anthony, Wes Covington, Crystal Covington, Michael Ryan Peters "Myth", Michael Knight, Marilyn Kallet, Mickey Stagg, and Virginia Woodmore. All your energies are buried in the coding of this story.

To the ones that had to leave before I could finish the story, I carry you with me each day, and I love you. James, Nana, Gran, Uncle Dick, Coach Paul Bass, Maria Mullins, and Angela Bartlett.

To anyone who read this book and these acknowledgments, thank you so very much. I cannot wait to see the big, big things you bring to the universe.

Love, love.
Christopher W. Pell

CHRISTOPHER W. PELL is a husband and father, a professor and a researcher, and a poet/writer/would-be rapper who was abducted by a passing story that needed desperately to be written. He lives in San Diego now with his family where he teaches, writes, and sees live music whenever possible. You might also catch him reliving his skateboard fantasies at the local ramps; he's the skinny old guy in a ton of pads.

We fully expect you will love Book Two of
The Twelve Rings: The Shining Beacons

Just Outside Nashville, Tennessee-Summer 2003
Last Session of Youth Camp

Months spent in summer heat ferrying kids on a pontoon boat has DuBell Jones ready to take off for college in the fall. The only thing keeping DuBell from screaming with joy is the obvious rising anxiety of his brother and best friend Paul Daisy. While DuBell is eager to explore a new city free from adult supervision, the coming of his birthday and the end of summer may be signaling an end to everything he and Paul have ever known. But how much distance from home is required for DuBell and Paul to experience freedom when members of the Mothers observe their every step and aim to expand the organization known as Pantheon? Tech guru, blogger, and secret agent Loni Lore-Walker (a.k.a. "Lolo Knows") is hip-deep in the intrigue alongside her former nemesis, the mysterious Sylvia Tate, prepping to keep as many well-trained eyes as possible on Paul and DuBell once the duo leave the city.

Is an invisible hand pulling strings across city and state lines to push an agenda for a contest worth untold fortunes? Or is the secret cabal surrounding DuBell and Paul betting on a contest that won't even exist?

Book Two of *The Twelve Rings: The Shining Beacons* returns readers to the cast of *A Chance For Heroes* seven years later and one step closer to the finish line of this epic story. In the second episode of *The Twelve Rings*, readers are treated to secret agents in the post Y2K tech boom, a funk music rechristening, high fantasy hallucinations, and a continuing story about brotherhood, finding love, and finally understanding dreams. If this story fails to keep readers' full attention the second time, we will travel back in time and fix it until it does. We fully expect you will love it.

–Pantheon

Visit **www.the12rings.net** for more about this book series and any related contest information.

Los Angeles, California-January 21, 2017
(The Twelve Rings National Launch)

After thirteen years of training and planning, Kendall Glidden, western controller of the Pantheon corporation, is ready to reveal the full power of the Twelve Rings contest coast to coast. The only hurdle left for Kendall to leap is securing corporate sponsorship at the national level. As Kendall faces a series of meetings to decide the fate of the contest launch, DuBell Jones and the other Pantheon agents await in the shadows, testing alternate endings in case plans go sideways. But how much control do the Pantheon agents possibly have when their members come under attacks from cyborg-enhanced villains? Tech guru and secret agent Loni Lore-Walker is trying to keep her husband, Tyrone "Supraman" Walker, safe long enough to find out, but she'll need the help of her former nemesis, the mysterious Sylvia Tate, to see them all to the end of their elaborate plans.

Can the invisible hand pull the final strings to successfully launch a contest worth untold fortunes, and what will become of DuBell, Kendall, and Paul Daisy if it does?

Book Three of *The Twelve Rings: The Pantheon's Delight*, reunites readers with the cast of *The Shining Beacons* thirteen years later, rocketing towards the finale of this epic saga. In the third episode, readers are treated to rival cyborg showdowns, funk-filled political parties, self-propelled challengers, and a fitting conclusion to a lasting story about brotherhood, growing older, and seeing your dreams fulfilled. If this story fails to keep readers' attention until the end, we will travel back in time and fix it until it does. We fully expect you will love it.

–Pantheon

Visit **www.the12rings.net** for more about this book series and any related contest information.